Hello!

You never know where inspiration might strike, but a holiday on a houseboat in the Isle of Wight seemed like a very good prospect and I wasn't wrong.

I fell in love with the island, instantly. It has so much to offer in such a small area and is like a little trip back in time to a more gentle era of English lifestyle.

Our houseboat was beautiful, the days warm and sunny. How could I not write a book set there? When I went back to do some more research, I fell in love a little bit more. If you haven't been, then I do urge you to take a trip.

Thank you for choosing this book, I hope you enjoy Cockleshell Bay and the characters I've created.

Love Carole :) xx

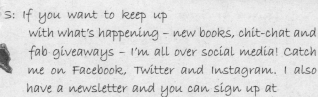

P.S: If you want to keep up with what's happening – new books, chit-chat and fab giveaways – I'm all over social media! Catch me on Facebook, Twitter and Instagram. I also have a newsletter and you can sign up at www.carolematthews.com. Look forward to seeing you there!

f www.facebook.com/carolematthewsbooks

🐦 @carolematthews

📷 Matthews.Carole

www.carolematthews.com

Also by Carole Matthews

THE CHOCOLATE LOVERS NOVELS

Carole Matthews

Sunny days & Sea Breezes

sphere

SPHERE

First published in Great Britain in 2020 by Sphere
This paperback edition published by Sphere in 2021

1 3 5 7 9 10 8 6 4 2

A CIP catalogue record for this book
is available from the British Library.

ISBN 978-0-7515-7216-2

Typeset in Sabon by Palimpsest Book Production Ltd,
Falkirk, Stirlingshire
Printed and bound in Great Britain by Clays Ltd, Elcograf S.p.A.

Papers used by Sphere are from well-managed forests
and other responsible sources.

Sphere
An imprint of
Little, Brown Book Group
Carmelite House
50 Victoria Embankment
London EC4Y 0DZ

An Hachette UK Company
www.hachette.co.uk

www.littlebrown.co.uk

Carole Matthews is the *Sunday Times* bestselling author of over thirty novels, including the top ten bestsellers *The Cake Shop in the Garden*, *A Cottage by the Sea*, *Paper Hearts and Summer Kisses*, *The Chocolate Lovers' Christmas*, *Million Love Songs*, *Christmas Cakes & Mistletoe Nights*, *Happiness for Beginners* and *Sunny Days and Sea Breezes*, which won Romantic Comedy Novel of the Year at the 2021 RNA Awards. Carole is also the recipient of the RNA Outstanding Achievement Award. Her novels dazzle and delight readers all over the world and she is published in more than thirty countries.

For all the latest news from Carole, visit www.carolematthews. com and sign up to her newsletter. You can also follow Carole on Twitter (@carolematthews) and Instagram (matthews.carole) or join the thousands of readers who have become Carole's friend on Facebook (carolematthewsbooks).

For Nikki Bloomer at Waterstones in Costa del Keynes who does so much for authors and always goes above and beyond the call of duty. Thank you for all your help and friendship over the years. Here's to more book sales and excuses for bulk purchases of Prosecco!

Chapter One

The ferry slips out of the port at Southampton and heads out into the choppy, grey waters of the Solent. The sky hangs low, malevolent and brooding, as grey as the sea, the peaks of washed-out clouds mirroring the white-tipped waves. I sit outside, alone on the rear deck – the only one foolish enough to face the inclement weather. The threat of rain whips in on the sea air and I wish I'd worn a coat more appropriate for the falling temperature. This is a smart, serviceable one for popping between city meetings, not for facing down the elements. The wind is finding all the gaps around my neck, up my sleeves, and cashmere isn't known for its waterproof qualities. But I left in a hurry and the last thing on my mind was my choice of wardrobe. Maybe it should have been. As it was, I just slung as much as I could in a couple of bags and left.

It's the end of March and there are rows and rows of empty bench seats which I'm sure are better utilised in the summer crossings. Now, long before the start of the holiday season, the ferry is probably only half full, if that. A few people brave the cold and come out to look over the rails towards the dwindling view of the port behind us, but soon hurry back inside to the

1

fuggy warmth of the onboard café. I bought a sandwich there, but it looks beyond grim and I can't face eating it. I could throw it to one of the cawing gulls that shadow the ferry, but they look huge and menacing and I feel so light, so insubstantial, so irrelevant, that they might lift me away entirely instead of just taking my disgusting sandwich.

While I further contemplate the many inadequacies of my stale-looking BLT, we pass the magnificent, floating city of the *Queen Elizabeth* – a Cunard liner in posh livery heading somewhere much more exotic than I am, no doubt. Yet, somehow, I still have the sense that I'm escaping. Perhaps there is no set distance-to-escapee ratio. A mile might be as good as a thousand, if you just want to leave everything behind you. I'm hoping less than twenty miles will do the job, as it takes in both a stretch of sea and an island destination. OK, it's not exactly Outer Mongolia, but that has to be worth something.

The Solent is a busy motorway of water, and vessels of all shapes and sizes bob, zip or lumber along beside us. The Red Jet speeds past and I know that I could have taken that, a quicker way to the Isle of Wight, but I wanted to feel the distance growing more slowly, the space opening up between me and my old life.

It sounds as if I know what I'm doing, as if there was a plan. But I don't and there wasn't. I only know that I had to get away to a place where no one knows me, where I don't keep having the same conversation over and over, where I don't have to talk at all, where no one looks at me with pity and thinks 'Poor Jodie'.

For something to do, I abandon my sandwich on the bench and cross to one of the rails, looking out to sea. I can't tell you if it's port or starboard as I'm a confirmed landlubber – but it's most definitely one or the other. The wind whips my long hair across my face and for once, I'm glad that I haven't spent money on an expensive blow-dry.

A few minutes later, the door behind me bangs and a hardy smoker joins me. Though he nods in my direction, he keeps his distance as he puffs away. I wish I smoked. It's years since I had a cigarette – a teenage flirtation – and I didn't much care for it then. Yet I'm tempted to pluck up the courage to blag one from him. I want to feel something, even if it's just burning in my lungs. However, before I can find my voice, he takes a deep drag, throws his butt into the water below and, with a theatrical shiver, disappears inside. Not as hardy as he looked, then.

Alone again, I stare down at the churning wake of the boat, mesmerised, listening to the deep thrum of the engines, feeling the vibration beneath my feet. My phone rings and I take it out of my pocket, even though I already know who it is. Sure enough, Chris's number is on the screen so I let it go straight to voice-mail. I don't want to speak to my husband now. I don't want to speak to anyone. What would happen if I dropped my phone into the sea? I hold it over the rail while I think, dangling it precariously. If it sank into the depths of the ocean would I, Jodie Jackson, simply cease to exist? Would I be so off-grid that no one could find me? No more Twitter, no more Instagram, no more WhatsApp. It sounds too appealing. If my phone rings again now, I'm going to throw it into the sea. I am. But I wait and wait and my phone, for once, stays silent. I switch it to mute and, still reluctant to give it a reprieve, put it back into my pocket. I suppose that I might need it for an emergency.

I try not to think, to keep my head empty as the sea slides by below me. And it nearly works. Behind me there's a shriek and two gulls are on the bench fighting over my cast-off sand-wich, having plucked it from its cardboard packet. I don't like to tell them that they'd probably be better off eating the box. The funnel belches black smoke and covers them in smuts of soot but they are too focused on the limp lettuce and the white, slimy fat on the bacon to care.

Then a sea fret rolls in and shrouds everything in mist, taking away any semblance of a view. I'm going to arrive at my destination engulfed in thick fog – both physically and metaphorically.

The ferry crossing is barely an hour long and, too soon, we're docking in Cowes. I'm sure it's usually a bustling place, but not today. The scene that greets me looks as if it's been filmed in monochrome. Even the colourful flags on the little sailing boats that line the entrance to the harbour are failing to compete with the mist, the forbidding light, and are bleached out to grey. Alabaster sand meets the silver sea, joins the battleship sky.

I came here on holiday as a child, just the once. I must have been seven or maybe eight. I remember playing on the beach with my older brother, Bill, burying our dad up to the neck in sand and sitting in deckchairs eating fish and chips from greasy paper. But that's all. After that we went to Spain every year. I don't remember much about that either. People say that the Isle of Wight is still like Britain was forty years ago. That sounds perfect to me. If only I could wind time back to then. I'd be two, would have the whole of the world ahead of me, and could make very different life choices.

Chapter Two

At the port, I take a taxi and look out of the window as we bump across the island to my destination. The driver is determinedly chatty. 'First time in the Isle of Wight, love?'

'Yes.'

'Business? Holiday?'

'Yes.' How can I explain that it's neither one nor the other?

'It's a great place. If you're looking for some tips on how to enjoy yourself, I'm your man.'

'Thanks.'

In theory, if I keep giving one-word answers, he'll stop speaking. After a few more futile attempts, he does, and I sink into my seat in silence. I'm glad he has the heater on full blast so it's cosy and warm, which thaws me out after my freezing journey.

It looks pretty enough here. Green. Lots of green. But then, compared to where I live in Inner London, so are most places. After a short while, we crest a hill and there's a rough layby marked viewpoint.

'Can we stop here, please?'

The driver pulls in. 'Do you want an ice-cream?'

'No.' The lone van looks as if it has few customers today. 'I'd just like to look for a moment.'

So I climb out of the cab and go to the edge of the fields to gaze out. A meadow of rather hopeful early wildflowers spreads out in front of me. Beyond that the lush, green pastures drop away, rolling gently towards the ribbon of sparkling silver sea that stitches the land to the vast blue-white sky. It's as if I've entered a different land. The mist has gone, the sun looks like it might be struggling to come out. Even on such a dull day, it's beautiful and I take a moment to breathe in the air, to admire the view.

Sensing the driver waiting patiently behind me, I return to the car. A short while later and I'm looking at the sea again as we drop down to the coastal road on the other side of the island. I check the address again, even though I've already given it to the driver and he hasn't, thus far, looked once at his satnav. A few minutes later, the taxi turns onto the curving harbour road and a sign says welcome to cockleshell bay.

He slows down as we pass a long line of smart houseboats and, eventually, he pulls up outside one that's rather smarter than the rest.

'Here you go, love.' He turns in his seat and I hand over a modest amount of cash for my journey and get out of the cab. The price of taxis is also quite different in London.

The driver joins me at the boot and flicks it open. 'Want a hand with your bags?' he asks as he lifts out my two bulging holdalls.

'I'm fine, thank you.'

'Nice place,' he observes with a nod at Bill's houseboat.

'Yes, it is.' This is the first time that I've seen it in the flesh. Although Bill's shown me enough photographs of it.

'Enjoy your holiday.' The driver jumps back into his warm car and buzzes off, leaving me standing there at the side of the harbour.

Holiday. That's not quite how I'd describe it.

I have a good long look at Bill's boat – my home for the foreseeable future. It's called *Sunny Days* and is painted cream and grey. It's not hard to tell that his lengthy and rather expensive renovations have only recently been finished. Everything looks shiny and new, even though the day is trying its best to stay dreary. My brother has clearly thrown a lot of money at his latest project, which is so typical of him. He has, of course, been too busy to visit it since it was completed, so I'm to be the first occupant. I think his plan is to use it as a weekend bolthole, but I can't see that ever happening. Bill runs his own company – the one that I work for too: WJ Design. I've been with him for years, ever since he set it up and I love working with my older bro. We lost Mum and Dad some years ago, so now it's just the two of us and, because of that, we've always been close.

Bill's company specialises in designing the interiors for hotels, office blocks, shopping centres and, though I say it myself, we're very much in demand. Which, as a result, leaves us little time for play. I'm marginally better at crafting a social life than Bill, who is a complete workaholic. My dear brother has more money than he knows what to do with and no time to spend it. At the moment, I'm feeling grateful that he has this folly as I had no idea where else to go and, when Bill suggested I escape to his houseboat, it seemed like the answer to my prayers.

The houseboat is solid, and sturdy on its moorings – I think Bill said it had been in service as a Thames Lighter. I don't even know what that is, but while the houseboat looks like it might have started out life as some kind of workaday tug there's not much evidence of that left now. Bill's team have worked their magic on it and now it's a houseboat fit for a queen – or a sister who's broken into little pieces.

I pick up my bags and walk up the gangway. As I do, I can't

help but note that the houseboat next door is not quite so chi-chi.

The entrance to Bill's boat is flanked by two bay trees in gleaming steel pots – so perfect that they look artificial. Where my brother has fancy, architectural plants, my new next-door-neighbours have instead a gas cylinder, a pile of wood, a tatty green and yellow wicker chair, a mountain bike and an abandoned shopping trolley to welcome their visitors. On shore by their boat there's a lean-to shed made out of a dozen different types and sizes of board. That too is filled with wood. No doubt it's individual, but it's also kind of an eyesore compared to Bill's fancy refit.

The owners seem to have taken shabby-chic to the extreme as this houseboat looks as if it's been cobbled together from stuff that was previously destined for the Tidy Tip and, as such, stands out in a row of pristine weekend places. The sides are covered with worn cedar shingles and one wall is painted a vivid purple. The window frames are many shades of bright blue and of every shape and size conceivable. There's an intricate totem pole carved from driftwood too with a kayak propped up against it and there are other attractive carved motifs on its shingle walls – a sunshine, a leaping fish, a tree. Though it sits uneasily next to the other boats – which with this one exception all look rather like Bill's – I admire its bold quirkiness and individuality. It's a hippy squatting in an office of accountants. Jed Clampett in the middle of Beverly Hills. In a world of grey, don't we need more colour? Just don't tell Bill I said that. Like me, he tends to favour the muted shades. The houseboat – *Sea Breezes* – doesn't look as if it's currently inhabited, so maybe no one lives there any more. There'd be no point asking Bill about his neighbours as I'm sure he hasn't a clue.

With a last appraising glance at *Sea Breezes*, I let myself in and, of course, my brother has worked his amazing magic with the interior too. I expected no less. I haven't seen any photographs of it completely finished inside and the ones I did see certainly didn't give any indication of just how lovely it is. If I hadn't been so busy with my own projects, I would have given him a hand, but the time was never available. Seems like he's done a pretty good job without me.

Dropping my bags in the hall, I catch sight of myself in the mirror. What a sorry picture. My long blonde hair hasn't benefited from being styled by the wind. It looks lank and lifeless. I used to get it coloured every eight weeks, cut every four weeks and would splash out on a professional blow-dry every week, but I can't remember when last I went. Whenever I look in a mirror, I see Bill looking back too. He and I share the same looks and, as kids, we were often mistaken for twins. My brother is only eighteen months older than me, so we're not very different in age – or outlook, or likes and dislikes. We're both tall, slim and are strawberry blondes – though my hair is highlighted with blonde and Bill's is now naturally highlighted with silver-grey. We both have green eyes – though there is no sparkle in mine any more. Once people used to remark on my eyes, including my husband. Now there are dark shadows beneath them and my skin looks as washed-out as the day. I've avoided mirrors for months. Now there is too much reflected there and I can't bear to look. I trace the line of my jaw, the curve of my nose, run my fingers over my long black lashes. I see my past, my present, my future staring back at me and it's all too much. When my eyes fill with tears, I turn away.

Going through to the main living area, I push all other thoughts aside and concentrate hard on appreciating it. There's a lot to admire. It's a huge space, flooded with light. On a sunny day, it will be incredible. The kitchen is fitted with white units and a huge Aga in a soft dove-grey colour – which does make me smile as I don't think I've *ever* seen Bill cook. I'm sure that the majority of numbers in my foodie brother's iPhone are for restaurants that he favours. The table is white, possibly a French antique, and has a distressed finish. To go with it are a range of beautifully co-ordinated mis-matched chairs in soft seaside colours – pink, pistachio, duck egg blue, lemon.

I walk towards the back. Again, my lack of boat-based terms evades me. I don't know if it's the bow or the stern, but it's the end of the boat that overlooks the sea. There's a comfortable living room with an oversized pale blue velvet sofa with navy sail-stripe cushions scattered over it. There's a range of accompanying eclectic accent armchairs and I remember Bill telling me that he'd sourced them through various up-and-coming designers, as we do with all of our work when we can. It's what gives our interiors an original edge. Every piece has been hand-picked and placed with painstaking care – Bill's forte – from the furniture to the artworks on the wall. There are giant sea charts on one wall and, on the other, a huge poster of Sean Connery and Ursula Andress on a beach. He's catching hold of her slender ankles as she does a handstand in her bikini – it's an iconic image and is perfect for the space.

In front of the span of bi-fold doors there's a telescope set up and I put my eye to it, but can see very little as it's all blurry. When I'm settled, I'll have plenty of time to work out how to focus it properly. With a bit of fiddling, I open one of the doors and step out onto the spacious rear deck. The wind has dropped and the air isn't quite as nippy as it was on the ferry coming over here, but I don't think I want to hang about out here too long today.

The view is breathtaking. *Sunny Days* is situated right in the middle of the curving sweep of the harbour, so has an all-encompassing vista. Bill certainly knows how to pick his spot. Right now, the tide is high and I can see that, at the mouth of the harbour wall, there's a circular, brooding fort ahead of us which is currently shrouded in low cloud. It looks as if it's floating on the water like a mirage. To the left, there's a line of moored boats, what appears to be a sailing club and a shack painted bright blue that's a café selling fresh seafood. To the other side, more sailing boats and houseboats, but not much else. Ahead of me, there's just the sea, the gulls wheeling in the air and the sturdy fort.

Out on the deck there's a dining table with four chairs which will be an ideal spot for breakfast or reading should the weather perk up. Beyond that is a small ramp which goes down to a wooden pontoon that extends out over the water and is home to two pristine, teak steamer chairs.

The only other human figure I can see in the harbour is a man out on a paddleboard in a wetsuit. Even looking at him makes me shiver. I guess these coastal types are more hardy than soft townies like me. Nothing on earth would persuade me into water that cold, that grey. I'm not even keen on venturing into the sea when the climate is tropical. I watch him for a few moments as he glides across the calm water of the harbour, before I retreat inside. Not my idea of fun, but he looks as if he's enjoying himself, anyway. It takes all sorts, I suppose.

My cursory exploration of this floor over, I scoop up my bags again and head downstairs to the bedrooms. There are only two, but they're both generously proportioned. The second bedroom is, as yet, empty, waiting to be finished. The master suite is, of course, beautifully furnished. My brother has impeccable taste and flair. He's so fussy, though, which probably explains why, at the age of nearly forty-four, he's still resolutely single. I don't think anyone could live up to his exacting standards. He says he might rent out this place, but I can't see him wanting to let strangers in here on a regular basis.

The main bedroom is the furthest away from the harbour road, facing the sea. Down here, all windows are traditional portholes and it does feel more boat-like. The theme is fresh, seaside-influenced without it being clichéd. There's a white bed-frame and crisp white linen topped with pale blue tweed cushions and a couple that are hand-stitched with delicate shell patterns. A rich, royal blue throw is meticulously arranged in a casual style. The bedside cabinets are stripped-back wood with glass lamps and white shades. The white dressing table has a Philippe Starck ghost chair in front of it – no doubt an original rather than a copy. It's all so pristine and wonderful.

Looking round, I like what I see. I can definitely be comfortable here, even if happy might be stretching it a bit. I can't exactly say that I feel any better or lighter, but some of the weight that's been pressing down on my heart and my head has lifted for a moment. Perhaps that's what sea air and some well-placed designer furniture does for you. I haven't lived on my own for years and it feels strange to be completely by myself without any detritus from another person in the house – or boat, in this case. All I can hear is the sound of the gentle waves lapping against the hull which is soothing, hypnotic. Perhaps I could learn to live again here. Heaven knows, the total solitude is appealing.

Then I hear the front door bang and a voice shouts, 'Coooooeeeee!'

Chapter Three

'What the f—?' I say to no one but myself. That made me jump out of my skin. Bill didn't tell me that anyone else had a key. Did I leave the front door open?

'Only me!' More shouting.

Abandoning my bags and any thoughts of unpacking, I take the steps two at a time to go and see who's invaded my space.

In the kitchen, there's a very buxom woman with bleach-blonde hair – as white as it possibly could be. Her red lipstick is also the brightest I've ever seen in my life. It's positively neon. She's wearing leopard skin print jeggings that give the impression of a boa constrictor trying to eat her. They're topped with a white floaty number that has a perilously plunging neckline, exposing a good deal of her comely cleavage. The outfit is completed by a pair of vertiginous red heels. Her nails are an inch long and also an eye-popping shade of red. She makes me feel very drab in my black trousers and grey shirt, but then my interest in my appearance has taken a back seat for some time now. This woman is far more glamourous – in a slightly alarming way – though she must be twenty years older than me.

Currently, she's determinedly loading shopping into my fridge from a carrier bag that states *Shopping is my cardio*.

'Just a few bits, sweetheart,' she says as if we've been friends for life. 'I thought I'd get you going. Cheese, hummus, pork pie – food of the gods – and salad.' She grimaces at the pack of three iceberg hearts. 'Though I can never see the point of lettuce myself.' She indicates her curves. 'As you can tell, I'm a confirmed salad-dodger. You're not vegan, are you? Joyless buggers. There's a nice loaf in the cupboard. Get some carbs down your neck, lovely. You're as thin as a chip.'

I stand there and gape. Who the hell is this?

'Cuppa, sweetie? You look knackered.' She bangs about with the kettle. 'How do you take it? Black, white? I've brought milk and sugar.' The woman holds them up for my inspection. 'You don't look like you take sugar.'

She gets two mugs out of the cupboard and crashes about with the kettle. All her bracelets jangle, dozens of them clanging together, setting my teeth on edge.

'Sorry,' I say, when I finally find my voice. 'But who are you?'

'Marilyn.' She looks at me as if I should have known this. 'I was named for Marilyn Monroe.' Like Monroe, she does a shimmy and a pout. 'My mother was a big fan. I'm a McConaughey, though.'

'And you're here because?'

'I've been doing for Bill,' she supplies as if it should have been perfectly obvious to me. 'Cleaning up after the builders and such. He's asked me to look after you while you're here.'

'Did he now?' Wait until I get on the phone to him.

'Probably forgot to mention it. He's such a busy man. I've never known anyone dash about so much. He runs around like a headless pony. Here, there, everywhere! He's done this place up lovely though.' She gives an admiring glance around the room. 'Asked my advice on most of it.'

I think if that had been the case there would be more considerably leopard skin print in evidence.

'Well, Marilyn,' I say. 'It's very nice to meet you, but I've actually come here to be *by myself*.' I try to address this as politely as possible. 'I don't know what arrangement you have with Bill, but I'm sure that I can manage.'

'You can be *by yourself* with me,' Marilyn tells me as the kettle boils. 'You won't even know I'm here. I'm as quiet as a squirrel. All I'm going to do is pop in every day and have a little run around with the hoover and the like.'

The thought fills me with dread. 'I'm really not intending to make very much mess and I'm perfectly capable of doing my own cleaning.'

'I'm sure you are, honey, but Bill's your big brother. He just wants to look after you. My kids are all the same. They're protective of each other. That's what families do.'

Yes, I think, but sometimes the people who should love you the most are the ones who cause you the most hurt. I sigh to myself.

'How did you want your tea?'

'I don't actually want any tea.'

'Of course you do. A cup of tea in time is as good as nine. White, no sugar?'

'Yes.' Some things in life you just can't fight.

Marilyn McConaughey-channelling-Monroe hands me a mug of tea that I'm not sure that I want and sits down at the kitchen table with her own. She has a kind face and a tan that looks as if it has come from a bottle.

'Come on, sit, sit.' She pats a chair. 'You must be tired after that long journey. Sit.'

There seems to be very little point in arguing about this too. Even though the trip here could hardly be classed as arduous, I realise that I am actually tired – emotionally as much as

15

physically – and a cup of tea would just hit the spot. Running away, it seems, takes it out of you. I sit down opposite my new and somewhat unwanted companion.

'The tea's wonderful.' I try a smile. 'Thank you.'

'I'm practically psychic when it comes to knowing what people want,' she says with a sage nod.

I'm sure.

It looks as if I won't get very far with convincing Marilyn that I don't need her here, but wait until I speak to Bill. I'll get him to call her off. He probably is trying to be kind, but I don't want someone 'popping in' every day. Especially not someone as chatty as Marilyn. I came here to be quiet, to see if I can find peace again.

'I'll tell you all about our lovely island so that you have a grand time while you're here. I know all the best places to visit.'

'I'm planning just to rest and read,' I tell her. 'Enjoy the tranquillity.'

Marilyn looks at me as if that's a completely alien concept. 'Nonsense. We have *all* of the things here. You'll love it. We've a garlic farm.'

'Right.'

'They have garlic ice-cream.'

Where was I without that in my life?

'That will put hairs on your toes.'

'Chest, I think you mean.'

'Why would you want hairs on your chest?' she asks, askance.

I'm not entirely sure that hair on my chest or toes would make me feel any better. In fact, I'm pretty sure that an excess of bodily hair in unwanted places would only add to my woes.

Then her face softens. 'Have you been through a rough time? I thought as much. Sure as eggs are peas, there's some man behind it. I know these things. Why else would you come here on your own? You're a beautiful young thing, but you look all frail and forlorn. There's no light in those lovely emerald eyes.'

The tears that are never very far from my eyes these days spring up afresh. I swallow down the emotion that's lodged in my throat. 'I just need some time alone,' I reiterate. '*Completely* alone.'

Marilyn reaches out and pats my hand. She crinkles her eyes and says kindly, 'Don't you worry, lovely. You can be alone with me.'

Chapter Four

Marilyn tells me about things to do on the island while I hurriedly finish my tea. She rattles them all off in a manner that the tourist board would be proud of. Apparently, as well as the must-see garlic farm, there's Osborne House – one-time seaside home of Queen Victoria – the Needles lighthouse and many other essential touristy experiences that Marilyn insists I must do. They all pass through my brain but don't stop. I'm not intending to spend my time sightseeing – although I'm not sure what exactly I'm planning to do with my time here. While she has a brief pause for breath, I seize my chance to speak.

'I must unpack,' I say, standing from the table. 'And I need to pay you for the shopping.'

She waves a hand. 'Oh, don't you worry about that. I'm to send the bill to *Bill*.' She laughs. 'See what I did there?'

I do. 'Well, thank you again for the tea.'

'I could make you some lunch?'

'I'm not hungry just yet, thank you. I think I might go out for a walk later while it's still light.'

'There's a nice café on the beach at the end of the next bay, Sandy Cove. Tiny place. Outside and all that. Lovely food.

Everyone goes there. It won't take long to walk there. It'll be a bit chilly today, but it will put some carnations in your cheeks.'

'I'll have a wander when I've sorted my stuff out.' In truth that won't take long as I've brought very little with me.

'Right.' Marilyn stands. 'I must get on too.'

'It really isn't necessary. The place is immaculate. We've used two mugs. I can manage to wash those up.'

Marilyn ushers me towards the stairs. 'I'll do that, young lady. You unpack and rest for a while. I'll be as quiet as a sausage. You won't even know I'm here and I'll close the door behind me when I'm gone.'

Resistance is clearly futile, so I say, 'Thank you.'

'Nothing is too much trouble.' Marilyn frowns at me with concern. 'You only have to ask.'

I take my leave while Marilyn is heading to the sink and retreat to my bedroom below deck – if that's the right term.

As I lift my bags onto the bed, for the second time, I catch sight of myself in a mirror. This time it's the one on the dressing table. Marilyn's right, I do look frail and forlorn. My face is pale, and I realise that my grey shirt does nothing to enhance it. I've never dressed quite like Marilyn, but even I realise that I could do with a bit of colour in my life. No wonder Marilyn looked at me with such pity. I turn the mirror round to face the wall.

I can hear her clonking about upstairs, her tottering heels tapping on the wood floor. I'll ring Bill as soon as she's gone. I can't cope with her. She's too colourful. Too brash. Too loud. She never stops talking and I know from just one meeting that I won't be able to turn her volume down to a manageable level. She has to go.

I've only thrown a few things in the drawers when I run out of energy and lie on the bed. I've a headache coming. A regular occurrence these days. Sometimes it feels as if I have too many thoughts in my brain and too little space in which to hold them. They clang against the inside of my skull, fighting for space, pressing against the back of my eyes ready to burst out in a shower of pain. I have some tablets, somewhere, but I feel too weighted down to get up and find them. Closing my eyes, I try to block out the tippy-tappy of Marilyn's heels and tune into the soothing sounds of the seaside instead.

I've just got my breathing under control and my eyes are feeling heavy when Marilyn switches on the vacuum. Believe me, Bill's boat doesn't need hoovering. There's not a speck of dust anywhere. She can only be a minute – five at the most. I'll grit my teeth until she's done. While she crashes and bashes about, I work on deepening my breath and, just when I think I might be starting to achieve a trance-like state, Marilyn starts to sing over the sound of the cleaner. 'Jolene'. It's not what I want to hear at the best of times and certainly not now.

With an exasperated tut, I reach for my handbag and pull out my earphones. I plug them into my iPhone and flick to the most soothing music I can find, but it's no good, I'm still competing with Marilyn who's joyfully murdering Dolly Parton. Giving up with the earphones, I lie there grinding my molars as she moves on to 'Islands in the Stream' at full blast, hitting almost one note in three. Then, when I think I'm about to turn into a screaming banshee, the hoover falls silent and so does Marilyn. I let out a relieved sigh and try to relax my clenched jaw.

A few moments later, she shouts. 'See you at the same time tomorrow, sweetheart! I've left my phone number in case you want me to pick anything up on my way in! Just give me a tinkle. Byeeeeeeeee!'

Then the front door bangs and the boat, as sturdy as it is, shudders.

I let out a long, wavering breath. 'Bloody hell. What a

whirlwind.' I have to ring Bill and get him to cancel her. I can't handle anyone so vibrant, so full of life, so happy.

Then I feel sorry for myself and I cry because I never know what else to do.

Chapter Five

When I've pulled myself together again and have dozed for a bit, I make my way back onto the main deck and curl up on the sofa in the living room with a soft blanket tucked round my knees. I'm perpetually cold, as if all the blood has stopped moving round my body.

Turning on my phone, I see that there are seventeen messages, only one of them from Bill.

I delete all the others, then call Bill back. 'Hello, bro.'

'You got there all right then,' he says. 'I was just beginning to wonder.'

'I'd have called as soon as I got here, but I've been talking to Marilyn,' I tell him. 'Or rather she's been talking to me.'

'Ah. Forgot to tell you about Marilyn. She's great, isn't she? Chatty.'

'*Very*.' I hope he hears the disapproval in my tone. 'I don't need babysitting, Bill. I don't need "chatty". I need quiet. Preferably silence.' I hug my knees to me. 'I'm perfectly fine.'

'You're not,' he points out. 'Otherwise, you'd be here at work with me doing the hotel refit presentation that I'm currently putting together.'

Guilt tugs at my heartstrings. 'Have I left you completely in the lurch?' Bill has been so good to me that I don't like to think of him having to take up the slack while I'm away licking my wounds.

'Of course you have. But that's fine. I understand and I want you to take this time to regroup. Stay there as long as you need. As soon as you're ready to get back on your game, I'll be waiting.'

'You're too good to me.' Just talking to my brother makes me come over all teary again. 'No other employer would put up with me running away.'

'I'm your brother first, employer second. All I want is for you to be happy again.'

'At the moment, I can't see that ever happening.'

'You never know what's around the corner,' Bill says. 'Good or bad. It's still early days.'

That's what everyone says. That's what I don't want to hear any more.

'Relax, kick back,' Bill continues. 'Do whatever you need to do.'

'I love you,' I tell him. 'What would I do without you?'

'Let's never find out.' Then he hesitates before saying, 'Have you heard from Chris?'

'He's left a ton of messages, but I don't want to speak to him.'

'You'll have to at some point.'

Bill's right, as usual. 'But not yet.'

'He's called me too, but I haven't replied either.'

'You won't tell him where I am?'

'Of course not. He'll get a piece of my mind when I speak to him.'

'Save your breath.' Chris only hears what he wants to.

'He is bang out of order,' Bill says, crossly.

'I know that, you know that,' I placate. 'I'm not sure Chris will have the same view.'

I hear someone else speak in the background then Bill says, 'Sorry but I have to rush off, Jodie. Anything else I can do for you, before I go?'

'Cancel Marilyn,' I beg.

'No. She's adorable. You'll get used to her. I want her to keep an eye on you.'

I tut at him as if we're children again. 'She's not adorable. She's annoying.'

'Give her a chance,' my brother pleads. 'For me.'

Bill has always looked after me. He's been the best big brother I could have ever had. He's been my protector, my champion. Yet even Bill couldn't shield me from what happened.

'I'm not going to be necking a bottle of voddy every day,' I assure him.

'Good to hear.' Then some tapping of keys in the background. 'I don't want to go, but I have to shoot,' Bill says. 'Meeting in five.'

'What?'

'The big eco-hotel project. First face-to-face. It's inching forward.'

I'm glad to hear there's some movement. We pitched to do the interior design for a fabulous new project of an eco-hotel set on the very edge of the New Forest. It looks amazing. This one has been on the back burner for an age as securing the planning permission has been a long, drawn-out process. 'That's something I really want to work on.'

'Better get your shit together pretty smartish then,' he teases.

'I love you,' I say again. 'Thanks for this.'

'How do you like the boat? Cool, eh?'

'It's fabulous. Amazing taste must run in the family.' Except for men. Bill and I both fall down on that front. I don't think my brother has ever had a relationship for longer than a year. I had great hopes for a few of the partners that Bill's had over the years, but as I've said he has very exacting standards and he's a workaholic – neither of those make relationships easy. Now I think he's become too used to doing his own thing. 'You've done a great job.'

'Yeah. I must get out there one day.'

'I thought it was going to be your weekend place for the summer? Party central.'

'That's still my plan,' Bill assures me. 'But we'll see how things go.'

What he means is that he won't be going anywhere over the summer if I'm not back in the office by then. He'll be working 24/7. The worst thing about this is letting Bill down. Well, it isn't the worst thing, but you don't know that yet and I'm in no fit state to explain it.

'*Sunny Days*, though?' I'm glad he can't see my nose wrinkling. 'I thought you would have chosen something more cool, more on message.'

'That was what the previous owner called it and, apparently, it's bad luck to change the name of a boat.'

'Is it?'

'Yes. You have to go through all kinds of rituals if you do – a purging ceremony to appease the sea gods.'

'Marilyn told you this, didn't she?'

'Of course.' Bill laughs. 'She knows everything. And everyone.'

Just my luck.

'Sorry, sis. Got to run. I can see the team assembling round the table.'

The offices of WJ Design are in a trendy area of Shoreditch and are very fancy indeed – which is only fitting for a design company. The main floor is furnished with an enormous table that is industrial chic teamed with brushed steel café chairs and we have a company breakfast here every morning. The rest of the office is open plan, except Bill and I – as senior partners – have offices that are glass boxes set at angles to each other.

We're lucky to have a great team of loyal staff and Bill will have to break the news to them that I'm not going to be around for a while. They know why – some of it, anyway – and they'll probably all make the right sympathetic noises but, equally, they'll more than likely be a bit pissed off that they have to pick up the extra workload. There'll be some very late nights at the interior design coal face and it will all be my fault.

I get a stab of regret that I'm not there at the sharp end of it, but I simply can't cope at the moment. It's all too much. Everything's too much.

'We'll speak soon,' Bill says. 'I'll be checking up on you every day.'

'I wouldn't expect anything else.' Then my throat tightens with emotion. 'Thank you for letting me come here. I didn't know what else to do.'

'I'm glad I could oblige. Fortunately, the timing was perfect. I can't wait to see it finished. Let me know when you feel up to it and I'll try to come over for the weekend.'

'I'd like that. You're the only person I'm going to miss.' That's not strictly true. There's my friend, Della, too. I'll be lost without her as well. She'll be furious when she hears that I've skipped town without telling her. That's another phone call I'll put off.

'Well, we'll all miss you. Hanging up now,' Bill says. 'Love you.'

Despite saying that I want to be alone, I miss Bill more than you can know and I'm reluctant to hang up the phone.

When he's gone, I'm not sure what to do with myself. I go to the back of the boat and the view has changed completely. The lone paddle-boarder has taken his leave, boats have come and gone, the tide is rushing out. The sun is starting its slow descent and I stand to watch the sunset with marvel. It's absolutely stunning. The golden glow lights up the living room and the rays spread out from the sun until they've tipped all of the clouds with a peach hue. Then they persist until the whole sky is ablaze with gold.

'Oh, man,' I say to myself. 'That's a sight for sore eyes.'

When the sun finally sinks below the horizon and the dusk is gathering, I realise that I haven't eaten. The café that Marilyn recommended will probably have closed a long time ago. So I rummage in the fridge to find what she has left me. Despite me moaning to Bill, that was really very good of her. I'm grateful now that there's a loaf and cheese as I rustle up a toastie.

I feel bad that I was off-hand with Marilyn and so I text her. *Thank you for the food, very useful. Jodie.*

Within seconds I get back. *No problem, sweetie. Mxxxxxxx* followed by a row of totally random emojis – a heart, a poodle, a snowman, two champagne glasses and a fish. Plus a dozen other things that I can't even identify.

I take my toastie to the kitchen table and nibble on it. I have no appetite, but I do try to remember to eat regularly. I used to love my food, but everything now tastes like sawdust. I eat just to stay alive and, sometimes, I confess that there seems little point in that.

Before long, I realise that I'm sitting in the dark and put the light on in the kitchen. As I do, I note that there are lights on in the boat next door. So it is inhabited, after all. I stand to the side of the kitchen window and have a little peek over in case I can get a glimpse of anyone, but I can't. I don't want my neighbours to think that I'm spying on them, even though I am.

As the night begins to close in and there's nothing but the darkness of the sea ahead of me, I take what's left of supper and sit in front of the television, letting *Celebrity Antiques Road Trip* go past my eyes.

This is what I need. No conversation, no company, no stress. No past, no future, only the present. Just myself and my thoughts.

Marilyn texts me again. *Four Weddings and a Funeral is on telly tonight. Best film ever. That Hugh Grant would so get it. Mxxxxxxx* A frog, a Canadian flag, a man surfing, three pandas and a glass of wine.

I shake my head, totally confused. Then think: actually, the last one might not be a bad idea.

Chapter Six

I don't sleep a wink. But then that's nothing new. I haven't slept in months. As advised, I stayed up until the small hours watching *Four Weddings and a Funeral*. What else was I to do? I'm sure Marilyn will quiz me on it. In fairness, though it's not my usual kind of film, I enjoyed it even though I cried through most of it – even the funny bits.

Now I lie awake listening to the creaks and groans of *Sunny Days* as it rises and falls on its mooring posts with the changing tide. When the light comes in through the portholes and I can hear the gulls calling, I get up.

There are more messages on my phone – the majority from Chris – and I delete them without reading. There's one from Della too and I promise myself to call her later. She'll be distraught that I didn't turn to her first before doing a runner.

The water in the en-suite shower is hot and plentiful. That, again, must be down to Marilyn as I didn't even think to look where the controls for the hot water or heating were. The boat is warm too, so the central heating must be on.

As I'm stepping out of the shower, I hear Marilyn's 'Coooeeeee!' as she bowls in and wince slightly.

Trying to put off the inevitable effort of conversation, I take my time getting dressed – noticing for the first time how loose all my clothes are on my frame – and then venture upstairs. Marilyn is already crashing about in the kitchen. Today, she's dressed from head to toe in peacock blue – a jumpsuit with a bold, exotic print that involves jungly leaves and parrots. The only exception is towering yellow heels that match the rubber gloves she's wearing. My eyeballs try to retreat into my head. So much colour is a shock this early in the day.

'Morning, darling!' She trills cheerfully and I wish she'd turn her volume down at least a notch or two. 'Sleep well?'

'Yes,' I lie.

Marilyn purses her scarlet red lips. 'An hour at best, I'd say. Look at you.' She shakes her head in despair at my appearance. 'You need some sea air on your ribs. And something to eat. Let me fix you a bit of breakfast. I brought some of my own jam for you to try. It's blackberry and apple from last year's pickings.'

'That's very kind of you, but I was thinking of walking down to the café you mentioned yesterday for my breakfast. It looks like a lovely day out there.' Sun is flooding into the living area and, once again, I congratulate Bill on having done such a great job on renovating this boat. It looks beautiful bathed in sunlight.

'It's fresh out there,' Marilyn warns. 'You'll need a big coat. The wind will cut right through you. It's as sharp as a banana. I think it's blowing all the way from Siberia or somewhere. It certainly feels like it. A drink before you go? The kettle's just boiled.'

'I'm OK, thanks.' She'll want to chat, find out why I'm here and I can't face it. 'I could do with some fresh air. I'll get my coat.'

'Anything in particular you want me to do while I'm here?'

'It's all immaculate, Marilyn,' I tell her, glancing around. 'Bill just wants you to babysit me.' Check that I'm still alive. 'Put your feet up and have a coffee. Read a magazine. Watch *Judge Rinder*.'

She laughs as if I've said something truly hilarious. 'Go on with you. I'm sure I'll find something to do. The sea spray plays havoc with the windows. And don't get me started on those ruddy gulls. I love them to bits but they're dirty things.'

I get my coat and button it up before I go out as I'm certain Marilyn would tell me off if I didn't.

'That's not a coat!' She looks at my neat single-breasted, dark grey cashmere affair with horror. 'You'll get draughts everywhere.'

'It's all I've got.' Though she's probably right. I've already realised that it's more city slicker than beach stroller.

'Scarf?' Marilyn says. 'Have you got a scarf?'

'I haven't.'

'You'll need one. A hat?'

I shake my head. I'm found wanting in the hat department too.

'You'll catch pleurisy,' she warns.

'It doesn't look too bad.' I peer out of the windows that the sea spray is supposedly playing havoc with.

She gives me a knowing look. 'Borrow mine.'

'I'm fine. Really. I'll see you tomorrow.' I head for the door.

'You know where you're going? You just walk along the esplanade and down the steps into the next bay. Go right the way along to the end. You can't miss it. If you go any further, you'll end up in the sea.'

'Thanks.'

'I can come and show you, if you like.'

'I'm sure I can find it. Have a good day.'

'Bye, lovely. You make sure you have a nice time. Give my love to Ida. They do a good crumpet. Homemade. None of your shop bought stuff. I'll see you tomorrow. Phone me if you need me. Byeeeee!'

I step out of the boat feeling as if I'm five again. I take a deep breath as I close the door behind me and all the talking stops. It's a long time since anyone fussed over me and I have to admit that I'm veering between finding it really annoying and quite liking it. She's no doubt very well intentioned, but it is like being bulldozed with love.

On the gangway, the wind nearly knocks me off my feet. Marilyn's right, of course. I do need a more suitable coat. And a scarf. A woolly hat wouldn't go amiss either. Gloves might be useful too. Once again, I rue that I departed my old life so woefully unprepared.

Chapter Seven

Thankfully, as I turn in the direction of the café, the wind is at my back and I get blown along rather than having to battle into it. Coming back is going to be fun, though. As the tide is in, I can't walk round to the next cove on the sand. Instead, hands in pockets, I walk towards the esplanade along the row of moored houseboats in the harbour, all looking pretty in their pastel shades.

They're all shapes and sizes, modern and traditional all thrown together. The one next door to *Sea Breezes* is enormous, painted bright white and is covered in bunting and wind spinners. The boat beyond that is a smart Dutch barge, then a big, square modern one with a Mondrian-style painting on the side. I walk along and have a good look at them all.

Then I head away from the harbour and, as Marilyn instructed, down the esplanade that runs along from Cockleshell Bay and into Sandy Cove. The sea front is old-fashioned, how seaside resorts used to be years ago. Smart Edwardian villas look out onto the sea, most of them now guest houses or holiday rentals rather than individual homes. Instead of turning up into the main street – I can explore that another time – I carry on along the promenade. There are some wrought iron benches that look in need of a fresh coat of paint after the worst of the winter and an art deco style shelter that offers some cover from the elements. At the top of the steps that descend to the beach, there's also a worn brass steampunk statue that seems incongruous in this setting.

As I pass by, the statue says, 'Morning!' and makes me jump out of my skin.

'God, you scared me half to death,' I say up at him.

'Oh, sorry.' Mr Steampunk raises his hat. 'You looked a bit fed up, so I thought I'd cheer you up.'

My mind might be elsewhere and he's higher than me on a raised plinth, but he makes quite a convincing statue. His skin is completely covered in bronze make-up and he's dressed from head-to-toe in clothing also painted bronze – a frock coat, top hat, retro rivet spectacles, and he's sporting a cane with a fancy handle. Now I look more closely, his plinth is a box covered with material and there's a small collection box at his feet. 'I thought you were actually a statue.'

'Well, my work here is done,' he says with a laugh and bows as he holds out his hat.

I look in my bag, fishing for change.

'Oh, I don't want any money.'

'Isn't that the point?'

'Well, yes. But have this one on me. I needed to move. It's freezing out here. You look like you need a big coat and scarf on.'

'So I've been told.' Everyone's an expert on my welfare – even statues.

'Nice to meet you.' He holds out a gloved hand and, after a moment's hesitation, I shake it. 'I'm George.'

'Jodie,' I reciprocate.

He stretches and jogs on the spot a bit. 'It's been slow here this morning and I'm not very good at standing still.'

That would seem to be a bit of a drawback for a living statue. I look up and down the seafront. There's no one else about but me. 'I'm sure you know your job better than me, but there doesn't seem to be much passing trade. It seems like a quiet spot.'

'That's why I like it. I used to be a living statue in Covent Garden,' he tells me. 'It was a nightmare. People kept pinching my bum.'

That makes me laugh and he looks hurt. 'I'm sorry.'

'The abuse that living statues have to suffer isn't widely appreciated. It's different here. Everyone's nice.' He nods towards the sea. 'The working conditions are better too. How many people can go to their office and enjoy that? You'd go a long way to beat this view.'

I follow his gaze. 'No. I suppose not. You can't earn much, though.'

He shrugs. 'Life's not all about money, is it?'

'No.' I can't really argue with that. I go to walk on, but he's not done with me yet.

'A bit early for a holiday,' he notes.

For goodness' sake, even the statues are chatty here. 'Yes. I suppose so.'

'Well, better get back to statueing in case anyone catches me relaxing. It would blow my cover. I might see you again?'

'You might,' I agree.

George strikes another pose and I can't help but smile as I walk away even though some of his bronze paint has rubbed off on my fingers.

I drop down the steps into the cove which is a small, perfect curve with a pleasingly sandy beach and a delightfully Mediterranean feel – even though it's clearly not quite at its best at this time of year. There are more holiday homes and a few beach huts advertising deckchairs and kayaks to rent by the hour, but they're all closed up for the winter. There's a small jetty with fishing boats tied up next to it and lobster pots stacked alongside the sea wall.

There aren't many people brave enough to be here today either, just a few ardent dog-walkers with their windswept pooches. A black and white cocker spaniel running about with its ears flapping wildly looks especially joyful. The wind is whipping up impressive waves and the cotton-wool clouds are scudding merrily across the sky. The sun is out in full force, but is not making one jot of difference to the temperature. Yet, it's nice. I surrender myself to the elements, letting the wind fling my hair around. Chris and I used to head straight to the Caribbean for holidays, so I haven't been on a beach in the UK in a very long time and I enjoy the forgotten feel of damp sand beneath my feet. Thankfully, I'd thought to throw some trainers into my bag, so at least I have suitable footwear if nothing else.

As I reach the other end of the beach, only a few minutes' walk, there's a couple ahead of me. They're strolling at the edge of the surf, the water lapping over the toes of their wellington boots. On the man's shoulders is a child of about two years old. A little girl with blonde hair and cheeks rosy from the cold. The perfect family. I watch them even though I don't want to. The couple look so happy, so in love. I feel a sucker punch to my stomach all over again and a rush of unwanted emotion threatens to overwhelm me. Will this ever pass, I wonder?

Thankfully, as I'm getting ready to turn on my heels and beat a hasty retreat back to the sanctuary of *Sunny Days*, I see the Beach Hut Café come into view at the end of the cove. This must be the place that Marilyn recommended. It's a welcome beacon with its stripy blue and white paint and strings of bunting which are flapping wildly like the cocker spaniel's ears in the stiff breeze. I make my way towards it, brushing the hot tears from my eyes.

Chapter Eight

The Beach Hut Café does what it says on the tin. It's a large and brightly painted beach hut at the very end of the cove, right on the sea front. Outside, there are a few tables and chairs in pastel shades, some of them sheltered from the prevailing wind by a low white-washed wall. The only covered area is a plastic awning on the side where there are more tables and chairs plus a couple of patio heaters – currently not switched on. At the back of the awning there's a bookcase with a good stock of well-thumbed paperbacks. There's plenty of bunting in evidence here too and lots of chalkboard signs dotted about with cheery sayings such as 'May your coffee be strong and your Monday short', 'Cake is always a good idea', and 'Congratulations! You made it out of bed'.

In the summer this place is probably rammed but, for now, it seems as if only the local die-hards are out and about. There are only a few other customers. Huddled at the back near the paperbacks is a man with a super-sized mug in his hands. At the front, two women in down jackets and bobble hats are deep in giggly conversation. I think of Della with a pang of guilt and how I should let her know where I am as soon as possible. I'm putting it off as I know she'll be furious when she finds out what I've done. She's been a big support to me recently and will see it as a personal failure that I've caved in.

I'm the only one brave or stupid enough to sit outside by the sea wall, but as I'm so foolhardy I can, at least, choose a table sheltered from the breeze. I peruse the menu and try not to let my eyes seek out the loved-up couple on the beach.

I'd had a few happy but ultimately failed relationships over the years. But none of them broke my heart and I knew that I'd never want to settle down permanently with any of them. I always went for high-maintenance men who weren't the marrying kind. When I met Chris, it was totally different. In a chance twist of fate, we happened upon each other when we took the last two seats in a crowded coffee shop. We laughed as we dashed to the seats and sat down at the same moment. Ice broken, we started chatting, hardly able to hear each other above the noise. So, when we reached the bottom of our respective cups and the café was closing, we exchanged numbers. The next night, we went for dinner. Instantly, I knew he was The One. I fell quickly and hard. I literally trembled when he called me. He was funny and confident – in hindsight, perhaps a touch too much. It's fair to say that Chris has never had a moment of self-doubt. His sense of self-belief is admirable. Unless, of course, you happen to disagree with him.

He's a handsome man, too – tall, broad. If you saw him, you'd know why the attraction was instant. He spends more time than I do in the gym, looking after his body – which he then usually ruins with too many business dinners and a liking for good red wine. He has a strong face with an abundance of freckles that I used to love to trace with my fingers and his horn-rim glasses give him a slightly geeky, intellectual look. Now, ten years later, his auburn hair is beginning to fleck with grey. But it suits him and gives him an air of maturity that I like.

From the beginning, we fitted together so well. We were both career-driven, so neither of us minded the hours that we put into our work. Chris was grinding away, steadily climbing the corporate ladder. I'd joined Bill in his company and was helping him to build it. Grabbing a few minutes with each other on a daily basis seemed to suit us both. Our weekends were spent playing hard with days out with friends, chic bars, boutique hotels, the best tickets at concerts. We were both happy. We laughed at our friends whose social lives ended when they started to have families and had sleepless nights to contend with, issues with babysitters, or the onslaught of unexpected fevers, tummy upsets, coughs and colds. We were smugness incarnate.

Yet, how I now hate Past Us.

Out of habit, I check my phone. A dozen more messages from Chris that all say exactly the same thing in increasingly desperate language.

As I was always so busy, he had a colleague, Meg, who he called his 'work wife'. How we laughed about that too. She'd be the one to accompany him to all the dinners and events that I couldn't make because I was at important ones of my own. I was really grateful that he liked her so much and that it let me off the hook. I don't think I find that so funny now either.

Meg's much younger than me – than Chris too. He's forty-two, like me. Meg is only twenty-eight. She has flowing blonde curls and legs like a colt. Even then, I didn't see a threat in her. There was no doubt that she hero-worshipped my husband, but what would she see in him as potential boyfriend material? He was an older, married man. Perhaps I was naive, but I suspected nothing. Chris and I were solid, happy. We had the same life goals. It was work that kept him late at the office, work that took him on regular overnight trips, work that took him to the theatre entertaining clients. It's no good looking at me like that,

I believed him. He was my husband, he told me he loved me on a regular basis, nothing he did made me doubt that. I loved him in return. I was a fool.

'What can I get for you?' The woman who comes to take my order is all smiles and wacky clothes. She's wearing a denim jacket lined with sheepskin, a Nepalese knitted hat with ear flaps and pom-poms, multi-coloured patchwork, hippy trousers and Doc Martens hand-painted with red roses. She's strikingly pretty, with olive skin and long, dark hair threaded with multi-coloured ribbons sticking out from beneath her hat. Another splash of colour. Again, I feel so drab in my grey, designer coat as if I'm blending into the background, a shadow. Which is fine. 'The soup of the day is roasted red pepper and tomato. Free refills on tea if you ask nicely.'

'Thanks, but I think I'll have a cappuccino and a bacon roll, please.'

'A very wise choice,' she says. 'Coming up in five.'

'Thanks.'

The family on the beach seem to have gone now, so I stare out at the sea until my bacon roll is delivered within the promised five minutes. Despite the vague feeling of nausea that seems to be my constant companion, I enjoy it much more than I'd anticipated. The bacon is crispy, smoky and on bread that's obviously freshly baked. The coffee is strong and creamy and that hits the spot too.

As I'm finishing, licking the last taste of bacon from my fingertips, the owner comes out again to wipe down the tables.

'It's certainly blowy today. Everything's covered in a film of sand,' she says as she stops at the table next to me. 'There are few downsides to having a café by the beach, but this is one of them. That and the gulls pinching customers' sandwiches.'

It's clear that she's not in a hurry to move on and I'm reluctant to be rude.

'Here on holiday?' she tries. 'It's a bit early in the season. I usual only see the locals at this time of year.'

'Not exactly holiday,' I admit. 'More of an extended escape from the rat race.'

'I empathise,' she says. 'That's kind of what brought me here too. I could have gone to art college in London, but I came over here instead and never left. Lucky me.' There's a certain amount of irony in her voice. 'Where are you staying?'

'At a houseboat in the next harbour.' I point towards it, unnecessarily. '*Sunny Days*.'

'Ah. That's been an ongoing project for some time. Finally finished?'

'It's my brother's boat, not mine. But, yes, he's finished it now.'

'And you're trying it out for size?'

'Yes. It's beautiful. He's done a very good job.'

'Your next-door-neighbour is a good mate of mine. Ned Haddon. I haven't seen him for a few days, but I think he's around at the mo. He's an artist, flaky as hell, obvs, but I love him to bits.'

'There were lights on last night, so it looks as if someone is there.' Just what I need, a flaky artist as a neighbour. Still, it explains the eclectic decor of the houseboat he lives on. It does look very arty. Hopefully, he won't be around much while I'm in residence.

'I'm Ida Ray. Maybe I'll see some more of you if you're here for a while.'

'I should think so. Marilyn said hi, by the way.'

She laughs. 'Is Marilyn cleaning for you?'

'Yes.'

'She can talk the hind leg off a donkey, but she's fabulous,' Ida says. 'She'll make sure you're OK.' She reaches into the pocket of her denim jacket. 'Here, I'll give you a loyalty card.

I don't give these out lightly, you know. Only to people that I want to see again.'

'I'm honoured.'

'See you then.' Ida flashes me a broad smile as she moves on to the next table.

The sun hides behind a cloud for a bit and it gets really quite chilly. The appeal of stoking up Bill's wood burner is calling. I wonder whether Marilyn will have finished yet and if it's safe for me to go back to the boat.

Chapter Nine

Instead of heading straight back to *Sunny Days*, I decide to explore the rest of Cockleshell Bay. I don't think it will take all that long. There's only one main street by the look of it and that rises up with a gentle incline away from the harbour. It's lined with a row of neat terraced houses and a handful of pastel-painted bed and breakfast places, most of which have their no vacancy signs out. That says to me that they're shut up for the winter and their owners have buggered off for a well-earned break in Gran Canaria. It seems unlikely that they're actually full as there seem to be very few people around.

Further up the street, there are a couple of interesting-looking cafés that must be serious competition for the Beach Hut in season. It looks to have a decent butchers and greengrocers too. There's a hairdressers and, of course, it has its share of estate agents. The rest of the shops are mostly filled with touristy fare – stuff that seems like a good idea until you get it home. I travelled a bit when I was younger, fresh out of uni, and eventually, stopped buying souvenirs altogether. What looks good in Peru should stay in Peru. Islington is no place for a replica terracotta soldier either. Cockleshell Bay is a pretty place though and I don't know why it should, but that surprises me. In a time when British seaside resorts are generally seen to be suffering, this town looks fresh, upmarket and as if it's more than holding its own.

I don't need any more food thanks to Marilyn but, after browsing what's on offer, I do pop into one of the two clothes shops to buy a wool hat with a ridiculously large pom-pom and matching scarf. If I'm going to be doing some walking on the beach while I'm here then I at least need to be warm.

Clearly seeing Marilyn and Ida with their cheerful style has influenced me as I go for bright red instead of my usual grey or black. I pick up some scarlet felted wool gloves to match. The backs are embroidered with butterflies and I'm not sure they're really me, but I'm prepared to give it a go. I'd like to think that I'm still erring on the side of tasteful. I can't see me wearing them in London though. If I ever go back.

What will Chris be thinking now, I wonder. Will he have turned to Meg in his distress? Probably.

I don't want you to think our relationship was all doom and gloom. We rarely argued and, when we managed to grab holidays together, we always got along well. That's probably why I'm so thrown by what has happened between us.

When I've exhausted window shopping, I turn and head back to Sandy Cove beach. I drop by the café again and ask for a coffee to go.

'In need of a caffeine fix so soon?' Ida quips.

'Not for me. There's a living statue just down the road, on the sea front. I thought I'd take one for him. He said he's cold.'

'Ah, George. He's a regular here. A proud bearer of the loyalty card. He likes a cappuccino, two sugars.' Ida kicks her coffee machine into life and duly makes one for me to take away.

The wind is still blowing strong and heading back is as much of a struggle as I'd feared, so I'm doubly glad that I splashed out on my woollies. They have helped to plug some of the draughty gaps in my clothing. It's not long before I climb the steps from the beach onto the esplanade feeling slightly breathless.

George is sitting chatting on his phone. When he sees me, he hangs up and jumps onto his box, striking a pose.

'Caught you slacking,' I tell him. 'I brought you coffee.'

He relaxes his pose and steps down to take it from me. 'That's lovely,' he says. 'I'm not feeling the statue love today. Might give up and go back to my day job.'

'What's that?'

'It's not *exactly* a job,' he admits a bit sheepishly. 'I'm writing a novel. Or trying to.'

'Oh. An author.'

'Well. Don't get too excited. I've been writing my *opus magnum* for the best part of five years.'

Perhaps he's not much better as an author as he is a statue. 'At least you can do that sitting down.'

'True.' George sips his coffee, gratefully. 'Hmm. Nice and hot.'

'Ida said it's what you like.'

'Thank you. This is very kind of you.'

'No problem. I didn't like to think of you being cold.' I move away as I've exhausted the extent of my chit-chat. 'I should go.'

'Have a nice day, Jodie.' He raises his cup to me. 'Thanks again.'

'No problem. Good luck with the novel,' I call as I walk away.

The wind is blustery, puffing in spiteful bursts. Some of the more lusty gusts threaten to blow me off my feet. I lean into it as I walk and am relieved when I finally see *Sunny Days* coming into view. That was a harder workout than any gym treadmill. Back on the gangway, I pause to catch my breath and notice that there's smoke curling out of the chimney of the eclectic *Sea*

Breezes next door. Ida's friend must have returned as I suspected. Though the blinds are all still closed.

Letting myself into *Sunny Days*, I strip off my inadequate coat and newly acquired hat and scarf and hang them in the hall. There's no sign of Marilyn and the houseboat is even more immaculate than when I left, if that's humanly possible.

On the kitchen table there's a note that says *See you tomorrow! Mxx* in big, loopy writing. There's a smiley face drawn beneath it and another plethora of kisses. Joy. It must be nice to go through life like Marilyn, untroubled by woes and perpetually sunny. There's also a big bunch of vibrant yellow daffodils in a vase in the middle of the table which, I have to admit, is very thoughtful of her. The colour is like a shot of sunshine.

I make a cup of tea and, while I drink it, reluctantly flick on my phone again. Nothing more from Chris, but one from Bill which simply says, *OK?* I message back *Fine*.

What to do with the rest of my day? The shelves are stacked high with books of all manner – romantic comedies, sporting autobiographies, several I recognise as winning literary awards of some sort. Probably bought by Bill but never read. I don't get much time to read at home and this should be a luxury, but my attention span is terrible. I'd put on the radio, but I can't bear to disturb the peace. It's as if too much sound hurts my brain. And all the songs make me want to weep. It's nice to hear the gentle shush of the waves, but the caw of the gulls sounds too much like a crying child and I wish they'd be quiet.

I take what's left of my tea and a blanket from the sofa and head out onto the top deck, which I've yet to explore. There's another couple of steamer chairs here and there are cushions for them in a locker. The cushions have still got the tags on and don't look like they've ever been used. I lay one out and settle myself under the blanket to do nothing more taxing than look out at the sea. George is right, it's a very beautiful view and, thankfully, the harbour is sheltered from the wind. It's so quiet and peaceful that I let a sigh escape. There's a plethora of yachts moored up, then the dark circle of the fort beyond and, further out to sea, there's an enormous cruise ship going by – probably filled with shiny, happy people enjoying their pre-paid drinks package. I sip my tea.

Chris and I did a cruise. A few years ago now. To the Caribbean. Waking up to a different island every day was blissful. We laughed, drank too many rum cocktails, danced the night away, were careless with our contraception. It was a wonderful holiday. I thought we had it all then.

Due to my largely sleepless night, it's not long before my eyes begin to grow heavy. The tide must be coming in or going out as I can feel a slight movement of the boat beneath me and that's helping to make me drowsy too.

Then, just as I'm edging into sleep, there's an ear-splitting noise which jolts me back to sitting and sets my nerves jangling. It sounds for all the world like someone starting up a chainsaw.

'What the hell?' I throw aside my blanket and go and look over the rail. Instantly, I can see who the culprit is.

Chapter Ten

Ida's friend, Ned Haddon, is on the back of the boat next door. He's busy attacking a lump of wood and, as much as I'd suspected, using a chainsaw to do it. Despite the cool of the day, he's just in a white T-shirt and dark trousers, ear defenders and protective goggles. He looks tall, broad-shouldered but, beyond that, I can't tell you much else.

This won't do. This won't do at all.

'Hey! Hey!' I shout down to him trying to attract his attention but because of the ear defenders and the nerve-shredding noise of the chainsaw he can't hear a word of it. Damn him.

Still, if he's chopping wood for the fire, hopefully he won't be much longer. However, as I watch it becomes clear that he's sculpting the wood rather than just hacking it into logs. It isn't a great leap to make me realise that those pieces on the boat are obviously carved by his own hand. When Ida said he was an artist, I imagined nice watercolour paintings of seaside scenes. Looks as if I was wrong. It appears that Mr Ned Haddon practises the noisiest form of art there could possibly be. Just my luck.

For some reason, I can't tear my eyes away. His body movements flow as he cuts through the wood, this way and that, almost in a slow dance and, despite being cross at the noise, I'm finding it mesmerising. Eventually, even the buzz of the saw finds a rhythm and, if I had ear defenders on too, it might be considered quite soothing. As I watch, a face starts to emerge in the wood. Chips of bark and sawdust fly everywhere, some bits somersaulting off into the sea. He's creating the face of a woman in the timber. I can see him shaping her cheeks, her eyes, her mouth. It's strangely sensual to see her emerging beneath his hands. The way he uses the chainsaw is just how an artist would use a brush. The machine he's wielding isn't your usual chainsaw, it looks to be lightweight and compact, clearly meant for the job in hand. It's bloody noisy though. Still, I'm riveted. His talent is obvious and I wonder how long he's been doing this or how he started. Let's face it, the chainsaw isn't the usual medium of choice for an artist.

As I'm leaning over the rail, staring down, he turns and catches my eye. He kills the chainsaw, tilts back his goggles and lifts his ear defenders. 'Hi there!'

'Hi.' I think this is the same guy that I saw out on the paddle-board in the harbour. Was it only yesterday?

Closer up, I can see that he's very good-looking. His hair's long, worn framing his face, and it's a rich toffee brown with highlights which look as if they've been put there by years of sunshine. His skin's bronzed too and I'm assuming that he must spend a lot of his time outdoors. He's lean, slender, but there are taut muscles in his arms and the shape of his body beneath his clothes hints at being toned too. I'd guess that he's younger than me, maybe mid-to-late thirties. His face looks young, care-free.

'I thought there was no one home,' he calls up to me. 'Is the noise bothering you?'

'Yes,' I admit. 'Though I confess that I'm interested in watching you too.'

'It's just something small I'm working on. Bread and butter stuff. You're here on holiday?'

'Kind of.' He doesn't need to know my business. 'My brother owns this place.'

'Ah. He's made a great job of it. Very fancy. I came over and looked through the windows when it was empty. I'm about to stop for a coffee. Want to join me instead of shouting at each other?'

I think not and consider telling him that I have things to do. Important things. But I don't. In fact, I don't even know what to do with myself to quell the restlessness inside me. Plus, call me nosy, but I'd also like to have a closer look at his work. In our line of business, you never know when inspiration might strike or when you could see something that could be useful for a future project. So I'm torn between my reluctance to talk to anyone and a need to know more about this unusual form of art. I also wouldn't mind seeing what his houseboat is like inside, compared to Bill's – purely from an interior design point of view, you understand.

While I'm dithering, Ned puts down his chainsaw. 'I have some new coffee that I'm going to brew, I'd be happy to share the experience. I'm only trying to be neighbourly. It's up to you.'

'OK,' I hear myself say. It's out of my mouth before my brain has a chance to fully process it.

He smiles up at me. 'Cool. Come right round. I'll see you in a second.'

Ned goes inside and I stand there frozen at the rail, panic building inside of me. I've lived in London all of my life, in my current apartment for five years and I've barely spoken to any of my neighbours. I wouldn't know who half of them are if I passed them in the street. I try to avoid bumping into them in our shared garden. And yet, here I am, in a quest for solitude, agreeing to coffee in the home of a stranger. I think I've gone mad.

Still, I can hardly tell him that I've changed my mind. I couldn't just not turn up and I have no way of calling him. I'll pop round there for long enough to knock back a coffee – the thought of which is quite appealing – have a look at his work and his boat, then I'll politely leave. And while I'm there, I'll reiterate my need for peace and quiet, which is, generally, not compatible with chainsaws.

Bracing myself, I take the blanket inside and throw it back on the sofa, before heading round to my neighbour's house for coffee. I can do this. This morning I talked to a fidgety statue and a café owner and managed that OK. The conversation will be strictly on the level of inane chit-chat. We'll pass the time of day and I'll find out a bit more about his work. This man knows nothing about me and I'd like to keep it that way.

Chapter Eleven

Ned Haddon's boat couldn't be more different to Bill's. Given the outside, I suppose that I'd expected nothing else. The front door's already open as I walk up the gangway and onto the deck. Inside, Ned is at the sink drying cups. He turns to me and grins. 'Welcome aboard!'

'This is an amazing space,' I tell him, genuinely surprised at how wonderful it is. The exterior might be a ramshackle hotch-potch of colour and untidiness, but in here you can tell, instantly, that it's the home of an artist. It's cluttered, filled with eclectic furnishings, clashing colours and is fabulously bohemian. Yet it isn't what I envisaged at all. Shame on me, I thought it might be a bit grungy and unkempt. Far from it. Ned's home is a veritable treasure trove of delights.

The main room is spacious and open, like Bill's boat. However, the kitchen looks as if it has been hand-built, more than likely by Ned himself, I'd assume. There are only a few cupboards along one side but the doors have been exquisitely carved with oriental symbols. Hanging above the small copper sink, there are myriad glass baubles in every colour you can think of, perfectly placed to catch the light. As a result, a rainbow is reflected across the room in the sunshine, which makes me think that every room should have its own rainbow. Ahead of me there's a wood-burning stove that's gently warming the room. I continue my appraisal and it's hard to take in everything at once.

Light floods in from the side windows and there's a huge sign saying caution: adult at play. One wall is made up of covered pegs adorned with hats – top hats, embroidered ones, a stetson, a faded red fez, a tricorn edged with gold braid – enough to require further study. The other wall is decorated with a mural made entirely of driftwood, delicate pieces interlaced to form a swirling design like the crest of a wave. There's a well-worn sofa in teal velvet opposite a blood red chesterfield, both of which have cosy-looking crochet blankets slung over them. A large rag rug covers the floorboards between them. On the far wall hangs a colourful cloth which is heavily embroidered with yin and yang symbols. In front of that is a crate with a bronze Buddha head on it and lots of candles in mosaic holders. Ned clearly favours rich, jewel colours and definitely has an eye for putting them together. Or maybe there's a female influence here? Ida never mentioned that he had a wife or partner, but perhaps there is someone in his life.

'You have a lot of lovely things,' I say rather lamely, when I realise that I'm still staring and haven't said much. In London, my apartment is minimalist, sparse, monochrome. I like to think it's stylish but I wonder, looking round at the warmth and cosiness in this place, if Chris and I ever really made it a home? Perhaps that was part of the problem. However, I shut my mind down before I can dwell further on it.

'Most of this stuff is collected from my travels over the years,' Ned gestures around the living area. 'Much of it old tat.'

'Treasures,' I correct. 'Memories. You must love it or you wouldn't hold on to it.' I'm generally not a hoarder. I'm the opposite. An enthusiastic thrower-outer. Yet there's one room in my home that's filled with memories and I wonder how I'll ever bear to part with the few precious possessions in there.

'I have one very modern luxury,' he says. 'A state-of-the-art, all-singing, all-dancing coffee machine. I have a friend with a café by the beach. She got it at trade price for me.'

'Ida? I had the pleasure of meeting her,' I tell him. 'I went down to the café this morning. She said you were her friend and my neighbour.'

'I've known Ida for years. We went to art college together. If you know who I am, then you have the advantage.'

'Oh, I'm so sorry. Here I am in your home and I haven't even introduced myself. I'm Jodie Jackson.'

'Pleasure to meet you, Jodie.' Ned shakes my hand and, with the work he does, I thought they might be rough, calloused, but his fingers are smooth, warm and strong. 'I apologise for the racket. I've been so used to either not having neighbours or competing with noise from the builders that I've got out of the habit of being considerate. I didn't think to check if anyone had moved in.'

'I'm not here permanently. Just for a while.'

'A holiday?'

'Kind of. An extended stay.' A week, a month, a year. I'm not sure. I just know that I can't go home yet. 'London was getting a bit much,' I offer, evasively. He doesn't need to know any more than that.

'I hate the place,' Ned says. 'I have to go over there sometimes – for work, for personal stuff, but it's my idea of hell. I scuttle back here as fast as I can.'

I never used to think of living in London in negative terms, but now I'm not so sure.

'It can be overwhelming,' I agree. 'I've come here in search of peace and quiet.' A bit passive-aggressive perhaps, but I think it's worth mentioning that.

He holds up his hands to show that my point has hit home. 'My bad. I'll try not to work if you're around. I do have a workshop that I can go to. I was just fiddling with some new ideas while I thought no one else was here.'

Ned turns his attention to the coffee machine, measuring out beans, grinding them, fiddling with levers, milk and cups.

'Do you mind if I look around?'

'Help yourself,' he says over his shoulder.

So I entertain myself by wandering round his living room, taking in all that's displayed there.

'While this does its thing, I'll just go and change my tee. I'm covered in sawdust.' He goes through a beaded curtain and disappears out of view while I continue my exploration of his personal possessions.

As I pass the back of the teal sofa, I glance towards what must be the bedroom and I catch a glimpse of Ned stripping off his T-shirt – beaded curtains, it seems, provide little in the way of privacy. His body is as lean and toned as I imagined and, without my bidding, my heart does a little skitter. My goodness. Being a chainsaw artist is clearly a good workout too. I avert my gaze and concentrate, instead, on an incense burner in the shape of a lotus flower. Much better for the equilibrium.

A few moments later, Ned comes out of the bedroom, pulling his T-shirt down, and I pretend to be absorbed in a line of fossils on a hammered metal coffee table.

'Almost there,' he says. 'What takes your fancy? Flat white, cappuccino, cortado? I can offer you all of the coffee-based joys. I even have chocolate sprinkles, if that's what your heart desires. However, this is good stuff, so I'd recommend it as unadulterated as you can take it.'

'I'm impressed. A flat white will be just fine.' He crashes and bangs a bit more and then delivers the perfect flat white.

'This is great.' I sip it appreciatively.

'I'm a man of many talents,' he says with a mischievous twinkle in his eyes. 'We can sit outside while it's fine.'

So, exceptionally good coffee in hand, I follow him out of the front door and we go round the outside of the boat until we reach the rear deck.

Chapter Twelve

I couldn't see from my lofty view on *Sunny Days* but, out here, there's a kind of porch with a bench that looks as if it's been made from an old door and painted in a bright shade of turquoise. It's covered with a floral throw, a range of eclectic scatter cushions and a coffee table made from the trunk of a tree. Next to the sofa there are two storm lanterns with well-used candles in them. There's a rocking chair painted in sunshine yellow and fairy lights are strung here and there. On the wall behind the bench, there are more examples of Ned's work – a mermaid's head, an octopus, a few different types of fish. At the front of the boat, there's a pile of silvered driftwood, obviously waiting for Ned to work his magic on it.

'I use a lot of driftwood,' he says, following my glance. 'I collect it from the nearby beaches when I can. I find it speaks to me.' He picks up a piece and holds it out to me. 'You probably think I'm mad, but I can already see the figure in that waiting to come out.'

'It's a real talent,' I tell him. 'I admire that. Your work is wonderful. Very accessible.' I run my hand over the smooth, worn surface of the wood before Ned lays it back on the pile with the other pieces.

'Here, sit down.' Ned quickly shakes the sawdust from the throw and cushions. If Ned feels as awkward as I do, then he doesn't show it. He stretches out his legs and kicks off his boots to reveal bare feet. I note that they're tanned to a nut brown. He has rather nice feet and nice hands too, now that I come to look. His fingers are long and slender, and I know from our brief contact that they're strong and soft. He sees me staring at him and smiles. I look away, feeling guilty at being caught assessing my host.

To deflect attention from myself, I turn to my coffee and sip it. The flavour is rich and deep flavour. 'This is wonderful.'

'I buy my beans from a little shop in Seaview. This blend is new in. It's grown by a women's co-operative in Peru. This is my first cup. Cheers.' Ned tries it too and nods his approval. 'Not bad at all.'

The sun comes out, making the water in the harbour sparkle like diamonds. In front of us is the part-carved sturdy branch that he was working on earlier. The small chainsaw is propped up in a metal box. He nods at the delicate face that's emerging from the wood. 'Thought I'd try to create some fairies with a seasonal flair – spring through to winter, that kind of thing,' he tells me. 'I go to a lot of festivals over the summer and do some carving there. I create them quickly, in about ten minutes, and sell them at the end of my demo. It's generally how I make my living over the summer and I like to have something new to offer for regulars, something that people can tuck into a corner of their garden. This is the type of sculpture that should go down well.'

'I've never been to a festival.'

'Seriously?' He looks at me, clearly amazed by my shortcomings in the festival department. 'Everyone should go to at least *one* festival in their lives. Put it on your bucket list.'

'Maybe I will.' Though I'm not sure that roughing it in a tent is my kind of thing.

'So what are you going to do with yourself while you're here?'

'I don't know,' I admit. I hadn't thought much beyond getting away. 'Read, walk, sleep.' Try to find who I am, who I was, again? 'Take some time away from work?'

'Which is?'

'I'm an interior designer.'

Ned smiles. 'No wonder you were so interested in all my "treasures".'

'You have a very good eye. The colour is your choice?' I stroke a peacock blue cushion next to me.

'Yeah. The brighter the better. Do you approve?'

'I do. It's all put together very well.'

'Did you fit out your brother's boat?'

'No.' I shake my head. 'Bill is very fussy. That's all his own work. He always likes to have a project on the go.' I think about inviting Ned over to look at *Sunny Days*, but stop short. Time alone, I remind myself. 'I work with him in his company. He's been good enough to allow me this time away.'

'So the world of interior design was all a bit much?'

From anyone else it could sound like he was taking the piss, but I feel that Ned is genuine. 'Our company does a lot of high-pressure projects – hotels, offices, bars, shopping centres. It's pretty full-on. I just needed some calm in my life.'

'Sounds like a plan.'

'I'm not sure how good it'll be. My brother has appointed me a babysitter while I'm here. She's possibly the most talkative person on the planet.'

'Marilyn?' he says.

I laugh. 'How did you know?'

'I saw her going in and out when they were working on the

boat. They were the most well-fed builders on the island. She's the very best in babysitter material. You're lucky.'

'She seems like a lovely person. I'm not sure that I can cope with her . . . exuberance . . . right now.'

'Marilyn's a great lady,' he assures me. 'I've known her for years and have nothing but admiration for her. She's one of life's optimists and is so kind-hearted. She'll do anything for anyone. Ida and I were at art college with one of her boys, Declan. We were best friends at the time.'

'That sounds like you're no longer friends with him?'

'It's a long story,' Ned says.

'I'm sorry, I don't mean to be nosy.'

'It's not that. It's just that she's had a tough life,' Ned says.

'I confess that I don't know much about Marilyn.' I don't like to admit that I've been trying to avoid her company. Even the bright colours of her clothes are too much for me to cope with. They make my eyeballs throb. 'We haven't had much chance to talk.' Which is a blatant lie and I now feel guilty that I've been trying to avoid her.

'What she's been through would have broken most other people – understandably – but she's still standing, still smiling. I don't know how she does it.'

I wait for him to tell me more.

'The McConaugheys are a big, boisterous family – well known round here. Marilyn's got six kids and more grandchildren than I can remember. Her daughter runs the local pub on the next beach along.' He nods in the general direction. 'It's a great place to go off season.'

I haven't been there yet and can't think why I would do. Even the thought of going out and socialising brings me out in hives.

'It was years ago now,' Ned continues. 'When we were still at college. But she lost Declan. To drugs. Christ, it was terrible. I remember it like it was yesterday. Marilyn tried everything – we all did – but she couldn't help him to turn it round. None of us could.'

'I'm sorry. I didn't know.'

He shrugs. 'Why would you? He was a great lad. The life and soul of the party. You can tell where he got it from. His mum's great company. Declan was a really gifted artist too. Had more talent in his little finger than I'll ever have. He just became too fond of the chemicals.' Ned sighs sadly. 'We all dabbled a bit. What student doesn't? But it got hold of Declan. It went from recreational to addiction too quickly for us to do anything to stop it. The amount of time I spent in Marilyn's kitchen trying to talk to him.' He looks across at me and shakes his head. 'It's a terrible thing to watch your friend suffer like that. How much worse must it be when it's one of your kids?'

'I can't begin to imagine.' I can feel the colour draining from my face, my head going light and my throat closing with emotion.

'It was fifteen years ago,' Ned carries on, oblivious to the nerve he's hit. 'But it leaves a mark on you. When you'd expect her to be crumbling, Marilyn was a rock for us all. I don't know how she kept going. I think I'd go to pieces.'

I'm about to. I'm frightened that I can't hold back the tears and I don't want to cry in front of a stranger. This is why I had to get away from work, from people who knew me. I'd keep breaking down in meetings, in the hairdressers, at the gym. Other people's pain is a doorway straight into my own. I can't watch films or even listen to music without welling up. I can't listen to stories of people losing their children in tragic circumstances.

I put my cup down and it rattles in my saucer. Jumping up, I say crisply, 'I'd better go. Thank you for the coffee.'

Ned jumps up too, startled by my hasty departure. 'What?' he says. 'You're leaving? I've said something wrong?'

'No, no. It's fine. I have things to do.' We both know that's a lie.

'Christ, I'm sorry. I shouldn't have gone on like that. You've come here to get away from your troubles and I'm telling you sad stories.'

'It's not that at all. Really, it isn't.' I make a bolt for the front of the boat.

'Jodie,' Ned shouts after me. 'I wish you wouldn't go.'

But I keep on walking.

'You know where I am,' he calls after me. 'I can offer wine as well as coffee.'

'Thank you,' I say over my shoulder while still hurrying away. 'I just need some time by myself.'

I rush down the gangway and back to the safe sanctuary of *Sunny Days*. I catch Ned looking after me as I flee, a concerned expression on his face. This is why I don't talk to people. My heartache is always there, just beneath the surface, and it only takes a tiny scratch to expose it.

Chapter Thirteen

I can't sleep. When I close my eyes I just relive everything, all over again. My heart is making the same agonising, groaning noises as the boat as it rises and falls. Then I realise that it's not only my heart and the keening sound is coming out of me. So at first light I get up and sit in the kitchen drinking coffee. I opt for instant even though there's an enormous coffee machine here too. It looks terrifying and perhaps I should have got some useful tips from Ned as he seemed to be quite a handy barista. Still, he's now on my growing list of People to Avoid.

Four cups of coffee in and I pluck up the courage to listen to Chris's stream of messages. He has been leaving them constantly since I left.

'Jodie. Just call me,' he pleads. Hearing his voice twists my insides into knots.

'That's all I ask. We need to talk.'

But do we need to talk? What is there to say? There are times when talking makes no difference at all. It can't change anything.

In among them is one from Della. 'Chummie, where the fuck are you? I haven't heard from you for days. You're not answering my messages on WhatsApp.' Her voice sounds tight with anxiety.

'I bumped into Bill at the gym at lunchtime and he said you're not in the office. He was very coy about where you *actually* are. What's going on? Call me, woman.'

Della's been a friend for about five years – my closest friend. We both joined a book group at our local library on the same evening and were both suitably appalled by the choice of book – a dry and heavy tome that made my eyes glaze over within minutes. It was clear that Della felt the same. When the other women began to drone on about what they saw as the literary merits of the book and we hadn't even started to read it, we both looked up and caught each other's eye. Our expressions were the same and both said that we were in the wrong place. Very quickly, we were exchanging 'kill me' messages with our eyes and sniggering into our hands. Then Della made indications towards the door and we both ended up sneaking out early. Instead of continuing our quest for literary appreciation, we headed to the nearest bar where we giggled like schoolgirls over too many glasses of wine. I'd joined the book group primarily to meet people outside work as I had pitifully few friends – I still do – so I suppose on that level it worked. I never did get into reading that much, though. I discovered that I just don't have the time.

However, Della and I clicked instantly – the way you do with very few people who cross your path in life. She's fun, has an acerbic wit and takes no prisoners. She's a tall brunette with curves in all the right places who oozes confidence. Whenever we go out together she turns heads. Della's a young-looking thirty-five, gloriously single and never short of admirers. She always insists that she's having too much of a good time to want to settle down. She's fun, feisty and loud. We're chalk and cheese, but somehow it works. Recently, she's been such a rock for me. I don't know what I would have done without her. But even my best friend couldn't help me pick up the pieces this time.

I *will* call Della – we usually text or speak a dozen times a day and, when work allows, we go to the gym near to both of our offices together at lunchtime. She'll be wondering what on earth's the matter and, if I don't contact her soon, there'll be hell to pay. My husband is a different matter altogether. If I never speak to him again it will be too soon.

I'm still at the kitchen table, listening to his messages over again when Marilyn rocks up. The door bangs open. 'Cooooeeee!'

I click the phone off, but not before she catches the end of Chris's message.

'He sounds like a right misery guts,' she says as she throws her glittery gold bag on the floor.

Today's outfit is no less eye-catching than her previous attire. She's wearing matching gold sandals, the leopard-print jeggings and a white floaty blouse. Her earrings and her multitude of bangles jingle-jangle as she moves. Her scarlet nails are immaculate and match her lipstick. Never has a cleaner looked more glamorous.

'You could say that,' I agree.

'And you look like you need some more coffee, Miss.' She nods at the coffee machine and pulls an alarmed face at it. 'I can't work this beggar.'

'Me neither.'

'Instant it is, then. Toast, too? I've brought fresh bread from the bakery. I got sourdough. I know what you London people like. Don't think about saying no.'

'Toast would be lovely.' I'm not even sure that I ate dinner yesterday, but my stomach growls that we didn't. 'No more coffee, though. I've had too much already. I'll have the jitters soon.'

A few minutes later, while I'm still staring at my silent phone, coffee and toast is put in front of me along with a small pot of jam. Today it's peach Prosecco preserve with glitter. And why not? In Marilyn's world, it's obvious that clothes and food should be as sparkly as possible.

She sits down with me, clearly to make sure that I actually eat it. I spread some of the glittery jam on the hot toast and, to my surprise, it really does taste rather good. I drink the coffee too. I daren't not. Hello, jitters, welcome back.

'You can talk to me, you know,' she says. 'There's not much I haven't seen or done. You shouldn't keep pain to yourself. It's not good for your humours.'

That makes me smile. 'We're not Victorian, Marilyn. I'll be fine. I just need . . . '

'Peace and quiet. So you keep telling me. Well, I think peace and quiet is very over-rated. You're young. You're beautiful. Whatever's happened, you need to get out there and start enjoying yourself again.'

'It's easier said than done.' I don't know that I feel young and beautiful. I feel as old as the hills. Is forty-two still classed as young? I know all too well that some doors are closing to me already.

'Of course it is,' she agrees. 'But that doesn't mean we should stop trying. I take it this is all because of him.' She shoots a glare at my phone as if it's Chris standing there.

'That's part of it.'

'Lover?'

'Husband,' I tell her.

She shakes her head. 'These men. I've cried a table over too many of them in the past. They're not worth it, darling.'

I'm sure she's right. Chris isn't worthy of my tears.

'I lost my husband ten years ago,' she tells me.

I wonder why Ned didn't mention that? 'I'm sorry to hear it.'

'He didn't die,' she snorts. 'Far from it. He decided he wanted to be a lady, shaved off his beard and moved to Hull. He's

67

Veronica now and very happy by all accounts. He took some of my best frocks with him. Bastard.'

That makes me laugh out loud, a proper guffaw, and it's a sound I barely recognise.

'You've got to pick yourself up, dust yourself down and get on with it. Whatever you've been through. Life's for living.'

I well up again. These days, my emotions are not under my control. 'It's more complicated than that.'

'Another woman?'

I nod. At least I think so. And more. So much more.

Marilyn puts her hand on my arm. 'I've known loss, proper loss, love. Loss that makes you wonder how you can even keep breathing. So I do understand some of what you're going through.'

And, because of Ned's revelation, I know that she does. She might not have lost her husband in the traditional sense of the word, but she has buried a son. She knows what grief can do to a person. She understands me more than she realises, but I can't confide in her. I can't offer my sympathy either. The words simply won't come out.

'But every day is an adventure. When you get up in the morning, you never know what it might bring. Sometimes it's wonderful, sometimes it's heartache. Those of us who are here should make sure we enjoy every moment to honour those who aren't.'

Once again, she touches on the root of my pain, but when it's clear that I'm not going to share any further, Marilyn stands up. 'Right,' she says. 'You get yourself up and out. A nice walk on the beach will be a tonic and it's quite mild today.'

'I went to the café yesterday,' I tell her. I don't want her to think that all I'm doing is sitting here brooding – especially when that actually sounds quite appealing. 'I met Ida and I bumped into the living statue on the seafront, George.'

'Oh, that's lovely.' She raises her eyebrows. 'Sounds like you had a busy day being all peaceful and quiet. George is a poppet. He's the world's most twitchy statue, I'm sure, but very sweet.'

'I met Ned too.' I don't know why, but I'm suddenly more coy. I already know Marilyn enough to realise that she'll read more into this than there is. 'We had a coffee together and I watched him work for a bit.'

'Oh, that Ned, he's as hot as butter!' Marilyn fans herself. 'If I were a younger woman, he'd have to watch himself.' She whips my plate and mug away, taking them to the sink. 'Clever boy too. I've got one of his sculptures in my garden under my apple tree. So lovely.'

'He definitely has a talent.' I feel myself flush. Perhaps I need to fan myself too.

Over her shoulder she adds, 'I'm glad you're getting to know some people. Friends are important.' She says it more pointedly than she needs to. 'Right, off you go. I need to get on.'

'Marilyn, the place is absolutely spotless.'

'That's because I'm looking after you.' She gives me a big, beaming smile and it's so hard not to respond.

'It is,' I agree. 'Thank you.'

'I won't rest until you're as happy as pizza.' And with that she whips a duster out of the cupboard and heads off to wave it at imaginary cobwebs.

Chapter Fourteen

Putting on my new red woollies, I head out to the beach. As Marilyn said, it's quite mild today, but there's still a gusty breeze from the sea and my scarf feels cosy and soothing against my neck. Perhaps there are healing powers in the feel of soft wool. I don't know.

My plan, such as it is, involves walking down to Ida's café again and putting my loyalty card to good use. It's a reasonable distance for a walk, but not too taxing on a body that feels fragile.

The sky is bright blue and the expanse of it seems so vast compared to Shoreditch, the built-up area of London where I work and where I'd normally be at this time of day. It's supposedly a chi-chi area now and it's full of creatives and start-up companies. There are also lots of trendy cafés, bars and restaurants where the beautiful and 'woke' people go which is fabulous, but there are precious few glimpses of the sky between tall and close-packed buildings. I walk aimlessly along the sand, hands tucked in my coat pockets. Marilyn is right, if I'm out doing things then my mind doesn't wander into difficult territory.

The beach is quiet again, but ahead of me I can see a man

doing yoga on the shore. Instantly, I recognise the toned and honed physique. Ned's bare-chested, so that's very much in evidence. Hot as butter, indeed, as Marilyn said.

So what to do? Do I turn round and pretend that I haven't seen him or do I brazen it out? As yet, he hasn't noticed me as he's doing a pose facing the sea which looks particularly strenuous. I've never taken a yoga class, so I'm afraid that I can't tell you what. He's wearing loose, patchwork trousers and his legs are planted firmly in the sand, arms stretched out towards each end of the beach. As I stand there dithering, he turns his head and sees me. Even at this distance, I can tell that his face lights up and that takes me by surprise. Chris and I were together ten years and it's a very long time since I saw anything approaching that kind of look from him.

Ned relaxes his yoga pose and shouts out, 'Hey. How goes it?'

Trapped, I can do nothing but walk towards him. 'I'm good. Thank you.'

He gives me a look that's too searching, too searing. And I avert my gaze before he gleans too much, but not before I've taken in that his eyes are the most beautiful shade of blue. They'd compete with any summer sky and I wonder why I didn't notice that before.

'Are you walking down to Ida's place?'

'Yes.' What else can I say? I could hightail it back to *Sunny Days*, but what good would that do? Marilyn will be crashing and bashing about there and I'll only be in the way or subject to more scrutiny – which I can well do without.

'I've all but finished here.' Ned picks up a T-shirt that's rolled into a ball on the sand. 'Can I walk with you?'

I must hesitate, as he adds, 'If you don't want the company, then just say. I'll leave you alone.'

But, suddenly, being alone isn't all that appealing. Perhaps

Marilyn is right about that too. She has a lot of annoying habits and it seems that always being right may be one of them.

'I'd be happy to walk with you,' I tell him and I like the grin he gives me back. It's easy to smile in return.

He pulls on his T-shirt – which I'm grateful for, as those abs-on-abs-on-abs were quite distracting.

'I've never tried yoga,' I say as a way of making conversation as we walk. 'It looks like fun.'

'And very good for you,' he says. 'It keeps the body supple and settles the mind.'

'Ah, yes. I could do with a bit of that.'

'I'm here every morning when I'm at home. You should join me. I don't profess to be any kind of expert, but I could show you some basic moves. It sets you up for the day.' He glances across at me. 'I don't know what's going on, Jodie, and it's none of my business.' Ned holds up his hands. 'But it's clear that you're hurting and if I can do anything to help, then I'm here.'

The kindness of a stranger makes my eyes prickle with hot tears. 'I do have a lot on my plate right now,' I admit reluctantly.

He gives me that warm grin again and his whole face glows with happiness. He seems like a man who is quick to smile and slow to anger. Which makes a change. I'm more used to being surrounded by alpha males – and females – who are, quite frankly, bloody hard work. Not my colleagues, I hasten to add, but a great deal of our clients who head up their own empires. Whereas Ned certainly appears to be someone who's very comfortable in his own skin.

I like that. I like that a lot.

Chapter Fifteen

We reach the café and George is by the wall, posing with his hand above his eyes gazing out to sea. 'Morning!' he says when he sees us.

'I don't think statues should chat quite as much as you do, George,' I note.

'Business is slow again today.' He changes position. 'Thought it might be better here.' He shrugs in a statuey way. 'Though I'm a bit bored.'

'Take a break. Join us for coffee,' Ned offers.

'I've only just started. I should do a bit more.' It's hard to tell beneath all his bronze paint and steampunk gear, but I think he's torn.

'We'll be over here if you change your mind.'

He does a mechanical bow before freezing into position again and that makes me smile.

Ned and I sit on the same table that I had the other day, sheltered from the breeze. Ida is clearing away crockery in the awning. She's colourfully dressed again with a full-length crocheted blanket coat over jeans covered in sewn patches – Stop, Love, smiley faces – and a black trilby keeping the ribbon dreadlocks in check. My red woollies seem somewhat twee now that I look at them again. Still, it's warm enough for me to risk taking them off while we have breakfast.

When Ida sees us she comes straight over and seems rather surprised to see me with Ned.

'I see you two have met,' she says and there's a slight crispness to her voice that wasn't there yesterday.

'I'm trying to be a good neighbour,' Ned says.

Ida leans over and kisses her friend warmly on the lips. There's a distinct possessiveness about it, as if she's staking her claim to him. 'Usual breakfast?'

'I'll have the veggie sausage bap for a change,' Ned says. 'And a flat white, too. Did you try that new coffee I gave you?'

'Love it,' Ida says. 'You have impeccable taste in coffee. In women? Not so much.'

Ned laughs and Ida turns to me with a smile that seems just a little too smug. 'For you?'

'Bacon bap and tea please.'

'Coming right up.'

Ned watches her go. 'You seem to have a very special bond,' I say.

'Yeah,' he agrees. 'We've been friends for a long time. We're like brother and sister.'

Hmm. I think by the way that Ida acts around him that she views him as rather more than a brother. 'Have you always lived here?'

'On the island? Yes. Born and bred. Ida's been here since she came over to go to art college – where we met.'

'When did you move into *Sea Breezes*?'

'I've been there about eight years, maybe more. I inherited some money when my parents died and took the opportunity to buy it. I could never really see myself living in a traditional, two-up-two-down terraced house.'

I can't imagine Ned like that either.

'*Sea Breezes* was a complete wreck when I moved in but I patched it up as best I could. It's got a sound hull. Nice and watertight. That's all that matters.'

'I think it looks great. I love the eclectic style.'

He laughs. 'That's a very polite way of putting it.'

'I mean it. The decor says a lot about you.'

'None of it was intentional. It kind of grew organically when I had some money to spare. It suits me – my lifestyle, my work. I like being close to the ocean.'

'I've only been here a few days and I can see the appeal.'

'Have you always lived in London?'

'Yes. Until now, I've liked the hustle and bustle. You can get anything you want at any time of day.'

'Except peace and quiet,' he teases.

'Except for that,' I concede.

Ida brings our breakfast and puts it down in front of us. She seems reluctant to leave and hangs back as Ned tucks into the food she's brought for him. 'Are you playing in the pub tonight?'

'Nine o'clock kick off,' he says. 'Coming?'

'Yeah,' Ida says. 'There's bugger all else to do round here.'

'See you later, then.'

She hesitates a bit more, but when there's nothing else to say, she moves on to another customer, newly arrived from the beach. I'm glad to see that they tipped some money into George's collection box and he's able to move again.

'Why don't you join us tonight?' Ned says to me between mouthfuls. 'I play in a band down at the Jolly Roger, the pub further down the other beach that I mentioned. It's pretty low-key, but there's usually a good crowd.'

'I'm not sure . . . '

'You'll not get a better offer today.'

'You're probably right about that, but I'm not really in the mood for socialising. I'll pass. Thanks for asking though.'

Ned points at the veggie sausage bap on his plate. 'You have no idea what you're missing.'

'I'm more of a carnivore.' I'd kind of expected Ned to be a vegetarian. It goes with the houseboat, the yoga, the arty job.

'Ah. This is a good substitute. Just because I've given up meat, it doesn't mean that I don't, on occasion, long for the taste of it.'

'I think the sea air must be giving me an appetite, as I haven't eaten like this in weeks.' I take my time and enjoy every last morsel of my bacon bap.

At work we have a breakfast meeting at the office every day, eight o'clock sharp. Bill likes to keep on top of all our projects. We put out a hearty spread of cereals, croissants, green juices and fruit platters for everyone to help themselves. Most of my colleagues are early gym bunnies and usually turn up with hair damp from the shower and flushed faces. Most of them are vegan, gluten free, teetotal, non-smokers. Bill and I are definitely the dinosaurs among them – two of the few meat-eating, alcohol-swigging oldies.

I glance at my watch. They'll be finishing up now and getting on with the rest of their day and I wonder who's been tasked with taking on my projects. I must ask Bill when I speak to him. Perhaps they might need my input. If only on the periphery. Then I realise that it's the first time I've thought about work since I've been here and I really don't want to do that.

Glancing idly back towards the beach hut, I see that Ida seems to be watching us both like a hawk. I'm not sure that she'd be so keen on me joining them at the pub. She seems to be quite possessive about Ned and that's fine. I'm in no rush to play gooseberry – here or anywhere else.

Ned and I talk about nothing in particular as we finish our

drinks. He's easy company and, for a short time, makes me forget my pain and that I shouldn't be enjoying life.

Despite my protestations, he insists on paying the bill for us both and I hope he gets mates' rates.

'Thank you. That's very kind.' I put my woollies back on as I watch George shoo a seagull away in a very unstatue-like manner.

'Walk back along the beach together?' Ned asks.

As I have nothing else to do, I say, 'Yes.'

Chapter Sixteen

The tide is in when we walk back, so we stroll along the edge of the sea. I pick up some pretty shells and, carefully dusting the damp sand from them, put them in my coat pockets.

Ned bends to skim stones across the waves with impressive skill. I tuck my gloves into my pocket too so they don't get sand on them before picking up a large rock and tossing it as far as I can into the sea. It makes a big splash and sinks beneath the water with a satisfying 'plop'. I'm so ridiculously pleased with myself, that I find another big rock and do it again.

'You need to practise your skimming more,' Ned observes wryly.

'I've never tried it,' I admit. 'Not a lot of call for it in Islington.'

'Want a lesson?' Before I get to consider it, he comes over and says, 'First, you find a nice, flat stone with a smooth surface.'

Following his lead, we hunt about for a bit and I show him a few possible candidates, but they are found wanting.

'This one's a good one,' he finally declares. The stone in his hand is a flat, dark oval and he passes it to me. It's ice cold in my fingers. 'Come right to the edge of the waves, as close as you can, and crouch low.'

The sand is wet, sucking at my boots, and I only just manage to dodge a couple of cheeky waves that edge further forward up the beach than the rest.

'This is the throwing action.' Ned demonstrates. 'The aim is to keep it low over the water. Real low.'

Despite my trepidation, I bend down, gripping my perfect stone.

'Right.' Ned comes behind me and crouches too. 'OK. Go.'

I draw back and let go of the stone as instructed. For all my effort, it plops and sinks in much the same way as my rock did.

'Here.' Ned hands me another stone that's deemed to be ideal. 'Let me show you.' Before I know what he's doing, he draws me close to him, my back against his chest, and takes my arm, moving it backwards and forwards. 'Like this.'

It feels nice being sheltered from the wind in the warmth of his arms and this is the first time that I've really missed physical contact with another human. Ned's body so close behind me feels strong, solid and reliable.

'Nice and low again,' he says. 'Right down.'

We crouch together and my knees, unused to such an extreme position, complain in protest. Though I feel a little unsteady, I stretch my arm as shown and let my stone fly. This time it does two bounces before diving beneath the waves.

'Yes!' I shout out and punch the air. But, having concentrated so hard on the technique of skimming stones, I hadn't quite noticed how close the waves were to my feet. The water laps over the toes of my boots and I jump back in alarm, overbalancing as I do.

'Jodie!' Ned shouts and jumps forward, trying to grab me before I fall and hit the sand.

But, of course, his timing is off and I go down with a wet splat just as he reaches for me. I grab his arm for balance and manage to pull him down on top of me. To compound it all, a perky rogue wave washes over us.

'Bloody hell!' I cry out. The water's freezing. It's like being up to the neck in ice. The sea finds all the little gaps in my coat, my clothes, and rushes in. My lungs are in such shock that I can't breathe out.

Ned, not very helpfully, collapses with laughter. He rolls off me and lies there on his back in the surf, arms and legs spread like a starfish, letting the sea surround him. I struggle to get up, gasping and flailing as the waves still roll in. In the end, I give up and flop down again next to Ned. Another wave buffets us and I let out a part scream, part laugh. Ned grabs my hand and as the next wave comes in we shout out together. Then we lie and let the sea wash over us until I start to hyperventilate as my lungs are freezing.

When we can bear the icy water no longer, Ned hauls me up and I stand there dripping and shivering, teeth chattering.

'That wasn't quite the plan,' he says. 'But it was fun.'

And though I'm nearly frozen to death, soaked through to the skin and I've got sand in all my important little places, I feel strangely happy too.

Chapter Seventeen

Ned puts his hand under my arm and ushers me back towards the path to the harbour and our boats. I've gone beyond shivering now and am into a deep, internal juddering. I'm pretty sure my organs are shutting down and I can't feel my fingers or toes.

'A hot shower,' he advises. 'I'm used to the temperature of the water – I surf and paddleboard – but you're turning a worrying shade of blue.'

I don't tell him that I'd watched him out on his paddleboard the other day and thought him a lunatic.

When we get to the door of *Sunny Days*, I fumble with my key as my hands are now completely numb with cold. Ned takes it from me and unlocks the door.

'Thank you.'

'I feel terrible,' he says. 'It's a very poor teacher who nearly drowns their pupil.'

'You didn't tell me it was *extreme* stone skimming,' I say through teeth that I don't have full control of.

He puts his hands in a prayer position and gives me an apologetic face. 'Forgive me.'

'Nothing to forgive, but I must get into the shower before I die.'

'Do you want me to come in and wait to make sure that you're all right?'

'I'll be fine. Honestly. But I need to get moving as I can feel icicles forming on my nose.'

'See you later?' He ventures. 'Come to the pub. I owe you at least two large glasses of wine by way of apology.'

'I don't know . . . '

'We're all nice. No one bites.' He makes an imploring face. 'Don't stay here alone.'

'I'll think about it.' I'm regaining the feeling in my toes and fingers and it's quite painful.

'I need to go down there and set up about seven, you can walk with me or I'll see you there when you're ready.'

'Maybe.'

'That will do for now. Go and get in that shower.'

'Thanks, Ned,' I say. 'That was kind of fun in a deeply unpleasant way.'

He laughs and then walks back towards *Sea Breezes*, raising a hand as he goes.

I hurry inside, stripping off my soaking coat and wet boots as soon as I'm in the hallway and dumping them on the doormat. I'll sort them out when I can fully feel my extremities again. Marilyn will be delighted that she'll have a sandy mark to clean up tomorrow.

I'm already pulling off my jumper as I head downstairs to the shower. I crank it up to as hot as it will go and hurry out of the rest of my clothes which are feeling colder by the minute. I throw them on the floor and promise to put them straight in the washing machine when I'm thawed out. Then I jump in the shower. I'm so chilled that I can't tell whether the water is hot or cold. But, soon, the feeling comes back and the water is like scorching needles on my skin. I linger as long as I can and then swaddle myself in a cosy towel to dry before pulling on my favourite snuggly joggers and hoodie with some slouch socks.

I throw my clothes into the washing machine and it makes me smile as I think of flailing about in the waves. It's years since I've done anything like that and I realise that, most of the time, my life is quite buttoned-down. When did Chris and I last get silly together? I can't even remember. We used to once, I'm sure, but it seems like a long time ago. Perhaps we've both been so consumed by our careers, by being chic and sophisticated that we've forgotten how to belly laugh for the sheer pleasure of it.

My mind wanders to Ned too and how kind he is. He has such a sense of fun and he's easy, relaxed company. Maybe it's all that yoga on the beach. Perhaps he's right and I should give it a go. Even rolling around on the sand has lifted my spirits.

Upstairs, I rescue my beautiful grey coat from the doormat. It's still wet through and caked in sand. I don't think cashmere is meant for dunking in the sea and I'm not sure that it will survive its very thorough drenching. I'll put it on the radiator to dry and then see if a there's a cleaners locally who can rescue it. I'm sure Marilyn will know these things. I'm going to have to go out and get another jacket. Again, I'm sure that Marilyn can tell me of a good place to shop.

I take the shells I collected out of the pockets and put them on Bill's shelf. He'll probably throw them in the bin, knowing my brother, but I like them. The delicate pink inside reminds me of a baby's skin. Then my heart plummets. That's something I don't want to be reminded of.

Chapter Eighteen

I text Marilyn. *Where can I go to buy a new, warm jacket? Have ruined my coat. J xx*

Instantly, she replies. *Have you? I'm not busy. I can take you out now? Mxx.* A pig, a smiley face, a ghost, a bikini and an umbrella follow the words.

No idea.

That would be great. Thanks. Jxx. I should have known that she would immediately come to my rescue.

Sure enough, about fifteen minutes later, Marilyn rocks up and toots her horn outside. I'm ready for her, so I go straight out. Marilyn's car is some sporty number, in banana yellow – of course – and she has the top down. Thankfully, as I'm coat-free, I've put on a couple of jumpers.

'You'll catch your death of cold,' she scolds. 'Where's your coat?'

'That's why we're going shopping,' I remind her. 'I had an unfortunate accident on the beach where the sea won.'

'Oh. I can't leave you alone for five minutes,' she tuts. 'And you say that you don't need looking after.' More tutting.

I decide, wisely I think, against telling Marilyn the part that Ned played in this.

'I want something plain and warm. Maybe a padded jacket.' I hope that implicit in that statement is 'no leopard-skin print'.

'Plain. Padded,' Marilyn repeats. She doesn't look impressed by this concept. 'You don't want something fancier?'

'No. Just serviceable.'

She raises her eyebrows at that. 'OK. There's an outdoor shop near to here. It's very boring.'

By that, I think she means none of its clothes are electric pink and covered in glitter. 'Boring sounds good.'

Marilyn shrugs her disappointment but, nevertheless, we set off in her sports car at breakneck speed. Obeying the speed limit seems to be viewed as an optional extra. The heater is cranked up to max and our hair is streaming out behind us. I feel like I'm in *Thelma and Louise*.

A few minutes later, we pull up at a shop that clearly sells all requirements for an outdoor life and is catchily called 'Outdoor Life'. I probably could have walked down here, given directions, and I think that Marilyn has just been glad of the opportunity for a bit of girly shopping. I must be such a disappointment to her.

'There are nicer shops in Newport or Ventnor,' she says. 'It won't take long to go either. Nowhere here takes long to get to.'

'This looks fine,' I assure her. I need a jacket, any jacket, not red-carpet couture. We get out of the car and head for the store, Marilyn clip-clopping ahead of me in chunky gold sandals.

When she pushes the door open, we're greeted by racks and racks of perfectly adequate outdoor jackets. Admittedly, most of them are in shades of navy blue and dark green.

'These look fine,' I declare.

Marilyn stares at me aghast. She definitely thinks I'm Mrs Drab from Drab Town.

'I want to be warm,' I tell her. 'I don't really care what I look like.'

She recoils as if I've slapped her. 'You should care,' she says. 'You're too young to give up on your appearance. You're as pretty as a saucer. You should make the most of it.'

My days of caring about designer clothes or the latest fashions are gone. What does it matter? Who will look at me here?

I head to the navy blue padded jackets. Like a flash, Marilyn shoots off in the opposite direction. Picking one in my size, I try it on. It fits perfectly. That will do.

Marilyn comes hurrying back. Clearly, she has other ideas as she's brandishing a sunshine yellow down jacket at me, the same colour as her car.

She leans against the clothes rail, clutching at a stitch in her side. I think she's run round the entire shop in record-breaking time. Obviously, she realises that my shopping mojo will be short-lived and has but one chance.

'This one,' she pants. 'Try this one.'

I grimace. 'I don't do yellow, Marilyn.' Though I realise it is one of her more favoured colours.

'Do yellow,' she puffs.

'Seriously, I'd need sunglasses to wear this.' I shade my eyes to make a point. 'It's burning a hole in my retinas.'

When I still don't budge, she thrusts it into my hands and gasps out, 'For me.'

So with a pointed sigh, I take off the perfectly nice navy jacket and slip on this thing the colour of Big Bird.

I make a fuss of wriggling into it. Yet, once on, it feels surprisingly soft and comfortable. I'm loath to admit that it even fits better than the navy one. The shape and style are flattering. The colour, though.

'It's lovely,' Marilyn says. 'Cheery. Have a look in the mirror.'

'I don't do mirrors.'

'There's a lot of things that you "don't do" that you should do.' She grabs me by the shoulders and steers me to the mirror.

Staring back at me is a very jolly-looking jacket. It's actually quite nice. The reflection of the yellow gives a glow to my pale skin. 'I look like a banana.'

'You do not.'

'It'll clash with the red woollies I've just bought.'

'Excellent,' Marilyn declares. 'Get it.'

'Can't I have the navy one?'

'No,' she says. 'Nice things will happen when you wear a yellow jacket. People will smile at you. And, if you're not thinking too hard about it, you might even smile back.'

I'm not going to get out of this place without it. I know enough about Marilyn to realise that. With a resigned breath, I say, 'I'll get it.'

She smiles broadly at me. 'Look, it's working already.'

Chapter Nineteen

We get back into Marilyn's sporty car that matches my new jacket. I don't just feel like a banana, I feel like a banana in a bowl of custard. Can't deny that it's toasty warm, though.

'Stop looking like the cat who got the sausage,' I tell her, using one of her tangled phrases. 'You got me to buy an outrageously coloured jacket. It's a small victory.'

'That's how wars are won.' She grins at me. 'One small victory at a time.'

I look out of the window while I smile.

'I like spending other people's money. I'm going to put Personal Shopper on my CV,' she says, somewhat triumphantly.

She'd certainly be a persuasive one. I never for one moment imagined that I'd be using her as my style guru.

'Come to my house for lunch,' she says as we hit the road again. 'I'm picking up two of my grandbabies on the way.'

While I'd very much like to have lunch with Marilyn, I'm not up to meeting grandchildren. 'I'm tired now,' I tell her. 'I need a quiet afternoon. But thank you for the offer. I do appreciate it.'

She tuts at me again. 'There's being quiet and there's being a recluse.'

'Another time,' I assure her. But not yet. Definitely not yet.

So Marilyn hits the warp speed button on her car and seemingly moments later we pull up at *Sunny Days*.

She turns to me. 'Are you sure you won't come for a spot of lunch?'

'No. I'm fine, thank you.' I give her a sideways glance. 'Besides, I have a fridge overflowing with food.'

I open the door.

'Make sure you take that nice new jacket for an outing. A walk will do you the world of good.'

'I might take it for a spin.'

'I'll see you tomorrow,' Marilyn says.

'Thanks for my shopping trip. It was very kind of you.'

She flicks a hand at me. 'It's what friends do.'

Climbing out of her car, I wave goodbye as she roars off down the road.

I know that Marilyn will check, so I eat some of the food from the mountain in my fridge and then, rather than doing as she instructed, mooch about for the rest of the day.

Flicking through Bill's books, I choose an historical novel featuring those troublesome Tudors and try a few chapters, but it's not gripping me and my eyes slide over the words. I sit out on the front deck and crane over the side to see if Ned's there, but he's not and his carving lies abandoned. The gentle sun on my face is soothing, the air is fresh and invigorating. I put the book to one side and watch the pretty little boats bobbing in and out of the harbour.

The day crawls round to supper time and, when the sun sinks, I go indoors, closing the blinds against the impending night, and watch *Pointless*. By the time I get home my general knowledge will be second to none, but I turn off the television before the news as it's always too depressing. I think about phoning Bill and Della, but don't really want to talk to either of them.

I'll want to talk about work with Bill and Della will only want to revisit old ground. As a compromise, I text Bill to say I'm OK and vow to contact Della tomorrow.

Marilyn texts me. *Don't forget to have dinner! Mxxxxx* followed by a face crying with laughter, a bag of fries, a skull and crossbones, a lipstick and some sunglasses.

I shake my head, bemused.

Sitting at the kitchen table, I eat more of the stuff that Marilyn keeps putting in the fridge – some scrambled eggs on heavily buttered sourdough this time. It still doesn't seem to have made much of a dent in it.

After I've cleared up, I peek out at Ned's boat. The lights are on and I can see him pottering about in the galley kitchen. I tear myself away as it's not nice to spy on your neighbour. But, as I do, I see the lights go off and, a few moments later, hear the door bang. Ned's out on the gangway with a guitar case slung over his shoulder. I duck back as he hesitates and glances in the direction of *Sunny Days* as he passes. He clearly thinks better of calling for me, as he then heads off towards the beach path and the pub for his gig.

I'd completely forgotten that he'd asked me, but I'm restless now and fidget about, unable to settle. I can't stay here by myself again, thinkingthinkingthinking. I'll go mad. A glass of wine feels like a very good idea and drinking alone is never as much fun when there's a warm pub and music calling. Part of me is intrigued to see what kind of songs Ned's band plays. I bet he's good at the guitar, too. He looks like he should be.

Before I talk myself out of it, I go and slip on my jeans and a jumper. Then I grab my shouty yellow jacket and, as my boots are still wet through, put on my trainers. I wrap the red scarf round my neck and pull on my matching gloves. They clash hideously with the yellow jacket, as I knew they would. Marilyn would love it.

A few minutes later, feeling slightly anxious, I'm heading out of *Sunny Days* in search of alcohol and company.

Chapter Twenty

The Jolly Roger is right on the beach, down at the far end of the broad sweep of sands of the next bay. I haven't been onto this beach before as it's in the opposite direction to Ida's café and, so far, my path has always taken me that way.

As it's dark, I walk down the road instead of crossing the sand which takes a little longer but I'm less likely to end up in the sea again. If I dunked this jacket, Marilyn would never forgive me. I hoped that I might be able to catch up with Ned, but he's nowhere in sight.

Although the evening can't be classed as warm, there's a hardy throng of smokers on the deck outside beneath the two Jolly Roger flags which are flapping in the breeze. Their laughter is caught on the wind and thrown out to sea. The pub looks like a theme park and is strung with multi-coloured fairy lights. There's a ship's figurehead painted in fluorescent paint that's shining out in the night, a spotlight on a sailor climbing up some rigging, and a large rowing boat planted with bold and brassy spring flowers.

George is standing at the entrance, striking a pose. 'Hey,' he says, relaxing as I approach. 'Good to see you. Great jacket. Makes you want to smile.'

'Thanks.' I think Marilyn must have him on her payroll. 'Evening, George. Are you coming in for the gig?'

'I'd be too hot in there with all this on.' He indicates his bulky steampunk outfit. 'And it takes an age to get all the make-up off. It would all be over by the time I was ready. Thought I might try to earn a few bob before I call it a night.'

For once, his box certainly seems full of change.

'I'm keen to get back to my book, too. I've got a great chapter planned.'

'So how's the writing going?'

'OK,' he says. 'One good thing about being a statue is that I've got a lot of time to think when all I have to do is stand still for the day. I might look as still as a stone but my mind is always busy.'

For the record, George never looks as still as a stone. It's harder to catch him still than it is moving. 'What kind of book is it?'

'Romance,' he says. 'Girl meets boy. Boy meets boy. Girl meets girl. It's quite modern.'

'I expected you to say that you were penning a dark, dystopian steampunk novel.'

'Oh no.' He shakes his head. 'Under this brash costume there beats a very tender heart.'

That makes me smile. 'I'm sure there does, George.' I'd like to know more about the man behind the mask. I guess we all have a public face, though George's is more extreme than most. 'How did you come to be doing this?'

'My own story's very dull. I wanted to be an actor, but I found that I was far too shy. I had crippling stage fright. I'd be so sick and all the words would rush out of my head. I stuck at it for a while, but I felt I was letting everyone else down, so this seemed ideal. I can make up my own little show and the audience have no idea who I am. I'm just anonymous.'

'They say all writers are frustrated actors too.'

'Do they? I hadn't heard that. The writing thing might suit me too, then.'

'I'd like to read it, if you've got a copy? Nothing on my brother's bookshelves is holding much appeal. I had a brief struggle with the Tudors today.'

He smiles brightly at me, his teeth shining out amid the bronze. 'I've never shown anyone my writing before,' he says. 'Seems a bit scary. I really have no idea if it's any good. Are you sure?'

'It's not too slushy?'

'I don't think so.'

'There are no cheating husbands in it, are there?' I don't want to spend hours reading something only to find that her man goes off with his co-worker who he laughingly calls his 'work wife'.

'Not a one,' he assures me.

'Then I'd love to. If you don't mind sharing it with me.'

'I'll drop a print-out of it off at the café for you.' He does a theatrical sweeping bow. 'Have a great time tonight.'

'Thanks.' George resumes his pose and, with only a moment's hesitation, where I think about turning round and racing back to *Sunny Days*, I brace myself to walk up the terrace and head inside.

Chapter Twenty-One

A wall of animated chatter hits me as I open the door of The Jolly Roger and there's a lovely warm fug in here, a crush of people around the bar. In the summer I'd guess it would be packed with tourists but, for now, it seems like the place to be if you're a local. The pub has very much embraced the seaside theme inside too. There are ships' wheels and a variety of life-buoys on the walls, ropes and upturned rowing boats hanging from the ceiling and those coloured glass balls in nets, which look great as decoration even though I've no idea of their original purpose. Storm lanterns with fake candles burning in them grace every table giving it a cosy air and there's the scent of freshly cooked seafood in the air.

It's ages since I've been to a good old-fashioned boozer like this. All the places around where I live are achingly trendy, mind-numbingly expensive and often soulless bars. Plus I haven't had anything alcoholic to drink for what seems like a very long time and I can feel that a large glass of wine is calling me. I've fancied one for days, but haven't succumbed yet. Now seems like the ideal time to break my abstinence. And why not? I don't care if it's good for me or not any more.

In the far corner I can see the band setting up on a small stage area and, feeling anxious, I make my way towards them. Right next to the stage, Ned and Ida sit together at a table looking very comfortable. I guess the people with them must be the rest of the band and their partners. As I draw closer, Ned looks up and sees me. I feel relieved as he breaks into his customary grin and waves me over to them. Is it my imagination or is Ida's smile a little forced when she greets me?

'Hi,' I say and I sound slightly breathless after my walk, mixed with a little nerves.

Ned pulls up a chair next to him. 'Glad you could make it,' he says. 'Didn't think you would!'

'I was in two minds,' I admit.

'New jacket?'

'Marilyn's choice,' I say, wrinkling my nose.

'It looks great.' Ned gives it an approving look. 'The colour suits you.'

Another one she's bribed to give me a compliment.

'I guess your clothes were ruined after our impromptu dip?' Ida shoots him a questioning glare. 'I was showing Jodie how to skim stones when the sea had other ideas,' he explains. 'We both took a serious dunking.'

His friend doesn't look mollified and I see again that she's quite possessive of Ned. Well, she has nothing to worry about from me. 'It was fun, if a little more wet than I'd anticipated.'

'I can only apologise again,' he says, but there's laughter in his voice.

'I survived,' I say. 'Not sure I can say the same for my coat.'

Ned grimaces.

'Before I sit down, can I get anyone a drink?' I ask.

Without hesitation, Ida holds up her glass. 'Red wine, thanks. Large.'

'Anyone else?' The other members of the band shake their heads.

'I'm good,' Ned says and shows me that he already has a bottle of beer. 'But let me go to the bar. After all, I owe you. One of the few perks is that we get free drinks in lieu of wages and we try to make sure we get well paid. I'll introduce you to everyone when I get back.' As he stands, he steers me to his chair and I take it, gratefully. There's quite a crowd in and seats seem to be at a premium.

It's not long before Ned comes back. He hands Ida her drink, then sits back down next to me and passes me the other glass. I take a good swig of the wine and it tastes like nectar on my tongue. I let out an appreciative sigh.

'Good?' Ned asks. 'I got something a bit nicer than house plonk.'

'I haven't been drinking for a long time. I'd forgotten how much I liked it.'

He has a cheeky twinkle in his eye when he says, 'Rehab?'

I shake my head. 'Nothing like that.'

'Let me do the honours, although you'll never remember them.' He runs through the names of the other band members and their wives or girlfriends and I try my best to commit them to memory – but Ned's right, I pretty much forget them instantly. They all nod or say hello in welcome.

'What kind of music do you play?'

'Mostly covers,' Ned says. 'Keeps the punters happy. Every now and again the budding songwriters among us chuck in a song or two. We try our best, but they're never as popular. People prefer George Ezra and Sam Smith to the Beach Bums,' he jokes.

'The Beach Bums?' That makes me giggle.

'Hey. Not my choice. I'm one of the new boys. I've only been with them for five years. Blame Tim for the cheesy name.'

'Time we got started, lads?' That's Jack. I think.

Everyone nods their agreement and Ned says, 'Work calls.'

They take their drinks onto the stage and set up. Ned plays bass guitar and that shouldn't surprise me as all bass players seem to be easy-going souls. Once they've done with some necessary man-faffing, they play some of the recent chart hits – not the dancy stuff, but mellow tunes. I'm halfway down my glass and the wine is taking the edge off my tension. Not that I want to get up and dance on the table, but it certainly seems to be untangling some knots that I didn't know I had. Ned is a brilliant bassist – another talent. His fingers pluck and slide over the strings with a casual expertise. The general hubbub in the bar quietens which is unusual as these days the aim seems to be to talk over the band.

Ida catches me looking at him. 'He's good, no?'

'Great,' I agree.

'He could have been anything,' she says. 'If he wasn't so flipping laid-back.'

'He seems very happy with his life,' I note. Then, perhaps emboldened by the wine, I decide to stick my neck out a bit. 'You both seem to get along so well.' They look good together, too. Ida and Ned would make very pretty babies. What's Ida? Thirty-five, probably? Lucky cow. She's probably got another five years to have children without expensive medical intervention. That's one of the first things that I usually think about other women. How long have they got to start a family? If they want kids, why don't they get started now while they can? I'd do things very differently if I had my time again. But who am I to give anyone advice? 'I would have thought you were the perfect match. Why haven't you got together?'

Ida narrows her gaze. 'We have. On and off over the years.'

'Oh.' I admit that surprises me.

'I'm his default setting. When there's no one else around, he turns to Good Old Ida.'

She says it as a joke, but I can hear the hurt behind it. I'm an expert in that.

'One thing Ned doesn't like is commitment,' she continues quite crisply. 'Variety is very much the spice of Ned's life. He likes to spread his love around and come the summer season, there's just too much choice for him.'

I don't know him very well, but he doesn't strike me as a player. But then, you might have gathered that I have pretty poor judgement when it comes to the character of men. I thought my husband was strong, loyal, faithful. Couldn't have been more wrong.

'He's a heartbreaker,' Ida says. 'You'd do well to remember that.'

'You have no worries on that front. The last thing on earth that I'm interested in is hooking up with a man. I'm finished with relationships.'

'You've been burned?'

'Oh, yes.' The wine has definitely loosened my tongue.

'Is that why you've come over here?'

She looks at me, expectantly, waiting for more juicy details, but Ida doesn't need to know anything else. No one does. 'It's a long story,' I say and turn my attention back to the band.

Chapter Twenty-Two

When they've played for half an hour or so, the band take a break. While the rest of them rush to the bar, Ned comes to join us again. I make sure that I move seats so that he's next to Ida rather than me.

'That was great,' I say to him.

'I enjoy it.' Ned takes a swig of his beer. 'I've played since I was a teenager.'

'Only because you thought that being a musician would get you more girls,' Ida quips.

Ned laughs. 'It kind of worked. For a while.'

Ida tuts at him.

'If you're going to pick on me, I'll go to the bar,' Ned says to her. Then to me, 'Another wine?'

'Yes, please.' I probably shouldn't. It would be wise to pace myself after being teetotal, but it tastes so good and I'm feeling more relaxed than I have in a good while.

'Ida?'

'I never say no.'

'So you're going to sing with us in the second set?' he asks.

'Damn,' she says. 'I walked into that one. Give me a break,

Ned. You know that I haven't rehearsed with you guys for ages.'

'It's the same old thing,' Ned points out. 'You'll ace it. You always do.'

'I'll think about it.' Ida frowns.

'You've got about fifteen minutes. Just do a couple of numbers with us. The lads will love it. What about "Beyond the Sea" and, maybe, "Love is Easy" for starters?'

Ida, I think, feigns reluctance.

'"Time after Time"?' he suggests. 'You know you love a bit of Cyndi Lauper.'

'It always makes me cry,' Ida says.

'I'll go and get some drinks while you decide what you want to do.' Ned moves towards the bar.

I turn to Ida. 'I didn't know that you're a singer.'

'Not so much these days,' she tells me. 'A few years ago, I used to be a member of the band. We played weddings, parties, pubs all over the island. Then Ned and I went through a "diffi-cult" phase and I couldn't do it. It was hard to watch him go home with someone different every night after the gigs.' She waits for my reaction, but I don't give one. 'Now my singing is very much confined to the shower. Though, once in a while, he manages to persuade me out of retirement.'

'This evening?'

She shrugs. 'I don't know. I usually like a bit more time to prepare. I'm more than rusty.'

'I'd love to hear you. I'm always in awe of people who can play instruments or sing. I'd love to be musical but I can't string three notes together.'

I don't know if my words have any influence on her but, after the interval, Ida takes to the stage with the band. She makes a show of being pulled towards the microphone and the partisan crowd cheer. Ida's clearly popular here. She sings the songs that

101

Ned suggested and, I'm no expert, but it sounds to me as if she has a really beautiful voice. The crowd in the pub clap and whistle so loudly that Ida is persuaded to sing two more songs. It's a shame that she's not a regular feature with them as I'd pay good money to hear her sing.

She comes off the stage, flush-faced and slightly hyper. I think, despite her initial reluctance, that she enjoyed it too. While the band play, I buy us more wine and we clink our glasses together.

'To you,' I propose. 'To more gigs with the Beach Bums.'

Ida laughs at that and says, 'I don't know if they'd have me back.' But I feel that she softens towards me, a little.

Too soon, the evening ends. The landlord calls last orders and the guys play their final song. I fuss with getting my jacket on with slightly unhelpful fingers as the band pack up their gear.

As I'm about to take my leave, Ned jumps down from the stage. 'If you wait for a few minutes, we can walk back together, Jodie. It's dark on the way home, you shouldn't go alone.'

'OK.' I admit that I hadn't been looking forward to heading off by myself as, much to my surprise, I feel a little bit wobbly on my legs, but I didn't know if Ned would be going home with Ida.

So, Ned packs up his bass, and kisses Ida on the cheek while I hang back and wait for him. I see her eyes flick anxiously at each of us and I know that Ida is still very much in love with him. Equally, I'm sure that it isn't reciprocated.

'Straight home, you two,' she says and there's an underlying tartness in her words.

'Yes, ma'am,' Ned says.

I don't like to leave Ida there looking so forlorn, but I don't think this is my business either. While I'm wrangling with an offer to walk Ida home too, Ned takes my arm and steers me through the remaining stragglers. Outside the pub the fresh air hits me and I suddenly feel a lot more drunk than I did when I was sitting down in the warmth. The pretty fairy lights swim before my eyes.

'Wow,' I say. 'That wine has hit me hard.'

'I was going to walk down the road,' Ned says, 'But we could take the short cut across the beach. It's a lot quicker. You're not wearing heels?'

'No.' I show him my appropriate footwear, but even the act of lifting one leg is a bit tricky and I topple over, which causes me fits of giggles.

'That's never a good sign,' Ned laughs as he catches me. 'I can phone a taxi. We'll be home in a minute.'

'The beach in the moonlight sounds wonderful.' I'm compos mentis enough to note that it's a full moon and that the sky is beautifully lit. Silver-tipped clouds drift across its shining face.

'I should remind you that this isn't Antigua. It'll be chilly down there.'

'I'm game, if you are.' I sound bold, adventurous. 'Besides, the fresh air might help to clear my head – unaccustomed as I am to strong drink.'

'Come on, then.' Together we head across the terrace of the pub and down the steps to the beach, Ned making sure that I find each step with feet that want to go off in different directions.

Chapter Twenty-Three

My head is definitely woozy while my body is delightfully numb. 'I shouldn't have had that last glass.' Maybe even the one before the last one was a bad idea.

'You looked to be having a good evening.'

'I enjoyed it a lot more than I expected.' Then an emotion catches in my throat. 'I've got out of the habit of socialising.'

'We'll have to see what we can do about that. Ida seems to like you. That's never a given. She seems to get on better with blokes rather than women.'

'She's feisty,' I say. 'Fierce. I admire her.'

At the bottom of the steps I hit the sand and, instantly, walking becomes a lot more difficult in my inebriated state. I, of course, find this hilarious.

Ned is on hand to steady me as I wobble again. 'And this seemed like such a good idea,' he says, which makes me giggly all over again.

'It's a long time since I've been on a beach at night.'

'It's better in the height of summer,' Ned says. 'With a cold beer and an open fire.'

'It must be wonderful. You never know, I might still be here in the summer.' I think I shay *shummer*. Someone's slurring their words, anyway. Then I wonder if I *will* still be here then. I might never go home again. This could be my new home. I've only been here a short while yet I think it's been very ther . . . thera . . . therapertic – good for me.

Ned hangs onto me as we start to cross the wet sand, pulling me close. It feels unnervingly good to have his arms around me, holding me tight. No one has held me like this for a long time and I know now that I have very much needed it. I lean into him and feel the warmth of his body against mine. We walk a few steps before I have an overwhelming urge to lie down, even though Ned is doing his level best to hold me up.

Perhaps he senses my reticence for walking as he says, 'You've ruined one coat already today. You're not going in the sea fully clothed again on my watch.'

'I'm more tired than I thought,' I admit.

'Is that what we're calling it now,' he laughs. '"*Tired*"?'

He relaxes his grip on me and, without meaning to, I sink to my knees. The wet sand is cold against the knees of my jeans and I can feel the damp seeping through. 'I'd very much like to build a sandcastle,' I tell him from all fours. 'I haven't done that for such a long time.'

'Are you sure?' he queries. 'Wouldn't you rather me take you to the nice warm houseboat that's waiting for you?'

'Sandcastle,' I insist. 'One fit for a fairy princess.'

With a bemused shake of his head, he drops down next to me. 'As it happens, I am the king of sandcastles,' he boasts. 'You came to the right guy. Sandcastles for fairy princesses are my speciality.'

'Really?' I'm quite impressed by that and briefly wonder how Ned became such an expert.

'OK. Get digging, sandcastle slave,' he instructs, 'otherwise we'll still be here at dawn.'

'I quite like the idea of that.' Wouldn't it be better than lying awake all night, tossing and turning? 'We have nothing to dig with. We should have brought our glasses from the pub.'

'Wait there. Don't move.' He points at me in a very forceful manner.

'I wouldn't dream of moving.' I'm not entirely sure that I can.

Ned sprints back towards the pub and returns a minute later with two large beer glasses. 'They hadn't cleared up smokers' corner. Whatever you do, I don't want you patting these too hard. A trip to A & E isn't on my wish list.'

'Don't pat too hard,' I repeat.

'Better still. You fill them with sand. I'll do the patting.'

'No patting for me,' I concur.

So while Ned makes a pile of sand in front of him, I start scooping the soft, damp sand into the beer glasses, enjoying the grittiness in my fingers. I pass them to Ned who does his most expert patting and tips the sand out onto the beach in a perfect flat-topped cone. Frankly, I am a sand-scooping machine and Ned is a patting genius and so we soon have a perfect circle of sandcastles round the main mound of sand. I lean back to admire our handiwork. 'This is looking wonderful.'

'A des res for any discerning princess,' he agrees. 'Now the tricky bit.'

I wait to be told what that is with bated breath.

'It's time to build them up around the mound.' I pass him the next beer glass and, with his free hand, he levels a little shelf in the side before up-ending his beer glass. I gasp with awe as the sand cone slides out of the glass and takes its place in the emerging castle.

'Fabulous,' I breathe.

Ned grins at me in the darkness.

Clapping my hands, I say, 'This is too good. Hurry, hurry.'

I fill more glasses and, while I'm waiting for Ned to pass them back to me, I start to shape the big hole I've created into a moat. What's a fairytale castle without a moat? I can feel the wind, chill on my face, but I'm not cold. It must be the wine as there's definitely a warm glow inside me.

'Last one,' Ned says. 'Want to do it?'

I look up and, in front of me, there's a magnificent sand structure. A circle of little sandcastles stand to attention around the central mound and more sandcastles wind their way up its side in a spiral until they reach the pinnacle. The one remaining sandcastle is ready to go on top.

'You do it,' I tell him, 'I don't want to spoil it.' So Ned tips out the sand, gently but purposefully.

The sand cone sits proudly on top. Ned studies it, carefully. 'Just missing one thing. We didn't bring a flag and it definitely deserves a flag.'

'It's brilliant.' I'm truly amazed. 'Did we really build that?' I have no idea how long we've been out here, but I've enjoyed every minute. 'I can tell that you've had practice.'

'Yeah,' he agrees. 'But not for a long time. My services are no longer required.' For a moment, his face slips and he looks terribly sad. I know how he feels. In every picture, every image I store of having my own family, building sandcastles is right there among them. Don't all families want to do that at some point, be happy and carefree with their kids just messing about on the beach? I push the thoughts away. Now isn't the time.

'You are my sandcastle-building hero,' I tell him.

'It just needs a beautiful princess,' he says. 'Care to volunteer?'

'Take a photo of me with it,' I instruct. 'How long will it last?'

'It'll probably be gone by morning.'

'Oh. That's too sad.'

'It's magical,' he reminds me. 'Nothing magical lasts for ever.'

I try to get to my feet, but it's harder than I remember. There are wet patches on my knees and my bottom.

'Let me give you a hand, sleeping beauty.' Ned hauls me up and I'm still wobbly but a bit less so than before. He holds me while I regain my equilibrium and I suddenly feel a little less drunk and more aware of how close he is. He smells of sweet beer, wood resin and seaside. I have an overwhelming urge to lay my head against his chest. 'Whoa,' he says. 'Steady.'

With some considerable help from Ned, I stagger to the sandcastle. It stands tall and proud in the moonlight and I can't believe we've just made that. It's so wonderful that I could cry. I think I might actually do so.

'Give me your phone, I'll take a photo.' I do as I'm told and pin on a brave smile while Ned clicks away. Then he takes a selfie with us both in it. He hands my phone back. 'They might be a bit dark.'

'At least we have it captured for all time now.' As Ned said, it will be gone tomorrow. No one will ever know that it was really here. All I have is a photograph that's too dark to make out all of its ethereal beauty.

'Time to go home,' Ned says. 'It won't be long before the sun comes up.'

I think he's joking, but maybe we have been here all night. Then I come over so weary that I can hardly move.

'Come on, princess.' I don't protest when he picks me up and throws me over his shoulder with so little effort that I might be a feather. I guess he's used to hauling heavy logs around.

'I *am* a princess,' I say as I dangle down Ned's back. 'With my very own castle.'

'You certainly are.'

Albeit, I'm a slightly slurry, drinky, teary princess.

Then he shifts me until he's comfortable and sets off across the beach. And I surrender to the pleasant indignity of being carried like a sack of potatoes, just glad that I don't have to do walking. I let my weight rest on Ned's back and my eyes close. I feel his strong arms holding tightly onto my legs as he carries me home to *Sunny Days* and I think that I might like it a little bit too much.

Chapter Twenty-Four

The sun is starting to rise as Ned gently lowers me to the ground at the door of *Sunny Days*. The sky is blossoming with lemon and lilac to gently chase away the night.

'Easy as you go,' he says as he rights me on my feet.

I fumble in my pocket for the key and, as I nearly drop it, he takes it from me and opens the door. As I go to thank him for a great evening, I stumble slightly. I don't know if I'm still drunk or just tired now. Ned catches me and his hands on my arms feel solid, capable. I want to reach round and hold him in an embrace. I want him to stroke my hair and tell me that everything will be OK. With Ned I could actually start to believe it.

While all this is still whirring through my mind, he says, 'Shall I put the kettle on?'

'Yes, yes. Of course.' I step away from him. He makes sure that I'm able to stand unaided before he side-steps past me into the kitchen. I flick on the hall light and blink at the harshness.

Sitting on the bench under the coat hooks. I pull off my trainers. I'm so exhausted that I could lie down here and fall asleep, but I make myself go into the kitchen, eyes rolling.

'Peppermint tea,' Ned says. 'I thought it would be for the best.'

'Lovely.' I take the mug from him and our fingers touch. Neither of us pull away.

Ned takes a deep breath. 'I can tell that you're working out some stuff,' he says softly. 'I can sense a sadness in your soul.'

That nearly has me undone. I'm tired, and emotional isn't far behind. 'I'm fine. Really,' I assure him. But I can tell that he doesn't buy it.

'Will you be OK by yourself?' he asks. 'I can always put my head down on your sofa.'

'No, no. There's no need for that. I'm fine.'

He smiles sadly. 'So you keep saying.'

'Though I don't think I've been this drunk since university,' I admit. 'I hope I haven't made a fool of myself.'

Now it's Ned's turn to say, 'No. Not at all. It's been fun. It's been too long since I built a sandcastle.'

'You have an exceptional talent.'

That makes Ned smile again and I realise that I very much like to see him smile. He has unbearably cute dimples in his cheeks. He steps towards me and, just as I think he might kiss me, he gives me a barely there, tender peck on the cheek.

'Goodnight,' he says. 'What's left of it.'

'Yes. Thank you again.'

I follow him to the door and turn the key in the lock behind him as he leaves. Then I switch off the lights and go back into the kitchen. I turn off the lights there too and sigh in the darkness, mind in turmoil. I don't deserve to feel happy, so why do I?

Sitting at the kitchen table in the half-light before dawn, I watch as Ned flicks on a lamp in his kitchen and he potters about at the sink, probably making himself some tea, and I wish he would have stayed here a little longer. I like Ned. A lot. He seems open, dependable. Not the type to keep secrets. I don't think he's the kind of guy who would cheat on his wife. Do you?

Eventually, his boat is plunged into darkness and I decide it's time for me to hit the sack too. The harbour looks mellow in the growing light and I stare out of the windows to the dark shadow of the sea fort for a while, my thoughts in free flow. They tumble slowly through my brain yet I can't quite catch any of them.

I head downstairs and pull off my jeans and jumper, hopping round on the floor as I do. Then, feeling more than a bit swimmy, I fall gratefully onto the bed and pull the feather duvet over me for comfort. For a brief moment, before sleep finds me, I imagine that it's Ned's arms around me.

Chapter Twenty-Five

I must have fallen into a deep sleep in a nano-second as the next thing I hear is Marilyn's dulcet tones calling out 'Cooooooeeeeee!'

'Oh, Lord,' I mutter to myself.

Opening my eyes, the bright light burns into my pupils, making me wince. I think I overdid the vino collapso last night and I should know better by now. There's a jackhammer in my head and a washing machine in my stomach. My eyeballs feel twice their normal size and I seem to have my face in a puddle of drool.

'Are you still in bed, sweetheart?' she shouts. 'Shall I bring you tea? Coffee?'

I stagger out of bed and to the door. 'I'll be up in a few minutes,' I manage to get out, even though my mouth seems to be filled with birdseed.

I'll never get any peace now that Marilyn's here, so I do more staggering until I find the shower. Leaning against the wall, I let the jets of hot water beat on my skin. It might make me feel better. I'm not sure.

The jeans I pulled off last night are covered in sand, as is the bedroom carpet. Marilyn will be delighted as she'll have something to do today. I get a flashback of Ned and me building our sandcastle and smile to myself. For a precious moment I left my cares behind. I look at the photo of us he took on the beach and it makes me smile.

Finding my cleaner jeans, I put those on instead. Then I scoop last night's clothes and half of the beach into the laundry basket. I brace myself to face Marilyn's relentless cheeriness.

'Hello, lovey,' she says as I appear in the kitchen. Very loudly. She's already doing something unnecessary with a duster. She stops and regards me critically. 'Drunk as a squirrel, I'd say.'

'I did have rather more than I should have,' I admit.

'My daughter said you were in the pub until late. With Ned.' She nods knowingly at that.

It's clear that good and bad news travel fast in a small community. I wonder if Ned and I were noticed heading onto the beach? Did anyone see that we were still there at dawn? Or was he spotted leaving *Sunny Days* as the sun rose? That would certainly set tongues wagging. I've already learned that everyone here knows everyone else's business. Just wait until Marilyn sees the sand on the bedroom floor.

'I forgot that your daughter works in the pub,' I admit. 'I would have said hello. It has a great atmosphere.'

'I usually try to get down there myself for the music nights, but I was on babysitting duties for one of the grandkiddies.'

'You missed a good night.'

'Next time,' Marilyn says. 'I'll be there. As sure as eggs are pigs. It does you good to let your heart down every now and again.'

'Hair,' I croak. 'I let my *hair* down.'

'That as well,' Marilyn agrees. 'A bit of breakfast for you?'

'No. Nothing. Thanks.' Then I add, 'Could you maybe turn the volume down? Just a bit?'

'Of course, love. Sorry.' Marilyn rolls her eyes at me. 'I'm such a noisy bucket. Everyone says so. Comes with having so many kids. You have to shout to make yourself heard.' But she carries on, her voice still just as loud. 'I came a bit later in case you needed a lie-in. Shall I put some coffee on?'

'Yes. I need three cups. Black and strong.' A few painkillers wouldn't go amiss too. There's a steady throbbing behind my eyes.

'Hair of the cat,' Marilyn says sagely.

'Indeed.'

But before she can fix me any coffee, there's a knock at the door.

'I'll get it,' Marilyn says and bustles out. When she comes back, she's all smiles and silliness. She announces, 'Visitor.'

Behind her is Ned, looking as tousled and as tired as I probably do.

'Rough night?' I ask.

'Probably had more to drink than I thought as well,' he admits. 'I brought you breakfast.' He holds out a brown paper bag and a thermos flask. 'A wholemeal fruit bagel and a Virgin Mary. I didn't think the vodka would be a good plan.'

'That's very thoughtful.'

'It's my way of saying sorry for keeping you up late.'

'No apology needed it. I enjoyed every minute.' Then I realise that Marilyn is still listening to every word and bite my tongue.

'I'm just heading to the beach to do some yoga and wondered if you'd like to come with me. It's a beautiful day.'

The way I feel, I think I might spontaneously combust like a vampire if the sun hits me. 'I'm not sure . . . '

'It will do you good,' Marilyn chips in. 'It's a great idea. Get some fresh air to blow those spiders' webs away.'

'I think I'd rather just . . . '

Marilyn ushers me to my feet. 'Get your nice yellow jacket on then. You'll need it. That sun's deceitful.'

'I . . . er . . .' I'm unceremoniously bundled out of the kitchen, coffee clearly off the menu. I can see that Ned's trying not to laugh. He hands me my jacket and, realising that protesting is pointless, I slip it on.

'See you later,' Marilyn trills. 'Don't rush back for me.' She pretends to return to her dusting while keeping an eye on us both.

I follow Ned out of the door. 'You're no help,' I say to him when we're out of earshot.

'She has the right idea,' he tells me. 'The fresh air will do you good.'

'Any sudden movement is making me feel queasy. I'm not sure yoga is going to be an option. Your constitution must be a good deal stronger than mine.'

He laughs. 'I'll find you a nice rock to sit on out of the breeze and you can watch me do all the hard work.'

Chapter Twenty-Six

When we hit the beach, Ned is true to his word. He finds me a flat, sheltered rock and, as it's slightly damp from the tide, he strips off his hoodie which he lays down for me to sit on.

'That's very kind.'

'Comfy?' he asks.

'Very.' The sun sparkles on a sea that's as blue as the sky, though the temperature is cool and I'm glad I put on my jacket. Marilyn was right. The sun, like so many things in life, is deceitful.

I try a tentative nibble of my fruit bagel and take an equally tentative sip of the fresh Virgin Mary. The sharp tang of tomatoes, Tabasco and celery salt tingles on my tongue. That's definitely waking me up.

Ahead of me, Ned kicks off his shoes, wiggles his feet into the sand and starts to stretch. Within seconds, he's taken off his T-shirt too and is bare-chested on the beach. I'm not entirely sure where to look now. I know that I'm supposed to be watching him, but it does feel slightly voyeuristic. How can I watch him and not check out those abs? His shoulders are strong, his arms also impressively muscled though his limbs are long and slender.

In fairness, there are very few other people on the sand to warrant my attention – the obligatory dog walkers by the water's edge and a couple of optimistic joggers. So, trying not to feel too guilty for staring, I settle down on my rocky perch and concentrate on Ned as he goes through his routine. He has such a calm, chilled air about him that it's relaxing even watching him. I'm sure this is as beneficial as actually doing yoga. It's certainly making me feel quite warm inside.

Ida says that he's a player but, again, it doesn't fit my impression of him. Obviously, she knows him considerably better than me, but he seems very caring and generous. Perhaps it would be more appropriate to class him as a 'free-spirit'. Or maybe this is his seduction technique?

'How are you feeling?' Ned looks over his shoulder as he performs some kind of standing pose. I hope he can't read my thoughts.

'Better.' I hold up the flask of Virgin Mary in a toast. A layer of coffee on top of it and I might just feel human again. 'This was a very good idea.'

'Fancy joining me in a few simple moves?'

'Hmm. I don't think so.'

He comes over to me and takes my hand. 'There was enough hesitation in that for me to think I'd be in with a chance.' He pulls me from my nice rock seat and, a bit half-heartedly, I pull against him. 'Resistance is futile. Marilyn and I are grinding you down.'

'Marilyn definitely is,' I laugh. 'That lady doesn't take no for an answer.'

'A woman after my own heart.' He stands me on the sand in front of him. 'Jacket off.'

'It's chilly.'

'You'll warm up in no time.'

I take off my jacket and toss it onto the rock. To make a point, I shiver theatrically.

Ned gives me a look. 'Now the shoes.'

'I'm very attached to my shoes.'

'You want to feel your toes connected to the earth.'

'I think I can manage without that,' I assure him. 'Isn't the sand cold?'

'Yes, but it feels amazing. Trust me.'

Still I dither. Who wouldn't?

'Shoes.' He says sternly and points at them. 'Might I remind you that last night it was *all* about the sand.'

Ah, yes. I realise that I'm not going to get away with this, so I take off my shoes. The sand is cold, damp as I'd expected, but Ned's right, it does feel surprisingly good against my feet. Enlivening.

'I'm not going to be able to move much in my jeans,' I remind him.

'We'll do some very easy stuff,' he assures me.

'And no sudden movements.'

He laughs at that and then composes himself. 'Mountain pose,' Ned says and looks as if he's essentially standing still.

I copy. I can do standing still. Even after a night of much and many wines. It would be hard to mess this one up. I sway a bit. Standing still does, actually, appear to be a slight issue.

Before I fall over from the effort of staying upright, Ned takes me through a few gentle stretches. My head throbs a little and the breeze keeps throwing my hair in my face.

'Feeling warmer?'

'I am.'

'OK, let's try a sun salutation. I'll run through it first.'

'Have you taught yoga before?'

'No,' Ned tells me. 'But I've been doing this for years and have taken enough classes myself to have some idea of what I'm doing.' While I stand and watch he goes through a series of bends. 'This is downward-facing dog.'

'I'm not sticking my bottom in the air in public,' I say, aghast.

'There's no one watching you,' Ned assures me. 'This is less inhibiting than a typical yoga class. All you've got is me, the sun and the sea. I'm not going to judge you and neither are they. Do it with me.'

He has a decidedly determined expression on his face, so I join him in a forward bend and I admit that all the blood rushing to my head feels fabulous.

'Nice and slowly,' he instructs. 'Let your breath guide you.'

I think I'd been holding it.

'Keep your body relaxed and light.'

Then I follow him in a lunge, as far as my jeans allow, and am glad that the sound of the waves is disguising my grunts. What comes next feels suspiciously like a plank and I try to avoid doing that as much as possible, but it soon ends and we lower ourselves to the sand for a back stretch. Then it's sticking my bottom in the air for downward-facing dog and I do feel rather stupid doing this in public. Another forward bend finishes it off. I follow Ned through the moves a few more times and, as I do, I think my body does respond better. My breathing settles into the routine too. Thankfully, he doesn't task me with doing anything more strenuous and soon stands to indicate that we're finished. He puts his hands in a prayer position at his chest. '*Namaste.*'

I copy. '*Namaste.*'

'It means the light in me honours the light in you.'

'That's lovely.'

Ned grins as he pulls on his T-shirt. 'That wasn't too bad, was it?'

'I rather enjoyed it,' I confess.

At the end of our little session, I do feel a little lighter, surprisingly supple and feeling as if everyone should start their day with yoga on the beach. My hangover might even have gone.

'I'm here nearly every morning,' Ned says. 'In all weathers. There's not much can keep me away. You're more than welcome to join me.'

'I can think of worse ways to start the day than with the wind in my hair and sea spray on my face.'

'We'll call it a date,' he says and then we both laugh a bit shyly.

'I'd better get back.' I pick up my litter and Ned collects his hoodie. I look towards *Sunny Days*. I should call Bill and let him know that I'm still alive, and Della too. I know she'll be worried about me. So will someone else. 'Marilyn will wonder what's happened to me.'

'Marilyn misses very little.'

'That, I've already realised,' I assure him.

Chapter Twenty-Seven

We stand at the gangway to my houseboat. Ned lingers, seeming reluctant to leave, and I feel strangely disinclined to part company too.

'Thank you,' I say. 'For making me do that. I have really enjoyed it. I'll see you tomorrow. Hopefully.'

He goes to turn away then pauses. 'I don't know what you're up to for the rest of the day, but I've got a commission to complete.' Ned runs a hand through his hair, leaving flecks of sand in it. 'If you want peace and quiet, I'll leave you alone. However, if you want some company, I can take you up to my workshop. If you don't mind the noise, you could come with me and watch me do it. If you'd like to see how I work.'

'I'd love that.' I've answered before I think. It's not that I've got any other plans.

'Cool.' He looks pleased.

'I need to make a few calls and then I'll come over?'

'Sure. I'm in no rush. It's only a short drive from here. Take your time.' He waves a hand as he wanders off and it takes me a moment to stop watching him and go inside.

I kick off my shoes at the door. If Marilyn has just finished

cleaning, then I don't want to incur her wrath. I resist the urge
to shout, 'Coooooeeee!'

She's packing her bag when I go into the kitchen.

'That was good timing,' she says. 'I was just about to send
out a search party.'

'I was persuaded against my better judgement to try a little
yoga.'

Marilyn nods towards Ned's boat. 'He could sell ice to canni-
bals, that one.'

'I like him,' I tell her and hope that it's not all round the
island before noon.

Her eyes narrow as she asks, 'Are you going to do some more
of that yoga with him?'

'I might. I'd like to. I've only got jeans and posh joggers with
me though. Neither of which are really ideal for exercising.'

This time her eyes light up. 'We could go shopping again?'

'Oh, I'm not so sure. Let me decide if I'm going to do it first.'
That should put off another alarming shopping trip.

'Well, let me know if you change your mind. You should do
it. It might be good for you. That Ned's a good lad, you know,'
Marilyn says. 'One of life's nice guys. He's had his wild times,
but I won't hear a word said against him.'

I wonder what the 'wild times' might have involved. 'He told
me about your son,' I venture. 'What happened and how he was
friends with him.'

'Ah. He was close with Declan. They were like brothers.'
Marilyn's eyes fill with tears. 'There's not a day goes by that
I don't think of my boy. I still see him everywhere and in
everything. Sometimes he's still so close that I feel him right
next to me and it surprises me that, when I turn to talk to
him, he's not actually there.' She shakes her head, bemused.
'A mother's love never diminishes.'

'No,' I agree.

'I thank Jesus, Mary and the holy hostess of angels that I had him for as long as I did.' She sighs to herself and I see a rare moment of sadness on her face. 'I'd better be going,' Marilyn says with a sniff. 'I've got to run round with Mr Sheen at Mrs Smith's house. I'll see you tomorrow.'

'Thank you, Marilyn,' I say softly. 'I do appreciate it. The place is spic and span, as always.'

She allows herself a proud smile at that. 'Dirty house, dirty mind.'

'So true.'

She clip clops from the boat and I watch as she sashays down the gangway and feel nothing but admiration for her. How does anyone get over the loss of a child? How do you continue through the rest of your days without them, still putting one foot in front of the other? How do you become like Marilyn, so relentlessly optimistic and cheerful, despite having life throwing at you one of the cruellest blows that it can?

Chapter Twenty-Eight

Alone again, I make myself comfortable on the sofa with a view straight out to sea and take a moment to watch the little boats bob about in the harbour. It must be a good day for sailing as there's lots of activity on the water. Before it sends me into a trance, I pick up my phone and call Bill at the office. 'Hey,' I say when he picks up.

'How's it going, sis? You sound quite chirpy.'

'I feel a bit chirpy,' I tell him, realising that there is, indeed, a modicum of chirpiness at my core. 'I've been doing yoga on the beach.'

'Yoga? Have you gone all hippy-chick on me?'

'I enjoyed it,' I tell him. 'Didn't think I would.' Bill will assume it's a class, so I don't reveal that I had a very personal and private lesson. I'll fill him in on that another time. My brother would like Ned – maybe a bit too much. I look across to Ned's boat and I can see him pottering about on the back. He'll be waiting for me and I should go round there as I promised. I can't wait to see him doing some more of his superb chainsaw carving. Perhaps I'll get Bill something for the boat.

'I'll never get you home,' Bill complains as I muse.

'I'm not ready yet,' I confess. 'I'm still up and down. But this seems to be a good day.'

'I'm glad to hear it.' Then Bill clears his throat. 'I don't want to rain on your parade, but I've had Chris on the phone. He's desperate, Jodie.'

'You didn't tell him where I was?'

'Of course not, but you're going to have to face him at some point.'

'I know. But not today.' And maybe not tomorrow either. I've no desire to speak to my husband.

I can hear the sigh in Bill's voice, but he lets it rest. 'Della's messaged me a dozen times too.'

'I'll call her,' I concede. I owe Della and Bill that much.

'Promise?'

'Right now,' I agree. 'As soon as I hang up. How's work? Are you all managing without me?'

'Managing, but not enjoying being without you,' my brother says.

'How did the meeting about the eco-hotel go?'

'They liked what we proposed and have asked us to provide some more detail before we go to the next stage,' he tells me. 'Now I have everything crossed. It would be a great project if we can get it.'

'It sounds so interesting.'

'You'd *love* it,' he assures me and it does seem right up my street. 'I definitely need you on board for that one if it comes in.'

I get a pang of longing. I miss Bill. I miss my job. I miss my colleagues. 'Keep me posted on it.'

'Will do. I have to run,' says Bill, who pretty much spends his life having to run. 'I'm due on site across town.'

'I love you,' I tell him. 'I'll be back soon.'

But, as I hang up, I wonder if that's really true.

Chapter Twenty-Nine

After talking to Bill, I take a deep breath and stare at my phone, summoning up the courage to call Della. I don't know why I've avoided my best friend. Normally, we speak or message a dozen times a day. Perhaps I just can't face being the bearer of yet more bad news. I'm sick of being miserable myself so heaven knows what it's been like for my friend. For whatever reason, I haven't taken her into my confidence and I should have. That's what best friends do. Then I put it off as I knew she'd be cross with me.

I tap her number. Della answers after one ring.

'Where the fuck are you, woman?' is her opening salvo. 'I'm out of my mind with worry.'

'I'm sorry. I had to get away from everything.'

'And you couldn't tell your best mate?'

I can picture Della in her office, pacing in her sharp, black suit. My friend works in a high-powered asset management company – one of those that work hard and play hard. Even at the gym, she spends half of her time on the phone and most nights she's out schmoozing ultra-wealthy clients. Della's been so busy that it's been difficult to see her lately – even before I absconded.

What else can I tell you about my friend? She's very much a live-for-today type of person. She doesn't give two figs for tomorrow and I admire that in her. I worry about everything, but I don't think she knows what the word means. I look back on a life lived with small regrets – I should have done this better, I should have said that, I should have tried harder – while Della has none. I'm a perfectionist, while Della works in broad brush strokes.

My friend owns a fancy black sports car that spends most of its time under a dust cover in a basement garage while she Ubers around town. She has an extensive collection of designer handbags and shoes that occupy a walk-in wardrobe in her spare bedroom. She earns a fortune and spends even more. Handily, she lives a couple of Tube stops from my place in an open-plan loft apartment that could have come straight from a flash American sitcom. Our offices are also a few streets away from each other so we can share the same gym. We're such different people, but I don't know what I'd do without her now.

'It all became too much,' I confide. 'I didn't really think it through. I just grabbed a bag and left.'

'And went where? Your brother was annoyingly tight-lipped.'

'I'm at Bill's houseboat. I'm sure I've told you about it. He's been renovating it for ages.'

'The one on the Isle of Wight?'

'Yes.'

'Fuck's sake, Chummie! Couldn't you have gone to Mauritius or somewhere? The Isle of Wight?' She puffs her disdain at me down the phone. 'That shows a distinct lack of imagination.'

'In my defence, it required minimum thinking and planning. This place was available and relatively close by. Mauritius would have been a step too far. I couldn't have managed that.' I couldn't have got on a plane or coped with the hubbub of an airport, but I can't explain that to Della who spends half of her life breezing both. I look out at the sea ahead of me, the strong fort on the horizon, Ned's boat comfortably close next door. 'Besides, it's lovely here.'

'I can come straight out to see you. Tomorrow. I can be on a boat or a plane or however the hell I get there.'

'There's no need. I'm fine. Really.'

'We could sink a few bottles, check out the local hot spots. It'd be fun.'

Does it sound bad that I couldn't cope with Della here either? She's too much of a whirlwind, too bossy. I don't want 'fun' — especially as Della's particular brand of fun is exhausting. I want calm. Besides, I feel I don't want to share this with her. It's just for me.

'I can bring my bucket and spade,' she teases.

'Can I pass for now? I need some time alone to think.'

'Don't stew by yourself, Chummie. I know that you and Chris have had some difficulties because of . . . well, you know.'

I take a deep breath before I say, 'It's gone to a whole new level. He's been acting very strangely . . . '

'It's not surprising,' she chips in. 'With all that you've *both* been through.'

'He's having an affair,' I say bluntly. 'I've suspected it for a while.'

There's a pause on the phone, but I can hear Della breathing deeply. Eventually, she puffs out, 'Wow.'

'I know.'

'You said nothing to me about it?'

'I wasn't sure. It was just a feeling.'

'And now you are sure? Do you have proof?'

'There were all kinds of things. Too many late night meetings, phone calls that he could only take in private. You know the kind of thing.'

'You could be reading too much into it. You're still not yourself.'

'I found a hotel bill. For a double room. He was supposed

to be at a conference that night. Yet he was miles away in some boutique love-nest. I confronted him,' I tell her. 'He told me it was all a mix-up, but I could tell that he was lying.'

'Shit.'

I feel bad that I haven't confided in Della. She thinks Chris and I are the perfect couple, so this has clearly come as a shock to her too.

'On top of everything else, I couldn't face looking at him, hearing his blatant lies.' I sigh. 'I had to get away.'

'Do you have any idea who it might be?'

'It's probably someone at work.' Someone younger, prettier, less needy, less tearful. 'That's where he seems to spend all his time these days. I think that Meg is the most likely candidate.'

'The work wife? Oh, Jo-jo. I thought that was a big joke?'

'Me too. Doesn't seem so funny now.' He used to talk about Meg all the time and now he hardly mentions her at all. Isn't that a telling sign? 'Probably the easiest way to have an affair is to do it in plain sight. I never used to question all the work-related dinners or overnight stays he had with her. Now I wonder exactly how long it's been going on.'

'Fuck.'

After the expletive, my friend makes a sympathetic noise and, at this moment, I wish that Della was here with me. She'd have handled all of this differently. She'd have marched into Chris's office and would have confronted Meg, made a huge scene. She'd have given Chris an ultimatum. I haven't done either. Neither would she have let it grind her down or tormented herself the way I have. She'd have given them both what for. I've hidden from this as I've hidden from everything. Perhaps I deserve to have my husband cheating on me.

'I wish you'd told me. I could have helped.'

'Yes, well, it's too late now. I bolted rather than deal with it and here I am in splendid isolation in the Isle of Wight.'

'But you're coming home soon?'

'I honestly don't know,' I confess. 'I need some space, some time to think about things without all the madness around me.' And I do feel as if I have stepped out of a maelstrom even though I haven't exactly had the peace and quiet that I sought.

'Then maybe you should stay out there for a while. All we want is your happiness. You know that.'

'I think all that Chris wants is his *own* happiness. I'm not sure that I come into the equation any more.' It's heartbreaking to have to give voice to these things. A year ago we were filled with such joy, such hope, such wonderful plans for the future we'd have together. It's frightening how quickly that's turned to dust.

'I'm absolutely sure that you're wrong,' she says. 'He loves you. Both of you have had a tough time.'

We have. A tough time in which we should have pulled together like loving couples do. Isn't it the hard times that define a relationship? Any couple can skip along happily when it's all hahaheehee. It's what happens when the shit hits the fan and your world crumbles beneath you that counts. That's when you find out whether you've got each other's back or whether you turn on each other instead.

For me, it's over, but for some reason, I don't feel able to share that with Della. It's too heavy a conversation and I should have the courtesy to tell Chris first.

'I should go,' I say. 'Leave you to your day.'

'I miss you, Chummie. Tell me you're going to be OK. Otherwise, I'm coming straight out there.'

'I'm fine. Honestly. I'm sure I'll be back soon.'

'Good. You and I need to have a bloody good catch up over a decent bottle of red or two.'

'We do,' I agree. I miss my friend.

'Love you lots,' she says.

But when I hang up, I have a strange feeling that I can't quite put my finger on. Della didn't sound her usual ebullient self. Perhaps she was just distracted because she was at work. Or maybe it was something more.

Chapter Thirty

I don't know if we need a picnic, but I make some sandwiches from the bread and stuff in the fridge that Marilyn has brought every day without fail. I could feed an army – possibly two – from this fridge. Wrapping the sandwiches in foil, I take them round to Ned's boat. He's outside putting equipment into the boot of his car.

I hold up my foil packages. 'I brought lunch. Is that OK? Marilyn puts half a supermarket of food in my fridge every day, so I thought I'd better start to make a dent in it.'

'All contributions gratefully received,' he says. 'I was going to stop and pick something up for us on the way, so you've saved me a job.'

'I did look at a bottle of wine and thought "no".'

'Chainsaws and wine don't generally mix,' he advises me with a grin. 'Probably for the best.'

'I'm not sure I'll ever drink again after last night.'

'It was a good evening,' Ned says and his eyes twinkle. 'You'll have to come to another one. Get to know the band properly.'

'I'd like that.'

'Jump in,' Ned says, opening the passenger door for me.

'Sorry about the mess. I would have cleaned up if I'd known I'd be having visitors. My other car is a Porsche.'

'It looks very much like a working car.' I try to be diplomatic.

I don't know what type of car it is – possibly a Corsa? But it's of vintage origin and is absolutely wrecked. Every panel is a different colour of purple and it's much-dented. It must be regularly used to transport his stock of wood as, when I climb into the passenger seat, the inside smells of tree resin, leaves and earthiness. There's soil in the footwell, a pile of clothes and empty sandwich wrappers on the back seat.

He throws a few more bits into the boot, slams it shut and then climbs into the driver's seat. We set off, gears grinding, and I settle back into my seat as we trundle through the lanes. The traffic is slower today and we crawl through pretty touristy villages with thatched cottages and abundant tea shops.

It's half an hour later when we turn off into a track in a wooded area that's barred by a metal barrier. Ned pulls up and then goes to unlock the barrier so that we can pass through. The further we travel along the track, the deeper into the woods we go. The trees tower above us, every shade of green you can think of, and the sun peeps through whenever it can. Eventually, we come into a clearing where Ned parks and we get out of the car.

'Welcome to my office,' he says, gesturing at the forest that surrounds us on every side.

'What a fabulous setting.' There's a lock-up barn on one side with an open area that's filled with some of Ned's work-in-progress. Next to that is a huge pile of logs – some the size of branches, but others that are enormous tree trunks. There's another area covered by a canvas canopy that I can see is Ned's main work area – there's a sturdy bench, stacked wood every-where and an inch of sawdust on the ground. But the most impressive thing is the number of Ned's sculptures that are dotted around. There's a magnificent sculpture of a fairy king that stands about three metres high, next to him is a wizard with a magnificent crown and another that's some kind of sprite sitting down, his long legs stretching out in front of him made of gnarled tree branches.

'He's a tree spirit,' Ned says, following my gaze. 'I'm thinking of writing a kid's story book about him or some poetry – if I ever get round to it.'

'He's amazing. He looks as if he's about to rise up and move. You should get together with George. He's writing a book.'

'Is he?' Ned looks interested. 'I might chat to him.'

On the other side there are more Green Men with long beards carved with leaves and flowers. Then there are smaller animal sculptures: a kingfisher on a log, a badger and a hare.

The most imposing piece is an oversized chair that looks almost finished. It stands about ten feet tall and looks as if it's come straight from a fairytale castle. 'This is incredible.'

'The giant chairs are one of my most popular sculptures. I've lost count of how many I've done for various places. They're really popular in woodland settings. This one has got to have a final sand – which is my most hated job. Then it goes to its new home in a country park on the mainland,' Ned says. 'Want to sit in it?'

'Of course.' He gives me a hand and I climb up the side of the chair using the carved footholds until I can swing into the seat. My feet dangle in the air and I feel like a kid again, dwarfed by this enormous sculpture. 'I love it.'

I sit and let my eyes close. Without too much persuasion, I could fall asleep up here. The forest is still, settled around us. The only sound the snatches of nearby bird song. I could forget my worries in a place like this.

'I'd better start some work,' Ned says, to bring me out of my daydream.

Reluctantly, I rouse myself as he holds out a hand to help me down.

When I make the jump down the final step, he catches me by the waist and lowers me. It feels as if the air crackles around us and I wonder if it's being surrounded by all these enchanting pieces.

'How did you find this spot?'

'I sort of stumbled on it. After art college I was doing some tree felling on the big estates around the island to make some cash before I could work out how to make a living out of being an artist. I landed up here on a short contract and got chatting to the landowner. He's a decent guy and we got on well. Towards the end of the job, I cut down a particular branch and I could already see the figure in it – a Green Man. I don't know what made me do it, but during our tea-break on shift, I took the wood and had a go at carving it. As I didn't have any other tools to hand, I used the chainsaw. It seemed like the natural thing to do. I never looked back.'

'It was clearly meant to be.'

Ned shrugs nonchalantly as if it's the kind of thing that everyone can do. 'Now I rent this space from the landowner – very cheaply. I help him to manage the forest and I get to keep some of the timber that we cut down. It works well for both of us.'

'Amazing.'

Then he seems bashful that he's revealed so much of himself. 'There's a kettle in the barn if you want to make a brew. Nothing fancy. Strictly builders' tea here.'

'Want one?'

Ned nods and heads off to unlock the barn. As I go to get our sandwiches from the car, he shouts over, 'Grab the cushion and blanket from the back seat too and you can sit on the bench over there.' He points to another seat that he's sculpted.

I do as I'm told and put the packages down on the bench in a shady spot with the multi-coloured blanket and cushion. In the barn, I clear sawdust sweepings from the work bench and make us a mug of tea.

When I deliver it, I ask, 'So what are you working on?'

He stands back so that I can see it properly. 'This is going to be a mermaid and it's destined for the garden area of a fancy new seafood restaurant in Cowes that's opening in time for the summer season.'

It looks like a figurehead from a sailing ship carved into a tree trunk and I can see that the mermaid is starting to emerge, rising organically from the wood. Her face is lifted to the sunshine but has yet to receive its finer features. The body curves down to the roots of the tree and Ned has started to cut in some scales for her tail. At the bottom, delicate fishes have been carved into the wood and I've no idea how he does such detail with nothing more than a chainsaw.

'It's beautiful already,' I tell him.

'There's a long way to go yet.' He rubs his chin as he regards his work critically. 'Let me do an hour or so and then we'll stop for some lunch. Does that suit?'

'Yes, perfectly.'

'You need to wear these.' Ned roots in his tool box and pulls out a pair of safety glasses and some ear defenders. I wrinkle my nose. 'Trust me. You'll thank me for them. Bits of wood fly everywhere and, unprotected, your ears will ring for days.'

So I put them on and settle on a nearby bench while Ned puts on his gloves and pulls the chord of his chainsaw, making it growl into life again. He lowers his full-face visor. Soon he's into his rhythm and it's like watching him dance. His body moves and sways and the sound of the chainsaw ceases to be an irritant and becomes more like music. It's not all hacking with a chainsaw, a lot of it seems to be fine-tuning. With a few carefully executed cuts and slices, the mermaid's tail takes shape and her features appear. I feel so privileged to watch Ned work and love the way his hands move over the emerging sculpture, bringing it to life.

Though Ned is working up a sweat as he works, I'm feeling cool sitting here in the breeze and the shade of the trees. So I curl up on the bench, pull the blanket over me and then tuck one of the cushions under my head. My eyes grow heavy as I watch him engrossed in his work and it's not long before I let sleep take me.

Chapter Thirty-One

Ned cuts his chainsaw and the absence of noise rouses me from my doze. Blinking my eyes open, I realise that I'm still wearing my safety glasses and they're digging into my head.

'Hey, sleepyhead,' he says softly. 'Ready for some lunch?'

'You've finished?'

'Nah,' he says. 'I've made good progress, but there's a way to go yet. A bit more shaping then I have to sand her down. That's going to take a while.'

'Do you do it by hand?'

'On something with such intricate carving, then mostly. It's a filthy job. I end up covered in fine dust.'

I cast my eyes over what he's been up to while I was sleeping. 'She looks amazing.'

'Yeah,' Ned agrees. 'Mighty fine. I think my client will be pleased.'

'I'm sure they will be.'

'It'll keep me in beer for the summer if they are.' He casts a glance at the sky and the gathering clouds. 'Lunch outside or do you want to retreat into the barn?'

I should have brought a jacket, but I'd rather eat al fresco. It makes a welcome change from a sandwich grabbed at my desk. 'I'm happy to stay out here if you don't mind me hogging the blanket.'

'Every woman I've ever shared a bed with has been a blanket-hogger. Why is that?'

I flush slightly at the intimate revelation. Then I get a strange feeling of jealousy or something similar to it when I think of the women who've had the pleasure of Ned's company in bed. A more pertinent question is: Why is *that*?

'Let me go and make us another cuppa,' he says. 'I'll be right back.'

When Ned's gone, I wrap the blanket round me and take a minute or two to get my eyes to focus. I must have been in a deep sleep as I have that groggy feeling of not quite knowing where I am. While Ned's still making the tea, I get up from the bench and go to have a closer look at the mermaid. I run my hands over the intricate carving. The wood feels warm beneath my hand, almost alive.

I'm still admiring her when he comes back and hands me a mug. 'What are you going to call her?'

'I haven't decided yet.'

'I'd love a mermaid named after me, but I don't think that Jodie is very mermaid-esque.'

'I was thinking Nereida, which is Greek for mermaid.'

'That's lovely. I might just change my name.'

Ned laughs. 'That's a bit drastic. I could do a more appropriate carving for you. It wouldn't be any trouble.'

'I'd really like that.'

'Let's call it quits for the sandwiches.'

'I'm not sure that a few rounds of cheese salad sarnies is adequate payment.'

'Maybe we'll think of something else,' Ned says.

And it sounds like a pick-up line, but from Ned it doesn't sound sleazy. I blush anyway.

'It was mesmerising to watch.'

Ned laughs. 'Well, it certainly sent you into a deep sleep.'

'We did only have a few hours' sleep last night after our sandcastle adventures,' I remind him. 'I didn't realise I was so tired, though. This tea's helping to revive me.'

'The sound does kind of send you into a trance,' he admits. 'I find it very meditative.'

'I'd love to have a go.'

'That can be arranged, but you'd need to put some safety gear on.'

'More?' I still have my safety glasses perched on my head.

'I always wear cut-proof trousers and gloves. I'd never work without them. You don't want any accidents with one of these bad boys. This chainsaw is smaller and more manoeuvrable than one for felling trees, but it's still lethal. If you hit a knot or dropped it, this thing would cut through your leg like butter.'

I grimace. 'Maybe not, then. I'm not good when it comes to danger.'

'I'll be right here with you to guide you.' Ned raises an eyebrow in invitation. 'I've got spare stuff. It won't take a minute.'

I get a rush of recklessness. When am I ever going to get another opportunity like this? 'Go on, then.'

Chapter Thirty-Two

I'm trying not to think what I look like in Ned's spare cut-proof overalls and gloves. But it gives us both a fit of the giggles. Ned is slim, but they're still baggy on me. And, as he's tall, the legs of the trousers pool round my ankles.

'Stop it,' I say to Ned as we get ourselves under control. 'I'm taking this very seriously.'

'Good. Because you don't mess with chainsaws. Put your safety glasses on.'

I do as I'm told.

'I'm going to start the chainsaw, then I'll stand behind you and help you to hold it. We'll just try some straight cuts.'

Ned isn't, of course, letting me loose on the beautiful mermaid. While I was putting on his overall, he chose a large tree branch and set it on end for me to practise on. He starts the chainsaw and it rips awake. I place my hands on it where he's showed me and hold the chainsaw. The strength of the vibration shocks me and I grip it tighter. Ned's hands fold over mine and he guides them towards the branch. I make my first cut, the teeth of the saw ripping into the wood with a ferocity that frightens me. It looks a lot more relaxing when Ned is in control. He holds me in the circle of his arms and helps me to move the blade. My hands and arms shudder and the blade is going anywhere but where I want it to. Ned steadies me and I lean my back into his chest so that I can feel how he shifts his weight. I'm trying to steer the chainsaw with my hands, yet I can tell that it's definitely a full-body movement that's required. And I'm glad that it's taking all of my concentration to control the saw as this proximity to Ned is quite distracting and not at all unpleasant.

When I've managed to make a few straight cuts, Ned guides the chainsaw in a curve which is much more difficult as I'm going across the grain of the wood and the saw feels as if it wants to bounce. He holds my hands tighter and we move together. Speaking is impossible over the noise, but I feel that we're communicating well and with a few errant cuts along the way Ned has encouraged me to carve out a heart in the tree branch.

When it's completed, he cuts the saw and the ensuing silence is a welcome relief and a shock. Reluctant to break the moment, I stay in the circle of his arms while we appraise my efforts.

'Not bad for a beginner,' Ned teases.

'It's brilliant and you know it,' I bat back.

'Yeah. Well done,' he agrees. 'Thinking of becoming my apprentice?'

'You never know,' I tease. 'This is so much harder than it looks. I can't begin to tell you how much I admire the standard of work that you manage to achieve. It's breathtaking.'

'You flatter me. Now for some well-earned lunch?' He moves away from me and, instantly, I miss the feeling of his arms around me. I was getting a bit too used to that.

We sit together on the bench together and I pass him a tin foil packet of sandwiches.

'Bliss,' he says. 'I'd call that a good bit of work.'

His face is soft in repose and I realise that I like looking at it very much. As we eat, the breeze dies and the sun peeps from behind a cloud. I lift my face and let the rays that are filtering through the trees fall on my face.

I don't know whether it's the company or the place, but this is the happiest I've felt in a very long time.

Chapter Thirty-Three

When we've eaten, Ned takes me to walk through the forest where he gets his wood from. 'I do this walk nearly every day,' he says. 'I check that the trees are OK and look at those that need felling. If they're old and in danger of falling or have become diseased, I tell the landowner and we usually take them down together. It keeps me in touch with them all.'

'It doesn't look like it's changed for a hundred years or more.'

'It probably hasn't,' he says. 'There are no public thoroughfares, so it's pretty much unspoiled.'

I hear a drumming noise and Ned takes my shoulders and angles me towards a tree ahead of us. 'Woodpecker,' he says. 'Just below the canopy.'

The bird has beautiful black and white feathers with a distinctive red flash on its crown and tail. We watch it drilling into the tree. 'I've never seen that,' I whisper.

'They forage for insects in the bark. Seems like a hard way to get your lunch.'

'Cheese sandwiches are definitely an easier option.'

We stand still, observing him until he flies away.

'We have red squirrels here too, but they're very shy. We'd be lucky to catch a glimpse of one of them.'

But catch a glimpse, we do. A few moments later, one scampers across the path. It's tiny compared to our usual grey squirrels and its striking chestnut colour stands out against the lush green of the leaves. Even as I let out a gasp, it shoots up the nearest tree and is gone from sight.

We watch for a short while, but Ned says, 'It won't come back now. They're the most elusive of creatures. That was a bonus.'

Indeed it was. Then we continue with our walk through shaded glades and green lanes until we come to a boundary fence. 'This bit's National Trust land. It's a very special place.'

So we climb over the low fence and come out into a broad meadow that's filled with tall grasses and wild flowers.

'They're only just coming out,' Ned says. 'In summer, this place is filled with all kinds of flowers and butterflies. We should come back then.'

The thought is quite appealing. We walk out through the meadows and towards an estuary.

'Ancient salt marshes,' Ned says, indicating all the little creeks that clearly only fill at high tide. 'You wouldn't think so now, but this area is rich in history. It was once a thriving port and it's seen the plague, French invasions, smuggling – all of life.'

The landscape is bleak, but stunning. Ned and I are the only people in sight and I could happily spend the rest of the day here.

'We should head back.' Ned sounds as reluctant as I feel. 'I've got a space to look at for a potential commission, so I have to leave carving for today.'

'Thanks for letting me share it with you,' I say. 'It's been fun.'

'It's been a pleasure to have you around. It's nice to have company for a change. Even though you did fall asleep,' he teases. His eyes meet mine when he says, 'Let's do it again, Jodie.'

'I'd like that.'

As we walk back through the meadow to the woods, I want to slip my hand in Ned's, so I keep mine firmly in the pockets of my jeans where they can do no harm.

Chapter Thirty-Four

The journey back to *Sunny Days* goes too quickly and Ned drops me off by the gangway.

'Thank you again,' I say. 'It's been brilliant.' As I'm not sure what else I can add, I get out of his car and make my way to the houseboat.

'See you in the morning for yoga,' Ned calls after me.

Grinning, I shout back over my shoulder, 'Wouldn't miss it for the world!'

I might even mean that.

He drives away and I give him an awkward wave. Then I let myself into *Sunny Days*. Marilyn's stamp is on it – the smell of Mr Sheen and Zoflora competes with the sea air. She's left a cheery note for me on the table.

Hope you had a nice time. See you tomorrow. George left his book here rather than leave it with Ida. Looks saucy! Mxxxxx

She's underlined 'saucy' three times and has drawn a line of emojis too – a heart, a smiley face, a flower.

Sure enough, George's neatly typed pages are sitting next to it. *Wild at Heart*. I smile to myself and flick through the first pages, hoping that it's not *too* steamy or I'll never be able to look him in the eye again.

If I'm honest with you, I wasn't sure how I was going to fill the rest of my day so this is a very welcome gift. I thought I was good with my own company. It turns out that I'm not.

Making myself comfortable on one of the steamer chairs on the top deck, I settle down to read George's novel. I don't know what to expect, but soon I'm right into the story and the words whizz in front of my eyes as I devour some more. It looks as if there's a lot more depth to George than he makes out and I hope that a publisher will take him on.

A while later, I hear a car pull up and realise that Ned has returned. I check my watch and two hours have gone past since I started George's novel. Not that I know much about book publishing, but I'd say that he has talent. When I've struggled to settle to anything, George's book has had me so engrossed that time has just disappeared.

I shiver and decide to make a cup of tea. Not that I'm looking, but I can see Ned pottering about on his boat and wonder should I offer him one too. I'm aware that I've already taken up a lot of his time today, but he's such easy company to be with and I'm finding my own company considerably lacking. Perhaps I could cook him dinner tonight.

As I'm dithering with indecision, another car pulls up and Ida gets out. She glances towards *Sunny Days* as she knocks on Ned's door and waits for him to answer. And, for some silly reason, I duck back out of view. I don't want her to think that I'm a curtain-twitcher, spying on Ned and who visits him – even though I actually am. I could offer dinner to both of them, though I somehow get the feeling that Ida wouldn't be overly thrilled about that. I'm sure she'd like Ned all to herself. She's still sporting her trademark eclectic and wacky clothes, but she looks a bit more scrubbed-up than I've previously seen her. She's wearing a very short dress covered in cornflower blue flowers with over-the-knee suede boots in a caramel colour and a washed-out denim jacket. Her long dark hair is flowing loose and is topped with a cowboy hat. Her legs are slim and tanned. I envy her casual, distinctive style.

While I'm still playing Peeping Tom, Ned opens the door and she throws back her head and laughs. Perhaps they're having a date night. I don't like how that makes me feel. I was beginning to think that Ned and I had a special connection between us, but perhaps I'm wrong. Maybe it's his way to make everyone feel like they're the only person in the world. He puts his arm round Ida's shoulders and pulls her to him as he leads her inside. My stomach turns to liquid. It doesn't look as if Ida will be leaving any time soon.

Well, I've been warned about him and I'd do very well to listen to that advice.

Chapter Thirty-Five

I can't even settle back into George's book. So it's another evening with just me and the telly. I put something on and watch it, mindlessly, while trying not to think what might be going on in the houseboat next door. That's none of my business. It really isn't.

I should get a hobby – something all-consuming. That's what I need. I'm beginning to realise that work shouldn't be my everything. Apart from going to the gym, I don't do anything. I go to work, I eat, I sleep, I repeat. Again, Ned has inspired me to do something creative. But what? I used to paint a bit, when I was doing my degree in design – a dabbler, nothing more. But I haven't picked up a brush in years. Or perhaps I could take up crochet or knitting – they're trendy at the moment, aren't they?

Then I think that, if I'd had those skills, I could have been making cute little baby clothes and that plunges me down into darkness once more. I close my eyes and push away the images that haunt my days and nights.

I might as well be straight with you as I can't go on like this. You know that I've lost a baby, don't you? I'm sure you've guessed by now that there was more to my flight than an errant husband. That, on its own, I could maybe deal with. It was simply the straw that broke the camel's back. Or as Marilyn would probably say, 'broke the chicken's leg'.

I'm sorry that I've been keeping it from you, but I can't even vocalise it. I had months of people – friends, colleagues – looking at me with pity and I couldn't bear it any longer. I even felt strangers were staring at me, knowing my pain. I've been a nightmare to live with. I realise that. Folks, even the kindest of them, soon tire of a weeping mess and that's what I'd become. I bet even you're thinking these things happen, get over it. I'd like a pound for every person who said that they'd had one, two, three miscarriages, before they managed to carry a child to full-term – as if that would make me feel any better.

It wasn't any old miscarriage. It was *my* miscarriage. It was a child we'd fought hard for.

Chris and I spent our thirties having fun. We went to all the places, did all of the things, experienced all the joys that life could offer and lavishly too. I'm the big hitter when it comes to earnings, but Chris has a good salary too. Money was no object. We never thought about children or wanted our lives to be interrupted by the patter of tiny feet. We were having funfunfun.

And then I saw forty looming and like every cliché there ever was, I started to look in every baby buggy that passed me. It was like a switch had been flipped in my head and I longed to feel soft, pudgy skin against my breast instead of Chris's muscular chest. Chris was initially horrified when I broached the subject of a baby. It had never been on our agenda and he didn't see any reason to change.

But the more I talked about it – and, once it was in my heart, it was a subject that I couldn't let go – the more he came round to the idea. The thought of having a child consumed every cell inside me. Yet in all our rose-tinted conversations about what having our own child would be like, I don't think we ever really touched on the practicalities of it all. We thought about what great joy a child would bring us and all the wonderful things we could offer it, but the actual nitty-gritty of day-to-day child-rearing never troubled our vision. We assumed parenthood would bring us nothing but pleasure and it would be a walk in the park. We didn't think about sleepless nights or the end of our social life. Colic or chickenpox didn't cross our minds. It was all just going to be lovely.

Like everything else, we assumed that conceiving our child would be a breeze. It used to be one of the things that Chris and I did best together. Another reason why I never saw Meg as a threat. Our sex life had never wavered. We might have been like ships in the night for most of the working week, but whenever we were in bed together we made the most of it.

Consequently, we'd thought we'd only have to drop in the idea of having a baby and one would automatically appear. Neither of us considered what hard work it would be even to get pregnant. I think it was a terrible blow to Chris, to his ego, when 'low sperm count' was mentioned. He'd always succeeded at everything he tried and this, something at the core of his masculinity, was the first thing that he couldn't do. Perhaps that was the initial chink in our armour. Did it affect his confidence more than I realised? In all honesty, I never really knew how he felt as we didn't really talk about it. It seems that we didn't talk about much that mattered.

Fast forward and two harrowing rounds of IVF proved to be fruitless. Yet, third time lucky, and we'd struck gold. When it finally happened all the anguish that had gone before – the heartache, drugs, the injections, the expense – all disappeared in a moment. I was pregnant – miraculously pregnant – when I was beginning to give up all hope of holding my own child in my arms. Chris and I were the happiest people in the world at that moment. I'm sure we were. What a future we would have with our own little family. At forty-two, I was terrified it would be my last chance of having my own child, and I'd been blessed.

Of course, I did everything I could to protect the growing life inside me. I ate the right things, read the right books, went to all the appointments, made copious notes of what they told me so that I wouldn't get a single thing wrong. I would be the world's most perfect mother. I breezed through morning sickness with a surfeit of ginger tea. Work was busy. Maniacally so. Maybe I should have slowed down, but I felt fabulous, like a powerhouse, full of energy and in awe of the tiny miracle inside me. I was blooming. I was an Earth Mother. Pregnancy suited me. Everyone said so.

But it turns out that I was too hopeful, too smug, too complacent, too sure that everything would be all right this time.

Chris was attentive – much more so than usual – but his late nights continued. Work, it seemed, didn't slow down simply because his wife was pregnant. The business trips with Meg didn't seem to abate. He was always in Birmingham, Belfast, Belgium – always meetings that were crucial for him to be at. I thought he was trying to cram all his work in so that he could relax a little when the baby came, so I didn't think to take him to task about it. Why would I? I was floating on my own little cloud.

We cleared out our spare box room – our general dumping ground – and painted it ourselves. We'd normally get decorators in, but we wanted to do this ourselves, together. After much deliberation over a mountain of colour charts we picked delicate shades of lemon and barely there grey. No pink here. My girl was going to be feisty and fierce, not a fairy princess or a unicorn fancier. She was going to be a plumber or a concert pianist or prime minister. But above all she was going to be happy. And loved. We laughed at our lack of skills with filler and paint, but we had fun trying. I got emulsion all over my enormous maternity dungarees that had plenty of room for expansion once my bump really started to burgeon and cared not one jot. I agonised over the choice of cot and buggy. I wanted my child to feel secure, loved, cossetted. I couldn't wait for her to see it all.

Everything in my world was wonderful.

Chapter Thirty-Six

When the pains came unexpectedly and much too early, Chris rushed me to hospital. We both sat white-faced, unspeaking as all the traffic lights were red and against us. I felt my child's life ebbing away and was unable to do anything to stop it.

My baby, my beautiful child, too fragile for life, was almost twenty weeks old when she died. To me, she was a perfect, tiny person who just hadn't made it and I never thought that it was possible to feel so much pain.

Everyone tells you that the first twelve weeks are the most risky time for a pregnancy. Once past that, I assumed I would sail through until I had a healthy, bouncing baby in my arms. Just another few weeks and my baby might have had a viable chance of survival. Yet the sudden end of my pregnancy, the end of my hopes, was classed as nothing more than 'late foetal loss'. How cold is that? I know the medical community have to have their terms, but some seem too stark, too brutal. When they told me that they couldn't feel a heartbeat, I think that my own heart stopped too and it hasn't ever fully restarted. There's nothing but a gaping void where it used to be.

Losing a child who came silently into the world was one of the most traumatic experiences I could ever imagine. I was too numb, too distressed to know what was happening. In the depths of my darkness, Chris dealt with everything. He had to as I'd simply ceased to function. It was as if my brain had shut down in order to block out the emotion.

If my baby had lived just a little bit longer to that crucial twenty-four weeks old where she would have been classed as stillborn, she would have had a name, a birth certificate, a death certificate, a proper funeral. She would have been buried somewhere nice where we could have visited her. We'd have had some record of her being here, however briefly. As it is, I have nothing to say that she ever existed.

We were told that there might not even be a reason that she couldn't stay, that it happens horribly frequently. I was convinced we had done something wrong, missed some crucial thing that would have saved her. One of the nurses told me that as a 'geriatric' mother I'd have a higher chance of miscarriage, which only made things worse.

We were dismissed from the hospital and told to wait until I felt 'emotionally able' to try again. But when would that be? A month, a year, never? While I floundered in my pain and loss, Chris seemed unaffected. The very next day, he left me alone and went back to work. As time went on and I still struggled, he worked later, stayed away more often. I felt everyone was looking at me and instinctively knew that I'd lost a child. I dreaded people pussy-footing around me or smiling at me with pity. I'd sit at my desk and be unable to stop the tears. My grief was like a raw, open wound.

At home Chris and I stared at each other blankly and wondered what had happened. There was nothing there but an empty nursery and a crib that had never been used. Nothing but the memory of a baby called Little Bump. And that's what

I can't come to terms with. Everyone else has moved on and yet my arms still physically ache to hold her.

I can't tell you any more. I can't bear it.

Chapter Thirty-Seven

When I wake the next morning, the gloom is still upon me. Yet, in the midst of it, I decide that I *have* to be more positive. You know the extent of my pain now, but wallowing in it isn't helping anyone – least of all me. I don't want this to be my child's legacy – leaving nothing behind but the hollow shell of a mother. I have to do something to climb out of this dark hole.

It's a small thing, but it's a start. Ned invited me to do yoga with him and I'm bloody well going to make myself do it. I peer out of one of my porthole windows and the day is bright and sunny. That has to be a good omen, right?

I can do this. Yoga could be the answer to everything. So I put on my joggers and lurk about in the kitchen, trying to see if I can catch a glimpse of him heading to the beach. I make a coffee and a piece of toast, all the time keeping one eye out for any movement on *Sea Breezes*.

When Ned eventually appears, it's with Ida. So it looks as if she's spent the night with him. I don't know why that should bother me but I can't tell a lie, it does. A little of my determination to be more positive seeps away. I should be pleased for them. It's clear that Ida is more than besotted with him and perhaps there's hope that Ned feels the same. Unrequited love is a bitch. I should know.

Ida flings her arms around him as she leaves. She makes quite the display of it, in fact. Ned watches her, leaning on the doorframe as Ida bounces away down the gangway and into her car. When it splutters away, he goes back inside. At that point, Marilyn rocks up – or more accurately, roars up – in the lean, mean custard-coloured machine. She screeches to a halt outside *Sunny Days*.

I open the door. 'Hey, Marilyn.' Her outfit is so bright that, once again, it makes me want to reach for my sunglasses. Her trousers match her car and a turquoise T-shirt is accessorised with beads that bounce enthusiastically on her chest.

'Morning, sweetheart!' she trills.

As usual, she's laden down with a bag full of cleaning materials in one hand and a bag brimming over with the shopping in the other.

'Blimey,' she says as she bowls in. 'You've got a face like a wet week in Weymouth, lovey. What's the problem?'

At that, I burst into tears.

'Now, now, now.' Marilyn dumps her cleaning stuff and the shopping on the floor. 'What's all this about?'

Before I can ward her off, she comes and wraps her arms around me and crushes me to her bosom – and the beads – while I sob. I can do nothing but succumb to her ministrations. She rocks me as you would a child, patting my back, stroking my hair.

'You can tell me all about it,' she says. 'I know all about everything.'

Which sounds like a sweeping statement, but I can well believe that Marilyn does. She is a wise woman in gold wedge-heeled sandals. I did one counselling session, after the baby, with a pinched-faced woman who seemed to have no heart. It left me more depressed at the end than I was at the beginning.

The cold counsellor told me I should talk about it. But to whom? In the following months, Chris and I were barely communicating. We couldn't even face looking at each other. I did nothing but weep while he looked at me dry-eyed as if I was a stranger to him. Perhaps I was, but surely any normal person would cry at the death of your longed-for child? I blamed him and he obviously blamed me. I could barely get out of bed in the morning. He spent twelve, thirteen, fourteen hours a day at work. Or so I thought.

I'd gone early to ante-natal classes as I was so eager to learn, but all the women I'd met there had now either had their babies or were due imminently. I was the only one who'd walked out of the hospital alone. They sent a sympathy card that each one of them had signed. So I assumed they'd been out to coffee together. A get-together to which I hadn't been invited because it would be too embarrassing, too traumatic, too awful to contemplate. They couldn't face me and my empty arms. I wouldn't have gone even if they'd asked me. I didn't have a baby, so I couldn't be in their club.

Marilyn steers me to the kitchen table and presses me into a seat. Then she sits next to me and, still holding my hand, instructs, 'Spill the peas.'

That makes me smile through my tears and blow a snot bubble out of my nose. Marilyn produces a clean, folded tissue which she shakes out for me and hands over. I duly blow my nose.

'I'm sorry,' I say.

'Don't be,' she chastises. 'A good cry never did anyone any harm.'

'It's *all* I seem to do these days,' I tell her.

'Then you must have good reason,' Marilyn decides. 'This

isn't just about this husband of yours. I can tell that. It goes deeper.'

'I lost a baby,' I say, flatly.

It seems pointless trying to keep this all in. My heart and my head are too full of pain to hold it all in any longer.

Chapter Thirty-Eight

'Oh, lovey.' Marilyn sighs with concern.

'It was a few months ago now.' I could tell you the exact amount of days, of hours, but that would be too sad. I will say that Chris and I spent the bleakest Christmas I'd ever known. We'd planned to celebrate in style as it was to be our last as a couple. How true that was, but not in the way intended. We didn't go out, we didn't even put up a tree. Presents we'd bought were left unopened. I bought everything for a Christmas dinner and then threw it all in the bin, uncooked. The start of the New Year which was to be such a fabulous and exciting one for us now held no hope. 'I'm struggling to come to terms with it.'

'Of course you are.' She pats my arm. 'The loss of a child is one of the most devastating things that can happen to you. Why wouldn't you be in pieces?'

It seems like a reasonable question.

'You need time to heal, to grieve,' she continues. 'Sounds like you've been trying to burn the handbag at both ends.'

'I think I have.' I give her a watery smile. 'I think that's exactly what I've been doing.'

'You could have done a lot worse than to come to the Isle of Wight for a restorative break. It's God's own country.'

'I thought that was Yorkshire?'

'That, too,' Marilyn agrees, dismissively. 'I'm taking it that it's caused a moan of contention between you and your husband?'

'Yes. He doesn't seem to have felt it in the same way. Hardly at all.' I can't even bring myself to tell Marilyn that Chris actually went into the office the day after his wife miscarried, the day after his child slipped away from them. What kind of man does that? How could he leave me when I could barely put one foot in front of the other?

'Men are hopeless with emotions,' is her verdict. 'They handle them in very different ways, but that doesn't mean they don't feel exactly the same.'

Chris was the one who had to tell all of the family, all of our friends what had happened. I couldn't face anyone. I wonder if he resented that more than he said. Again, neither of us gave voice to our feelings.

'We didn't even give her a name,' I confide. 'I wanted to call her Charlotte after my mother. Chris never met my mum, so wasn't keen. He wanted to call her Beth for no good reason and we couldn't agree. I don't even have a photo of her or anything. I've only got the picture of her first scan.'

'You won't get over it,' Marilyn says. 'You'll just learn how to live with it. My boy's been gone for twelve years now and he was the apple of my pie. I still chat to him every single day. He might not come through my front door any more, but he still lives on in my heart and always will.'

'I don't know if I'll ever stop wondering how my baby would have grown up.'

'You won't. You'll see something and you'll think how they would have enjoyed it. You wonder where they are and what they would look like.'

'That's why I've stopped looking in mirrors because I wonder if she would have grown up to look like me.'

'Trust me, it will become less painful with time.'

I hang my head. 'I don't think I'll be able to bear it.'

'You will. It's early days yet. And you can have another child,' Marilyn says bullishly.

'I'm on the wrong side of forty, Marilyn. Let's face facts. This one took three rounds of IVF and now I don't even have a husband.'

'It's definitely over between you?'

'I'm pretty certain that he's seeing another woman.'

She purses her lips. 'It's hard to forgive, but maybe he's just not thinking straight either.'

'You think I should give him another chance?'

'Depends if he wants one.' She shrugs. 'If he keeps on denying it or blaming you, then bin him. If he confesses all and asks for forgiveness, then you'll have to see if you can make it work.'

I put my head in my hands. 'I can't even bring myself to speak to him at the moment, let alone think whether I want to repair our relationship.'

'Children are a blessing and a heartache,' she says. 'You'll have far worse to face than this when you have a family. It's how you deal with it will tell whether you've got a future together or not.'

'You're lucky you've had so many children.'

'Luck?' Marilyn laughs. 'I didn't plan to have so many kids. There were things that I wanted to do for myself, but my husband only had to take his trousers off and I was pregnant.'

I guffaw at that. 'I don't think that's how it happens, Marilyn.'

'You don't say?'

Then we both have a good giggle together.

'That a good sound to hear,' Marilyn says. 'Laughter is the greatest healer.'

'Time,' I correct. 'Time is the greatest healer.'

'Time and laughter.'

She's probably right.

'I've dedicated all my life to my kids,' she adds. 'You've had your fantastic career too.'

'I'm not sure that was the best thing. If I'm honest, Chris and I never really prepared for the baby to change our lives.' Oh, we bought pretty things, painted the nursery in pastel shades of Farrow & Ball, but we never really had a clue how it would affect us. We always assumed that any child would just fit in with our lifestyle. How foolish to think that. Was the baby trying to tell us that we just weren't ready to be parents? The hospital could offer no reason for why I'd miscarried. In my blackest moments I wonder was it the baby sensing that we weren't fit to care for her. I don't know.

As we're talking, I hear Ned's door bang and we both watch him make his way towards the shore. I wonder if he remembers that he invited me to go to the beach to do yoga with him. If he does, you'd think he might glance this way. I kind of will him to. But he doesn't.

So much for my psychic powers.

'You should go with him.' Marilyn is clearly better at reading minds. 'I thought you were going to give that yoga thing a go?'

'Not today. I'm emotionally drained.' I smile at her.

'I brought you a present.' She goes to one of her many bags and delves in. A moment later, she puts a carrier bag in front of me. 'Ta-dah.'

I give her a puzzled look. 'What's this?'

'You won't know until you open it.'

Now it's my turn to dip into the bag. I pull out the contents. 'Wow,' I say, slightly stunned. 'Wow.'

'I knew you'd like them,' Marilyn says, proudly.

'Wow.' In my hands there are silver glittery leggings and a neon pink vest top. 'Wow.' There really are no other words.

'Just the thing for your yoga sessions.' She looks more excited than I feel.

'I don't know if I'm going to do it yet,' I hesitate to point out.

'You are,' she says in a tone that brooks no challenge. 'That Ned won't know what's hit him when you turn up on the beach in those.'

I think we can both agree on that.

'This is very kind, Marilyn.' And it is, despite the fact that I'll probably look as if I'm emulating Jane Fonda, The Early Years.

'Go and try them on,' she urges. 'I can't wait to see you in them.'

I'm really not going to get out of this, am I? Still, I look at the silver glittery leggings and can't help but smile.

'There,' she says, satisfied. 'You look better already.'

'Thank you for that chat. I think I needed it.' I've been like a pressure cooker building up a head of steam, ready to blow at any moment.

'My pleasure. I'm always here for you.' Marilyn stands and plants a noisy kiss on top of my head. 'You'll be OK. I can feel it in my bones.' Then she goes and hefts the rest of the shopping onto the work surface. 'My only degree is from the University of Life, but it comes in handy sometimes.'

'I'm sure it does.' Marilyn might be able to talk for England, but she's proved to be a very good listener too and I'm grateful for that.

She cheerfully bangs about with the kettle and stacks more food in the fridge. If I do ever go home from the Isle of Wight I'll be about ten kilos heavier and will have to up my gym game. I wonder what the good people of LifeStyle gym in Shoreditch would think of my new workout gear?

'I saw Ida leaving Ned's boat this morning,' she says over her shoulder.

'Yes, so did I.'

'She looked a bit worse for wear. I hope they weren't up to what I think they were up to.' Marilyn shakes her head in dismay. 'That poor girl's always carried an umbrella for him.'

'Yes. I'd gathered.' You only have to see the way she looks at him to realise that. I'm also slightly worried that I, too, might be carrying an 'umbrella' for him.

'Shame, as it would be nice to see them both settled,' Marilyn continues. 'Ida might think he's the bee's elbows but I'm not sure Ned feels the same about her.' She gives me some side-eye. 'I think our Ned's got other fish to chip.'

That's as might be, but it didn't stop him from spending the night with her though, did it?

Chapter Thirty-Nine

I am feeling positive and energised after my talk with Marilyn. Plus two well-aimed coffees and a fresh Danish pastry haven't hurt either. These were also courtesy of Marilyn – who I may now refer to as Saint Marilyn. She really does have a heart of gold despite having seen a good deal of heartache herself. I should aim for that too. I feel she understands me when no one else does.

It's a beautiful day. The sun is shining, the sea is sparkling like diamonds and there's not a cloud in the sky. Thanks to Marilyn, I have a fridge full of food, not a speck of dust anywhere, new glittery workout pants and some small hope for the future. On a day like this I should count my blessings. I'm not going to mope around. I'll walk into town or along the coast. I might even sit down later and actually read some more of George's book. I feel better already.

When Marilyn has nearly finished banging around with the hoover accompanied by her singing 'A Million Dreams' from *The Greatest Showman* at the top of her voice, I emerge from downstairs modelling my new yoga outfit. I give her a twirl.

'What do you think?'

'Oh, my,' she says. 'You look like a little princess. You like them?'

'I love them.' That might be stretching it a bit, but the leggings actually fit me very well and, while the vest top is rather more plunging than I'd normally choose and doesn't really cover all that much, it will do perfectly well for any future yoga session that I might or might not attend on the beach.

I go over to Marilyn and give her a big hug.

'What's that for?'

'To say thank you for being you.'

'I'd have trouble being anyone else. Are you going to do some yoga?'

'I think I've missed the boat on that one,' I say. 'Seaside pun intended. I thought I'd pop down to the café. I've been reading George's book and have really enjoyed it. I might bump into him and tell him so.'

'Sounds like a plan,' Marilyn says. 'It's a lovely day.'

It is. So much about it is right.

I put my sensible clothes back on, topped with my cheery jacket. If Marilyn carries on like this, there'll be no black or grey left in my wardrobe. As I leave *Sunny Days*, I kiss goodbye to Marilyn and set off down the seafront, a tiny kernel of lightness in my heart.

Chapter Forty

The walk down to the Beach Hut Café is bracing. The sea air is cool, gusty and blows me along the front.

George is on his podium and, even more than usual, is struggling to stand still.

'Hi, George.'

'Hi, Jodie. How's it going? I've had a terrible morning. There's hardly anyone around due to the wind and then, when someone finally came along, her cockerpoo did a wee up my leg.'

'Oh, George.' I try not laugh. 'That's terrible.'

'Hazard of the job.' He sounds very doleful. 'Its owner had some Wet Wipes, so she cleaned it off. She was terribly apologetic and put five pounds in my box. But it wasn't very nice.'

'You must have been doing a very good job of being a statue, if that's any consolation.'

'Do I smell of wee?'

'Not that I can tell.' Though I don't think I want to sniff too closely. 'Want to abandon your post and join me for a coffee?' He looks forlornly at the one fiver in his box. 'I'm buying.'

'I don't think anyone would miss me for a short while,' he

says and jumps down to join me, bringing his money box and podium with him.

'Short cut across the beach?' He nods in agreement. 'I'll carry your podium. You might need a hand free to hold onto your hat.'

He gives it to me and I tuck it under my arm. We drop down the nearest steps and walk together along the sand towards the café.

'I'm enjoying the book immensely,' I tell him. 'So many twists and turns. It's a triumph.'

Even beneath all the metallic make-up I can see that he's pleased. 'You think so?'

'Yes. Have you sent it off to any agents yet?'

'I have a list of six and I'm going to be sending off three chapters and a synopsis later today. That's what they ask for. It's nerve-wracking,' he admits. 'Part of me doesn't want them to see it in case they don't like it. If it comes bouncing straight back, then I'll have to re-think my career plan.'

'Think positively,' I say. 'It could be just the thing they're looking for.'

'I hope you're right. It's horrible when you really set your heart on something only for it to be thwarted.'

'I know.' More than George can imagine. 'But life goes on. If it doesn't happen this time, then you can try again.' It's good advice that I should take myself.

George smiles and then says, 'Oops. Mustn't crack my make-up.'

We laugh together and that only makes it worse and George clutches his face to try to stop it moving as we giggle.

By the time we reach the café, we've managed to get ourselves under control again. There are only a few customers and Ida is in the hut, slumped on the counter. When she hears us, she lifts her head from her arms and, tentatively, opens one eye. She looks pale and as if much wine was taken and very little sleep was had. She's still wearing last night's clothes.

'Late night?' I ask, even though I know. I don't want Ida to think that I'm spying on Ned. Especially when I am.

'More like an early morning,' she says, sleepily. 'Your neighbour is *such* a bad influence on me.'

'I'm glad you had a good time.'

'We should have asked you to join us,' she says, sweetly. 'I didn't think.'

The implication being that Ned didn't either. But that's OK. I'm cool with that.

Ida yawns. 'Usual cappuccino, George?'

'Yes, please.'

'To drink in or take away?'

'We're staying,' he says.

'And for you, Jodie?'

'I'll have the same. Throw in a couple of flapjacks too, please.'

Ida stands up and looks as if she regrets the sudden movement. While we watch, she makes our coffees, scowling at the coffee machine and the amount of noise it makes. She hands over a tray bearing our drinks and flapjacks.

'Thanks.' We go to my favourite table and we tuck in together.

It's funny to see George eat as you get a peek of his white teeth and pink tongue which look incongruous in his bronze face.

Delicately, he wipes a crumb from his lip. 'Don't want to smudge the make-up. People are very quick to point out if there's a bit missing.'

When he's finished, he drains his cup, folds his flapjack wrapper and tucks it inside, then replaces the lid. Finally, he pops it back on the tray. All done as methodically as one of his statute routines. 'Thank you. I'd better get back to it. I'll probably just set up here.'

173

George takes his plinth and goes to stand at the entrance to the beach.

'Good luck with the book,' I call after him. 'I'll keep my fingers crossed.'

I finish my own coffee, pick up the tray and take it back to the counter. Ida has returned to her head on hands position. 'Thanks.'

She looks up, reluctantly opening one eye. 'No worries.'

Her head goes down again, so I put the tray on the nearest table. Not chatty at the best of times, clearly Ida is in no mood for conversation.

As I leave, George is already back in statue mode. He nods to me before striking a pose. So I head off back towards *Sunny Days* wondering what to do with myself today but, for the first time, the thought doesn't fill me with dread.

Chapter Forty-One

As I reach the houseboat, Ned appears from the beach path and heads to *Sea Breezes* and, out of nowhere, my heart does a little flip. He holds up a hand in greeting and I wave back, then wait while he walks up to me. He's wearing board shorts and a white vest top. His feet are bare and covered in sand.

'Hey.' His ready smile brightens. 'How are you doing today?'

'Good,' I answer. And I think I might well mean it.

He flicks a thumb towards the ocean. 'I thought you were going to come and join me on the beach.'

I don't like to tell him that was exactly my plan and that I changed my mind when I saw him emerging with Ida.

'Look at this!' Ned holds his hands towards the sky. 'You missed a lovely morning.'

'Tomorrow,' I promise. And I think I might well mean that, too. I'm going to have to give those glittery leggings an airing or Marilyn will give me grief. 'If it's not bucketing down. Or blowing a gale.'

He takes in my coat and trainers. 'Looks like you've been on a mission.'

'Not really,' I admit. 'I walked along the seafront and

bumped into George. We went down to the café and chatted for a bit.'

'He seems unsuited to the work of a statue,' Ned observes.

'Yeah.' Can't help but agree. 'He's sending off his novel today. Perhaps he'll have better luck with that.'

'Was Ida OK? She had a skinful last night.'

'She seemed a little delicate.'

'I should text her. She was in a bad way. That woman can drink me under the table.' Ned checks his watch. 'What are your plans for the rest of the day?'

'Nothing much.'

'I've got a meeting on the other side of the island. I've just got time to run round the shower and throw on some clean clothes, then I'm off. You could come along for the ride if you want to. It'd be a chance to see a different area, do a bit of touristy sightseeing. We could grab a bite of lunch.' I must look hesitant as he adds, 'I'd be glad of the company.'

'If you're sure I won't be in the way.'

'I'll have to leave you in a café with a coffee for half an hour while I meet the Powers That Be, but if you're OK with that, then I think we're good to go.'

I must confess that I like the idea of spending the rest of the day with Ned. I'm in a good frame of mind today and an outing sounds like fun. 'I'd very much like to join you.'

'Give me ten minutes,' he says. 'Come in and wait.'

So I follow him onto *Sea Breezes* and, while he goes through to the bedroom and bathroom, I mooch about in his living room and check out some more of the treasures from his travels. There's a wicker stand with a collection of marionettes heaped on one shelf, below them is a storm lamp and a reclining Buddha. On the top shelf there are copper singing bowls stacked together and an enamelled pineapple that says *Aloha Hawaii!*. What I *don't* do is glance anywhere towards where Ned might be changing. The last thing I need is another glimpse of that honed torso.

I hear the pump of the shower turn off and, true to his word, he emerges just a few moments later. As he comes into the living room, he's pulling a white T-shirt over his damp hair and I make myself look away. That body is a sight to behold. I feel a pull deep inside me and think my reaction shows that my hormones are still completely scrambled.

He claps his hands then grabs a portfolio case and his car keys. 'Ready to rock?'

I nod that I am.

'Let me show you what the Isle of Wight has to offer!'

So I follow him out to the car and he opens the door for me. Ned throws the portfolio on the back seat and it lands amid the plethora of clothes and empty sandwich packets that are still there from my last trip. He slides into the driver's seat. 'Sorry about the state of the car. I keep my Lamborghini for best.'

I laugh at that. 'Last time you said it was a Porsche.'

'Ah,' he says. 'Did I? Time to fess up that I don't have a garage full of high-end performance sports cars?'

'I'd kind of gathered that.' I turn to him and smile. 'I can't see you in a Porsche. Or a Lamborghini.' We have many clients who do drive such cars and they are definitely a certain breed. Ned isn't one of them. 'You seem more of a low-key sort of person.'

'That's me,' he agrees. 'What you see is what you get.'

But is it, I wonder? Does he realise that I saw Ida leaving his place first thing this morning? Is that an indication that Ned's life isn't as straightforward as he likes to make out? I notice that he hasn't yet texted her. Still, it's none of my business. I have no hold on him. He's a free spirit.

'I'm just grateful for the chance to explore,' I tell him. 'This is very kind of you.'

He starts the engine and slams the car into gear – not without some effort and grinding noises – and we set off.

'We're heading for Alum Bay,' he tells me. 'I might have a commission there, if I'm lucky. I've got some sketches in my bag and photographs of similar things I've done over the years. It would be a big one if I can get it.'

'Fingers crossed.'

'Yeah.' Then Ned switches on the radio and I settle back in my seat. The DJ's chatter and the pretty scenery wash over me. It takes an hour of relaxed driving to get to our destination. The Isle of Wight might be small, but the roads are too and there aren't that many of them. We go right across the middle of the island, mostly through pretty, unspoilt countryside and cutesy villages.

The car is warm and cosy. The sun coming through the window makes me feel sleepy and I'm relaxed in Ned's company. There's not the need for constant chatter and, without even realising it, I doze off.

Chapter Forty-Two

The car stops and I open my eyes, blinking against the sudden blaze of sunlight. Ahead of me the sea is shimmering and we're parked by a small theme park – The Needles Landmark Attraction.

'We're here,' Ned says. 'Welcome to the Needles.'

I rouse myself and we get out of the car. Even this looks like it's from the sixties, but not in a bad way.

'Want a coffee to wake you up?'

'That sounds like an excellent plan.'

'I'm going to take it personally if you keep falling asleep on me.'

'Sorry,' I say. 'I don't know why I do.' Perhaps it's part of the healing process that my brain grabs every opportunity it can to shut down for a few minutes. 'Take it as a compliment about how relaxing I find your company.'

'I'm glad that you do,' he says and that makes me flush.

Ned steers me to the nearest café – possibly the only one – and gives me his portfolio to hold while he queues to buy me a cappuccino. I sit in a window seat looking over the main thoroughfare. There's an old-fashioned sweet shop, the obligatory arcade of slot machines, a carousel and a few other shops selling seaside paraphernalia. None of them are busy today, but I bet you can't move here in the summer.

He delivers my drink. 'I got you a double shot of coffee,' he says. 'I shouldn't be long. I'll ping you my phone number in case you decide to go for a wander. When I come back I'll show you the sights properly.'

'I hope it goes well for you,' I manage to say, still feeling a little dazed.

'Thanks.'

So Ned dashes off, portfolio under his arm and I sip the scalding, double-strength coffee which does, indeed, start to restore me to full wakefulness. I stare into space, enjoying being still. The tang of sea air is mixed with the smell of fresh coffee and the seagulls here look like bullies, swaggering along the pavement looking for scraps of food.

I check my phone and Chris has called a dozen times again. The frequency is tailing off, but the messages are no less heart-rending. I can't listen to them. Not today when I'm feeling so much stronger.

For the first time, I wonder what he's doing, what he's thinking. Has he told Meg that I've left? Does he really miss me? Or is it simply shock at my abrupt and unexpected departure? I thought we had a good marriage – strong and steady. We were never lovey-dovey, always draped over each other, or joined at the hip – but it worked, or so I thought. It is a blow to see how quickly that has crumbled away.

Half an hour later, I'm still sitting deep in vacant contemplation, and no nearer to an answer, when Ned returns and slides into the seat opposite me. 'How did it go?'

'Well,' he says, with a degree of conviction. 'I think they liked my idea. In fact, they were quite enthusiastic. I'm ninety per cent certain that they'll go for it.'

'That's great. Can I have a sneaky peek at your proposal?'

'It's for a series of leaping dolphins on the beach.' He whips a piece of paper out of his case and scoots it across the table to me. 'Ta-dah.'

I take in the skilled pencil drawing. 'It's fantastic.'

'They seemed to think so too. I've got a verbal commitment. I just need to wait for the final confirmation and, of course, the contract.' Ned gives a sigh of what might be relief. 'I hate this bit of the job.'

'Perhaps you need an agent to do it for you.'

'When I earn enough to warrant one that would be a great idea. I'm gradually increasing my earnings so that they meet my living costs and this one will really help. It's a generous sum. Which means, on the strength of me landing this, I'm going to show you a good time. No expense spared.'

'What does that involve?'

'I don't want you to burst with excitement, so you'll have to wait and see.'

I drain the dregs of my coffee. 'Sounds great.'

'Prepare to be amazed and astounded,' he says and I follow him outside.

Chapter Forty-Three

'This was my favourite place when I was a kid,' Ned says, talking animatedly. 'I thought the Skyride was the most exciting thing I'd ever done in my life. It probably was.'

He takes my elbow and steers me towards a chairlift that could best be described as vintage. A rainbow-coloured string of seats and accompanying dangling legs go by above our heads. There's none of your high-tech stuff here. This is straight out of the 1970s and looks fairly basic.

'My plan is go down to the beach and I can show you where the sculpture will eventually go. Does that sound OK? You're not scared of heights?'

Right now, I don't feel scared of anything. 'No. Let's do it.'

Ned pays for our tickets and we go through the barrier. I can feel excitement building as we wait patiently for our turn to hop on board. When one of the chairs comes round we jump on and he pulls down the safety bar. We're close together and Ned puts his arm across the back of the chair, protectively. And I'm glad that he does as, with a certain amount of juddering, we're whisked away from the café and the arcades and out through the treetops. It's lovely to be so high in the canopy and I feel that I could reach out and touch the leaves. Then we come out of the trees and over the edge of the cliffs, the wind whipping around us as our legs hang high above the beach.

'Alum Bay is famous for its coloured sands,' Ned tells me as we shudder and chug our way down.

All around the bay I can see the cliffs made up of multi-coloured layers of sand – crimson, tan, graphite, saffron and lemon – and it's so beautiful. I can see why this is such a popular destination.

'I think it's one of the prettiest places on the island. Plus you get a great view of the Needles.' He points across the bay and there's the familiar row of the striking bright white stacks of chalk, eroded into pillars by years of wind and sea. They jut out into the milky, turquoise sea and finish at a jaunty red and white striped lighthouse.

When the chairlift reaches the bottom, Ned helps me as we step off. Then, side by side, we walk along the beach, dwarfed by the bright, multi-hued cliffs. His arm brushes mine as we go.

'As long as I get the go-ahead, the sculpture will be just about here,' Ned says, showing me the allocated spot. I can tell that he's really proud to be doing this, and why shouldn't he be? He has a real talent and the more people who can see his work the better.

'If we go out on the boat we'll get a better view of the bay and a close-up of the Needles. Up for that?'

'Yes.' It's a sunny, sparkling day, I'm at the seaside and I feel as if I'm ready to take on the world.

At the jetty, we have a choice of two boats: a high-speed rib or a more sedate cruiser.

'Want to go fast?' Ned asks.

'Yes, please.' Today is a day for excitement, trying new things. So we climb onto the rib, don lifejackets and strap ourselves in. As it's still a long way from peak season, there are only a couple of other customers and it feels like a private trip. When we're all settled, the rib roars into life and I cling on as it bounces out into the waves. The taste of the salty breeze is on my lips and the sea spray on my face sends my spirits soaring. We speed across the water at an exhilarating rate and my stomach lurches as we crest the waves.

Ned looks over at me. 'OK?'

'Great!' I shout in reply.

Soon the engine throttles back and we're bobbing beneath the towering cliffs, the tops dotted with sea birds standing like statues. More sedately, we tour the Needles and the lighthouse and the guide points out sites of historical shipwrecks in this treacherous area before we head back to the beach.

Ned lifts me down from the rib and I'm aware of his warm hands on my waist. I feel flushed and slightly hyper when my feet touch the sand once more. And when the chairlift whisks us back up to the top of the cliff, I'm conscious of sitting so close to Ned, the length of his thigh against mine. His arm rests casually along the back of the chair again, brushing my shoulders. If I relaxed back just a little bit, I'd be leaning against him. I try to keep upright.

We skim the trees once more as we return to the station at the top of the cliffs. Ned takes my hand to help me off the chair as it slows for us to step off.

'That was brilliant,' I say.

'Can you bear any more excitement?'

'Of course.' I think we're both feeling slightly giddy.

We head to the arcade and play the slot machines, spending an age waiting for pennies to drop on the Penny Waterfall with no luck. After too many attempts, Ned manages to hook me a pink teddy bear from the Crazy Claw toy grabber. I'm pretty sure he'd been aiming for the purple dinosaur but it evaded his grasp at the last minute.

The bear shoots out of the dispenser and Ned hands it to me, proudly. 'Not everyone has the skill and dexterity to do this.'

I hold the tiny pink bear to my chest and stroke it. It's unbearably tacky, but still manages to make my heart ache. 'It's gorgeous.' I give the bear a kiss on the head. 'I am in awe of your prowess.'

He laughs. 'That was my intention.'

Then Ned takes me to the sand shop where there are rows of wooden boxes offering all the different coloured sands from the cliffs. We choose glass bottles to fill with all the shades we can.

'They started doing this in Victorian times so we're carrying on an ancient tradition of our forefathers,' he says with mock solemnity which makes me giggle. 'Apparently, Queen Victoria had one on her mantelpiece.'

'I bet she did the mermaid-shaped bottle.' I kind of wish I'd done that one too.

I like the way Ned is making his creation in a haphazard manner. The sand is going everywhere and is all mixed up in the bottle.

'Why don't we swap?' I say to Ned. 'I'll do this one for your treasure trove and yours can be for me to keep on Bill's boat. That way we'll remember this day for ever.'

He looks up at me and I can't read the expression on his face but his eyes soften and he smiles back at me. I turn from his gaze and refocus on my sandy stripes, even though I'm doing mine in a much more controlled manner. Unlike Ned, I frown as I concentrate on spooning sand into my bottle, intent on not spilling a grain and then carefully shaking the bottle to make sure that it's all level before starting on the next row. I like to think that I'm creating classical art rather than modern.

When we've finished and paid, we exchange bottles – Ned's

with his wonky stripes, mine that are millimetre perfect. 'I'll treasure it,' I say. 'This has been a lovely day.'

'I have yet to reveal my *pièce de résistance*,' he informs me. 'Come this way.'

I follow Ned to the fish and chip shop, where he orders for us both and they wrap our meals in paper for us to take away. Clutching them, we head back to the cliff and find a suitable bench to sit on that overlooks the sea. The chips are hot and burn my fingers. The fish is fresh with crisp, golden batter and smells of the sea.

I don't really want to think about my husband – not while I'm having such a great time – but I can't help but wonder why Chris and I didn't do days like this? We very rarely had time to be free and easy, as each minute of our day was accounted for. The only real quality time we spent together was on our holidays and then we went to exclusive resorts in exotic locations where we lay on sunbeds all day and let waiters bring drinks to us. Would he have even enjoyed sitting on a bench on a windy clifftop eating fish and chips from paper? I don't think he would have. In fairness, I'm not sure it would have been high on my list of 'must-dos', but I've loved every minute.

We finish our al fresco meal in silence – not awkward silence, but quiet, companiable silence. Then, as we've exhausted all the delights of the Needles attraction, we head to the car. I sleep all the way home and only wake up as Ned pulls up outside *Sunny Days*.

'Home again,' he says.

Yawning, I say, 'You must be a very smooth driver.'

'Or you're a very tired lady.'

'Relaxed, I think. Plus I'm not accustomed to all this fresh air.' Or the delicious carb-loading from the fish and chips. 'I need to get an early night.'

We both climb out of the car.

'Thank you for today, Ned. It's been really brilliant. Just what I needed.'

He steps forward. 'I've enjoyed it too. Thanks for coming with me.' He brushes my mouth with his lips, the lightest of kisses.

And I want more. You know that. I know that. I think Ned knows it too.

But, before I can get carried away, I step away from him and say, 'I should go.'

I think Ned looks slightly disappointed. Perhaps he hoped that this would carry on until the evening. But where would it end? Only this morning Ida was coming out of his houseboat. I haven't forgotten that.

I don't need this kind of complication in my life. So, even though there's a long-forgotten yearning in the pit of my stomach and I'd like nothing more than to lie down with those strong arms around me, I grab all that's left of my willpower and say quite firmly, 'Goodnight, Ned.'

Before he can answer and before I can change my mind, I turn on my heel and head to the safety of *Sunny Days*.

Chapter Forty-Four

I sleep soundly for the first time in months. As I lie awake now, luxuriating in the comfy bed, in no rush to get up, I can still feel the touch of Ned's lips on mine. It thrilled me right to the core. I can't deny it. The sand bottle that he made is next to me on my bedside table, alongside the pink teddy, and I smile to myself as I look at them. It might have ended more abruptly than Ned wanted – more abruptly than I might have wanted it to as well – but it was a good day. A very good day.

I let myself soak in bed and, as I'm drifting in and out of sleep, Marilyn arrives.

'Coooooeeeee!' she trills.

Now it makes me smile rather than setting my teeth on edge and I realise how much I look forward to seeing her every day. I must remember to thank Bill for insisting that she stay.

I shower quickly and, as the sun is streaming through the portholes, I think that I might join Ned on the beach for a spot of yoga. With only the briefest of shudders, I pull on my tight silver leggings and skimpy neon pink vest. You know that I'm an avoider of mirrors and I really don't want to see what I look like in these. I hope Ned has his sunglasses on.

I head up to the kitchen, taking the stairs two at a time.

'Morning, lovely,' she shouts as I enter the room. Then her smile broadens as she takes in my outfit. 'Well, someone's looking a bit lively today.'

'If I can catch him leaving, I thought I'd join Ned for some yoga on the beach.'

'You definitely look the part.'

'You think?' I smooth down my vest, wishing that it was a little more substantial.

'Oh, yes. That boy won't know what's hit him. He'll be like jelly in your hands.'

'We had a lovely day out together, yesterday. Ned's a lot of fun.'

'That he is,' she agrees. 'If I was twenty years younger – actually make that thirty – he'd have to watch himself.'

I laugh at that. 'Poor man wouldn't stand a chance.' Marilyn is still a very attractive lady and can certainly carry off her enthusiastic dress style.

Today she's wearing yellow leggings – bought from the same shop as my silver glittery ones, I reckon – teamed with fuchsia pink heels and a matching floaty, floral top. There's a plethora of necklaces clanking on her bosom and her arms tinkle every time she moves due to the amount of bangles she's wearing. Her earrings are like chandeliers. I tell you, she's completely wasted as a cleaner. Marilyn should have an altogether more glamorous job.

She catches me taking in her outfit and says, 'We look like twins.'

It's true to say that my style has changed considerably since she came into my life.

'You look lovely,' she says, earnestly. 'They show off that sexy

189

figure of yours that you keep hidden all the time. You shouldn't hide your light under a shovel. Get a look in that mirror.' She nods towards the one in the hall.

'I'll take your word for it.' If I catch sight of myself, I might never leave the boat.

Marilyn tuts, but breezes on. 'I've brought you some dinner for tonight.' She points at a casserole dish next to the stove. 'Goulash. You need a good meal inside you. I've seen more meat on a fisherman's pencil.'

I have a quick look in the casserole dish. 'It smells wonderful.' There is, however, enough food for about fifteen hungry people. Marilyn is definitely a feeder.

'You'd have been proud of me yesterday,' I counter. 'Ned and I had fish and chips at the seaside and I ate every single bit.'

'Good for you.' She winks at me. 'It's definitely given you daisies in your cheeks.'

I don't even correct her mentally now. I just accept that Marilyn has her own way of speaking.

She grips her trusty duster and spray polish. 'I can't stand chatting today. I need to get on. I've got my three girls coming over today and they're bringing all my gorgeous grandbabies. It will be bedlam, but I love it. I was up baking a Victoria sponge and the goulash at four o'clock.'

'I do appreciate it.' I might even invite Ned round to help me eat it – for the next three nights judging by how much Marilyn has brought for me.

'You should come over.' She says it with a studied nonchalance. 'They'd love to meet you.'

'Yes, that would be great. But not just yet.' I sigh at Marilyn. 'In all honesty, I don't think I could cope. I'm sure it's a fun house and it sounds filled with love. I'm just not sure I could handle being knee-deep in kids.'

'It might kill or cure you.'

'Yes.'

'My middle one has got her hands full with three kids under the age of five. She popped them out one after the other. And my littlest grandbaby has cerebral palsy. She's adorable but she needs a lot of one-to-one attention.'

Which makes me realise that I only ever thought about having one child and even that looks as if it might be an impossible dream. Having a brood of them just didn't occur to me. Yet Marilyn's acceptance of all that life has thrown at her is, somehow, making me feel better about myself too.

Sometimes I wondered whether I'd ever survive this – and that was before my husband went off with another woman. There were days when I literally thought it would be better to step in front of a Tube train. Some days I don't know what stopped me from doing it. Now I feel there is some hope shining through. I might not be able to have another child, but I can still have a good and fulfilling life.

'There's Ned heading off to the beach.' Marilyn nods towards the window. 'Off you go. Have some fun. Watch him or he'll be having you put your legs behind your head.'

I give her a look. 'That wasn't really in my plan, Marilyn.'

She waves her duster at me and guffaws. 'Go on, you saucy madam. I'm talking about yoga! I don't know what you're thinking of. You're so cheeky.'

Marilyn walks off, rolling her eyes at me as she goes.

So I slip on my trainers and walk down to the beach. As I do, my phone rings and it's Bill.

'Hey, bro.'

'Hello, little sis. Is this a good time to talk?'

'As good as any.' I pause on my walk and lean against the sea wall. 'The weather is unseasonably warm and I'm just heading to the beach.'

'Now you're making me jealous. I will come out there at

some point, I promise. I've just got a couple of issues that I need to check with you.'

'OK.' While he talks and I tell him what he needs to know, I realise how much I miss him. I miss his constant, quiet caring and I've probably not fully appreciated that over the years.

When he's finished talking about work, I say, 'I do love you. You know that?'

'Where did that come from? Are you going doolally being out there on your own?'

I laugh. 'No! I don't think I've ever been as sane.'

'You're doing OK?'

'I am,' I tell him. 'Surprisingly well.'

He sighs before saying, 'I don't want to burst your bubble, but I've seen Chris. I bumped into him at a restaurant last night.'

'Was he alone?' It pains me to ask.

'With another bloke. No women.' Bill pauses. 'I know this is none of my business, sis, but he's going out of his mind with worry.'

'I'm sure he is.' Sarcasm central. 'You didn't tell him where I was?'

'No, no, no. I just said you were safe and taking time to relax.'

That's true enough. But the very mention of my husband makes me wobble again. I might feel slightly more steady – both physically and mentally – but I realise that I'm still not ready to face real life. 'I can't deal with it all yet, Bill.'

'I know. I'm not rushing you. Take as long as you need. That's what escaping to the Isle of Wight is all about. You're having a good time, though?'

'I'm loving it. I'm very pleased that you bought your holiday home here.'

'And I'm glad that someone is actually using it.' I hear the office door slam. 'Got to go, sis. My Uber is outside. Catch you tomorrow.'

'Love you,' I say and, as he hangs up, I get another tug of love for my brother.

What do I do? I miss Bill terribly, but I'm not ready to leave and the longer I'm here, the more I want to stay.

Chapter Forty-Five

Ned is well into his yoga practice by the time I arrive on the beach. He's wearing a pair of black board shorts and not much else.

'Hey,' I say to him. 'Here's your most reluctant pupil.'

He stops mid-pose and his eyes pop out on stalks when he sees me. I feel myself flush under his gaze.

'Marilyn bought them for me,' I offer by way of explanation.

'You look great,' he says and carries on staring. It's certainly having more impact than my usual attire. 'I thought you might stay in bed after our busy day yesterday.'

'Not much chance of that with Marilyn around. She likes to be up with the pigeon.'

Ned looks at me, puzzled.

'Lark,' I correct. 'Up with the lark.' Good grief, she's got me doing it now.

'Ah. Ready to do some yoga?'

'Ready but not overly willing.'

'We'll start you off gently then,' he says. 'Just do what I do.'

Without having to be told, I kick off my shoes and, hesitantly at first, I follow him through some stretches. We're in the lee of the sea wall, sheltered from the constant breeze. The waves are benign today, rolling in gently to caress the shore. The sun is high and there's some welcome warmth from it. Though the cold never seems to bother Ned.

I feel stiff, unyielding, as I start to bend and stretch, but Ned is patient with me and I'm sure we're only covering a quarter of what he would usually do. I've become so tense, my muscles so wound up that I can't even stand still without aches and pains.

'Everything hurts,' I complain to Ned. 'I'm sure I used to be more flexible than this. I thought I was reasonably fit. Nearly every lunch time I went to the gym with my best friend, Della.'

'The body holds onto emotional pain,' he says. 'I don't know the details, but I can tell that you've been through a lot.' My eyes fill with tears and he quickly adds, 'Technique doesn't matter at all. We should just have some fun. This is about moving, laughing, feeling good about yourself. See if you can do a handstand?'

I burst out laughing. 'I haven't done a handstand since I was about seven.'

'Then it's about time that you did.' With consummate ease he flips onto his hands and walks a few steps before flipping back again.

'Show off.'

'Do it,' he says. 'Even if you fall, the sand is soft. I'll stand here and catch you.'

I chew anxiously at my lip. 'I daren't.'

'You can do anything. I promise I won't let you fall. It's all about trust.'

'Trust is something I have very little left of,' I tell him, cryptically.

'Consider this as you starting to fight your way back.'

I'm weakening. There is a certain appeal to giving it a go,

though I'm totally out of my comfort zone. 'I don't know what to do.'

'Bend forward, hands on the floor – you need a bit of momentum – then kick up your legs one at a time.'

'You make it sound very easy.'

'It's mind over matter. Come on, try it.'

I stand, dithering, then against my better judgement, I bend and put my hands into the cool sand. My boobs threaten to break free of their scant neon pink casing.

'Pull in your tummy tight,' he instructs. 'Kick up.'

I manage to kick up one of my glittery-clad legs and then wobble and topple over into the sand. Ned catches me. I lie on the sand laughing. 'That was pathetic.'

'No, you were nearly there.' His face is earnest, encouraging. 'Do it again.'

'I might not have enough energy left for a second attempt.'

'Don't be a wimp,' he says. 'Come on.'

So I brush myself off and bend over once more. I plant my hands more firmly and tighten every single muscle that I can.

'Kick up,' Ned shouts.

Kicking my legs, I suddenly feel air between my body and the ground and then Ned grabs my ankles, holding me fast.

'That's it,' he shouts. 'Hold your tummy in tight! Don't sag in the middle.'

'I'm doing it!' I should triumphantly. 'I'm actually doing it!'

Then I think I must sag in the middle or I was too confident too soon as, suddenly, I start to collapse. Ned tries valiantly to save me before I hit the deck. Instead, we both tumble onto the sand, me pulling Ned down on top of me. We fall in a heap together, laughing.

'High five,' he says. 'You did it.'

'Very briefly.' But despite my reticence to accept praise, I'm quite proud of my handstand, even though I only managed to hold it for a nanosecond and the exertion has left me gasping for breath.

'It's a start.' Ned brushes sand from his chest and I become aware that he's half-naked above me. I feel all the blood rush to my face and I'm sure it was already bright red enough from the handstand. We hold for a moment, neither of us seemingly wanting to break away.

'That was fun,' I say.

'You did well. I think you've earned yourself a hearty breakfast. What do you say? Have you eaten yet?'

'No.'

'Shall we walk down to Ida's?'

'That would be lovely.'

He pushes himself away from me, then offers me his hand and helps me up too. And, as we walk along the beach together, I wish that he was still holding my fingers in his.

Chapter Forty-Six

We take what I've come to think of as my 'usual' table, the one by the wall that's slightly sheltered from the sea breeze. Even after a few visits it feels like mine and woe betide anyone else who sits here. I'd have to chase them away. As it's warm and sunny, the café is suddenly busier and I guess as the weeks go on everything will be gearing up for the summer rush of tourists.

Ida, as always, doesn't look that pleased to see me with Ned. She's clearing another table when we turn up and gives me the side-eye. Ned, of course, is totally oblivious. She gives my loud yoga gear a thorough appraisal too and, though I'm growing to love my sparkly silver leggings, I wish I'd brought a cardigan to cover my skimpy top. By the time she comes to take our order, her smile is firmly back in place.

'Hey,' she says. 'You two look happy.'

'Starting the day with yoga on the beach, why wouldn't we be?' Ned answers.

'Lucky you.' She pulls a face at him. 'I've been here since eight.'

'Business is picking up, though?'

'Yeah. The madness begins.'

'Are you still going to be able to make the Spring Oasis Festival next weekend? You know you love it.'

'As long as I can organise cover for the café. I'm struggling a bit to get someone. It's deffo in my diary.'

When I look blankly at them both, Ned fills in, 'It's one of the most popular gigs on the island. It attracts an older crowd. Definitely the Waitrose of festivals. The chemical toilets are the best you'll ever find.'

That makes me smile. 'What better recommendation can you want?'

'It's important,' Ida says. 'Never underestimate the sheer awfulness of festival facilities.'

Ned laughs. 'You should come. You said you'd never been to a festival. This is your moment.'

'I think I'm too old to start going to festivals,' I laugh.

'Never. This would be your best introduction. It caters for a more mature vibe.'

'Old!'

'Grown-up,' he corrects. 'It's full of well-behaved people and great street food. I have a spare ticket. Your tent's big enough to hold another person, isn't it, Ida?'

Ida looks torn between agreeing that it is and thus landing herself with an uninvited guest and lying that it isn't. 'Yeah, sure.'

She couldn't really have said it with less enthusiasm.

'I'm not sure it's my thing,' I say, diplomatically – even though it sounds quite appealing.

'There are some good headliners this year,' he adds. 'Can't remember who, but at least I'd heard of them.'

'Philistine,' Ida mutters.

'It's great for me as it brings me in a chunk of early money before the festival season starts in earnest. It helps to fill up my coffers after the winter. The band plays there and I do some sculpting demos. I sell a lot of stuff and usually pick up a bunch of commissions too.'

'Isn't it too cold to be camping at this time of year?'

'The weather has always been very kind. Sometimes it's been like the height of summer. There's no Glastonbury-style mud here either. Well, not much.'

I confess that I've never been brave enough to go to a festival before. I'm more of a five-star kind of woman and it definitely wouldn't have been Chris's kind of thing – he liked luxury all the way. The thought of sleeping in a tent would give him hives. Yet, that handstand must have made the blood rush to my head as I find myself seriously considering it.

Ned beams up at Ida. 'You'd be happy to share?'

Again the dilemma of both wanting to say no and yet not appearing to be churlish. I don't want to put Ida's nose out of joint, but I find myself really wanting to experience festival life – even if I just do it once, I can tick it off my bucket list. Though, if I'm honest, it was never actually on my bucket list.

I risk saying, 'I'd love it. If you wouldn't mind?'

She takes a deep breath. 'OK.'

'Cool,' Ned says. 'Looks like we've got ourselves a road trip.'

'What do I need to take? I don't have a sleeping bag or anything.'

'Don't worry. We can sort it. The band are all seasoned campers. They'll have some spare stuff kicking about. Other than that, pack minimally.'

Another couple walk up from the beach and settle at a table. Ida clocks them and whips out her pad. 'What can I get for you?'

We both order – scrambled egg on toast for Ned and pancakes for me – and Ida moves on to the next table.

'You'll enjoy it,' Ned says. 'I promise you.'

And, no one is more surprised than me to find that, already, there's a buzz of excitement in my tummy.

Chapter Forty-Seven

I spend the rest of the day pottering about doing nothing in particular. I read some more of George's book and really enjoy it. I do so hope that he gets a positive response.

Later that night, I sit on the top deck of the boat with a welcome glass of white wine and watch the ever-changing landscape. Silently, peacefully, the tide slides out. Sea birds settle down before darkness falls and *Sunny Days* sighs as her hull shifts into a new position in the water. The sky is ablaze with golden clouds and raspberry splashes, all perfectly reflected in the still water of the harbour. Again, I think that perhaps I'd like to paint this.

As I start my second glass and am feeling more chilled, I call Della. I haven't spoken to her for days and she sounds a bit crisp when she picks up.

'Chummie.'

'Is this a bad time?'

'No, no.'

'Are you at home?'

'Yeah.'

That's a rare thing for her. 'I thought you might still be at work or heading for a bar. It's nice that you've got an evening to yourself.' I can picture her lounging on the sofa in her grey cashmere pyjamas. Della's the only person I know who does casual in cashmere.

My friend's apartment is too cool for words as well – rough brick walls, sanded floorboards and all industrial-style fittings. I'll admit to helping her furnish it, which is probably why I like it there so much. It's a great space for entertaining too as the kitchen is huge and there's room for a table that seats ten. Not that Della is at home all that much and she's like Chris in that she definitely prefers restaurants to cooking. The place is so spacious that there's always a faint echo behind her down the line. 'Have you got time for a quick catch up? We haven't spoken properly for a while.'

'Sure. It's the perfect time. How are you doing?' she asks, but there's a distance in her voice. Perhaps she's still cross that I've skipped to the Isle of Wight.

'Good,' I say. 'Feeling much better. I think the sea air is suiting me.'

There's a little pause before she says, 'What have you been up to?'

'Walking on the beach, reading, watching afternoon television – lots of adverts for incontinence pants and pensions.'

'Sounds riveting.' Again an off note.

'I'm really enjoying it. I've even done a bit of yoga.' I get a flashback to my attempted handstand and tumbling onto the sand with Ned and it makes me smile. 'I managed a handstand. Kind of.'

'Good Christ,' she says. 'Now I've heard it all. Should you be doing that so soon after . . . '

She doesn't need to finish her sentence, but we both know what she means.

'Too late to consider that now,' I admit. I'm sure that

everything, physically, is fine now. But surely it's a good thing that I didn't even think about it?

'Ooops,' she says.

I can't put my finger on it, but Della sounds distracted. 'Is everything OK?'

'Yeah, sure. Why wouldn't it be?'

'All good at work?'

'Busy as fuck, but otherwise same old, same old.'

'I think I agreed to go to a festival this afternoon,' I confide. 'Can you imagine? Me, camping and everything?'

'Are you sure you're just in the Isle of Wight? It sounds as if you've been abducted by aliens. Yoga? Festivals? *Camping*?'

'Maybe this is the new me?' I must admit that I've been feeling excited by the prospect all afternoon.

'I think I like the old wine bar/gym bunny better. Who are you going with? You can't go to a festival on your own.'

'Some of the local people have invited me. I've made friends with the guy in the boat next door and a woman who runs a café on the beach.'

Then I hear a man speak in the background and, although Della must cover the phone with her hand, I hear her whisper, 'I won't be long.'

I feel a stab of hurt. So that's why she doesn't seem keen to chat. 'Have you got someone there? I didn't realise. You should have said. I can call back tomorrow.'

'There's no one here,' she answers too sharply.

But I know that there is. She's there with a man and hasn't said. It isn't like Della. Now I feel weird. Perhaps because I haven't been entirely open with her, she's paying me back this way. As much as I love my friend, it's definitely something she would do.

'Well, I'd better go anyway,' I rush out. 'Marilyn has left me a casserole and it's in the oven.'

'Lucky you.' Again quite crisp.

'Shall I call you tomorrow?' I venture. I wonder if she's actually still working but didn't like to admit it and he's one of her colleagues? Or perhaps she's picked someone up in a bar? Or, more likely, has got herself another Tinder hook-up. It's a bit early for it, but I wouldn't put anything past Della. She could have just told me I was interrupting, though. We usually tell each other everything – or we used to. Is she jealous that I'm having a good time without her?

Then I think I hear a voice again and can't let it go. 'There *is* someone there.'

'There's not,' she insists. 'It must be the telly. Don't be paranoid.'

Perhaps she's right. I'm reading too much into everything. Once you've been burned, it leaves a lasting scar. 'I'm sorry. I'm being an idiot.'

'Yeah. But I still love you, muppet.'

'Sorry. Now I feel foolish.'

'No need. Look, I'd better go. Stuff to do. I'll phone you,' Della says.

'Tomorrow?'

'Yeah. Bye, Chummie.'

And, with that, my best friend hangs up. I'm unsettled for the rest of the evening and don't know why.

Chapter Forty-Eight

In the wee small hours, I lie in bed and fret about Della's call. I think she's more pissed off with me than I imagined. It's not like her to behave like that. I thought she'd be pleased for me that things are going well here but obviously not. Perhaps she thinks it's ridiculous that I can't face my troubles like a grown-up. Everything with Della is black and white. She's had a blessed life, every advantage, and has never been through anything like I have. As such, I'm afraid that my bestie has very little empathy. Normally, I like her uncompromising feistiness, but not when I'm on the receiving end of it.

I jump out of bed and fly upstairs to see Marilyn when I hear her welcoming 'Coooooeeeee!' An extra cheery one today as if she can sense my distress.

Today she's rocking a scarlet red jumpsuit and silver accessories. She smells like an explosion in a perfume factory. The now-obligatory bag of shopping goes on the work surface. I'm going to have to start running every morning simply to keep pace with the amount of calories Marilyn tries to get in me during the course of a day.

'The goulash was lovely,' I tell her. 'I froze the rest.' For the next time ten people turn up unexpectedly. 'And washed your dish.'

'You didn't have to do that,' she tuts. 'That's my job. I'm looking after you.'

'And very well too,' I say. 'I do appreciate it.' Though she can still make my ears ring with her chatter, I do look forward to seeing her.

'You look a bit out of sorts this morning.'

'Had a weird conversation with my best friend last night. I'm sure it's nothing, though. Just me being a bit sensitive. I felt like she couldn't wait to get me off the phone.'

Marilyn raises her eyebrows. 'Could be just a touch of the blue-eyed monster? Perhaps your friend would like to be on holiday by the sea.'

'You're probably right. I thought as much myself.'

'Why don't you invite her over for the weekend? You could do with some company.'

'I can't do this weekend. At least I think not. Ned and Ida invited me to go to the Spring Oasis festival,' I explain. 'I'm hoping I have your approval. Della thinks I'm mad. If you tell me it's a bad idea, then I might well change my mind.'

'Oh, you must go. It's lovely,' she declares. 'It's in a fabulous setting in the woods. If the weather's kind to you, it's like a little slice of heaven. They usually have great bands and all kinds of quirky acts. I haven't been for a few years – I'm always on babysitting duty as at least one of my kids is there every time. I think two of the girls have got tickets for this one.'

'I'm worried.'

'You're always worried,' Marilyn points out.

'I know. I'm nervous but do you know what, Marilyn, I actually feel a bit happy too. And then I feel guilty about that.'

She gives me a sideways glance. 'It is OK to start to live your life again.'

'At what point, though? How long am I supposed to grieve for? I feel as if it might be for a hundred years.'

'And there's nothing wrong with that. It will always be there with you, but it doesn't have to define your life. There are times when I'm at a concert or out for a meal and I think, "Ah, my Declan would have just loved this" and it makes me sad to think that he's not still here to share moments like that with me. It's only natural. But *life* is for the living. You're still allowed to have fun and this seems like the perfect opportunity for you to put your brightest lipstick on and dip your nose into the water again.'

'Toe,' I correct.

'Yeah, that as well. While you're at it, dip all of your bits in the water,' she advises. 'You might find you like it.'

Chapter Forty-Nine

I continue to worry if I've done the right thing until the weekend comes. But, as Marilyn suggested, I put on my brightest lipstick and take a few deep breaths. Actually, I didn't have a bright lipstick, so I bought one from the local chemist in a shade that would make Marilyn proud. It's red. The reddest red I've ever worn.

There's a knot of anticipation and dread in my stomach which meant I couldn't touch any breakfast. Don't tell Marilyn. She's arrived early to wave me off, bless her, and is now fussing round me.

'You've got a jumper and a jacket? It might be cold in the evenings.'

'Yes, I have.' I've also checked the weather forecast and it looks like it's going to be glorious for the Spring Oasis Festival.

'Don't forget your sleeping bag,' Marilyn reminds me unnecessarily.

I decided I couldn't do a borrowed sleeping bag and did some clickclick shopping online and had one delivered yesterday.

Marilyn is stressing as much as me. 'Have you got toothpaste? Toothbrush? Soap? Deodorant? Clean knickers.'

'Yes to all of those things.'

Other than when he popped by to tell me of the arrangements for the weekend, I haven't seen much of Ned this week. I haven't had another yoga session with him. I don't know whether he's been up extra early or if he's been too busy but I've heard him sculpting on the back of his boat and I find the noise comforting rather than irritating. It's nice to think that he's close by, even if I can't see him.

Now I watch out of the window as he walks down the gangway before he knocks on the door for me. He looks ready for a festival in cut-off khaki pants and a black T-shirt, but then he always looks festival-ready. His brown hair is as messy as usual and there's more than a hint of stubbly moustache and beard, which suits him.

When I open the door, Ned gestures at his battered car. 'Your chariot awaits, madam.'

The car looks packed to the gills and I wonder whether there's actually still room for me. I'm glad that I've only got one bag and my brand new sleeping bag.

'Ready to rock?' he asks.

'I feel terrified,' I admit.

'It'll be a blast,' Ned assures me. 'We'll make a hippy chick out of you yet.'

'Wish me luck, Marilyn,' I say as I grab my stuff and head to the door.

She comes after me and hugs me tightly. 'Be careful,' she warns. 'Don't eat cakes with *funny stuff* in them.'

'I'll try not to.'

'Look after her.' She wags her finger at Ned. 'You'd better bring her back in one piece. You'll have me to answer to if you don't.'

'I'll treat her like porcelain,' he promises.

Ned takes my bag and we head to the car. Thankfully, the front seat is empty and I climb in, sliding my sleeping bag between my feet.

From the back seat, Ida's voice says, 'Hi' which makes me jump. She's tucked in the corner with bags and boxes piled around her. I recognise the shape of Ned's guitar and I assume his chainsaw must be in here somewhere too. 'It's a good job you travel light.'

'So it seems.'

'This isn't half of it. One of the guys in the band is taking Ned's stock of wood in his van. He'll get through so much stuff this weekend.'

'Are you sure you're OK there? We can swap if you like?'

'I know my place,' Ida says. Slightly barbed. 'Besides, it's only half an hour over there. Cramp won't have set in by then, if I'm lucky.'

'I'll go in the backseat on the way home. I promise.'

'It's a deal. We'll be getting very cosy with each other. My tent's very small,' she tells me. 'I hope you don't snore.'

'I don't think I do, but I probably won't sleep a wink.'

'You won't need to. It does kind of carry on during the night. There's lots to do.'

'I am very grateful to you for having me, Ida.'

'I'm not sure that I had much choice,' she says. 'But we'll have fun. Once we get a few bottles of wine down our necks we'll be best friends.'

'I hope so.'

When Ned's finished squashing my bag into the boot – sounds as if there was a serious bit of re-arranging going on – he slides into the driver's seat. 'Ready to hit the road, ladies?'

Tension curls in my stomach. 'As ready as I'll ever be.'

Ned touches my knee and I daren't even look round to see whether Ida has clocked it or not. 'Relax,' he says. 'Kick back. Enjoy the ride.'

Marilyn is standing at the end of the gangway, waving her duster and brushing a tear from her eyes. You'd think I was going off on a year-long, round-the-world trip, not an overnighter a few miles away. She blows me a kiss and I wave back.

'Just drive,' I tell Ned, 'otherwise Marilyn will chase after us and bring me back.'

So we set off and joggle along the lanes across the island. I'm not entirely sure where we're headed and I don't feel inclined to find out. I'm going to go with the flow. That will be my motto for the weekend. Wherever we're going, it's green and pleasant and, even though I've not been up for long, my eyes feel heavy with sleep. It definitely must be the effect of Ned's driving. This time I fight to stay awake. I don't want Ida to catch me drooling.

Soon we join a queue of cars heading into the festival camp site and it's certainly buzzing. There are thousands of people converging on this place for the weekend. Ned is obviously known to the gate security staff as he's waved through without a ticket check. We park up and then start the unenviable task of unloading all the stuff to take to our pitch.

I confess to feeling that a nice comfy hotel is seeming like a much better option at this point.

Chapter Fifty

Ida stretches when we get out of the car. 'Thank God the drive wasn't longer,' she mutters.

I must first of all tell you that Ida looks amazing. She's clearly got this festival chic covered. Her cute denim playsuit is topped with a multi-coloured cardigan crocheted in granny squares that grazes the top of her bright pink Doc Marten boots. Her dark hair is threaded with a multitude of ribbons in all shades of pink and she's wearing a floppy cream hat. There's a row of glittery sequins gracing the top of her cheeks and curling up to her eyebrows. While having her own individual style she also blends in perfectly with the sea of frilly tops, glossy wellies and floral headbands. I, on the other hand, look set for a day at the office and stick out like a sore thumb.

Ned loads as much of our stuff as possible into a small truck that's been in the boot of the car while Ida and I carry as much as we can. We look like we are planning to stay for at least two weeks rather than overnight. Laden down with bags, we haul all our stuff across a field and up a hill to find our allocated campsite and, with a bit of huffing and puffing, eventually find our spot. With some more faffing and swearing, we pitch our tents next to each other. Ned goes back to the car for another load.

As I stand back and admire our achievement, Ida throws some cushions on the ground in front of the tents and, when Ned returns, he cracks open a bottle of white wine, ready-chilled.

'Might as well get this party started,' Ned says as he pours out our wine into plastic wine glasses before flicking the top off a beer for himself.

We clink cheers with each other.

'You've done this before,' I note.

'Just once or twice,' Ned agrees. 'I tend to spend the whole of the summer on the festival circuit.'

'I used to,' Ida says. 'Mostly as Ned's groupie.'

They exchange an intimate look and, for a moment, I feel like the gooseberry here. Or a perhaps strawberry, if I was Marilyn. It's clear that they've shared many happy times together.

'Since I've had the café it's been much more difficult. It was touch and go whether I could make it this year. As it is, I feel very guilty leaving it for the weekend. It's worse than having a bloody baby.'

I wince at that, taking the barb right to my heart, but I don't think either of them notice. If I had a baby, I certainly wouldn't be here. I take a slug of wine to help me regroup.

'Who's in charge?' Ned asks.

'My friend, Fern, is helping me out. She's just back from London and between jobs. I'm hoping she'll stick around for the summer. If she's doesn't I'll have to put an ad out on social media.'

For one mad moment, I think about volunteering to work in the café for the holiday season. But I'm not sure Ida would be thrilled with that idea and I know that Bill would go bonkers. He's trying to play it down, but I know he's desperate to have me back in the office. We're a good team and I should get back to him as soon as I'm feeling able. And I do feel OK at the moment. Is that because I'm doing nothing much more than chilling out, filling my days with lots of nothing? I wonder if I could manage being thrust back into the hurly-burly of normal life again? I don't know. Maybe it's too soon to tell. My hormones still feel very unreliable and I can burst into tears at the drop of a hat.

'I'm texting her every five minutes,' Ida continues, 'which must be driving her mad. She was a restaurant manager in London – real high-end place. I'm sure she can cope with knocking out a few cheese toasties. Though that coffee machine has a mind of its own and, generally, favours being an evil bastard.'

As if prompted by the thought, she immediately texts her friend.

We make use of the cushions to sit and watch the river of people, as colourful as a flock of parrots, meandering from the tents down to the festival field, everyone in high spirits. It's as soothing as watching the waves roll in.

Ned says, 'Do you want to polish off that bottle and we'll walk down to the festival? I need to have a word with the organisers and find out where I'm going to set up.'

'I'm in,' Ida agrees and knocks back the contents of her glass.

As a novice, I say, 'I have no idea what the score is, so I'll do as I'm told.'

When we've finished the bottle, with a little help from Ned, we walk across the camping field until we come to the festival proper. As Marilyn said, it's in a beautiful setting, but I still hadn't expected anything as lovely as this.

Just inside the entrance there's a huge sculpture of a tree decorated with lights and colourful wind spinners.

'One of mine,' Ned says. 'I've got quite a few more pieces scattered around the site. They sit very well in the woods here and the organisers seem to be happy to keep buying them.'

'You'll have to show me.'

'It would be my pleasure,' he says. 'We've got plenty of time.'

In the main area that's like a village green, there are dozens of food vans serving every kind of cuisine you can think of. I'd expected the usual burger vans and chips, but there's Persian food, a Chinese noodle kitchen, curry, posh mac 'n' cheese and vegan food in many varieties. Alongside them are several bars – an Airstream caravan serving cocktails, a red London bus already busy doling out Pimm's. So we pick up some food and a gin cocktail and avail ourselves of a stripy picnic bench while we eat.

There are three music stages and one of the bands is already in full flow, filling the green with raunchy rock tunes played with raucous enthusiasm. The atmosphere is light, cheery and chilled.

'There's festival central.' Ned points to the official tent. 'That's where I need to be. Can I leave you ladies to it?'

'Sure,' I say. 'See you later.'

'I'll call when I've finished and we can meet up at one of the bars for a drink. You should take in the Lost Woods,' he advises me. 'There's all kinds of quirky stuff goes on there. Just wander and see what you come across.'

'Thanks. See you later.'

So Ned heads off and I walk through the gathering crowds with Ida. We stop and watch fire-eaters, jugglers, men on giant bikes, people on tall stilts and festival-goers trying their hand at slacklining.

'This is such a great vibe,' Ida says. 'Anything goes. Just let your hair down. What goes on at the festival, stays at the festival.'

'I'll bear that in mind.' I think we're more comfortable in each other's company though it may be due to a few glasses of reasonable Pinot and a fancy gin.

She lights up a joint and takes a toke. 'Start with this.'

I hold up a hand. 'Thanks, but I don't . . . '

'Do it.' She pushes it at me, so I take it and tentatively inhale. I go to hand it back.

'Another one,' she insists. 'More deeply.'

I do as I'm told.

'More of that later,' she says, having another puff herself.

I wait for something to happen, but don't feel any different. Then a peacock with its tail fanned out wanders in front of me and I do hope that it's real.

'There are parrots in the trees too,' Ida says when she sees me gaping at it. I'm so relieved that I'm not imagining it.

We carry on taking in the sights and sounds, sharing the odd puff which I do think is making me feeling mellow. When Ida stops to chat someone she knows, I decide that we need to part company.

'I've got something I want to do,' I say to her. 'I'll leave you with your friend and catch up with you later?'

'Cool,' Ida says. 'Have fun.'

If the rest of the festival is anything like what I've seen, then I'm sure that I will.

Chapter Fifty-One

When Ida turns back to her conversation, I wander away, rather aimlessly, just enjoying being here until I reach an area filled with stalls selling all manner of festival-type stuff. This is what I want. Each one of them is offering a range of floaty clothing in floral and tie-dye prints or hats, headbands, beaded sandals. There are sarongs, harem pants, ponchos, angel wings in all shapes and sizes. I'm going to splash some cash to get my festival swag on.

I lose myself going from stall to stall, trying on dresses, skirts, strappy sandals, floppy hats and embroidered jackets to my heart's content. If anyone tells you that shopping isn't fabulous therapy, then don't believe them. At the last stall, I slip into a curtained changing area and put it all on. I look in the mirror and a very different me stares back. This is a woman that I don't know and I quite like the look of her. She looks young and carefree. I've chosen a pale blue chambray dress embroidered with flowers. It's short, probably a bit too short, strappy and falls in tiers to mid-thigh. Each of the tiers is edged with white broderie anglaise. I've bought beaded, strappy sandals with blue and pink spangles all over them and a washed-out, vintage denim jacket. It takes ten years off me, I'm sure. That could also be due to the wine specs but I don't care.

Then I find a stall with a face-painter peddling their skills and have some glittery daisies painted on my cheeks and set off the look with a floral headband. I've completely discarded my designer office-wear look and am now a fully signed-up festival-goer. So in another rush of recklessness, I consign the clothes I came in to a carrier bag. If I were bolder, I'd throw them in the nearest bin. I think for my first attempt at this new style it isn't half bad.

As I'm wondering where to head next, Ned calls. 'I'm at the Woodland bar. Do you want to make your way over here? There'll be a cold and colourful cocktail waiting for you.'

'I'm on my way,' I tell him.

So I head down to the woods, a spring in my step and flowers on my cheeks. I feel light, free and as colourful as one of the Oasis peacocks. It's strange to remember what this felt like. Even before the baby, I haven't been this happy for a very long time. Maybe I need to wear sparkly clothes and flowers all the time.

The woods are spectacular, decorated with quirky yarn bombs – flowers, mandalas and pom-poms in the trees. As I head further in, there's another area where the trees are adorned with musical instruments – trumpets, guitars, flutes and drums – that people play as they pass by.

The Woodland bar is set in a clearing draped with natural garlands and blowsy paper flowers. Wooden benches surround fire pits, loaded with wood ready for the cooler evening. The bar itself is in a marquee and is already busy and I weave my way through the throng of drinkers. Ned is waiting at the bar, already halfway down his beer. He glances up and then does a double-take as he sees me.

I sashay up to him and give him a twirl, flaring out the skirt of my dress. 'I found my inner hippy! You like?'

He looks me up and down and I flush under his intense scrutiny.

'Wow.' He seems genuinely stunned at my transformation and just continues to gape at me.

'Say something. Too young? Too much?'

'Just perfect,' he eventually says. 'You look fantastic!'

Relief floods through me. 'I do?'

'Amazing,' he says. 'Do that twirly thing again.'

I do and, call me shallow, but I like the way that Ned looks at me. When I've finished twirling, I stand still in front of him and our eyes meet.

'Beautiful,' he says softly.

Then Ida crashes in, throwing herself on the stool next to Ned, and the moment is lost.

She tosses her hat onto the bar. 'Fuck,' she puffs out. 'This place is totally *mad*. I know *everyone* here. Get me a drink before I die.'

Reluctantly, Ned's eyes leave mine, but they say that we have unfinished business, and he turns to Ida. 'What do you want?'

'Rum,' she says. 'Something with rum in it? And an umbrella.'

'For you, Jodie?'

I look at the list of cocktails chalked up on the board, but I can't concentrate. I keep thinking of how Ned looked at me and I want, very much, to experience that again. 'I don't mind. You choose.'

Then Ida seems to realise that I'm actually there and recoils slightly. Her eyes blink a lot as if she can't quite believe them. 'Blimey, look at you.'

'I went shopping.'

'And some. Wow. Seriously getting into the festival groove, girlfriend.'

220

I feel self-conscious again. 'If you can't beat them, join them.'

'Go girl,' she concludes, though she sounds a little put out. 'You look amazing.'

Ned orders drinks for us all and passes them to us when they arrive. 'Mojitos, ladies.'

I sip the sharp, refreshing cocktail, enjoying the hit of rum, lime juice and cooling mint. 'Delicious. Thanks.'

'Glad you approve of my choice.'

'Can't stay long,' Ida says. 'Places to go, people to see.'

She seems completely hyper, like an excited child.

'I've got my first demo in an hour back at the Village Green,' Ned says. 'The band are on the Peacock stage tonight.'

'That's a great slot,' Ida says. 'You'll ace it.'

'Will you be joining us for a few numbers?' Ned asks.

'No. I'll be there purely in the audience,' Ida tells him. 'I'm here just to chill out this weekend. This is likely to be my only time off until September, so I'm going to make the most of it.' Ida downs her drink. 'In fact, I'm outta here. I'll catch you both later.'

I don't know if she feels in the way or if she's just too animated to keep still, but she flits off again like a butterfly. Gratefully, I take the stool next to Ned. 'I don't know where she gets her energy. I'm exhausted just watching her.'

'There are two ways to do festivals,' Ned tells me. 'You can run round like a headless chicken and try to fit everything in or you can kick back, accept that there's too much to take in on one visit and vow to come back next year.'

'I think I'll go for the kicking back option.'

'Sounds like a plan. When we've had our drinks we can take a slow stroll and I'll show you some of the sights. But there's no rush. Take your time.'

'That sounds lovely,' I say. Then I take his hand and squeeze it. 'Thank you for making me come along. You and Ida have taken me under your wings and I do appreciate it.'

'You're easy company to be with, Jodie,' he says and I'm glad to see that look in his eyes again.

Chapter Fifty-Two

We finish our drinks and head out into the fray, walking round the festival site together. I'm sure I'd be totally lost and over-whelmed without him. I enjoy it when Ned takes my arm or touches my back as he steers me to look at this or that.

Like Ida, he seems to have a lot of friends here and there's a constant stream of hugs and high fives as we go. We take in an area of tents set deep into the woods offering various therapies – massage, reiki, tarot readings – and there's an area with a hot tub and sauna. We drift in and out of the various music stages, relaxing as we watch a few bands who Ned knows.

The range of experiences and workshops on offer is simply mind-blowing. I think I'd need a week to see them all. Besides all the other stuff, there's a comedy tent, a craft corner and lots of activities for families. I'd like to try the aerial yoga and the gong sound bath, but I'm not sure that I'm ready for Shamic Spirit Trance Dance.

On the Village Green, we both spot George. He's standing on his plinth posing in a new costume of top hat with feathers in it and military-style frock coat. He looks very smart and we watch as he goes through his routine for his audience. When the crowd thins for a moment, we walk up to him and I say, 'Hey, George.'

'Oh, hiya!' He waves enthusiastically, then remembers he's supposed to be a statue and freezes again.

'Business looks good?'

'Brilliant,' he says out of the corner of his mouth. 'I've got some new moves today.'

He leans right over to the side, defying gravity.

'Wow.' I give him an encouraging round of applause.

'Poles that go up from my boots into my trouser legs,' he confides. 'Saw it on YouTube. Quite easy to do when you know how. You've got to have a little something extra. I've got strong competition here.'

'Looks like you're holding your own. Maybe you can catch up with us later for a drink when you're off duty?' I still wonder what he looks like under all that bronze paint. 'Ida's here too.'

'I'd like that,' he says. 'I'll try to find you.'

'I've got a demo starting soon,' Ned says. 'We'll catch you later.'

'Good luck,' George says and gives us a mechanical bow before resuming his pose.

We leave George behind and head over to the area in the centre of the Village Green where Ned's already set up earlier. Someone from the band has brought his wood and chainsaw so, while I hang round feeling like a spare part, he organises himself. Already a circle of people is forming to watch him and I take a place on the grass beside them.

As soon as Ned starts his chainsaw, it attracts more people and, before long, there's quite a crowd. A few minutes in and Ida sits down next to me.

'He won't forgive me if I don't watch him once,' she says. 'Though I've seen him do this a thousand times, I still enjoy it.'

'Me too.'

He carves a bird for his first piece and then, as the sun warms up, he strips off his top, showing his ripped abs with his trousers slung low on his hips. For some reason, even more people stop to watch. I think Marilyn would come up with some very colourful ways to describe him. As he works, I become mesmerised, paying far too much attention to how he moves, his body shifting as he manoeuvres his saw, how he coaxes the wood into shape. It's hypnotic and Ned is very easy on the eye. Then I catch Ida giving me side-eye and check myself.

'You should hook up with him,' Ida says as nonchalantly as if we were talking about the weather. 'He's a great lover. Some of the best sex I've ever had was with Ned.'

I'm not sure if she's telling me this because she really wants me to know or because she wants me to know that *she* knows. If you know what I mean.

'Just don't give him your heart,' Ida continues. 'Ned likes variety and he loves to be loved. If you're looking for commitment, he's not the one.'

'I'm not looking for anything,' I tell her. 'I want some time on my own.'

She shrugs. 'Just offering some friendly advice. It's up to you whether you take it or not.'

We both look over at Ned who is finishing his next piece – a carved wood sprite. Instantly, someone from the audience buys it from him and he fires up his chainsaw again to start another piece. The sun on my face is making me feel sleepy and the buzz of the saw begins to sound like a soothing background noise of bees.

'I'm off again.' Ida brushes grass from her clothes. 'I'm sure I'll catch up with you both later, at some point.'

The next few sculptures Ned does are snapped up too. Then, the last piece that he carves is a small, oval-shaped statue of a mother and baby curled together. The figures are so entwined that I'm unable to tell where one ends and the other begins. It's beautiful and makes a lump come to my throat. Surprisingly, there are no takers for this one and, yet, I think it's the best one he's carved. Ned thanks the crowd for watching before packing up his chainsaw.

As people drift away, I slip under the rope and go over to Ned. 'Well done.'

'Thanks,' he says. 'Felt a bit rusty as it's the first one of the festival season. Takes me a bit to get back into my groove of doing these.'

I pick up the statue of the mother and baby. It's surprisingly weighty and, as I hold it to my chest, the permanent ache that has been in my arms for the last few months disappears. I trace my fingers over the face of the baby and the wood feels warm, alive beneath my touch. As it always does, the emotion catches in my throat as I say, 'I'd like to buy this.'

Ned raises his eyebrows. 'You would?'

'Yes, please.'

'Let it be my gift to you.'

'That's not necessary . . . '

'I'd like you to have it,' he insists. 'But let me finish it for you properly. The ones I do for festivals are a bit rough round the edges. I want to sand this down so it's nice and smooth. I'll put it somewhere safe and do it when I get back to the boat.'

'OK. That's very kind of you.' I'm reluctant to hand the statue back. Just the few moments of holding it has eased something in my heart.

When I do part with it, Ned packs the carving away carefully in a box. 'Ready to head out into the fray again when I've put this lot away?'

'You bet.'

Ned grins at me. 'Are you having a good time?'

'The best,' I tell him. And I am. Maybe it's the alcohol, or the puff, or the company, but it's a long time since I've felt so relaxed.

He laughs out loud. 'Then my work here is done.'

Chapter Fifty-Three

If you haven't been to a festival, then do. It's a revelation. I wish I'd started my festival career much earlier in life as I think I've been missing out. I see all the people dancing to African drums or doing yoga in the fresh air or trying their hand at a new craft and wonder why I've spent so much of my life sitting in an office worrying about the placement of furniture and architectural plants. I'm too uptight, too embarrassed to join in with some of the more quirky activities, but we pick up great street food as we go – halloumi wraps, chickpea curry, blackberry flapjacks, the best salted caramel ice-cream I've ever tasted.

I feel so much lighter, freer, surrounded by the sights and scents of the festival – it's a delightful assault on the senses. There's every kind of music that you can think of and we pause at the different stages to take it all in. We get up and dance like mad things to a crazy Balkan disco band called Circus Folk, then there's country music from The Shires and I feel a bit teary at the emotion in their songs.

Darkness is gathering when we say goodbye to the music stage and Ned persuades me to join a sound meditation. We sit on huge cushions opposite each other under the cover of an open-sided, Moroccan-styled tent. Following instructions from the workshop leader, we take each other's hands and look into each other's eyes. I love the feel of my fingers intertwined with his and gazing so intently at his face makes my heart start to beat faster and my temperature rises. Just when I think I can bear the intensity no longer, people begin to dance around us tinkling little bells and shaking tambourines while chanting. They are so earnest and sincere in their endeavours, it's all I can do to stop giggling.

'Take it seriously,' Ned whispers, trying to supress his laughter too.

'I can't.'

We sit until my shoulders start to shake and tears of laughter start to stream down my face.

'Come on,' Ned whispers. 'We'll try something else. You're completely rubbish at meditation.'

And we burst out of the tent, cackling like teenagers.

'That was pathetic,' he says. 'Let's find something that's more your level.' So he pulls me along until we find an area in the woods with a Pop-up Hula Disco. 'Perfect. This will do.'

I pull against him. 'I haven't hula-hooped since I was about seven.'

'It's like riding a bike,' he insists as he drags me into the clearing. 'You never forget.'

The trees are lit with fairy lights and there are disco balls hanging from the trees making the woods look as if they're filled with shimmering butterflies. There's a wooden boat that provides the DJ platform and he's pumping out old skool funk and disco music. We're given hula-hoops that glow with LED lights and Ned's right, it only takes me a minute or two to remember how to get the hoop twirling round my hips.

I hold up my hands and still the hoop spins. 'Oh, yes. Go me. Haven't lost my touch.'

It's fair to say that Ned has pretty good hip action too. I lose myself to Barry White, the Bee Gees, James Brown and the Commodores. All oldies but goodies.

We're breathless and laughing even harder when we leave the woods.

'That was a first for me,' I tell him, still panting. 'It was great fun. Thanks for making me do it.'

'It's good to be out of your comfort zone every now and again. It's also good to hear you laugh,' Ned says.

'It's a sound that been too rare in recent times,' I agree.

'Glad we could fix it.' And I like that he takes my hand as we head to the stage where he's playing this evening with the Beach Bums.

Chapter Fifty-Four

Ida's already there with the rest of the band when Ned goes to set up. We find a vacant hay bale and sit on it together. She seems a little tipsy though not overly so, yet she's all smiles and happy face. I'm glad that she's having a good time. Though I fail to see how you couldn't have a wonderful time at this place.

Ned and the band perform a mellow set – covers of songs by Jack Savoretti, Adele and Paloma Faith. Ida wanders off and brings us back two cartons of bean chilli which we eat with wooden spoons and two glasses of white wine in plastic glasses. Both of them hit the spot. There's a good kick to the chilli and the wine goes down way too easily. I go to the nearby bar and get us a refill.

As the families with children drift away, the atmosphere changes with the evening vibe taking over. The sun goes down, there's the heavy smell of weed in the air and everything feels more moody.

'We should have brought blankets down,' Ida says, 'but there's no way I'm walking back to the tent until I have to.'

The night air is cool but it's helping to keep my head clear.

Once again, I find myself watching Ned far too closely.

When the band performs their last number, the crowd go wild and give them a rapturous round of applause which is well deserved. Ned packs away his bass and jumps down from the stage.

'Excellent. That was a great set.' Ida says. 'Now you've finished work for the day, we can hit the hot spots.'

Ned rests a hand on my waist. 'Enjoy it?'

'Yes. Very much so.'

'What are we waiting for?' Ida raises her arms and dances. 'Let's find somewhere to boogie.' Then her phone rings and she rolls her eyes before answering, 'Hey.'

When the caller speaks, I see the expression on her face fall, her shoulders droop.

'Fuck,' she breathes into her phone. 'OK. I'll be back as soon as I can.' Ida hangs up.

'Not good news?' Ned asks.

'The café. It's been broken into. Bastards.' Quite rightly, Ida is furious. 'What the fuck is wrong with people? That was the police.'

'Did they say what was missing?'

'Nah, but they want someone to meet them there. The window's busted and the door's been kicked in. That will need to be fixed. More frigging expense. I'll call Fern and get her to go back if she can, but I'll need to head out straight away.'

'I'll drive you there.'

'How many beers have you had?' Ida says.

'Shit.' Ned rubs his forehead. 'Too many.'

'I'll get a cab,' she says. 'Besides, you've got to be here for tomorrow.'

'Are you sure? I can see if one of the lads in the band is going your way?'

'A cab won't take long. I don't want to put anyone out.' Then she sighs heavily and you can see how very pissed off she is. 'I'd better make tracks.'

'Call me as soon as you get there. Let me know what the damage is.' Ned is as distressed as Ida is. 'I can come over as soon as I'm done here.'

'You're a pal,' Ida says, tearfully. 'I hope we can still open tomorrow. I can't afford to lose a day's takings.'

Ned pulls her close and hugs her. She stays there in his arms, eyes closed, head against his chest.

When she pulls away, she says, 'Sorry to break up the party. You'll bring the rest of my stuff back? I can't be arsed collecting it now and Jodie will need the tent.'

'Of course,' Ned assures her. 'I don't want you to go back alone.'

'I'll be fine.'

I hug her as well, although we're more awkward. 'I hope it's not too bad.'

'Thanks. Enjoy the rest of your evening.' She gives me a knowing look. It's obvious that she thinks Ned and I will sleep together. 'Don't do anything I wouldn't do.'

'Can't you come back later?' I ask. 'You might be able to.'

'I doubt it. I'll have to see how it goes. Don't let this spoil your first festival. Eat, drink, be merry.' She punches a number into her phone and orders a cab to meet her at the main gate. 'See you, guys.'

Ida waves over her shoulder then marches away looking angry and crestfallen. It's a shame that she's had to leave like this. It wasn't how any of us saw the evening panning out.

'That's a bummer.' Ned looks torn as he watches her walk away and I know that part of him wants to go with his friend to help her out. When she's out of sight, he turns back to me. 'But she's right, we should still make the best of it.' Ned slings

233

his arm round my shoulder. 'Looks like it's just you and me, kid.'

That fact hadn't been lost on me either.

Chapter Fifty-Five

With nightfall the mood of the festival becomes much darker. Everyone seems to be drinking more, including me and Ned, and behaving with more abandon. The myriad coloured lights come on and the acts on display seem more risqué, sexier. There are fire-breathers, burlesque dancers, contortionists, a steam-punk jazz band and circus acts in minimal costumes. There's an abundance of feathers, body paint, PVC and Goth clothing. I look for George among the crowd, but can't spot him. I hope he's taken time off from statue duties and is having a wonderful time somewhere. I should have taken his number so that I could call him but, if I'm honest, part of me is enjoying being alone with Ned.

The woods are lit up with coloured lights and there's the scent of incense in the air. There are pagan masks painted in fluorescent colours that glow in the dark as we work our way through tunnels of entwined trees. We come to a clearing where there are performance poets in bondage gear strutting their stuff around a welcoming firepit. The Antipoet are edgy, funny and clever. Ned and I sit and listen to them put the world to rights in their own individual style. We laugh until our sides hurt and, when their set ends, to rapturous applause, I don't want to leave.

But, as there's so much still to experience, we move on. Deeper into the woods, the air is heavy, charged – it smells earthy and fecund. We stop to watch a couple doing a tango so intimate, so erotic that it stirs feelings in me that I haven't had for a very long time. Even when Chris and I were trying for a baby, it all became very mechanical. We lost the spontaneity, the love too in some ways. Perhaps that was when the rot really started to set in? I just know that as I look at Ned standing next to me in the darkness I have a yearning that I thought was all but gone.

The music continues and Ned leads me onto the makeshift dancefloor and any show of reluctance on my part is distinctly half-hearted. He twirls me round until I'm dizzy and the fairy lights around us are a blur. I throw my head back and laugh. Then the music slows and he pulls me into his arms and we sway together in time to the rhythm. I can feel the heat of his skin through my dress, feel the warmth of his breath on my neck and I could happily stay like this all night.

It's two in the morning when the band packs up and, reluctantly, we drift away from the dancefloor.

'Time for sleep?' Ned says and I nod my agreement. I'm tired, happy and aware that Ned keeps my hand in his.

We head back to our tents, wandering across the fields and away from the main festival area. In the darkness, it takes a bit of effort to find where we pitched them so many hours ago and when we do find the spot, only one of our tents is there. Ida's tent is still in place, but Ned's has obviously been stolen.

He stands and stares at the empty space where his tent used to be. 'Damn.'

'That's awful,' I say. 'Who would do such a thing?'

'It's fairly standard at some of the festivals, but we don't normally get anything nicked at this one.' He pulls out his phone. 'I'll call one of the lads and see if I can bunk in with them.'

'It's gone two in the morning. They'll probably be fast asleep by now.'

Ned laughs. 'Knowing that lot, they'll be partying all night. I doubt they'll even go back to their tents.'

'Ida's is still here.'

'Thank Christ for that. She's got enough on her plate without her stuff getting stolen from here too.'

The words feel thick in my throat when I say, 'You could squeeze in with me.'

He looks at me intently and I'll swear that the air crackles around us. 'You're sure?'

'I've never even camped before. I was kind of relying on Ida being here. I don't really relish being left alone in a tent.'

'OK. Sounds like you've got yourself a roommate. Thanks.'

I feel slightly shocked at what I've just done. I think it's the first time I've invited a man to spend the night with me before.

'Shall we sit and have a nightcap before we retire?' Ned asks. 'My booze might be gone, but I know where Ida keeps her stash.'

'That would be nice.'

So Ned goes into the tent and passes out a couple of cushions and a blanket which I spread out on the grass. He appears a moment later with a bottle of rum and two shot glasses. 'Festival essentials.'

We sit side-by-side and he pours us shots. Clinking glasses, we down them. My stomach is knotted with tension as I think we both know what's coming. Our movements are too conscious, our looks too filled with knowing. Ned refills our glasses and we go again. A few stragglers wander back to their tents in the same field and raise their hands in greeting as they pass. The

237

music from the festival drifts softly across the sky. The night is clear, cold and the stars are out. Ned takes off his jacket and puts it round my shoulders.

A text comes in and Ned checks it. 'From Ida. She says they've busted the window, the door and the coffee machine has gone. Some of the crockery is smashed and the chairs that were on the patio are now, mostly, in the sea.'

'That's awful. Poor Ida.'

'I'll swing over there tomorrow when I get back and see if she's OK. Give her a hand to put it right.'

'You're very kind.'

'Ida's a good mate,' he says as he returns her text. 'We go back a long time. We've been there for each other when our worlds were falling in for one reason or another.'

'It's none of my business but I get the impression that Ida would like it to be rather more.'

He sighs. 'I know. We've had a lot of fun together over the years. Sometimes too much fun. Occasionally, when one or the other of us is feeling lonely, we spend time together.'

Perhaps that's why I saw her coming from Ned's boat the other morning.

'We shouldn't,' he continues. 'It only complicates matters between us. We're mates. That's all we're ever going to be.'

'She loves you, I think.'

'Yeah,' he says. 'Sadly unrequited. Ida's a great woman. High-maintenance though.' He laughs softly at that and pours us two more shots. 'We've tried being in a relationship together. Briefly. It's never going to work. Ida might think she loves me, but I'm too laid-back for her. I drive her mad. She'd want me to be striving to be some fancy artist. Whereas I'm just happy pottering along as I am.'

'And then you give her a late-night booty call?'

'That sounds a lot worse than it is. It's just something we've fallen into. We comfort each other. It's not ideal, but Ida knows the score.'

'I guess there's a difference between knowing it and believing it. Is it nice to keep her hanging on? To always know that Ida will come running?' I'm teasing, but there's truth in my words. Ida says that's Ned's a player. Perhaps this is why.

'That's not how it is. It's a long time since we've done that.'

'The other night?' I know it's not my business who Ned sleeps with, but perhaps the booze has loosened my tongue, as I can't help myself.

'She came over because she was feeling down. We spent the night drinking and she fell asleep on my sofa. There was nothing more to it.' He looks at me and seems sincere. 'I really wish she'd find someone else. Someone who would love her as she deserves. That can never be me. You can't make your heart love another, can you? It just happens.' He turns to me. 'Sometimes when you're least expecting it.'

I study the contents of my glass. 'Have you never been tempted to settle down?'

'I nearly did,' he admits. 'A few years ago now. She came over from the mainland for the season and I fell heavily, quickly. By the end of the summer Liberty found out she was pregnant. I was delighted and really thought we could make a go of it. However, Libs realised that she wasn't quite as much in love with me as I was with her.'

My stomach is knotted when I ask, 'What happened to the baby?'

'We had a lovely little girl called Skye.' Ned pulls out his phone and scrolls through it. 'She's four now.'

He hands the phone to me. There's a photo of a little girl who's the very image of her father. She's dressed as a fairy. 'She's adorable.'

'Yeah.'

'No disputing her paternity either.'

'No.' He laughs. 'She's like me too. Definitely a chip off the old block, if you don't mind a sculpting pun.'

'Where is she now?'

'Back on the mainland. They live up in Northampton. Liberty went back to live with her parents to have the baby which was a godsend. They helped her to do all of the things that I should have been there to do. Eventually, she hooked up again with her old childhood boyfriend. He's a great bloke and treats Skye like his own. The only downside is that I don't see my girl often enough.' He looks sad as he talks. 'It's been six months now. Liberty feels that it disrupts their life. They've got a kid of their own now too – a little boy. Libs says he gets upset if I want to take Skye away for the weekend. I've no idea if that's true, but I go along with it. I can hardly stay at Liberty's place with them all. Let's face it, I'm not great father material.'

'You'd be a wonderful dad,' I counter.

'I'm not so sure. I live from hand to mouth. Skye has a much more stable life with Libs and Adam. He's a good bloke. Got his own business that has something to do with advertising on the internet. He's funny and he's kind to them both. Libs could have done a lot worse. At least there's not some total arse bringing up my kid. He'll do right by her. They're not short of a bob or two either, so they have a comfortable house and a great lifestyle. I don't want to be the one who messes that up for them. I figure that Skye will have more to do with me when she's older and can make her own choices.'

'She's your daughter,' I point out, needlessly. 'She should be in your life.'

'It's not an easy situation. I don't want to fight with Liberty. I have a good relationship with her. I help her when I can. I might not see Skye as much as I'd like, but I love her to bits. I hope she knows that.'

I give him his phone back. I wonder will I ever have pictures of my own child to show people with pride shining in my eyes, as Ned's are. This is the moment to tell him that I lost a child, that I've been desperate for a baby for the last few years. I should explain to him the cause of my sadness and why I think it's so important for him not to let his own daughter slip away.

But, instead, he turns to me and takes my face in his hands and pulls me closer. His lips cover mine and they're warm, soft and taste of rum. We kiss and kiss and kiss until my head spins and the moment for my confession is gone.

Chapter Fifty-Six

Without speaking, we move into the tent – the rum, shot glasses, the cushions, all forgotten – in our haste. We undress, tearing at our own clothes and each other's as we fall onto the sleeping bags in the cramped space, lips still exploring as we do. We bang our heads, elbows, knees and, as we clutch at each other, try to smother the laughter at the comedy of our coupling so that we don't wake the entire campsite.

As I'm tugging off Ned's jeans, my dress, with something approaching lustful abandon, I realise that I didn't know if I would ever feel like this again. All I want is this man inside me. After the baby, I couldn't bear Chris to touch me. I resented him. I blamed him. And I certainly didn't want another baby with him. I pushed Chris away and he, as it turns out, seemed to be more than happy to go. I should feel guilty that I'm about to sleep with another man, be unfaithful for the first time in my life, but I don't. Technically, I have a husband but, emotionally and physically, we are so far apart that I don't feel married any more. He's with someone else, so why can't I be? I feel alone and, if only for tonight, I don't want to be. And I like this man who's nearly naked in front of me. I like him a lot.

I'm thinking all of this, but not thinking it. My brain feels totally separate to my body which is lost in the heady sensation of being in Ned's arms, my skin against his skin. It feels so familiar and yet so strange. I thought my body might be too tense, too uptight, too reluctant, but it isn't. When we've finished wrestling out of our clothes in the confined space, Ned moves above me in the tiny tent, the sounds of the festival still in the background, kissing me tenderly as we make love. I surrender myself to him and enjoy every minute. Ida's right, he's a very skilled and caring lover.

When we're sated, we lie in each other's arms. Ned strokes my hair until, eventually, he drifts off to sleep. Then I curl up on my side and have a little cry – it's not happy tears, nor sad, but more release and relief. The rain starts to fall, at first pattering on the canvas above us, then increasing to a soft persistent downpour. I listen to it and it feels like it's cleansing my soul. Ned sleeps on, unaware, and I'm glad that I don't disturb him; this is time for me to listen to the rain, to reflect. This night has proved that I can heal the emptiness inside me and that I can learn to love life once more. He's helped me to feel normal again when I had actually lost sight of what normal might be. And, for that, I'm truly grateful.

Chapter Fifty-Seven

Outside I can hear people chatting and laughing. There's music playing and it's clear that the campsite is getting ready for the new day.

Inside the cocoon of our own tent, my eyes are open and I'm looking at Ned, trying to fix this night in my memory, when he wakes up. His hair's tousled from sleep and he looks even more attractive. I move closer to him, fitting my body along the length of his. Ned's arm snakes round my waist and he holds me tight.

I kiss him. 'Thank you,' I say. 'For last night.'

He grins at me. 'My pleasure.'

'It was a big deal for me,' I tell him. 'I thought you should know that.'

'It was quite a big deal for me too,' he teases, but he doesn't fully understand what I mean. How could he?

I realise, too, that this wasn't anything to do with sleeping with Ned as some kind of tit-for-tat for Chris's cheating. All it's done is highlight that the cracks in my marriage have become a chasm. Plus, I have genuine feelings for this man. Would my stomach flip so readily as the mere sight of him, if it was nothing but a casual fling? He's funny, laid-back and caring. I didn't know that I needed that in my life, but I do.

'I should thank you for the pep talk too,' he says. 'It made me appreciate that I should do more to keep in touch with Skye. I don't want her growing up not knowing who I am. I'll call Liberty and talk to her about it.'

'I'm glad. You should.'

'I couldn't bear it if anything happened to her and I wasn't around. You're right. I shouldn't take the bond between us so lightly.'

'She's four,' I say. 'Plenty of time to make amends.'

'No time like the present, though,' he says. 'I'll try to get over to the mainland to see her as soon as I can. But for now . . . '

His mouth covers mine and we make love again. This time it's slower, softer and I'm amazed at how comfortable we are together so soon. Afterwards, we lie in each other's arms until we can put off getting up no longer.

Due to the lack of space, Ned pulls on his jeans first and goes out of the tent while I dress. I try my second festival outfit of a tie-dyed vest top and harem pants with an elephant print which seemed much in evidence. Outside there are still the shot glasses, the cushions, Ida's rug. They're all wet from the rain and I'm not sure there's anywhere to dry them. With all that's going on in her life, I'm not sure that a couple of soggy cushions will register.

Hand in hand, Ned and I walk in the damp grass and join the queue for the showers. I feel bad that Ida's misfortune has meant that we could spend this time alone, but I feel as if I'm walking on air this morning. It sounds so stupid and shallow, but you can't believe what this has done for my confidence. And, if this was just a one-night stand for Ned, I can cope with that too. I know it's not love, I'm not that gullible, but it was certainly done with care and affection.

Ned squeezes my hand. 'OK? You look deep in thought.'

'I'm good,' I say. 'In fact, I feel great.'

'In need of breakfast?'

'Oh, yes. I'm starving.' Clearly, love makes you hungry as I'm ravenous.

When it's our turn in the showers, the water is hot and plentiful and I'm grateful for that, too. I emerge refreshed and ready to meet the day.

We go down to the festival field and hit the street with all the food stalls. We grab full English burritos for brekky and Ned says, 'I have a surprise for you.'

Once again we head into the woods, Ned leading the way. The earth smells intense and fecund after last night's rain. 'This is a secret part that not many people find.'

Beneath a large oak tree ahead of us there's two sofas, a coffee table and a well-stocked library. Next to it is a dining table and two chairs.

'I have a reservation,' Ned says.

'For us? Seriously?'

'I know all the right people,' he says with a twinkle in his eye. 'We might not get waiter service, but it's a very exclusive spot.'

He produces cutlery and napkins from his rucksack and holds out my chair for me. Then, in our oh-so-secluded al fresco dining room, we eat our burritos which are the messiest thing I've ever had to tackle.

Ned laughs as he wipes round my mouth with a napkin and I lick the remnants of egg and baked beans from my fingers. Beneath the table, our feet are entwined and, my hormones must still be running high, as I could throw him to the forest floor and make mad, passionate love right here. I so want to be with this man again. Perhaps we could extend this fling to more than one night. Ned certainly doesn't seem to be in a rush to leave.

That's when I get my first twinge of guilt. I should sort this out with Chris. Our relationship is over, that's clear enough, but we should make the split formal, decide what paths we will take for the future. I'll definitely speak to him this week to set things in motion. It has to be a divorce. I can see no other way. We had such hopes for our future, yet we've both left our marriage in a heap of dust.

'I've got a few more sculpting sessions throughout the day.' Ned breaks into my thoughts and I shake myself back to the present. 'And the band are playing this afternoon. Are you happy entertaining yourself?'

'Yes, sure. I'll have a wander round and then I'll head back for your sessions.'

'I don't expect you to come and watch me.'

'I'd like to.' I say. 'I enjoy seeing how you work.'

He leans in and kisses me again. Within a second my body is on fire for him. No wonder Ida finds him so addictive. I should remember that this is a relaxed relationship – the way Ned likes them. It's best for me too. There's so much going on in my head that I'm probably not making good decisions. Though I have to say that spending the night with Ned seems to be one of my better ones.

So I spend the day drifting aimlessly round the festival while Ned goes off and does his thing. I do some outdoor yoga, along with about a hundred other people, and am glad that I bought the harem pants – a flirty little dress wouldn't have worked quite so well for this. The yoga clears my head and sorts out some of the aching muscles, both from last night's activity and, for what was left of the night, sleeping on the floor.

Heading into one of the many workshops that are on offer, I make a felted corsage. I pin the little posy to the collar of my denim jacket, feeling very proud of my achievement as I'm the least crafty person in the world.

When Ned starts to do his sculpting sessions, I sit on the grass near the front. Once again, I'm hypnotised by the way he moves and how he creates his sculptures so effortlessly. I'm pleased to see that he sells all of his pieces and, from the notes he's jotting down between works, I'm guessing he's got more openings for commissions too. Later, I listen to the band do their set at the end of the afternoon and then, too soon, it's time for us to pack up and go.

Ned loads his sculpting stuff into the band van along with the instruments, while I wait patiently. People are drifting away from the festival, heading back to their normal lives and I feel a little bit sad to be leaving. This has been a great experience and a bubble of happiness for a couple of days.

As if reading my mind, Ned glances up from his work and says, 'Glad you came?'

'It's been really brilliant,' I tell him. 'Every minute of it. I don't want it to end.'

And I realise how much I mean that.

Chapter Fifty-Eight

It's pushing into evening when Ned has finished at the festival field and we head back to the campsite to gather our belongings and pack away Ida's tent. After the gloriously unseasonal weather, the rain has now settled in. At first a steady drizzle but, by the time we get back to the tent and start to take it down, it's a relentless downpour. Within seconds, Ned and I are soaked through to the skin. My hair is plastered to my head and I don't think that the glitter daisies on my cheeks are faring too well either.

We hurry as much as we can and haul our stuff to the car across a field that's already wet after last night's rain and is now rapidly turning to mud. We slip and slither and the truck wheels sink into the mire. Ned is muttering darkly. My poor flippy-floppy, beady sandals will be ruined and I can now see the attraction of festival wellies.

I'm shivering by the time we load up Ned's car and when we get inside, he puts the heater on full blast.

'We'll be home soon,' he says, which is optimistic as we join a massive queue of traffic that's inching out of the car park. We sit there for ever, but he holds my hand while we do.

'I'm not going to be able to check up on Ida tonight,' he says. 'We'll be later back than I thought. But she seems OK. I called her earlier and, though she's thoroughly pissed off, she thinks she can get the café open by tomorrow. Someone came today to reglaze the window and fix the door.'

'That's good news. I'll pop in tomorrow too.' I want to ask what she'd think if she knew how Ned and I had spent the night, but I don't. If it was a one-off, she might never need to know. Though, if I've learned anything about Ida, it will be the first thing that she asks me when I see her and I'm not sure how I'll handle it.

We eventually get going and Ned plugs in his iPhone and mellow music fills the car as we head back to Cockleshell Bay. The thing is, I really don't want this to end. The nearer we get to home, the more I dread saying goodbye to Ned. We're slowly slipping out of the delicious cocoon we've been in and, quite frankly, I'd be happy to stay there for ever.

The sun is going down and the dusk is gathering in when we pull up outside *Sunny Days* and *Sea Breezes*.

Ned kills the engine and turns to me. 'Home.'

I sigh. 'The first thing I'm going to do is jump in a hot shower.'

He takes a lock of my straggly hair and twines it round his finger. 'Can I join you?'

'Yes,' I say without needing to think. I didn't want this to end and it looks as if it won't. 'I've got food too. Thanks to Marilyn. We can have dinner afterwards.'

His smile widens. 'Give me five minutes. I'll throw my stuff inside and then I'll be right with you.'

We climb out the car and he gives me a brief but passionate kiss before we unload our stuff from the boot and go our separate ways.

250

'Don't be long,' I tell him.

'As fast as I can,' he agrees.

I'm singing to myself as I head down the gangway to *Sunny Days*, bag in hand. Ned surely must stay the night with me again? To be honest with you, I can't wait to lose myself in the comfort of his arms once more. As my dear Marilyn might well say – I'm making play while the sun shines. It makes me feel a little bit scared but more than excited too.

Unlocking the door I kick off my ruined shoes as I step inside. There's mud all up the legs of my trousers, but I don't care. It was all worth it. If you want to know, I just can't stop grinning. I thought that Ned and I might have the one night together and then we would go back to being simply friends, but I get to hold him again. I can't tell you how happy that makes me.

Then I flick on the light and get the shock of my life.

Chapter Fifty-Nine

My heart is pounding in my chest and my mouth is dry when I ask, 'What the hell are you doing here?'

My husband is standing, as large as life, in the kitchen. He's wearing his favourite dark jacket – the one I bought him years ago on a trip to Rome because he'd forgotten to pack one and it was cooler than expected. There's a bag at his feet, so he must have only recently arrived and he looks tired, drawn. Though I've known him for years he seems like a stranger to me.

Chris frowns at me. 'I thought you'd be pleased to see me.'

'You should have contacted me first,' I say. 'I left for a reason.'

Perhaps I should be pleased to see Chris, feel grateful that he's made an effort to pursue me. Shouldn't I want to go him, hold him, kiss him? Is that what he expected? Did he think I would run and throw myself into his arms? Instead, I'm rooted to the spot and feel nothing but cross with him.

'I've been trying to get a reply from you since then,' he points out. 'I've been going out of my mind with worry. You've just cut me out, Jodie. That's not fair.'

'I think we've gone beyond "fair".' I might sound calm, but I'm shaking inside. How dare he just turn up out of the blue like this? I had bloody good cause not to have been replying to his texts or calls.

He runs a hand through his hair, clearly exasperated that he hasn't had the reception he anticipated. 'You owe me an explanation for your sudden disappearance, at the very least.'

'I needed to get away.' I'm aware how lame that sounds. 'I wanted time to myself to think.'

'You couldn't have "thought" while you were at home?'

'You, of all people, know what I've been through. I couldn't handle it any more.'

'What *we've* been through,' my husband corrects, coolly.

'If you've only come for an argument,' I say, wearily. 'Then you might as well leave. I don't have the energy.'

Chris takes in my appearance. 'Where the hell have you been? You look terrible.'

In fairness, he isn't used to seeing me muddy and bedraggled – or in clothes that teenagers and hippies favour.

'Is that glitter on your face?'

I have to supress a smile at that, despite the gravity of the situation. 'I've been to a festival,' I explain rather grudgingly. 'For the weekend.'

'Jesus,' he exclaims as if I've told him I've just flown to the moon and back on a unicorn.

'It was fun. And now I'm dirty, tired and want nothing more than a hot shower.'

Chris steps forward and holds out the enormous bouquet of red roses that he's had behind his back. 'I brought these.'

My heart sinks at the sight of them. Does he think that a bunch of flowers will make it all right again? Quite obviously. I take them and put them on the table. 'Thanks.' But my tone lacks grace. 'I'll put them in water in a minute.' Assuming Bill has a vase in his cupboards. 'Who told you I was here?'

'I managed to get it out of Della.'

Thanks, Chummie.

'And how did you get in?'

He looks slightly abashed. 'There was a key under one of the pots by the front door.'

Was there? Who knew?

'I just came on the off-chance,' he continues. 'I'd waited long enough, Jodie. I've booked a couple days leave from work. I thought we could talk. Try to sort things out. I'm hurting too, you know.'

He comes to me and pulls me close. I don't want to be held. Not by Chris. I don't protest, but I feel stiff and unresponsive in his embrace.

It is, however, at that point that Ned knocks lightly on the front door before pushing it open.

On seeing us in our clinch, Ned recoils in horror and, not knowing what else to do, I stand frozen in Chris's arms. I'm all too aware what this must look like. Ned's expression darkens and he looks from me to Chris and back, stunned.

'Ned . . . ' I eventually offer, but that's all I can manage. What do I say? What do I do?

'Hey,' he replies crisply when there's nothing more forthcoming. 'I'm obviously interrupting.'

'No . . . no . . .' But we both know that he is.

Chris and I break away. Now I feel as guilty as hell. My brain is in freefall and, while I stand there still not knowing quite how to deal with the situation, Chris steps forward and holds out his hand. Still confused, Ned shakes it.

'I'm Chris,' he says. 'Jodie's husband. I thought I'd surprise her.'

He's certainly done that.

Ned looks to me for an explanation. 'Husband?'

What can I say to defend myself? In the heady atmosphere of the festival, it was all very well to think of myself as free

254

and available, that I could love Ned without thinking of the consequences. But I'm not. No matter how much I wish that to be true, no matter how much I believe that our marriage is over, Chris is my still very much my husband. I can hardly deny it. Oh, fuck.

'I'd say it was a big surprise.' Ned's tone is sharp, hurt. 'You didn't expect this at all, did you, Jodie?'

'No,' I admit. 'I didn't.' What else can I say?

'Looks like your plans for the evening have changed.' He backs towards the door. 'I'll leave you to it.'

'I'm *really* sorry, Ned,' I say and I hope he hears all that I mean by those words. 'I'll talk to you tomorrow.'

'I'm busy tomorrow,' he bats back. 'Have a great time together. Nice to meet you, Chris.'

Chris comes to me and slips his arm round my waist, possessively. His smile is chilly. 'Nice to meet you too, Neil.'

Ned throws me a look before he leaves. It's disappointed, crushed, angry and I don't know what to do. I'm distraught and want to rush after him to explain all that has happened, *all* of it. But I can't. I'm frozen, physically and mentally, and don't know what I can do to make right this bloody mess.

Chapter Sixty

'I need a shower,' I say to Chris. I don't want to face this situation at all and I definitely don't want to do it covered in mud with hair like rats' tails. 'Make yourself useful and put the kettle on. I won't be long.'

But I am a long time. I linger in the shower, washing the muck from my feet, scrubbing the remains of my once-beautiful glitter daisies from my cheeks, listening to the steady rhythm of the pump chugging the water away. In the bedroom, my festival gear is thrown on the floor and it looks silly, girlish. I don't know what I was thinking. I'll wash it and put it straight in a bag for the charity shop. I look out of the porthole and see the lights on in Ned's boat. Should I go round there now and explain? I couldn't care less what Chris thinks. He doesn't have the moral high ground here.

I drag on my jeans and go to face him. Upstairs, Chris has set the kitchen table. The roses are in a vase and he's lit two candles. Chris never does this. I want to throw the roses into the sea.

'I've ordered a takeaway,' he says, overly bright. 'I found a menu in the drawer. Chinese. Your favourite dishes.'

'Thanks.' I don't tell him that there's enough food to feed a dozen armies in the fridge and freezer.

'You must be hungry.'

I realise that I haven't actually eaten since breakfast, but I've not much appetite. I feel sick to my stomach. This takes me right back to the days after the baby. That gnawing, empty feeling has returned with a vengeance. How quick it is to resurface.

'Bill's boat is amazing,' Chris says, talking as if nothing has happened. He pours me a glass of wine and I knock some back. It tastes like vinegar even though it's a decent bottle. 'I had no idea.'

'He's worked hard on it.'

'You look very comfortable here. You might never have come home.' He glances across to *Sea Breezes*. Ned is pottering about in the kitchen, but he doesn't look our way. 'You've made friends too?'

'Yes.' No point denying that either. 'Everyone has been very kind.'

Chris's expression says *some more than others* but he doesn't voice that opinion. I wonder if he can sense that Ned and I have been intimate – much as I could tell when he'd been sleeping with another woman?

The doorbell goes and I flinch, but it's just the takeaway delivery. Chris pays and dumps the carrier bag on the counter. I pull out two plates and put them on the table along with the cartons. The food smells delicious, but the thought of it makes me want to hurl.

We sit at the table like two strangers and the irony of how we first met isn't wasted on me. How did we come to this, I wonder? I glance at Chris and can tell that he's thinking much the same. We lost it all along the way and, for a moment, my heart tightens, craving the love it once knew.

For something to do, I spoon some fried rice and black bean chicken onto my plate, but push it around with my fork. The atmosphere is, needless to say, strained. Even James Bay on the iPod does nothing to soften it. I'm here with my husband yet, all I can think of is the look of disappointment on Ned's face.

We both pick at our food until Chris slides his hand across the table and covers mine. 'I know that I've messed up. We didn't talk enough after . . . '

He can't even continue. He can't say our baby's name because there wasn't a name given.

'. . . but I want to get back to how it was before.'

'How were we?' I genuinely want to know. 'How long *before*? Were we really happy then?'

Chris looks shocked. 'I think we were. This has taken a terrible toll on both of us. Understandably.'

'Yet, while I was grieving for the loss of my child, you were sleeping with someone else.' It's the first time I've said that aloud and Chris looks taken aback.

'I wasn't.'

'Don't do this, Chris. I'm not stupid.'

'Neither am I,' he says and makes a point of looking towards Ned's boat again.

He's right. Neither of us are innocent now. So what does that mean? Should I be more understanding about what he's done? There's no doubt that I pushed him away. I couldn't bear for him to touch me. I could hardly bear to look at him. Is it any wonder that he sought solace elsewhere? I know from how Ned made me feel that it's a heady mixture.

'I was grieving too, Jodie.' His face is sad. 'No one seemed to notice that.'

'You hid it well,' I spit back.

'All the focus was on you and how you'd suffered. Everyone

258

turned away from me. Including you. What was I supposed to do?'

'Stick by me? Support me? Love me?'

Chris drops his fork to his plate and rakes his hands through his hair. 'Don't you think I'd do that if I could turn back the clock? I handled it badly.'

I tut at that.

'*Very* badly,' he continues. 'But I was in uncharted territory too. I was floundering as much as you were. But men are meant to pull it all together. Well, I couldn't. I'm sorry about that.' He gets up and slams his chair in. 'I wish I still smoked. Fuck.'

He gave that up when I found out I was pregnant. Chris marches to the back of the boat and goes out onto the deck, slamming the door behind him.

I sit there, head in hands, and, when I glance up, Ned is staring back at me. Our eyes meet briefly and then he closes his blind, shutting me out. I deserve no better. There's a headache forming above my eyes and I massage my forehead which doesn't help at all, so I swallow down what's left in my glass of wine. I follow Chris out onto the deck. I stand beside him and we both look out to sea.

'It's beautiful out here,' he says, leaning on the rail.

The sun is gone and the very last vestiges of light are fading. The clouds are dark, bruised after the rain. The sea in the harbour is still, smooth, like black velvet. I've got used to how wonderful it is since I've been here and I try to see it again through Chris's eyes. As I should everything else.

'I can see why you came,' he says.

'I didn't know where else to go,' I offer.

'I wish you'd been able to turn to me. I didn't realise how bad things were.'

'You're right,' I say, softly. 'We do need to talk. I don't want

259

all our memories of the baby to be ones of pain and heartache. We have to remember some good.'

'We were so full of hope for the future.' Chris's voice breaks with emotion. 'What went wrong?'

'We lost our child,' I say.

Then we hold each other tightly and cry.

Chapter Sixty-One

We should talk now, I suppose, but Chris and I are both too emotionally exhausted, so we go to bed. A few hours ago I would have told you that the chances of us sharing a bed were somewhere between slim and remote, but here we are. I consider sleeping on the sofa, but I think we're both just too weary to consider making up a bed.

When I turn off the light, he moves towards me and tries to kiss me, but I say, 'Nothing has changed.'

So he sighs and turns over. With minutes of his head hitting the pillow, Chris is fast asleep. No matter what is going on in our lives he's never lost the ability to sleep heavily. Worry doesn't keep Chris awake at night. He calls it 'the sleep of the just'. I'm not so sure.

Despite not having slept much in the last couple of days, I'm wired and wide awake. My brain refuses to turn off. Even though I'm lying next to my husband, I'm thinking about what I was doing last night and can still feel Ned's hands on my body. If it's shown me one thing, then it's that I understand now why Chris was tempted to have an affair. It doesn't mean that I like it, but I can see how it might have happened. Should we talk about that or leave it unspoken between us? Do I need to know details or would that simply make it worse? I'm assuming that it's someone Chris works with – the most likely candidate being Meg – as he doesn't have time to meet anyone anywhere else. She's the one he goes away with when his job requires it. She's the one who stays overnight in luxurious hotels with him. I suppose the temptation and the opportunity is always there. One too many drinks at the bar, a willing partner – I understand that now.

Chris needed someone to comfort him and I was so consumed with grief that I couldn't do it. I get that. I found no comfort in counselling but maybe we should have gone together. Perhaps that would have helped. Yet I realise now that we have very poor communication in our relationship. We've jogged along happily enough, but as soon as something like this has hit us, we're thrashing around, helpless.

I listen to the rise and fall of *Sunny Days* as it shifts with the incoming tide, the creaking of its hull against the mooring posts, until the grey light of dawn peeps in the windows. The thoughts going through my mind are as restless as the movement of the ocean.

When I can bear lying here no longer, I leave Chris sleeping and get up. I grab some clothes and, as quietly as I can, pull them on in the bathroom. I can shower later. I tiptoe upstairs, push my feet into the trainers by the door and slip on my jacket. So early in the morning, it's still cold outside and the sharp air wakes me up in seconds.

I glance over at Ned's boat, but there's no sign of life and I assume he's still sleeping. I hesitate outside *Sea Breezes*. What if I knocked? Would he talk to me now? I walk up his gangway and dither for a few moments at the door, but can't make myself do it. Instead, I slink away, defeated and desolate, and head down to the beach. I need to get up my nerve, as I'd like to see him today so that I can at least try to explain the situation with Chris. Actually, I'd just like to see him.

The sunrise is beautiful, the sky washed with splashes of lemon, peach and blueberry. As I take the steps down onto the sand, I can see Ned on the beach ahead of me, just out of the reach of the waves. He's standing in a warrior pose, feet planted in the sand, arms stretched out to the horizon. He looks strong, grounded, yet even from here, I can tell that his body is more tense than usual. Though my heart lifts to see him, I hadn't expected to find him on the beach and thought that he'd still be in bed.

I shiver, wishing I'd put on my scarf and gloves. It's so chilly that even Ned's wearing a hoodie and joggers. The wind is ruffling his hair and I have the overwhelming urge to smooth it. I walk over the damp sand towards him and, as I approach, he turns.

'Hey,' I say, softly. 'Early bird.'

He relaxes his pose, but I notice that his familiar smile is absent. 'Couldn't sleep.'

'I didn't expect you to be here, but I'm glad that I've seen you. I went to knock at your door, but bottled it.' I try a smile, but it's not returned. 'I wanted to explain about last night.'

He looks at me, still cross. 'A husband, Jodie? You didn't think to mention that?'

'It's a difficult situation.'

'I bet.'

'Chris and I have been going through a very tough time in our relationship.'

He raises his eyebrows.

'I thought it was all over between us. *Firmly* believed it,' I reiterate. 'He's been having an affair with someone else.'

'So you thought you'd try it too? I'm a revenge fuck? Thanks. That makes me feel *so* much better.'

'No, it's not like that at all. You misunderstand me. What happened between us is different. I hadn't expected or planned for that to happen. For both of us, it was something spontaneous.'

'It's my golden rule, Jodie. I *never* mess with married women. Never. You made me break it unwittingly. That's shameful.'

'I know. I'm sorry. I do have my reasons.' All of them pathetic, though.

'Have you told him about us?'

'No,' I admit. 'We are the world's worst at talking. There is so much unsaid between us. It's not just the affair. There were other things.'

'And now you've kissed and made up?'

'Far from it.' How can I explain that my husband thinks that a Chinese takeaway and some red roses will fix everything? He couldn't be more mistaken.

'I can't be part of this, Jodie. My life is pretty uncomplicated and I'd like it to stay that way.'

'Shall we walk to Ida's and have a coffee? I can tell you more about it. I want to.'

'No.' Ned holds up his hands. 'I'm out of this.'

'But . . .'

'No,' he reiterates. 'Is your husband still here?'

'Yes, but . . .'

'This is not my problem and I don't want it to be. Whatever's wrong, you need to sort it out between you.'

I could tell him; this is another opportunity to let him know why I'm here, why Chris and I have fallen out of love, why I'm a shadow of the person I once was. But I can't bring myself to voice it. I don't know if I could hold it all together.

Then Ned faces me square-on and adds in a softer tone, 'I can tell that you're hurting and I wish that we could be friends. I'd love to help you, but I can't be in the middle of what's happening with you and your husband. I'm angry at you for deceiving me.'

'I didn't mean to . . . '

'I really like you, Jodie. For the first time in many years, I've let my heart get involved. I felt something for you. I thought that we could . . . ' Like me, Ned can't finish his sentence either. 'I wish you well. You're a wonderful woman. You just need to get your head and your life sorted out.'

'I'm sorry, Ned. So sorry.' I step towards him, but he holds up a hand.

'I don't want your husband seeing us hug and come round to bloody my nose. I'm a lover, not a fighter.'

'Chris isn't like that.'

'Sometimes people aren't quite what they seem,' he says pointedly.

'You've been so kind to me, Ned.' There's a ball of emotion lodged in my throat. 'You coaxed me out of my shell at a time when I really felt that I never wanted to speak to anyone ever again. Our night at the festival gave me back something that I thought I'd lost.'

He looks at me sadly. 'For what it's worth, I enjoyed it too. And this sounds like hippy-shizzle, but I felt we connected on a level that I hadn't experienced before.'

'We did,' I say with hope.

'You need to fix whatever's broken with your husband,' he says, flatly. 'My advice is to go home, make your marriage work.'

He makes it sound so easy. But what do I do? It's clear that Ned doesn't want me to stay here now and I don't know if I want to return home. I'm in limbo, purgatory, stuck here between heaven and hell on earth, not knowing which way to turn.

Chapter Sixty-Two

'I'll say goodbye, then.' I hold out my hand to shake Ned's.

'We can't do that,' he says. 'Not now that I know what you look like naked.'

That breaks the ice and we both manage a weak laugh.

'Come here.' Ned pulls me towards him. 'I just hope your husband isn't the jealous type.'

'He's a good man,' I tell him. 'Mostly. I don't know if we have a future together.'

'Only you can decide that.' Ned holds me tightly and I cling to him, wanting to stay in the circle of his arms. I feel such comfort, such warmth, such strength from him. If Ned asked me to stay now would I abandon everything and try to make a new life here? I don't know. My brain's too mashed to be able to consider the implications.

'You're going back to the mainland?' he asks.

'No. I don't know. Probably. Yes.'

Ned grins. 'I'm glad that you're clear about that.'

'My head's all over the place. I can't run away for ever, I suppose. For one thing, I have a job to go back to.' And a husband.

'I hope you resolve your problems,' Ned says. 'A quiet life is a good life.'

'Thank you for showing me that. I'll try to do some yoga when I'm back in London.' I attempt a smile but, inside, it feels as if a little bit of my already-battered heart is breaking. I feel too fragile to deal with this as well. 'It'll probably be inside some air-conditioned industrial unit rather than on this beautiful beach.'

'You'll be OK.' He holds me away from him. 'You're stronger than you think.'

I'm not sure if he's right about that or not. Only time will tell.

'I should go and say goodbye to Ida too.'

'Tell her I'll see her in a while,' Ned says. 'I'll bring my tool-kit.'

I nod.

Call me foolish, but I'd imagined leaving all my problems behind me and staying here for the rest of the summer with Ned. Maybe my heart would have started to heal by then. Perhaps Ned and I could have made some kind of relationship together. Chris could have declared his undying love for his new lady and I could feel less guilty than I do now.

But none of it is to be. Life, I've discovered, is never as straightforward as we hope.

'Goodbye, Ned,' I say again. 'Introduce yourself to my brother, Bill, if he ever manages to come here. You and he would like each other.'

'Take care of yourself, Jodie. It's been nice knowing you.'

'Yeah.' I turn away and walk down the beach. Tears roll down my face and I swipe them away with my hands, but I make myself march on.

Chapter Sixty-Three

I think Ida is cross with me too. But she seems to be cross with everyone and the world in general.

The café has only just opened and, as yet, there are no other customers. Which is just as well as Ida's still clearing up after the break-in. She's currently wielding her broom in a ferocious manner, sweeping broken glass and crockery from the deck and cursing under her breath as she does.

As I step up from the beach, she spins round. When she sees that it's me, she relaxes slightly and pauses to lean on her broom.

'Bastards,' she says by way of greeting. 'Look at the frigging mess they've made. If I catch hold of them, I'll string them all up by their bollocks. How can you live in a place as beautiful as this and still want to destroy it?'

'I'm sorry, Ida. This is awful. Is there anything I can do to help?'

'No. I've got it.' Her hair is tied up in some kind of top-knot with bits sticking out everywhere, the remnants of her festival ribbons still entwined. She rubs her neck. 'I've still got the red mist in front of my eyes,' she admits. 'I feel the urge to hurt someone. Badly. I work bloody hard. I don't deserve this.'

'No. It's dreadful.'

'We had to fish most of the chairs out of the sea yesterday. At least the tide hadn't carried them away. Some little shit had painted "COCK" in massive capitals on the hut, but I covered that yesterday with a fresh coat. I'll bloody well "cock" him if I catch hold of him.'

'You got the window and door fixed?' Looking at them you wouldn't tell that anything had happened.

'Yeah. I know a good local company. They came out yesterday. Charged me handsomely, though.'

'Will your insurance cover it?'

'I think so,' she says. 'You can never be sure these days. They'll probably make me beef up my security. CCTV cameras and the like. More expense.'

'Ned says he'll swing by later and bring his tool box.'

She looks at me sharply. 'You were with him this morning?'

'He's on the beach doing his yoga. I just bumped into him.'

'Oh.' She returns to her sweeping, but is less determined with it. 'You had a good time at the festival?'

'Yes. It was great fun.'

'Did you and Ned get it together?' she asks more frankly than I'd like. It's not that easy to dodge a question like that, but I had expected it from Ida. Perhaps she realised all along what would happen between me and Ned when she left us alone.

'I don't really want to talk about it, Ida.'

'So you did.' She shrugs. 'I can tell when he's got that glint in his eye. I've seen it a *million* times before. It won't last, but enjoy it for the summer.'

I'll never know whether Ida is right or not. From what I've seen of Ned, he doesn't seem to be the lothario she's making him out to be. Perhaps he was in his youth, but then we were all young and reckless once.

'I'm not staying,' I explain. 'I'm heading back to the mainland. I've really come to say goodbye.'

Ida looks taken aback. 'What's brought this on?'

'I'd rather not talk about that either. It's complicated.' She'll find out soon enough, from someone – probably Ned – that my husband turned up unannounced. Maybe they'll share a bottle of wine – or more – and laugh at my discomfort. I hope not, but you never can tell.

'Bugger,' she says. 'I thought you were going to become a permanent fixture.'

'Seems not.' I risk a smile at her. 'I wouldn't mind a last cup of tea before I go, if you've got the necessary . . . '

'I have. Can't offer you coffee – only instant. Bastards nicked my fancy-dancy machine.'

'Tea will be fine. I can finish sweeping for you while you make it?'

'OK.' She hands over her broom and I take up where she left off. Ida disappears inside the hut. I sweep the shards of glass and china into a dustpan, then tip the mess into a black sack.

A few minutes later, Ida returns with a tray of tea and I take my favourite seat in the shelter of the wall. I look out to sea, drinking in the view. The cove looks pretty in the morning light, more like somewhere on the Mediterranean. The gentle waves lap at the rocks as the tide edges its way back in.

'They smashed a load of crockery,' she complains, nodding at another couple of sacks by the hut. 'But I've got enough to be going on with until I can get a delivery.'

'Will it affect business?'

'We had to close yesterday and that hurt. The weekends are my busiest days. But we should be able to manage.'

'That's good to hear.' I pour my tea. 'Thanks, Ida. Won't you take a minute to join me?'

'Nah. I'm too wound up to sit down. I've got stuff to do.'

So she stomps away and I nurse the cup to me, warming my cold hands. Another customer arrives and Ida serves him. I keep hoping that Ned will change his mind and appear, but he doesn't.

As I'm finishing my tea, my phone rings and I wonder if Chris has woken up and found me gone. He'll be worried if he has. But the screen says that it's Della.

'Hey,' I say when I pick up.

'Chummie! Where the fuck are you?'

'Still on the Isle of Wight,' I tell her.

'Are you coming back any time soon?'

'Yes,' I say.

'Well, bloody hurrah for that!'

I might be feeling sad to leave, but Della has the knack of making me smile.

'We can hit the gym again. And the bars. Maybe the bars more than the gym.'

I force myself to laugh. 'Sounds like a plan.'

'Have you seen Chris?' she says and I can hear something strange in her voice.

'Yes, I have, and I've got a bone to pick with you. He turned up at the houseboat last night. I believe it was you who told him I was here.'

'Guilty as charged. You need to sort this out, Jodie. Neither of you can go on like this.'

'I know. Part of me would like to stay here and avoid it for ever, but I know that's not fair. Though it's largely down to Chris whether I come back or not.'

'What did he say?'

'Not much. We haven't really discussed our options yet, but

I get the impression that he wants me to come home.'

'You have to be sure,' she says. 'It's hard to pick up the pieces.'

But isn't that what you're supposed to do when you're married? Should I try again or should I stay here and send Chris packing? To be honest, I don't know if I'm coming or going.

I hear Della clear her throat. 'So did you sleep together?'

'In the same bed, but that's all. Even that seemed weird. It's a long time since we were . . . together . . . like that and there's too much distance between us. I don't know if he's still seeing another woman. He denied there was anyone else, but I don't know if he's telling the truth.'

'I'm sure you're imagining it,' Della says and she sounds very convinced that she knows best.

'I don't know. Maybe you're right.' Is it simply a sign of how I feel about Chris that I can believe that of him? Perhaps he has been working late as often as he's said and it is all in my head.

I'm not going to confide in Della that I've spent the night with Ned. She's my best friend, but I owe it to Chris to tell him first if we decide to put all our cards on the table. Besides, it's not something that I want to gossip about. Della will be scandalised and we'll, no doubt, have a good giggle about it, but I don't want that. What I had with Ned was special and I can't share it. Not even with my best friend.

'I'd better go,' I tell her. 'I'm currently in a beach café having a cuppa. Chris will be wondering where I am.'

'Lucky you,' she says. 'Think of me with my nose to the grindstone. And keep me posted with where you're up to. I need to see you as soon as you're back. I miss you, Chummie.'

'Miss you too,' I say and then we both hang up.

So that's it. Looks as if I have one foot here and one foot already on its way home.

I take my cup to the hut where Ida is banging around inside, still in a crotchety mood.

'Can I have a coffee to take away for George? I should say farewell to my favourite statue.' I'm hoping that he'll already be on duty.

'I don't even know if he likes instant coffee,' she grumbles. But she makes him one, anyway, and hands it over.

'I'll be off then,' I say when I've paid. 'It's been really nice meeting you, Ida.'

She puts her hands on her hips. 'So that's it? You come into our lives, make Ned fall in love with you and then sod off again?'

'I hadn't quite planned it like that,' I admit. 'But this was always going to be a temporary arrangement until I got my head together.'

'And have you done that?'

'No,' I confess with a laugh. 'I'm sure you over-estimate Ned's feelings for me. He's just been very kind while I've been here.'

'I know Ned better than you do. Much better. I'd like to believe otherwise, but I think he's fallen hook, line and sinker. I know I said he's a player and he was, once, but he's not like that now. He'll be gutted that you're leaving.'

I realise that Ida still doesn't know about the small matter of my husband and how I've disappointed Ned. Well, all in good time. She'll find out soon enough. I can't bring myself to tell her about my deception, that I've burned my bridges with Ned, when it had all been without intent to cause harm.

'I've been jealous of you,' she says. 'I can't deny it. But I've never seen Ned's eyes light up for me the way they do when he looks at you.'

This is all too difficult to hear. I don't want to cause any more pain than I already have.

Ida comes out of the hut and hugs me. She smells of patchouli

273

oil and seaside. We might not have been the best of friends, but we could have been, and I'll miss her.

'I've got used to you being around. Come back for a holiday,' she says. 'Soon.'

'I will,' I promise. But, somehow, I don't think that's going to happen.

Chapter Sixty-Four

I walk along the seafront and think that I'll be sad to leave this place. I'll miss the endless sky, the sand beneath my feet, the tang of seaweed in the air, the gentle pace of life.

Sure enough, as I approach the esplanade, George is standing there on his plinth, arms stretched out to the sea. He can't earn much, if anything, at this time of day, but here he is as I'd expected.

He jumps down when he sees me and beams, showing his white teeth in his bronze face. 'Hey.'

'Hi, George.'

He rolls his shoulders. 'Sometimes I forget that it's better to do poses where I don't have to hold my arms up.'

'I'm sure you could move when no one's looking.' There are actually a decent number of joggers, dog walkers and early morning strollers already out, but I don't think they'd mind.

'And break the living statue code?' he teases.

I laugh and hand over his drink. 'Ida got broken into at the weekend and her fancy coffee machine was nicked. That's instant.'

'Thanks.' He wrinkles his nose as he tastes it, but glugs it down anyway. 'Is she OK?'

'She's angry more than anything,' I tell him. 'The damage isn't as bad as it might have been.'

'I'll pop along later,' he says. 'When I've dumped this lot and I've scrubbed up. See if I can help.'

'I'm sure she'll appreciate it. How did it go at the festival? You looked to be very popular.'

'It was a good vibe,' he agrees. 'I felt I got my statuing mojo back. The new costume helped. I needed a new lick of paint.' He runs his hands over his coat, proudly. 'Did you enjoy it too?'

'Yeah,' I say. 'I did.' Too much, I think.

'Sorry I didn't find you later, but I got in with a good crowd in the evening and time ran away with me.'

'As long as you were having fun.'

'Yeah, there were some great bands on. Besides, it looked as if you and Ned could manage without my company.' He gives me a statue-style wink.

'It was that obvious?'

'Not that it's my business, but are you and he an item, then?'

'No,' I say sadly. There was a moment when I thought we might have been, but I've blown it. Though I can't say that out loud. 'I've actually come to say goodbye. I'm heading home today.'

'You're going back to London? So soon? I thought you were going to stick around, at least for the summer.'

'So did I, but something came up.'

He looks as crestfallen as a statue can. 'I'll miss our chats.'

'Me too. I've nearly finished the book. I've really enjoyed it. I hope it goes well.'

'I haven't heard anything,' he says with a shrug that aims at nonchalance but fails. 'But I've not given up hope just yet.'

'Keep at it,' I advise. 'We all deserve our dream.'

'Sometimes your dreams come true and sometimes you have to change what your dreams are. I know that already.'

And he's right, of course. My dreams, such as they are, seem to be ever-elusive.

While I'm musing on it, a dog walker passes by and George freezes into position, cup of coffee in hand. I do the same. The man smiles at us and tosses a coin into George's box. We both laugh once he's gone.

'The start of a new career,' George says.

'I've got a job waiting for me.' And a husband and a brother.

We sit for a moment together and enjoy the view in silence. I take in the vast, unbroken blueness of the sky and I wonder how I'll manage with the little glimpses I get of it in London. Little boats bob about on the ocean. A couple of hardy people swim at the edge of the sea. It'll be freezing in there, but still I envy them.

Then I stand and try to hug George, but I can't really get near to him because of his costume and we both end up a bit embarrassed. We shake hands instead.

'I'll see you around,' I say.

He gets back onto his plinth. 'I hope so.'

So I walk away, back towards Cockleshell Bay for the last time. When I turn round George is looking after me, hand held up in a frozen wave. I wave back and walk faster, the wind making my eyes sting.

Chapter Sixty-Five

When I get back to *Sunny Days*, Marilyn is swishing round the mop. Her favourite thing.

'Hi, Marilyn.'

'Where have you been?' she says, clutching her chest. 'Your man was standing here in nothing but his pants when I turned up this morning. Nearly gave me a heart attack!'

'Sorry, I should have texted you to let you know.' Though I should imagine that Chris was equally surprised to find a buxom Marilyn Monroe looky-likey dressed in a gold lamé jumpsuit letting herself into the houseboat at the crack of dawn along with a cloud of *Joie de Vivre* perfume mixed with *eau de Cif*.

'I thought you'd brought one of those Chippendales home from the festival. I can tell you, I didn't know where to look.'

'But you *did* have a good look?'

'You bet I did!' she laughs.

'I gather Chris introduced himself.'

'Once we'd both got over the shock.' She lowers her voice. 'He seems very nice.'

I don't remind Marilyn that looks can be deceptive. 'He turned up unexpectedly last night.'

'Ah,' she says. 'I bet that was a lovely surprise.'

It was a surprise, that's for sure. I'm still trying to judge whether I find it 'lovely'.

'He must have been pining for you. You know what they say about absence making the legs grow fonder.'

'I do.' No point arguing with that. Absence might as well make any part of the body fonder.

'But where have you been, sweetheart?' she continues. 'We were both worried. I sent a text.'

It bounces in as she speaks and I hold up my phone, so that she can see I've only just received it. They never fail to make me smile. This one has a pig, a balloon, a bottle of champagne and a poodle emoji attached to it.

'I went down to the café to see Ida. She had a break-in over the weekend and had to leave the festival early. There's quite a bit of damage so I went to see if I could do anything.'

'Poor lamb! She wasn't hurt?'

'No, she was with us at the festival when it happened. It's just the mess really and the coffee machine's been nicked.'

'I'll pop by later and see if I can do anything to help.'

'I'm sure she'll appreciate it. She's feeling very unhappy today. I hated her having to rush away like that.'

Marilyn raises her eyebrows. 'So she left you and Ned there? All by yourselves?'

I feel myself flush and nod in lieu of a reply. Marilyn glances downstairs to make sure that Chris isn't within earshot.

'You've been getting on very well with Ned,' she observes. 'A bit too well?'

Thankfully, Marilyn has lowered her usual volume and is using her inside voice and I do the same. 'Yes.'

I'm sure that she knows we've slept together and, if I'm so transparent to Marilyn, then Chris must be pretty certain too. Perhaps he's prepared to forgive and forget and I'll need to do the same thing if we have a chance of rescuing our relationship.

'Does Ned know about . . . ?' She gives a theatrical nod towards where Chris might be.

'He does now. He's really angry with me. It's all getting a bit too complicated. A very good reason as to why I should go home.'

She looks at me, shocked. 'You're leaving?'

'I have to. Much as I've enjoyed it, I can't hide here indefinitely. As you've said, life goes on. I have people who rely on me. I've got work to do and I need to face my difficulties head-on.'

'Not head-on,' Marilyn advises. 'Walk beside them for a while and see how that feels. Don't let them overtake you. That's the key.'

'Very sound advice.' I look at her and smile sadly. 'I'll miss you, oh wise woman.'

'I'll miss you too, sweetheart. Who'll look after you when you get home?'

'I'll be fine,' I promise her. 'I'll make sure my cupboard runneth over with bread.'

'I'll text you every day to check,' she says. Then, 'You've seen Ned today?'

'On the beach.' It twists my inside when I add, 'I said my goodbye to him.'

'What did he say?'

'Not much.' What could he say? I'm married. I have another life.

She whispers now. 'Do you love him?'

'I don't know, Marilyn. I don't know what I feel about anything.'

'Then don't make any hasty decisions. You might fix things with your young man. A camel *can* change their spots.'

'I think you'll find that it's a leopard who *can't*.'

'Whatevs,' Marilyn says. 'You know what I mean.'

And that's the lovely thing, I do. Despite her always getting her words tortured and tangled, I know exactly what she means. I've warmed so much to this kind-hearted lady since I arrived feeling bleak, lonely and on the edge of despair. I still might not be sorted out emotionally, but she's done wonders for me during my stay and I'm going to miss her terribly.

'You've helped me so much,' I say. 'Even when I thought I didn't want your help.'

'Go on.' Marilyn wipes a tear from her eye. 'You'll make me blub and I've not got my waterproof mascara on.'

'You've been a good friend to me.' I go and hug her tightly. I would have liked to have been a mother like Marilyn – perhaps with less exuberant taste in clothes. 'Say you'll come and see me in London.'

'No, no,' she says. 'I hate the mainland, especially London. It's not my cup of coffee at all. You'll just have to promise to come back here.'

Chris appears at the top of the stairs. Marilyn's face falls. I do believe she's quite disappointed to see him fully clothed.

'Come back?' he asks, after hearing the tail-end of our conversation.

I break my embrace with Marilyn and turn to him. 'We should go home.'

He looks surprised. 'Now?'

'Yeah. Let's strike while the Hoover's hot.'

Out of the corner of my eye, I see Marilyn wink at me. She's taught me well.

Chapter Sixty-Six

I pack while Marilyn cleans *Sunny Days* from top to bottom. She goes about it in a very determined manner and the odd sniffle or strangled sob comes from her direction when her back is turned.

I've not got much, but it seems to take me an inordinate amount of time to fold it and put it back in my bags. It doesn't seem to be two minutes since I arrived here and, despite my earlier bravado, I don't feel that I'm ready to leave. Chris, it seems, is in a different frame of mind.

'Come on, Jodie,' he urges. 'If you hurry, we can catch a lunchtime ferry. We'll miss rush hour on the other side then. Otherwise, it'll be hell getting into London.'

Out of heaven and into hell, I think.

I look out of the window at the harbour ahead of me. Cockleshell Bay looks particularly inviting today. The sea sparkles, the clouds are gloriously white and fluffy, the black-headed gulls wheel and call on the breeze. I've never wanted less to be heading to a city. Chris, it seems, can't wait. Should we linger just a little longer and I could maybe show him some of the island or explore parts that I haven't seen? I've barely scratched the surface myself. But he doesn't seem interested. He simply wants to spirit me away as soon as possible. It's probably for the best. I don't think I could face bumping into Ned again.

Downstairs, I take some deep breaths before I start to dissemble my life here. I throw my clothes into the case, even the glittery leggings from Marilyn. The only things I leave behind are the sand ornament that Ned made for me and the garish pink teddy bear he won on our day out at the Needles. I'd love to take them, but I can't. How would I explain my desire to hold onto them to Chris? So, with a last fond look, I hide them both in the depths of the wardrobe and close the door.

When my case is packed and I can delay no longer, I hug Marilyn once more and we both shed a tear or two. While we hold on to each other, Chris takes the bags and goes to get the car which is parked further down the road.

'I hope it works out for you, sweetheart,' Marilyn says with a tearful sniff.

'Thanks, Marilyn. You've been brilliant. I couldn't have asked for anyone better.'

'Go on with you. It's been my pleasure. You need taking care of, Jodie. Be kind to yourself too.'

'I will.' I give her a tight squeeze. 'I'm going to go now, before I find it too hard to leave.'

We go to the door together and, when I step outside, I see that, propped up against one of the bay trees, is the mother and baby carving that I'd asked Ned if I could have. It's such a beautiful sculpture that I'm teary all over again. When I pick it up and cradle it in my arms, it fits just perfectly. The weight and the warmth of the wood is comforting against my body. Ned has sanded it until it's wonderfully smooth. I can't tell you what the wood is, but I think that Ned has probably oiled it too as the colours are rich and deep.

'What's that?' Marilyn asks.

'It's from Ned.' I glance over at *Sea Breezes*, but there's no one there and his car has gone. 'He started working on it at the festival and I said that I'd like it.'

'It's beautiful,' she says, stroking the baby's head. 'A lovely memory for you.'

I can't speak I'm so overwhelmed, so I just nod and hold the carving closer to me.

Chris pulls up in the car and I turn to Marilyn, unable to disguise my sorrow at parting.

'Goodbye, sweetheart,' she says and cries again.

'Oh, don't,' I say with a sob. 'I can't bear this.'

Chris honks the horn.

'I'd better be going.' So, sculpture still in my arms, I climb into the passenger seat.

Chris stares at it. 'What on earth's that?'

'The guy next door is a wood sculptor. He made it for me.'

His face tightens. 'Did you tell him about the baby?'

'No. I saw him working on it and asked if I could buy it from him.' I don't say that Ned seems to have left it as a gift for me. 'I love it. You don't?'

My husband shrugs. 'If it makes you happy, then that's all that matters.' He doesn't look as if that's what he feels. 'Ready to head off?'

'Yes.' I look back at *Sunny Days* which I've enjoyed so much as a temporary home and the beautiful view of the harbour as we drive away. Marilyn is waving furiously and I wave back.

Chris and I don't speak as we hit the road and turn inland, but he rests his hand on my knee. It's heavy, oppressive and I can feel the sweaty heat of his palm through my jeans, but I don't feel able to move it. Then we wind our way through the green and pleasant scenery of the Isle of Wight back towards the ferry terminal.

'It's OK here,' is Chris's verdict. 'A bit twee.'

'You've hardly seen anything of it. That's a harsh judgement.'

'Did you get out and about much?'

'A bit,' I admit. I think of the day that Ned took me out to his hideaway in the forest and to the Needles and what fun we had. It's a shame that I didn't see more of the island too. 'But I would like to see more one day.'

'I'd rather go to Bali,' is Chris's opinion.

Chapter Sixty-Seven

We undertake the rest of the journey in silence and, thankfully, it's not too long before we're at the port of Cowes. Chris joins the lines of cars waiting to be directed on board our ferry back to the mainland. My heart is in my boots. I don't want to stay and I don't want to go. Tell me how I'm going to start to sort that one out in my head?

While we wait, Chris and I try to make conversation, but each attempt falls flat. We give up and both turn to our phones for solace. I check some work emails from Bill and Chris busies himself with texting. Thankfully, we're soon waved on board.

'You're going to put that thing down?' he says.

My sculpture has been nestled on my lap, giving me a degree of comfort. Reluctantly, I leave it on the passenger seat. Chris and I get out of the car.

Chris stretches as if we've been on some mammoth journey. 'Some lunch?'

'Not for me.' I've been beguiled by their sandwiches before, which offer much and deliver little. 'I'd rather stand outside as we leave, if you don't mind.'

'OK. It's a nice day for it. You go outside and I'll get us some coffee.'

So I head to the back of the ferry and, with a feeling of déjà vu, I stand on deck. As the ferry sets sail, I watch the Isle of Wight disappear into the distance. The little boats, the chic apartments, the fancy restaurants grow smaller, become more indistinct, as we leave the harbour and head out into the Solent. I feel numb when I suppose I should feel happy.

I'm going to miss Marilyn, Ned, George and even Ida. But especially Ned. I can't bear to think of him, yet can't stop the images of his body above mine. I take out my phone and look at the photo of us by the princess's sandcastle we built on the beach. We're both grinning at the camera – me a little drunkenly. I should delete it, no good will come of keeping it. It will only serve to remind me, when I should be doing my best to forget. Yet, I can't make my finger press the button.

The weather has taken a sudden turn for the worst. As we cross the open water, the clouds are heavy and low. The sparkling sea turns from turquoise into a writhing mass of slate grey, choppy and unsettled. Big splots of rain fall, exploding on the water like tears falling from the sky. The ferry ploughs on regardless. I stare unseeing at the waves, not caring that I'm getting wet. We pass the other Red Funnel heading back to the island and every fibre of my being is telling me not to leave. The boat is close, so close, that I feel I could jump from here right onto it and go straight back. I hold my breath for a long moment, wondering if I could make it. But, of course, I stay where I am.

A while later, as the houses and boats of Cowes are tiny dots on the horizon, Chris joins me at the rail.

'My God, the queue,' he complains as he hands me a coffee.

'Thanks.' The coffee is lukewarm and bitter. I try a smile but fail.

'You're soaked. Did it rain?'

'Yes.' I hadn't realised that it had stopped as suddenly as it started.

Chris slips his arm round my waist and pulls me to him. I try not to tense in his arms.

'Cheer up,' he says. 'Everything will be better once I've got you home again.'

But will it? I wouldn't like to say. I can only hope that Chris is right.

Chapter Sixty-Eight

The traffic is hell on the way back into London and everything looks so crowded and grimy. We are both frazzled by the time we park in the next street to our apartment – and it takes us ten minutes to find a space.

'I don't know why we live in London,' I say.

'We love it,' Chris declares. 'We wouldn't want to live anywhere else.'

I'm not so sure. I've got used to waking up to the sound of the sea birds and the still, sparkling water of the harbour, the gentle pastel sunrises, the magnificently technicolour sunsets. This all seems so bland, so monochrome in comparison.

'Let's go to our favourite restaurant tonight,' Chris suggests. 'You'll enjoy that.'

'Sounds like a great idea.' I have to make an effort otherwise I'll be sinking again.

We lug our bags round the corner to our place. I have Ned's sculpture tucked carefully under my arm. Chris unlocks the main door and then pushes it open with his foot. Our apartment is in a beautiful Edwardian house that's been split into four flats. We're on the top floor and have a view over the houses and chimney pots behind us. There's a small garden with a high wall that we have access to, but rarely go in it as we don't know our neighbours and it would be awkward if we bumped into them. Even though it's ours, it feels like an intrusion to go in there if someone else is using it. We all chip in to pay for a gardener who maintains it for us and, when I do venture out there, seems to do a good enough job.

We climb the stairs to our front door and Chris lets us in. 'Home sweet home,' he says.

I follow him inside. The first thing I notice is the absence of scent. My home smells of nothing in particular. There's not the freshness of sea air nor the bitter tang of seaweed exposed by the receding tide. I must get some reed diffusers or something. Seaside fragrance.

'Tea?' Chris says as he throws the bags on the floor. He's already at the Quooker tap.

'Yes, please.'

Our living room is large, open plan and with high ceilings. While the outside of the house is still pretty, the interior is another matter altogether. All indication that it ever was Edwardian inside has been obliterated by a succession of unsympathetic builders and most of the period features are long gone. We have shiny new oak floors, white walls and, in here, there's an enormous L-shaped grey sofa. Our artworks are minimal, abstract and mostly leaned up against the walls, so that I can move them around as the whim takes me. The windows are covered by white slatted blinds and I go over to the bay to put Ned's beautifully carved statue in prime position. The blinds hide the view of the street and the skip that's permanently parked across the road from renovations that have been going on for as long as we've lived here. Our opposite neighbour seems to be extending up, down and sideways.

I gaze out and watch the traffic negotiating its way through double-parked cars. A man in a white van shakes his fist at a vehicle he decides is too slow. It seems strange to be back in my sleek, stylish home with the shushing sound of the waves and the plaintive cries of seabirds replaced by shrill police sirens and the constant thrum of traffic.

I look at Ned's sculpture in its new home and feel that it connects me to both the baby and Ned and, for that, I'll treasure it for ever. I wonder where he is now and whether he's thinking of me as I'm thinking of him.

Chris jolts me out of my daydreaming by bringing me tea and I take it, gratefully.

'Thanks.'

'You're going to put that statue there?'

'Yes,' I say. 'For now.' But I suspect this will be its permanent home.

He smiles at me, uncertainly. 'I should probably have mentioned this before now.' He takes a deep breath. 'I need to tell you that I cleared the baby's room.'

'Oh.' That makes me feel sick to my stomach.

'I thought it was for the best,' he rushes on. 'Too much of a reminder. I've put the stuff in storage. Just in case . . . '

In case we need it again? I wonder if that will ever be necessary.

'I'll go and look.'

He puts an arm on mine. 'Is that wise?'

'I can't avoid it for ever.' So I walk along the hall and into my now-empty nursery with Chris on my heels.

The cot has gone. The one that we spent so long choosing and spent an inordinate amount of money to have a paint finish free of toxins. How stupid when we live in one of the most polluted cities in the world. Will Chris and I ever be able to try for another baby? We seem a million miles away from it, at the moment.

I feel as if I need some time alone here, but Chris wraps his arms round me. 'We could repaint it? If you like. Or leave it as it is for now?'

The room's still the pale yellow and soft grey that we chose with such care and such hope.

'Say something?' Chris urges.

'That's fine.' Before it was a nursery this was our general dumping ground. I'll expect it will become that once more.

He holds me tight. Tighter than I want to be held. 'You're home with *me* now. I'll make this right, Jodie. It might take a while, but I promise you I *will* make it right.'

I lean back against his chest and try to relax. After a few moments, I manage to find some peace and it's nice to feel the warmth there.

'Don't shut me out,' Chris whispers.

'I'll try not to.' I squeeze his hands.

I have to give this my best shot too. We married, for better, for worse. It's just that you never really appreciate how bad the worse can be. And I can't think of much worse than the death of a child. Even a child who was with us so fleetingly.

Chapter Sixty-Nine

Chris has booked a table at Night Owl. Our favourite restaurant and go-to place for celebrations – birthday, anniversary, any excuse. It's ruinously expensive, but worth it as the food is great and the atmosphere second to none.

I sit and look at myself in the mirror on my dressing table. I think I look better than when I left. My skin is no longer the colour of uncooked pastry and I do believe I've got a sprinkling of freckles. I've certainly put weight on due to Marilyn's minis-trations. Everything I've tried on to go out in tonight is tight. The waistband of the black trousers I settle on is cutting into my waist. While I'm thinking about Marilyn, I text to say that we're home safely and thank her again for all that she's done for me. I get back the usual row of random emojis from her – bikini, dinosaur, taxi, sheep, cocktail glass, flamenco dancer – which makes me smile. I miss her already.

Then I text Bill that I'm back at home and I'll be in the office tomorrow, but I don't get one in return so I assume he's out, probably entertaining clients, and has his phone turned off.

'We need to get moving, Jodie,' Chris shouts from the living room. 'Table's booked for eight and they'll let it go if we're late.'

My wedding and engagement rings are in a dish next to my hairbrush and I pick them up and slide them back onto my finger. I look down at them. We had such hope, such expectations when we signed up for all of this. And, to be fair, we've both had a pretty gilded existence. Everything has always gone according to plan, all swimmingly and tickety-boo. Until, of course, we decided to have a baby. Who knew that the thing which you think should come most naturally in your life could be the most difficult and emotionally painful thing to achieve?

'Jodie!'

I slip on my jacket – unfortunately, not my cheery, yellow padded one – pick up my handbag and join Chris who's fidgeting by the front door. 'We'd better put a spurt on.'

He hurries me out of the building and we walk down the road to the hustle and bustle of the high street. The smell of diesel fumes makes me feel slightly queasy as we walk. Chris takes my hand which may be romantic or may be to make sure that I'm walking as fast as he is.

Fifteen minutes later and we descend the stairs into Night Owl. The place has a relaxed, sophisticated vibe which, as I've said, you pay handsomely for. Its décor is vintage, tasteful and I wish our company had tendered for it. I don't know why we missed out on this one, but we did. The tables are all bathed in candlelight and they serve the most enticing cocktails. There's usually live music, smooth jazz or something like that and it always feels quite decadent in here – a touch of nineteen-twenties Berlin in London. Chris orders a Negroni cocktail.

'I'll have the same. Thanks.'

When the waiter moves away, my husband says, 'You're drinking again?'

'Yes. I thought I might as well.'

He leans in close to me. 'The doctor said there was nothing

wrong with either of us. Not really. There was nothing wrong with the baby either. It was just one of those things.'

'"One of those things"?'

'You know what I mean.' Chris sighs at me. 'Don't pick me up for using the wrong words. I'm trying to be positive. The doctor said we could try again in a few months. If that's what you want.'

'No,' I say. 'It isn't.'

'There's nothing to stop us. I'll do anything you want to make you happy.'

Chris can't imagine, with the way we are, that we could embark on the hideous circus of IVF again, could he? It's not simply a matter of me falling into his arms once more. He seems to have forgotten all the horrors that trying for a child entailed – as we both did when I finally fell pregnant.

'This isn't just about you,' he says, slightly barbed. 'We both wanted the baby.'

I take another swig of my cocktail before I say, 'I'd like to give our child a proper name, something other than "the baby".'

'What, though?' Chris spreads his hands. 'We never could settle on a name.'

'I still like Charlotte.'

'Lottie,' he says. 'Let's agree on that.'

'Lottie,' I concur and feel a little lift in my heart. My child, my beloved child who slipped away from me, has a name and you won't believe how much better that makes me feel. She's someone: Lottie Jackson, a proper person.

'Does that make you happier?'

'Yes. It does.' It may seem like a small, inconsequential thing to Chris, but it means the world to me. I smile across at him and say, 'Thank you.'

He squeezes my hand. 'We'll be all right,' he assures me.

If he says that enough times both of us might believe it.

So we order food and I have another cocktail. As we eat, Chris has two more and we listen to the band before we walk home. We're both more relaxed in each other's company than we have been in a long time.

'I'm going back into work tomorrow,' I say as we reach our front door. 'I texted Bill earlier.'

'So soon? Now I'm back, I should go into the office, but don't you want another couple of days to yourself?'

'No.' I shake my head. 'I've already had too much time off. I know Bill's going mad without me. I should get right back into it.' Besides, what would I do kicking around the flat by myself?

We let ourselves in and, as we throw off our coats, Chris checks his watch. 'Tea or shall we turn in?'

'It's late,' I say. 'We should go to bed.' I want to be fresh for the morning. I want everyone in the office to know that I'm back and on form. After my lazy time in the Isle of Wight, it's going to be a shock getting up, out and in work for our daily eight o'clock breakfast meeting.

I turn for the living room. 'I'll be with you in a minute.'

His lips brush mine. 'Don't be long.'

While Chris heads to the bedroom, I go in the opposite direction. I just wanted a last look at Ned's statue before bed. I don't switch on the light as we left the blinds open and there's more than enough ambient light to pick my way over to the window. The streetlights shine directly on the wood, making it glow. I pick up the sculpture and rock it gently in my arms. The shape is smooth, the perfect weight which fits so comfortably against my chest. I wonder where Ned is now? I picture the houseboats, *Sunny Days* and *Sea Breezes* nestled together, Cockleshell Bay, the moon on the water. It may not be far, but we are half a world away. I miss him. I can't tell you otherwise. Kissing the baby's head gently, I put it back on the windowsill.

'We've called you Lottie,' I whisper. 'Goodnight, beautiful. Sleep tight.' Finally, I have something tangible to remember Lottie by and I can't tell you how much I cherish it.

Chris is still undressing when I go into the bedroom. It feels weird seeing him naked and I avert my gaze. His body is strong, toned, due to the hours he spends at the gym but, where it was once so familiar, it looks like the body of someone I don't know any more. We're polite, uncomfortable with each other as we use the bathroom. We have two sinks and even brushing our teeth side by side seems too intimate after our time apart.

I spend forever prevaricating over what to wear for my return to gainful employment and realise how drab my wardrobe is when I used to think it was sophisticated. All my dresses are fitted bodycons in shades of grey, black and beige. I think back to the festival and my glittery cheeks, my flirty little dress that was too short for a woman of my age. I didn't know that fun, carefree person was lurking inside me. After flicking through my wardrobe a dozen times, I settle on a white shirt and black trousers. I'm going to look like a waitress in a high-end restaurant. Too late to do anything about it now. I need to find my inner Marilyn and embrace it.

When I eventually climb into bed beside Chris, I try to keep some space between us. He's naked beneath the sheets and that's usually a sign that he wants to make love. It's funny how you fall into these unspoken habits when you're married. Sure enough, when I go to turn off the light, Chris turns towards me and his hand snakes beneath my T-shirt and his mouth is on my neck.

'Jodie,' he murmurs. 'I've missed you.'

'Not now, Chris.' I move away from him. 'I have an early start.'

I can see the disappointment, the rejection written on his face, as he takes his hand from my skin. 'It's not just that, is it?'

'We've had a lovely evening,' I say, calmly. 'Very lovely. I'm not ready for this. Let's take it slowly. We have a long way to go to rebuild our relationship.'

My husband flops onto his back with a sigh. 'You're never going to forgive me, are you?'

'Don't spoil it.'

'Wanting to make love to my own wife shouldn't be "spoiling" anything.'

Then he snaps off the light and turns over. Within minutes he's asleep but I lie there awake, listening to music thumping out of a house from further down the road and a couple having a full-on row outside. The language is more than colourful, but at least they are both saying what they think.

Chapter Seventy

My journey to work isn't far, a few stops on the Tube, but I hadn't really ever stopped to consider how hideous it is. I close my eyes and try to let the rhythm rock my body and not consider how squashed I am, how the people getting on and off jostle me as they squeeze through to the door, how bad the smell of stale food and body odour is. There's a young man watching porn on his iPhone and another picking his nose with more enthusiasm than is necessary. I'd forgotten how disgusting it can be.

I should make the effort to walk to the office now that the mornings and evenings are light, but I wouldn't feel safe to do so alone in the dark of the winter.

Chris was up and gone first thing. I kept my eyes closed as he moved around the bedroom. Him trying not to make a noise, me pretending that I was still asleep. He left quietly and without saying goodbye.

When I emerge from the Tube, Bill texts me. *Are you on your way? B xx*

5 mins, I punch in and step out a bit more.

Our offices are terribly trendy and are in an old warehouse

that's been renovated. It seems like a long time since I was last here and take a deep breath before I enter. Our breakfast meeting is laid out in the office every morning – a fine spread to set us up for the day and to give us chance to touch base with our colleagues. We have a catering company who comes in and does it for us.

I feel both excited to be back and daunted by the prospect. Yet I needn't have worried as, when I open the door, a great cheer goes up. My colleagues are all gathered round the table and they all applaud me. One of them quickly lights a tiny candle that's set in a holder on top of a pile of croissants.

Bill comes and hugs me. 'Welcome back, sis. We've all missed you.'

And, of course, I'm instantly teary. I blow out the candle and they all hug me while I try to hold it together.

'Thanks, guys. It's good to be back.' And, at this moment, I really mean it. We have a wonderful, creative, fun team here and I should be grateful that I love my work.

'Let's get breakfast,' Bill says. 'We can fill you in on where we are with various projects.'

I'm handed the croissant – minus the candle – and a cup of strong coffee. I need both. I can't deny that I'm tired. I wanted to be firing on all cylinders today, but I slept fitfully while Chris snored next to me. We take our seats at the table and I listen as various colleagues give updates on the project they're working on. Business is booming, which is good to hear.

When it's Bill's turn, he says, 'I need to set up another meeting with the consortium for the eco-hotel. I'm aiming for next week or maybe the week after. It'll be down in the New Forest site, Jodie. Are you OK to come along with me?'

'Try keeping me away,' I reply.

'We'll take the car rather than the train. It'll be an early start too as I'd like to get ahead of the traffic.'

'No problem. I can't wait to get stuck in.'

'I'll show you what we've already been given, but this is the first time we'll see the full plans and the site itself. If you can put some rough ideas together over the next few days, so that we've got something to show them, that would be great.'

'Will do.' I'm eager to get cracking on this as it's been brewing for a while. I'm sure we can do a great job with the interior design. It's right up our street and I'm glad that Bill feels able to trust me with it. If we get it, it will be a feather in our cap. Or as Marilyn would probably say 'a feather in our eye'. It makes me smile to think of her. Marilyn won't be wearing a drab black and white outfit today, that's for sure. I get an unbidden pang of longing for my friend – and, of course, for Ned.

Bill must see the shadow cross my face as he frowns at me and leans in to me. He lowers his voice. 'Sure you're OK?'

'Yeah.' I nod vehemently. 'Fine.'

The meeting breaks up and I head to my office. Bill follows me and closes the door behind him.

'It's good to have you back, sis,' he says when we're alone. We hug each other. 'I genuinely mean that. I'm lost without you.'

'You're never without me.'

'You know what I mean.'

I take my place behind my glass desk and run my hands over the surface. It seems like a long time since I've been here. Bill sits on the scarlet velvet sofa that's by the window.

'Good to be home?' he questions.

I wrinkle my nose. I can't lie to my brother. 'Parts of it,' I admit.

'Things still not good with you and Chris?'

'It's going to take time.'

'But you felt like your break on the Isle of Wight did you good?'

301

'Brilliant,' I say. 'I think I've left a little bit of me there. It's a fabulous place, Bill. You should try going out to your own houseboat. You might like it.'

We both laugh.

'I hope we get this eco-hotel project,' Bill says. 'I've got my eye on a chateau in France that I'd like to renovate.'

I shake my head at him in disbelief. 'Do you *never* stop?'

'No!' He smiles at me. 'You're good in yourself though?'

'Yeah. I feel a bit weird being back here, like I've got jet lag.'

'It will take a few days to settle in again, I'm sure. Anything else?'

'We've called the baby Lottie,' I tell Bill with a happy sigh. 'And I don't want us to ever forget her. She might not be with us, but I want her always to be part of this family.'

'I was looking forward to being a doting uncle,' he says. 'I mourn her loss too, Jo.'

'I know. We all do.' Though I am guilty of forgetting how this has impacted on other people.

'Will you try for another baby?'

'I don't think so.' I shrug. 'Chris and I are miles away from that. I'm going to concentrate on my work for now and see if he and I can patch up our relationship.'

'It would be sad to see this destroy you guys,' my brother says. 'You were always good together. I hope you sort it out.'

'Me too,' I agree.

He stretches and says, 'I'd better move or I'll be asleep on here. This sofa is too comfortable.'

'Late night?'

'Early hours,' he tells me.

'Schmoozing?'

'Dating,' he counters. 'A guy I met online.'

'Hopeful?'

He shrugs. 'Yeah. Maybe. For now.'

302

'Don't sound too enthusiastic.'

'He was nice,' Bill adds. 'We had fun.'

'I want you to find someone to love,' I tell him.

'I don't have time for love.' Bill pushes himself out of my sofa and comes to kiss the top of my head. 'I'll leave you to it. Shout if you need any more details or input. I'm in most of the day.'

'Thanks, Bill.' We exchange a smile. 'For everything.'

Chapter Seventy-One

I try to concentrate on my work, but fail. My mind keeps drifting to Cockleshell Bay, to Ned. I wonder what Marilyn is doing now. She'll be missing the work and having someone to fuss over but, knowing Bill, he'll still be paying her. I hope the weather is good so that George isn't out being a living statue in the rain. I hope Ida has got a new coffee machine and is less cranky.

I sit and look out of the glass box of my office, feeling as if I'm in someone else's life. It will take a few days, a few weeks, maybe even a few months, to get back to it.

Before I hit the pile of documents that Bill has sent to my computer, I pick up my mobile and call Della.

'Chummie,' she says. 'Where are you? Back in the land of the living?'

'Yeah. Yesterday.'

'You came home with Chris then? He wasn't sure that you would.'

'Me neither.'

'Is all well between you?'

'That might be stretching it a bit,' I say. 'But we're working on it. I was calling to see if you're hitting the gym at lunchtime.'

'Yeah,' she says. 'Why not?'

'OK. I'll see you there. One-ish?'

'Sounds good to me. Got to dash. Laters.'

I hang up and smile. I've missed Della too. She's always so energetic and so upbeat, she never fails to cheer me up. I can't wait to see her again at lunchtime – a bright spot in my day.

So I drag my mind from its reverie and work meticulously through the papers for our meeting next week with the eco-hotel people, wanting to make sure that I'm up to speed and can support Bill. I jot down some ideas that I can flesh out later. This is a very exciting project and I'm glad that my brother trusts me to be part of it. Eventually, the company are looking to roll out hotels across the country and abroad, so it's a big deal for us.

The alarm on my phone goes off just before one which gives me time to grab my gym bag and head out to meet Della.

'Back in an hour,' I shout to Bill as I pass his office.

'You're liking the project?' he shouts back.

'Love it!' Then I'm out of here and dash down the street to the gym that's virtually equidistant between my office and Della's.

I quickly change and head for the exercise bikes where we always warm up. There's a bank of them that face a huge window overlooking the street. They're nearly all occupied, but Della is already pedalling away and the one next to her is free.

'Hey,' I say when I get to her.

She stops her machine and comes to hug me. 'I'm not sweaty yet. Just started.'

'I'm out of practice,' I say.

'It'll be like riding a bike,' she assures me and we both giggle. Then she holds me away from her and scrutinises me. 'Looking good, girlfriend! The seaside clearly suits you.'

I realise that I've really missed my best friend. Della always knows the right thing to do, the right thing to say. 'I wish you could have been with me. It's lovely over there. Bill's boat is amazing and the location is beautiful.'

'But it's *England*,' she pouts. 'I only do exotic locations. If you'd gone to Bali, I would have been straight on a plane.'

'Chris said pretty much the same,' I say. 'You should both try it. You might be surprised.' But, in truth, I'm not entirely sure that the Isle of Wight would suit Della or my husband at all.

'I've not got long,' Della says. 'We'd better get at it. You have no idea how many people I had to scare off to keep this bike free.'

So we climb onto the bikes together and begin our usual routine. If I come here in the evening, which I do occasionally, I'll do some weights or maybe a spin class too. However, at lunchtimes, Della and I just do the bikes then the treadmills so that we can catch up on our gossip. Chris insists that we can't be exercising properly if we've got time to chat so much, but it works for us. Most people here just stick in their earphones and block out everyone else.

I try not to think of my long walks on the beach or my yoga sessions with Ned, the sun on my back, the endless sky and sand on my feet. Instead, I pedal furiously.

'Is Chris glad to have you back?' Della asks a little breathlessly.

'I assume so. He wouldn't have come out to ask me to return home if he wasn't.'

'Were you surprised that he came out there?'

'Yes.' I think of our embarrassing reunion and how Ned walked in unexpectedly too. I'm not going to share that with Della though. It feels wrong.

'What did he say?' she asks.

'Not too much, so far. We need to sit and talk but we're both putting it off.'

'Did he beg? Swear undying love?'

'Kind of.' I don't know why I'm being so cagey with my answers. Perhaps because I think I'll cry if I start divulging too much. 'I'm glad you told him where I was – I think. It's brought things to a head.'

'I didn't have much choice,' my friend says. 'He forced it out of me.'

'Well, I'm back now.'

She glances sideways at me, puffing away. 'Did you ever ask him whether he'd been seeing anyone else?'

'Not directly. We're both shying away from it. I'm still sure he has, though. And, let's face it, he could have been up to anything while I've been away. I'm sure Meg would have been happy to comfort him.' Della knows exactly what I think of Chris's colleague.

She rolls her eyes sympathetically and says, 'Cow.'

Yet, it also makes me think about my own night with Ned. I wasn't exactly blameless when I was away and am glad that my face is reddened from cycling as it hides the flush of pleasure that I feel. It doesn't take much and I'm back there imagining his body above me, his mouth, his hands, on me.

'I'm sure Chris was a good boy,' Della pants.

I snap my attention back. 'I don't know. You might be right.' Though I have my nagging doubts. 'He tried very hard when we got home. We had quite a romantic evening at Night Owl.'

'Oh.' For some reason Della sounds a little bit put out. 'That sounds nice. I didn't know he was the romantic type.'

'You know Chris well enough by now,' I say. 'He's not normally. But I think he's prepared to give our marriage his best shot. I am too.'

'We should go out one night, hit the bars, go crazy,' Della says, huffing and puffing like a steam train as she pedals faster. 'To celebrate the return of my best Chummie. This week?'

'Maybe. I've got a lot to catch up on. I can see me pulling a

307

few late nights. I'm going down to the New Forest with Bill to look at an important project next week. It'll be full-on and I want to make sure I'm up to speed.'

'I'm kind of busy too,' she admits. 'Another time, then. Soon, though.'

'Yes. Definitely.'

'Lunchtime torture same time tomorrow?'

I nod. 'Wouldn't miss it for the world.'

So we spend another fifteen minutes on the exercise bikes while Della tells me about work and how she hooked up with a couple of guys on Tinder in the last few days. We laugh at the disastrous outcomes of both of them.

'One guy only wanted to use the back door,' she says, widening her eyes. 'First date. Cheeky bastard.'

'You're kidding me.' I look at her, scandalised.

'I wish. There are some real weirdos out there.'

'You didn't let him?'

'Of course not. What do you take me for? Told him to jog on. And when he'd jogged on, jog on a bit more.'

'You're terrible,' I tell her. 'But you should be careful. You don't even know these men. They could be axe murderers.'

'They're all just after sex. But I can't complain. It's not as if I'm looking for a husband on there. I like getting low down and dirty with strangers. Even the rubbish ones add variety,' she laughs. 'What can I say?'

I think of my night at the festival with Ned and how tender and caring it was. I'm not ready to confide in Della yet. It's too soon, too raw.

'You don't think you'll ever settle down?'

'Nah. You wait, when I meet the man of my dreams he's bound to be hooked up with someone else or be gay. When you get to my age, they all come with baggage.'

'Love is never straightforward.'

'Ain't that the truth, sister?'

'You've never met anyone you really liked?'

'Not on there. But there's someone.'

'Oh, yeah. Who?'

'It's complicated,' she says with a puff of breath. 'Of course it is.'

'Where did you meet him?'

'I can't even be arsed to talk about it,' Della is dismissive. 'It's all too annoying. Let's ditch the bikes and punish ourselves on the treadmill for a bit.'

'OK.' So I let the subject drop. If it goes anywhere, Della will tell me in her own sweet time. She's rubbish at keeping secrets, so I'll get it out of her at some point.

Then she ups a gear on the treadmill, pounding away as if she's running the London Marathon, and I can't keep up with her and talk at the same time.

When we're in the shower, after our session, I think that I am lucky to have Chris. We've been through a terrible time and, if I'm honest, neither of us has handled it well. If we both want to though, we might well just weather the storm. I vow to make more effort to get our relationship back on track. I get a sudden rush of affection for my husband. I need to put Ned out of my mind and concentrate only on going forward. My marriage can survive this if I try hard enough.

After I've towelled myself down, I text Chris. *I love you. J xx*

But he doesn't text me back.

Chapter Seventy-Two

I get home later than usual from the office. There was nothing pressing, I simply wanted to take my time and make sure that I've gone through everything that I've missed before next week.

I've just emerged from the Tube when Chris calls me. 'Where are you?'

'About five minutes from home.'

'Good to hear it. How's your first day been?'

'OK. It's good to be back.'

'I just wanted to check your ETA. You've not eaten?'

'Just grabbed a sandwich after my gym session, that's all. Do you want me to pick something up? I haven't given dinner a thought.'

'Sorted,' Chris says. 'I'll see you in five.'

He hangs up and a few minutes later, I'm opening my front door. There's a wonderful herby smell wafting from the kitchen and the living room is bathed in candlelight. On the table, there's a single red rose in a bud vase.

'You can make a habit of this,' I say. 'It looks and smells lovely.'

'Ready meal,' Chris admits. 'Marks and Sparks Gastropub have done the catering.'

I peel off my jacket and hang it in the hall, feeling more tired than I'd like to admit. I wonder if Chris has romance on his mind as a hot bath and an early night might be more on the cards for me.

As I go into the kitchen area, Chris pours me a glass of wine and hands it to me. It's red, heavy and hits the spot. I sigh as it works its magic.

'I thought we'd celebrate your first day back at work.'

'Thanks. It went well. Bill's keen to get me right in the thick of it. We're off to the New Forest next week for the day for a project we're both keen to handle.'

'Sounds good. It'll give you something to get your teeth into.'

'Yeah. My mind is buzzing with ideas.' Another swig of wine before I say, 'I texted you earlier. No reply?'

He glances at his phone and sees my earlier message. 'Sorry, Jodie. Missed this one completely. My day was madness.' He grins at me as he reads it. 'That's nice to know.'

'I was worried,' I admit. 'I thought it might have been for another reason.' In these days of instant technology, it's easy to read something into a message, or lack of it, that isn't there.

'No. I love you too. Of course I do.' He comes to snake his arm round my waist, pulling me close so that he can plant a kiss on my mouth. Then the pinger goes.

'Dinner is ready.' Chris opens the oven and a cloud of mouth-watering steam billows out. So he dishes up and says, 'On the menu for this evening are lamb shanks with honey-roasted root vegetables and some kind of potato thingy. I forget. Threw the wrapper in the bin.'

I laugh. 'Sounds amazing. Potato thingy is my favourite.'

At the table, we sit opposite each other in the candlelight and the atmosphere is decidedly less strained than when we did this on *Sunny Days*.

I eat heartily and, whilst it may not exactly be home-cooked fayre, it still tastes pretty good and is very welcome. 'This is lovely,' I say. 'Thank you. My sandwich with Della seems a long time ago.'

Chris looks up at me. 'You saw Della today?'

'Yeah. Usual gym stuff. I ache all over now. I'll be as stiff as a board tomorrow.'

He forks food into his mouth and chews thoughtfully before asking, 'Did she say anything?'

'About what?'

'I don't know.' He shrugs. 'What do women talk about? What's she up to these days?'

'You talked to her while I was away.'

'Only to find out where you were. Is she seeing anyone?'

'Her usual Tinder disasters.' I laugh. 'I don't know how she does it. There seems to be a different bloke every week if not every night. The things she was telling me she did with one guy. I can't even repeat the story. It would make your hair curl.'

Chris looks suitably horrified.

'She doesn't have any trouble pulling men, but I wish she'd find someone nice. I'd hook her up with Bill if he wasn't gay.' Then I think again. 'Actually, I love her to bits but wouldn't wish her on my worst enemy. I think Della would be a whole new level of high-maintenance. We're going to have a long overdue night out, next week sometime if we can both make it.'

'I'm out with clients tomorrow night,' Chris says, taking a swig of his wine. 'Will probably be a late one.'

'I'll stay on at the office as well, then. I have more than enough to keep me busy.'

When we've both finished, I sit back and massage my tummy. 'I'm fit to burst.'

'It's good to see that you have your old radiance back.' My husband clutches my hand across the table.

'Some of it,' I agree. 'I'm certainly in a better place than I was.'

'I know that you don't want to discuss it now, but we *can* try for another baby.'

I go to speak but he presses on.

'I feel that I've learned a lot these past few months. I've grown up, Jodie. This has changed me, has changed both of us.'

Is that what I want to hear? There's still an emptiness inside me, a longing. But do I want to go through another pregnancy? I'm not sure that I can face it. What if it ends in heartbreak once more? It's taken its toll on me – on us. If I were to lose the baby again I might never recover.

'No pressure this time,' Chris continues when I don't offer anything. 'No IVF. If it happens, it happens. None of the stress, but all of the fun. And, if we can't have a child, we're still happy, aren't we? We can go on ludicrously expensive exotic holidays, take up ridiculous hobbies, get a cat!'

'I don't like cats,' I point out.

'Not a cat, then. But we can do other things. That's the point I'm trying to make. If there's a void there, we can fill it.'

'I thought that you'd met someone else,' I confess. We may as well confront this now. 'I was sure that's what you'd done.'

Chris looks away from me. 'I think we've *both* done things – and said things – that we bitterly regret.'

So he suspects that Ned and I have been intimate. I'm not surprised. How could I be? Yet, it seems that this is as close as we will come to both admitting our failures as husband and wife.

'All I want now is a fresh start.' Chris looks at me earnestly. 'No raking over old ground, no mud-slinging, no recriminations. What's done is done.'

So that's it? What happens on the Isle of Wight stays on the Isle of Wight?

'We are where we are,' Chris concludes. 'I just want you and me to be happy again.'

313

'I'd like that too.' And I feel a relief that, whilst we haven't aired or shared our secrets, we seem to have turned a page.

'Come to bed,' he says.

'The washing-up?'

'It'll wait until morning.'

So we go to bed and Chris is gentle, caring, holding me as if I was precious china. I try my very best to relax and not push him away. And I keep my eyes wide open so that I see my husband above me, because I'm frightened that if I close them, I might see someone else.

Chapter Seventy-Three

If getting back to normal means that Chris and I work late every night and hardly see each other, then we're pretty much back to normal. I'd like to say that I've settled back into my life seamlessly, but I still miss waking to the stillness of the harbour, walking on the beach and the peaceful blackness of the nights. Ned. I'm sure it will pass.

I get through mountains of work, batter the exercise bikes with Della most lunchtimes and exist on whatever food Marks & Spencer provides. I do manage to finish George's book and thoroughly enjoy it. I even have a little weep as, after all her trials and tribulations, the heroine gets her man. I hope George gets his own happy ending too with a book deal. I text Marilyn every day and get chatty ones in return with the usual slew of random emojis – today it included an alien, a kiss, two surprised eyeballs and a vampire. She tells me about George, Ida, all of her kids and their children, but doesn't mention Ned at all and I don't ask.

I've been home for over two weeks now. Chris and I haven't made love again. It wasn't a great situation last time as I was just so tense and we've both avoided it. But I have to admit that things are gradually – very gradually – getting better between us. When Chris eventually comes home at night, he cuddles up in bed with me. And, while I can't say that I'm entirely relaxed with him, the memories of Ned holding me are slowly fading. So that has to be a good thing, right? Given time, I suppose, he'll be a distant memory. Of course, I think of him every time I hold the mother and baby sculpture – how could I not? It still brings me such comfort and I'm grateful to him for it. I never contacted him to say so – I daren't – but I hope that he knows somehow.

Today, I'm going down to the New Forest to see the site of the eco-hotel with Bill and meet the directors. I think the ideas I've put together are some of the best that I've come up with for any project and can only hope that they think so too. I have everything crossed.

I've hardly slept a wink as I've been going over my presentation in my head and, even though Bill's not picking me up until six o'clock, I've been wide awake since four. This is a big deal for our company and a lot of our team's salaries are riding on it.

As I go to slide out of bed, eager to start the day, Chris reaches out for me. 'Not yet,' he murmurs, pulling me back. 'Snuggle up.'

'Five minutes,' I say as I rest my head on his shoulder. 'I'm too wired to lie still.'

'Eco-hotel?'

'Yes. I'm buzzing.'

'Why the ungodly hour?'

'Bill wants to get ahead of the traffic.'

'Wouldn't the train have been quicker?'

'Probably, but we need to drive out to the site too, so he wanted to have the flexibility. If it goes well, we might stay down there and have dinner with the clients.'

'You'll be late home?'

'Yeah. We have a full day. I'll text you when we're leaving.' Then I start fidgeting.

'Go,' he says, kissing my forehead. 'I don't want to stand between a woman and her work.'

I slip out of bed and pull on my dressing gown. Coffee before my shower, I think. 'What are you up to today?'

'Not much.' Chris bunches the duvet round him. 'A quiet-ish one in the office.'

'Want coffee?'

'No. I'm going to get my head back down for another hour. Wake me to say goodbye.'

'OK.' I get my clothes out of the wardrobe so that I don't disturb him raking through the rack and take them through to the main bathroom. If I get ready in here then he won't hear me.

I have an extra strong coffee, then another. There's not much in the fridge and I think how much I could do with a Marilyn at home. I find a yoghurt that's still, just about, in date and make do with that. I'm sure Bill will want to stop for a break on the way down and I can grab something then.

When I've showered and dressed, I run through my presentation again. Then Bill texts me to say he's parked outside and I gather my stuff together. I put my head round our bedroom door and see that Chris is fast asleep again. He'll need to get up for work shortly but, for now, I decide not to disturb him. I stand next to him at the bed and look at his handsome face, soft in repose. Why is the connection not there any more, I wonder? Is it still because of losing Lottie or is there more to it than that? I could be looking at a stranger rather than my husband of ten years. As I plant a gentle kiss on his forehead, I vow to try harder to make this all right.

317

Chapter Seventy-Four

'Hey,' I kiss Bill as I get into the car. I take in his crisp white shirt, his dark blue suit. There's a jacket and matching tie hanging on the hook on the rear door. The quiff in his hair is still damp and his neat beard is freshly groomed. 'Looking sharp.'

'Feeling sharp,' he says. 'You?'

'Hell, yes. Let's do this.'

He slips the car into gear and off we go. It's a beautiful sunny day and Bill has Freya Ridings on the iPod. I'm looking forward to spending the entire day with my brother. It's something that we do too little of. What socialising we manage to fit in is generally worked around client dinners.

'This is nice,' I say. 'I don't see enough of you outside the office.'

'I know. We should do more.' He manoeuvres the car through the traffic that's already building. 'You sold me on my own houseboat. Maybe we should do a long weekend out there at some point in the summer, hang out on the beach, have barbeques, drink beer. You, me, Chris. Maybe my new beau – if it works out. I'm planning to take some holiday this year.'

'You *never* take holiday.' In all the years we've worked together,

I don't think Bill has ever had more than a day or two off work. He thinks the place will collapse without him. Mind you, I used to think that too. 'I'll believe it when I see it.'

'Let's put it in the diary,' he says. 'Then it's written in stone.'

'Yeah.' But how can I do that? How can I go and stay there when Ned is next door? This would be a good moment to tell Bill about my time there, but I don't.

'Everything's OK again between you and Chris?'

'We're trying our best,' I tell him. 'I hope that it's enough.'

Then we turn the conversation to business, which is much safer ground, and talk through our proposal. Bill is as keen to get this contract as I am, if not more so.

Freya Ridings gives way to Jack Savoretti as we head out of London on the M3 towards the New Forest National Park and Brockenhurst, our ultimate destination. As we skirt past Southampton and head further south, I realise how close we are to the Isle of Wight. I could hop on the ferry and be there in an hour. I wonder what Ned is doing now. Is he on the beach enjoying some al fresco yoga? Needless to say, despite my good intentions, I haven't done any since my return.

The morning sun coming through the glass warms my face and I kick back and listen to Bill as he talks about future plans for the company. However, as his voice flows over me, my mind still keeps drifting back to dangerous territory. I'd love to feel the sand between my toes, splash in the waves, laugh with Ned over some stupid little thing.

'You're quiet,' Bill says when he realises that I'm not responding in the right places.

'Sorry,' I say. 'I've a lot on my mind.'

'Want to talk about it?'

I shake my head. 'Not much.'

'You're still not quite yourself yet.'

'No,' I agree.

'We've not loaded too much on your plate too soon? I can get someone to assist you. Kade's workload is pretty light at the moment.'

'I can manage. To be honest, it's been a welcome distraction. Like you, I really want this project.'

'Together we're invincible.' Bill grins. 'They won't know what's hit them, sis.'

My heart swells with love for my brother. He's always kind, always here for me. 'I hope you're right.'

Chapter Seventy-Five

We meet our clients at Twitchell Grange – one of their boutique hotels that's already been established for several years in the New Forest. This is a great place too. While the outside looks traditional – mostly Victorian, I'd say – the interior is contemporary and chic.

There are three directors here today. Two men, one woman. They all look scary, like they might eat puppies and kittens for breakfast, and my nerves go on full alert. We shake hands as Bill makes the introductions, then go to settle ourselves in the private sitting room that's been reserved for us. We have a welcome coffee, exchange pleasantries while I try to eat a warm, fresh croissant elegantly. Bill has the advantage of having met them before, but this is my first time and I can tell that they're checking me out. And why wouldn't they? There's a lot of money at stake here.

While they're refilling our cups and chatting to Bill, I have a good look at their chosen style of décor for this hotel. Where we're sitting, there's a purple velvet sofa and lime green side chairs, mixed with traditional checks in plum and grey. The floor is blonde oak and the traditional chandelier is complemented by modern glass wall lamps. Whoever put this together has done a great job. Two huge windows look over the traditional gardens and flood the room with light.

Once we've had our coffee, it's my turn to talk. So I hand out brochures and send my project to the waiting screen on the wall.

'I thought I'd run through a few of my ideas to give you a feel for our work. I've put some storyboards together.' I click my first computer-generated slide which gives an overview. 'I'm calling this particular look Woodland Boho.' Which raises a smile and I feel a moment of relief. 'The setting you've chosen is fantastic and I wanted to make sure that we utilise that to the very maximum. My designs bring the outside inside, so that transition between the forest and the indoor spaces of the hotel is as seamless as possible.'

I flick up my first design for the reception area. 'I see it as rustic, but contemporary. Soothing rather than busy with a contained use of natural materials. The walls here are rough lime plaster painted white, the floors a dark traditional oak. The main trees in the New Forest are oak, ash, beech and elm, so I've taken my palette from that.' I use my pointer. 'The reception desk would be informal, a lengthways slice through a large oak trunk and following the contours of the wood.'

'We're taking down as few trees as possible to respect the ancient woodland.' The one female director, Eleanor Garten, looks across at me. 'And then we'll replant the same number in the grounds.'

'That's good to know.' In the centre of the reception area there's a planned glass enclosure that's open to the sky, within which there'll be a specimen tree planted. 'The trees that are felled can be used throughout the hotel, so nothing will go to waste,' I explain.

322

Eleanor again. 'We want this hotel to be completely carbon neutral.'

'That's been at the forefront of our minds and I don't think we'll have any difficulty achieving your aims. To complement your ethos I've designed the rooms to feel as natural as possible. This is my rough idea for the main lounge.' I flick to the next slide. The architects have created an amazing space. Floor-to-ceiling windows all along one wall will look right into the forest. 'Once more, I've tried to emphasise the outdoor feel. The floor in here is wood, but this time parquet-style, combining the different natural colours. One wall is clad in dark brick and features a heavy wood fireplace topped by a statement mirror. Contemporary globe lights will hang from the rafters and one wall will be entirely lined by open bookshelves. The colour palette for the furnishings is autumnal shades and I'd like to source some mustard and rust-coloured velvet sofas. The side tables will be wood with a sixties, Ercol-vibe.'

'That's stunning,' Eleanor says. The others nod in approval though she seems to be the one taking the lead. It's obviously Eleanor who I have to impress.

Behind their heads, Bill winks at me. He's beaming from ear to ear. This is going well. He's largely leaving this to me, other than chipping in every now and again to clarify something. We work well as a team and I'm glad that he's trusted me with this contract which I know means so much to him.

'We'll move onto the bar area. I've gone with the theme of "rest".'

'I was actually thinking of calling it something similar to that,' Eleanor pipes up. 'That would work.'

'Here I see cosy seating set into chunky wood banquettes with soft furnishings in shades of the forest – juniper, fern, moss, pine. Lots of plants, trailing ivy, evoking a real woodland feel.' In the bar, folding doors will open right out onto the terrace. 'The tables will be marble and I've sourced this particular one from Italy.' I show them a dark green marble veined with black that looks like the roots of trees. 'I thought to give it a modern twist we could use neon signs with keywords like rest, relax, enjoy.'

They all nod again. 'It's good.'

So, buoyed by their enthusiasm, I press on to present what I've envisaged for their bedrooms, including the main suite which is like a fairy glade fantasy with rough-sawn wood on the walls and leaves, birds and butterflies painted on the ceiling. The colour scheme is moss green, lilac and cream. And I have to say that I'd love a room like this myself.

They applaud when I finish going through my ideas which brings a satisfied flush to my cheeks.

'Great work,' they all agree.

Eleanor says, 'I'm sure you'd like to get out to the site to see progress as soon as you can but, before we do, I'd like to show you this.' She gets out her phone and flicks through it. 'I recently discovered this artist and I've commissioned a piece from him for my home. I think it would be great if we could incorporate some of his designs – ideally within the hotel and in the grounds too. Let's see if I can get this thing to work.'

She waves her phone at the screen. 'He's a great guy. I saw him at a festival last year.' A moment later, an image pops up.

My heart literally misses a beat. I can do nothing but gape at the smiling photo on the screen. It's Ned. Of course, it is. He'd be perfect for this project. I don't know why I haven't considered that before.

'Let me find some of his work.' She flicks another image and a range of Ned's sculptures pop up. 'He works entirely with a chainsaw, but what he produces is astonishing.' She scrolls through them and Ned's work fills the room – some of the sculptures are already familiar, others I've not seen before. 'Good, aren't they?'

I nod, wordlessly, feeling the colour drain from my face as I stare, transfixed.

She turns to me. 'You don't like it?'

'I love it,' I breathe. 'It's perfect.'

'He's my new find. I'm telling all my friends. Though I've a mind to keep him all to myself,' she adds with a conspiratorial laugh.

I should tell her that I know him – but, perhaps, not how well. It would surely help my credibility, if I told her that I already have a sculpture as a gift from him, that he's Bill's houseboat neighbour – yet I can't. I can't bring myself to speak at all.

'I'll give you his contact details,' she says while I stand there like a fool. 'He's called Ned Haddon. Get in touch with him. I'm sure he'd come up with something exciting. He's very easy to work with.'

When I still fail to respond, Bill says, 'Right. We will do.'

She flicks back to Ned's photo. He's smiling out at the camera, his face open and happy – a look I've seen so often. My heart is still beating erratically and I don't know how my legs are managing to support me. I feel as if I need to sit down.

'Makes you want to take up wood sculpture,' Eleanor quips with a wink to me.

'I think we're done here,' one of the men says. 'Shall I get them to bring lunch in?'

'Great,' Bill says.

While they organise lunch and pop out to make some calls, Bill and I are left alone. I fall into the nearest chair. Instantly, Bill's next to me, looking at me with brotherly concern. 'OK?'

'Yeah,' I say. 'Sudden rush of blood to the head. I should have had more breakfast.'

'Lunch is on its way,' he says as he studies Ned's face on the screen.

Bill looks at me again and, I know that at some point later today, he's going to want more than my glib answer.

Chapter Seventy-Six

After lunch, we're in the car heading to the site, following Eleanor and the other directors of the hotel chain who are leading the way.

I still haven't quite managed to regain my senses. Sitting in the car, I'm unsettled, palms clammy, stomach churning. All I could do was pick at a few things from the buffet they provided.

Bill navigates out of the grounds, onto the main road which is bordered on both sides by open heathland. He slows to a standstill as the wild New Forest ponies which flourish in this area wander across the road in front of us. While we wait patiently for them to cross, he turns to me.

'Do you want to tell me why you looked like you'd seen a ghost when they showed the photo of that chainsaw sculptor guy? I thought he looked familiar.'

'He's your neighbour at the houseboat.'

'Is he?'

That makes me laugh and eases some of the tension. 'Oh, Bill.'

Bill chuckles too. 'How am I supposed to know? I've hardly been there.'

'You'd like him,' I say.

'Would he like me?'

'No. He likes ladies.'

'Too bad. He's as hot as hell.' Bill looks at me more closely. 'Do I take it from your reaction that you think so too?'

I nod.

'And do I also gather that he likes you?'

'Rather too much.'

'I see. Does Chris know this?'

'No,' I confess.

We both fall silent as the ponies wander away on the other side of the road and Bill pulls away again.

'You got to know him while you were on *Sunny Days*?'

'He was the one who showed me how to do some yoga,' I confess. 'We used to go to the beach in the morning.'

'I *knew* there was more to that particular madness.'

'We just fell into hanging out with each other.' I make it sound as if it was the easiest thing in the world and, in truth, it's hard not to be at ease with Ned. 'I got drunk with him and we built sandcastles on the beach.' That night is etched so clearly in my memories that, if I think hard enough, I can still feel the sea breeze on my face and taste the salty night air. 'I went to the Spring Oasis festival with him.'

Bill looks at me, blankly.

'It's a big deal on the Isle of Wight,' I assure him. 'Ned's a lot of fun and made me laugh when there wasn't a lot to find funny.'

'I feel quite jealous,' Bill says. 'It seems he made quite an impression on you.'

'He was there when I needed someone to take me out of my misery.'

'Where I'd failed?' My brother sounds sad.

'No one failed,' I correct. 'Least of all you. It was just a horrible, horrible time.'

328

'Did you . . . ?' He looks at me, pained. 'I can't even bring myself to ask my little sister.'

He doesn't have to spell it out. 'Just the once.' I've never hidden anything from Bill and I don't want to start having secrets from him now.

My brother frowns. 'That's really unlike you, Jo.'

'I know. I didn't mean it to happen, it just did. He was there right when I needed someone's arms around me.' It was so much more than that, but how do I begin to explain that to Bill, or to Chris, or even to myself for that matter. 'I like to think that I'm not the cheating kind and this is the one and only time I've ever strayed.'

'You've been under a lot of pressure. It's not hard to understand why you're acting out of character.'

'I don't even know what my "character" is any more.' I rub my fingers over my forehead. 'I think it would have gone further, but then Chris turned up to bring me home.'

What would have happened? I know we'd have spent another night together and then what? Would I have begun a relationship with Ned? I like to think that I would never do that to Chris, but I honestly don't know.

'Have you spoken to him . . . this guy . . . since?'

'Ned.' I shake my head. 'No.' I let out a long, weary breath. 'Since I've been back, I've done my best to forget him. I'm really trying hard with my marriage.' And I am. It surely must be easier for Chris and me to work on our marriage than to throw it all away and start again? That's not to say that I'm not beset with doubts. 'I thought I was dealing with it.'

'Until you saw him again?'

'I didn't expect it. I was so shocked to see him. And yet Eleanor Garten is right. Ned would be perfect for the project. I should have thought so myself.' I think I've been trying so hard to push him out of my mind that it didn't click until now. 'His

329

work is truly amazing. You should see it. You'd fall in love with it too.'

Bill gives me a wry glance.

'Stop it,' I admonish. 'I've behaved very badly and I'm trying to making amends.'

'Chris suspects, though?'

'Yes. He's said as much. We've both decided to put it behind us. I'm pretty sure he'd been seeing someone else at work – for quite some time. Meg's my prime suspect. He hasn't mentioned her at all and he used to talk about her all the time.'

'A sure sign,' Bill agrees.

'We haven't actually discussed anything properly, but I think that's over too. He's been very attentive since I got back. I couldn't ask for more.'

'You think you can patch it up.'

I look at Bill, bleakly. 'I thought so.'

'Can you work with this guy if we get him to do some stuff for the hotel?' Bill asks. 'His work did look like a brilliant fit. Or will it be too complicated? I can deal with him or there'll be other sculptors we can approach.'

But no one quite like Ned. 'Let me think about it,' I say. 'We've got time.'

'You'll be blown away by the site.' Bill's back in business mode. 'I can't wait for you to see it.'

'Are we nearly there yet?' I tease. He was always the one to be saying this as a child. He was the one impatient to be at our destination, just as he is now.

He keeps his eyes on the road when he says, 'One last question. Do you love this Ned?'

'I don't know,' I admit.

'Actually two questions,' Bill adds. 'Do you love Chris?'

'I don't know that either.'

Bill reaches for my hand and squeezes it. 'Life is short,' he says. 'You of all people know that. Don't spend it with the wrong person.'

But that's easier said than done, isn't it? I've made vows to Chris, we have shared history, shared highs and lows. Our foundations have been rocked, but we can recover. Can't we? I had fun with Ned – more than I should. I look at him, even in a photograph, and my insides liquefy, my heart yearns for him.

Yet last time I saw him, he was angry with me and I don't know what else, if anything, he feels for me at all. Is that worth throwing everything away for?

Chapter Seventy-Seven

The site of the eco-hotel is right on the edge of the New Forest. Work has already begun and the main building is up to first floor level, so we can walk through the shell and get an impression of how the rooms will be.

The place is overrun by tradesmen and we dodge them as we go. Even though it is, literally, a building site, we can still tell where the huge windows will be, how the light will fall into the rooms.

'It's going to be stunning,' I tell Eleanor. 'You must be very excited.'

'The place is cutting edge in terms of build and technology used to run it,' she tells me. 'If it goes as we plan, then we'll roll out the same design and ethos worldwide.'

I make notes as we progress through the space. Then we go out into the grounds and walk down towards the towering, ancient trees of the forest. I remember that the last time I walked through the woods, it was with Ned at the festival. Now that my mind has been opened to him again, I can't stop thinking about him.

'Some of this is our land where it joins the forest. We're

planning to have tree-houses here. High-end luxury but, again, eco-friendly.'

I drag myself back to the conversation and try to concentrate.

'They're not on the design brief?' Bill says.

'No. We've not put that out to tender yet,' she says.

Eleanor's right, I think that it would be a wonderful job for Ned. I can just imagine him sculpting furniture to go inside too. 'I'd like to have the chance to show you some ideas for those too,' I offer. 'My mind is spinning already with the possibilities.'

'We've certainly liked what you've shown us so far.' Eleanor seems very much to be a woman who knows what she wants. 'I'll send the details over when they're finalised.'

My brain continues to whirr as we walk round the edge of the forest and they show us the planned sites for the tree houses – it flits from Ned to work and back until I feel quite giddy.

Thankfully, we're soon wrapping up the tour but, before we leave, we take one final pass through the hotel.

When we return to our cars, Bill says to the directors, 'Can we take you for some supper? We could reconvene at seven. I'll book a restaurant of your choice.'

'We'll meet you back at Twitchell Grange later and eat there. Does that suit?' It's Eleanor who suggests it and her colleagues nod in agreement. 'I'll sort out the table.'

'It's fine by me,' Bill says.

We all shake hands. 'Until later.'

Bill and I watch them walk away, all smiles.

When they've gone, I sag against the car and Bill blows out a relieved breath. 'I can't tell you how much I want this project.'

'It's all about the chase with you,' I tease.

He laughs. 'You did well. Thanks, sis. Your ideas blew me away. They seemed to be suitably impressed too – as well they should be. Eleanor seems to be running the show and she's definitely on board with your vision. I don't know what that sea air did to you, but you're definitely on your game.'

'Maybe the rest did me good. You think we'll get it?'

'I hope so. It may come down to price, but it looks like they're prepared to spend big bucks to achieve their concept. A project this high-end won't come cheap. This will be their flagship eco-hotel. I don't think they'll cut corners. Have you done any costings?'

'Not yet but, after seeing it all today, I have a better idea of where we're going now. I really want to throw myself into this one. I've never felt so passionate about a project.'

We climb into Bill's car. 'We'll head back to the hotel and work for a couple of hours until it's time for dinner. You have stuff you can do?'

'Always.'

Before he guns the engine, he says, 'Thanks for coming back, Jo. The business is better with you in it. I don't know what it is, but we just seem to spark off each other. Don't run away again. Whatever you need, just talk to me, we can make it work.'

'Thanks,' I say to him. 'I'm not out of the woods yet – which, I fully appreciate, is a terrible pun while we're sitting in a forest – but I'm getting there.'

'Good to hear it.' Bill kisses my cheek. 'Come on, let me buy you a *huge* gin. You deserve it.'

'I'm not going to argue with that,' I laugh and we head back to the hotel through the forest roads, dodging wild ponies on the way.

Chapter Seventy-Eight

While Bill works in the private sitting room, I go out in the garden to phone Chris. I find a bench beneath a tree that's in blossom and settle in the shade.

'Hey,' he answers after a couple of rings. 'How's your day?'

'Good. But we're staying down here and taking the clients out to dinner.'

'That means it went well?'

'We hope so. They seemed to like our presentation.'

'What time do you think you'll be home?'

'Could be midnight. Maybe we should have stayed overnight, but I haven't got anything with me. It's a long drive for Bill.' I'd offer to share, but my brother is the worst passenger you can imagine. Control freak that he is, he needs to be in the driving seat. 'You'll sort dinner out for yourself?'

'Yeah. I'll probably stay late here too.' I can hear the buzz of his office behind him.

'I'll see you later, then.'

'Safe journey,' he says and then hangs up.

I stare at my phone for too long. Sadly, I still don't get the warm, fuzzy feeling I used to when I spoke to my husband. Now there's just an emptiness where that should be. Will it ever come back? Can you force something like that?

Bill is focused on his MacBook when I go back into the sitting room and so I get mine out too. I try to look at work stuff, but my mind can't settle. Seeing Ned up there on the projector has filled my brain with images of him and I decide not to fight it any longer. I wonder if he has a website. I'm surprised I haven't done it before, to be honest, but I Google him now. I convince myself it's work, research.

Sure enough, there's a website and the same photo I saw earlier smiles out at me. My heart flips once more. This is bad. I manage to tear my eyes away from his face to scroll through the gallery of his work. Ned's portfolio is more extensive and even more appropriate than I imagined. It would be great to work with him, but could I do it? Would it be wise? Even if he'll agree to come on board, should I risk the contact with him? Should I get Bill to do it? Or, as my brother suggested, should we look at someone entirely different?

When I've looked through Ned's site more times than I really need to, I Google *wood sculptors* and check out the top three that appear on the first page of searches. Their work is good, no doubt about it, but it doesn't have the finesse or the magical quality that Ned's sculptures do. Damn.

I hadn't realised but Bill has come to look over my shoulder. 'Not in the same league as golden boy,' he says.

'No.'

'Want me to contact him?'

'I don't know. I'm trying to get that straight in my head. This is my project and I should be professional enough to run with it. Let me think about it?'

'It's just about time for dinner.'

I check my watch and Bill's right. I don't know where the time has gone.

So we head to the dining room to meet our clients again and have a productive and fun dinner. I like Eleanor; she reminds me a lot of Della. She's a fun, feisty and no-nonsense person. I think I'm going to enjoy working with these guys – at least, I hope we get the opportunity to do so. The food in the restaurant is superb and the wine flows, for me at least. And, while they don't come outright and say that we've got the contract, the directors of the eco-hotel are making all the right noises.

We're both happy when we get back in Bill's car and, accompanied by the sounds of Will Young for most of the journey, drive back to London. I close my eyes, letting the soothing music calm my troubled soul while Bill chats away, telling me of some new contacts he's made, and I try not to think too much about Ned.

Chapter Seventy-Nine

It's gone midnight when we pull up outside my apartment, but I see that the lights are still on.

I kiss Bill. 'See you in the morning, big bro.'

'I might not make it for the eight o'clock meeting,' he says with a stifled yawn.

Yet I know that he will. It's been a long day, but Bill has boundless energy and will be at work before any of us. I, on the other hand, might struggle a bit more.

I gather my belongings. 'Well done. It's been a good day.'

'The best,' he agrees. 'Even if we don't get the contract.'

'We will,' I assure him. 'I feel certain of it.' Then I get out of the car and wave as he leaves.

Letting myself into the apartment as quietly as possible, I tiptoe down the hall in case Chris has dozed off on the sofa. But there's no one in the living room. There is, however, a bouquet of flowers in a vase on the kitchen counter – though still in their cellophane wrapping. They look like they came from a supermarket. I go to make a cup of tea and find two wine glasses in the sink, one of them bearing a lipstick stain. My heart goes cold. Meg?

'Hey,' Chris shouts from the bedroom as I'm staring at the glasses. 'Come and say hello.'

I go through to him. He's sitting propped up in bed with his laptop on his knees. 'Sorry, I thought you might be asleep.'

'Nah. Still working,' he says. 'Nearly done, though.' He reaches for me and pulls me down to sit down next to him.

I frown when I ask, 'Have you had company?' I hate how suspicious that makes me sound.

'Ah, yes. Della dropped by.'

'Della?' That wasn't the answer I expected. 'She knew I was going down to the New Forest today. Did she forget?'

'No. She brought flowers for you as she knew today was a big deal.'

'Oh, that's nice of her.' And unusually kind. Though it makes me smile to think of her in a supermarket. Definitely not her style. She'd normally get her assistant to phone an upscale florist to deliver.

'She stayed for a quick glass of wine. I'd only just got home.'

It's unlike Della to pop in like that. She and Chris rub along when they have to, but they're not exactly over-keen on each other. They both have strong personalities and tend to clash. Plus Della tends to have very little patience with the male of the species, anyway, and Chris does like to do a bit of mansplaining.

'It all went OK?'

'Yes,' I say. 'It couldn't have gone better. We're just waiting for them to give us the go-ahead now.'

'You think they'll choose you?'

'I hope so. My designs really suited their plans. I gave it my best shot.'

'Then you can ask no more.' Chris's lips find mine. 'I missed you today. Come to bed.'

'I'm just going to have a quick cup of tea and a shower,' I tell him. 'I feel dehydrated and crumpled.'

'OK.' Chris looks disappointed. Perhaps my husband has love on his mind, but it's late and I'm tired.

'Do you want some tea?'

He shakes his head. 'Don't be long.'

So I go back through to the kitchen and make myself some peppermint tea and down two glasses of water. The last thing I want for work in the morning is a hangover. While I drink my tea, I hold my sculpture tightly to my chest and sway with it as I look out over the street below. There are moments when I think that everything will be all right again, that I'll slip back into my old life once more. Then there are other times when I feel like I'm living someone else's life, when I want to be back on *Sunny Days*, watching the vast expanse of impossibly blue sky and feeling the sand beneath my feet.

When I hit the shower, my daytime euphoria is seeping away and melancholy has crept in once more. In the bedroom, Chris has settled down and is fast asleep, laptop still open on the bed. I tidy it away, slide in next to him and, though I know it's wrong, I feel relieved that he's not awake.

Chapter Eighty

Chris is grumpy when he wakes up and is stomping around the flat. Sometimes he's best left to his own devices as he crashes and bashes his way out of a bad mood. Today it's taking longer than usual. Every cupboard door in the kitchen is slammed. Everything is done with an accompanying huff. I find myself pussy-footing around him until I can bear it no longer.

'Everything OK?'

He's shovelling cereal into his mouth as if it's his last meal while he stands at the kitchen counter. 'Yeah.' Furious munching.

'Did you not sleep well?'

'I slept fine,' he snaps.

'Is something at work worrying you?'

'Stop fussing.' His bowl and spoon clatter into the sink, chinking against last night's wine glasses as they go. Perhaps it's just a hangover. Something that a couple of Ibuprofen would fix. Maybe he and Della had more than the one glass.

I'm not entirely sure what's changed overnight, but something most definitely has. Was it because he was in the mood for love and I managed to duck out of it? Again. I should try to repair the damage. 'Shall I cook dinner for us? As I was so late home yesterday, I'm planning to leave on time this evening.'

'I might be stuck in the office. Can't say until later.'

'You'll let me know?'

'Don't I always?' he says with an exaggerated sigh and, though he kisses my cheek, it's cursory. 'See you later.'

He grabs his laptop bag and as I shout 'Have a good day' after him, my husband slams out.

What was that all about?

Still unsettled, I pour out some muesli, splash it with milk and then push it away from me. I can't eat. So, instead, I gather my stuff and slip on my coat ready to hit the Tube. Then I notice that Chris has left his phone on the table next to my still-wrapped bouquet from Della.

'Damn,' I mutter. That will put him in an even worse mood. He'll feel like he's left one of his limbs behind. I'll call him when I get to the office and tell him where it is. He'll be in a blind panic when he realises he doesn't have it with him. I could take it to work with me and arrange to meet him at lunchtime to hand it over.

I don't know what makes me do it, but I pick up the phone and punch in Chris's passcode to open it. The phone doesn't open. I wonder if he's changed it? I try another number and that's wrong too. My heart beats more rapidly with each successive failure. I have three attempts before I manage to unlock it. He must have changed it and not told me.

Eventually, I'm in and Chris's messages pop up on the screen. There are the usual slew of work-related exchanges and the normal run-of-the-mill texts from me but, what stands out more, is that the majority of messages are to one person and one person alone. And I know that person so well. It seems as if Chris does too. I feel sick as I read the plethora of text messages between them – increasingly intimate, increasingly graphic.

It isn't Meg that I need to worry about. The woman I've suspected for so long is innocent after all. The texts from her are, indeed, all about work and nothing more. Instead, it seems as if my husband and my best friend are having an affair and have been for some time.

While I was grieving the loss of our child, the two people who I cared most for in the world have been sneaking around behind my back. The knowledge feels like a sucker punch to my stomach. I feel for a chair and sit down, heavily. My mind spins. Della and Chris.

I scroll through the texts – most of them more explicit than I could have imagined – with an increasing sense of despair and anger. There are photos too that show infinitely more of my friend than I'd like to see. Some of them from last night. There's a selfie of them together in our bed. My husband has sent an actual dick pic. I close them down.

I knew that there was someone, but I didn't have any idea that it was Della. All the time that Chris has been pretending to be solicitous, to want to get our marriage back on track, to even try for another baby and yet he's been sleeping with my best friend throughout it. I still can't quite get my head round that. I've become used, to a certain extent, to the rollercoaster of emotions. We've both gone through that. What I can't cope with is the lies. And not just one lie, but a sustained and separate life over months and months that has become one great big lie. I don't know how long I sit there for, almost catatonic, but, eventually, my phone rings and jolts me back to the present.

I glance at my mobile and, on the screen, it's Chris's office number. Behind that is his smiling face on my wallpaper – a photo I took when we were on holiday in the Maldives some years ago when we were happy, in love and any thoughts of starting a family together were way ahead in the future. It's my favourite photo of him, but now his grin just looks duplicitous.

He's obviously arrived at work and has realised his phone is missing. I can imagine how much he must be panicking and for more reasons that I'd previously thought. I don't answer. I can't. What would I say if I picked up?

It rings and rings, but I let the call go to voicemail.

Chapter Eighty-One

I'm not entirely sure how I get to work, but I do. I must have, as usual, gone on the Tube then walked the rest of the way. Yet I remember none of it. The breakfast meeting was a blur. Now I'm sitting here in my glass box of an office feeling as if my life has been turned upside down once more and I'm questioning everything that I knew before.

Because I'm late, Bill has already been into the office and has left again. I'm glad of that as he'd instantly tell that something was wrong. All my colleagues are busy and I catch snippets of chat and laughter, but I can't bring myself to go out and join in with them. I hide away, pretending to be busy. Instead, I go through the motions of working – I move papers around, tap computer keys – but none of it registers. My mind simply isn't on the job.

Now I know why Della was at my place last night and it wasn't just to deliver flowers. How many times have they been together in my home and in my bed? I can't bear to think of it.

While I'm sitting and brooding – a flurry of thoughts racing in my brain, all of them difficult to catch – a text pings in. It's from Della. *Hi, Chummie. Gym as usual? Dxx.*

The audacity leaves me breathless. All this time, while I thought she was my sanity when I was losing my mind, and throughout it all she was sleeping with my husband. I don't even know how to begin to confront her. Well, it looks as if I have an hour to think about it.

I text back: *Def. See you soon. Thanks for the flowers, btw. J xx*

My pleasure. Love you lots. D xx

Pushing down nausea again, I then watch the clock around until lunchtime. If someone gave me an excuse – any excuse – I'd not go at all. Yet another part of me wants to see if I can tell that she's the other woman in my husband's life, if there were any signs that I missed. With heaviness in my heart, I grab my things and head to the gym.

When I arrive, Della is already pedalling away on an exercise bike. She's her usual cheery self.

'Saved one for you, Chummie!' she trills over the thumping music. 'Been here working my lard arse for the last fifteen minutes.'

I climb on next to her and, with extreme reluctance, start pushing the pedals.

'You look a bit glum,' she says with a frown. 'All OK?'

'Fine.' I pin on a smile.

'Yesterday went well?' she asks.

'Yes. It was very thoughtful of you to drop in with those flowers for me. Very kind.'

'My pleasure. Just a little something to cheer you on. I know that it was a big deal for you.'

'You and Chris had a nice evening?'

'I grabbed a quick glass of plonk with him,' she says,

beaming at me. 'Seemed rude just to cut and run.'

I think of the steamy content of their text messages – long discussions about what they did and what they might do next time they meet, the photos of them in my bed – and seethe inwardly. But what to say? How do I challenge my best friend with this? Do I do it now or wait until I've had it out with Chris first? Believe me, I've stewed over this all morning and am no clearer. I have no idea what the etiquette of these things might be.

Della chitter-chatters on about her day and stuff that's going on at work, while I pedal furiously. Emotional pain, it seems, is quite a good motivator for working out.

'What about Mr Complicated?' I ask, keeping my voice as level as possible.

I think I see her flush, but it's hard to tell as she's quite red in the face already. 'Still complicated,' she says. 'I'm hanging on in there, but still having fun while I do.'

'More shagfests with strangers?'

She laughs. 'Whenever I can!'

I wonder if Chris is aware of that? Does he think he's the only one? I wonder just how many men she's sending pictures of her naked and pouting? Not only has she put him at risk by sleeping around with other men, but me too. I feel sick. Sick and angry. Bile is burning my throat.

We move through our usual routine and head to the treadmills.

'I can't stay long today,' I say. 'Stuff to do.' The longer I'm with her the more I want to slap her smug, lying face and I hate myself for feeling like that. I should come clean with her and tell her that I know, tell her that I'm aware she's lying bare-faced to me. But I can't bring myself to do it.

After ten minutes of pounding the machines, we head to the showers. As we strip off our gymwear, I look over at Della.

There's no denying she's all woman. She has curves in all the right places and, only too well, I can imagine her and Chris together.

We enter our separate shower stalls and I have a quick wash. Della is obviously luxuriating in her own shower, as she often does. She's singing softly, 'Nothing Breaks Like a Heart.' I guess we'd both know about that.

Getting out, I dry myself, anger still simmering inside me. I'm furious with her and with myself for not being able to address this directly. When I'm dressed and Della is still happily singing away to herself, I notice that she's left her locker key on the wooden bench outside the shower with her towel. Without really knowing what I'm doing, I sneak up and take her key.

Inside her locker there's her clothes, her handbag, her phone. I scoop them all out. First I put her phone down the loo. Nothing but a top-of-the-range iPhone for Della. For good measure, I flush it. I'm quite horrified at what I've done, but quite pleased with myself too.

Back in the changing room, I open the nearest window and tip the contents of her handbag into the street. Della's purse, many lipsticks, tissues, Kindle, lunchtime sandwich, all hit the ground one after the other with a pleasing clatter or thump. Her favourite Prada handbag goes swiftly after them. Then I follow it by tossing out each and every item of her clothing – blouse, jacket, trousers, ridiculously expensive designer shoes. I watch as her bra and knickers – Agent Provocateur – are caught on the breeze and flutter down to the pavement. There are some rather startled people passing by – especially the ones who have to dodge her pants.

That should tell her that I've found out about her affair with my husband.

Della's singing stops and I hear her turn off the shower. 'Are you still there, Chummie? You've gone very quiet. Chummie?'

But I don't answer her. Instead, I pick up my own things and walk out of the changing room, head held high.

Chapter Eighty-Two

I'm back at my desk, head in my hands, wondering what on earth my next move should be, when Bill bowls in. 'Ta-Dah! I have news,' he announces. 'Good news! Excellent news!'

I look up. 'We got the contract?'

'We did, indeed,' he says. 'You aced it, sis. Eleanor just called. They *loved* the designs. She wants us to develop some ideas for the treehouses too. It's full steam ahead.'

'That's fantastic.'

He stops and grimaces at me. 'Your mouth is saying the right words, but there's not a lot of enthusiasm behind them. I thought you'd be thrilled.'

'I am. Really, I am.'

'So, what's the problem? Is there something I need to know about?'

I sag. 'Trouble,' I tell him. 'Big trouble.'

He sits on my sofa, crossing his long legs. 'Want to tell me about it?'

'I might cry.'

'I can deal with that,' he says. 'I'm a gay man. We like a good cry.'

Taking a deep breath, I launch in. 'I found out that Chris has *definitely* been having an affair.'

Bill raises an eyebrow. 'You thought as much.'

'It's been going on a lot longer than I imagined. And it's with Della.'

'Whoa!' Bill says, eyes widening. 'Your best mate?'

'I believed so. It seems not.'

'Oh, Jodie.'

'I know. What can I say?'

'How did you find out?'

'Chris left his phone at home this morning.' I still have my husband's phone – though I was tempted to throw that down the loo as well. Opening Chris's photo cache at a relevant and quite graphic photo – a selfie of Della naked and on top of my husband – I slide it across the desk. 'And – shame on me – I looked at it.'

Bill picks it up and his eyes go even wider as he looks at the screen. 'Wow.' He blinks a lot, clearly as stunned as I am. 'Good job you did. What a pair of bastards.'

'I could have forgiven him. I *had* forgiven him. But not now that I know it's Della.'

'What did she have to say for herself?'

'I didn't even confront her,' I admit. 'I just didn't have the heart. But I did throw all her clothes out of the window at the gym followed by her Prada handbag.'

Bill guffaws. 'You did *what*?'

'I flushed her phone down the loo too.'

Now he really laughs and I join in a bit too. 'It was wrong of me.'

'I think it was the perfect response,' Bill says.

'I feel so stupid, so humiliated.'

'None of this is your fault. You shouldn't feel like that.'

'I'm not exactly blameless.' Bill knows of my own indiscretion and I'm not proud of that either.

351

'It's hardly on the same scale,' he says. 'You had a reckless one-night-stand. Your husband has had a devious, systematic, long-running affair with your best friend while you've been grieving. He couldn't do anything more hurtful. Shitbag.' Bill is more furious than I've ever seen him. 'What are you going to do now?'

'Leave him.' It's the first time I've articulated it – to myself even. 'What else can I do? It's over between us. It probably has been for a long time.'

'Oh, sis.' Bill comes to my desk and I stand up while he wraps his arms round me. 'You can stay at my place, if that would help.'

'I might. I need to consider my options.' I'm still not thinking straight, I'm sure. 'I'll head home early. I'm no use to you here, anyway.'

'What else can I do?' Bill wants to know.

'Nothing. I need to sort this out myself.' Much as I'm dreading it.

'Call me later,' he instructs. 'I'll only worry about you.'

'I will.'

He holds me tightly and we rock together. 'I'll be fine,' I assure him. 'I've got through worse.'

And I have. I've faced the most terrible tragedy and survived. I should remember that.

Chapter Eighty-Three

As it happens, I get caught up with work and don't leave the office until six o'clock. The last-minute flurry of emails and calls that I had to deal with temporarily took my mind off my troubles. Now it all comes rushing back to me and a darkness that I hoped had started to dissipate threatens to swamp me again. Trying to dodge people as I go, I walk through the streets crowded with commuters, all the workers pouring out of the surrounding offices at the same time. It's grey, raining and I've forgotten my umbrella. Everyone has their heads down and I get shouldered more times than I'd like.

When I get to the Tube station, it's closed due to an 'incident'. That usually means either a stabbing or that someone has jumped in front of a train. It's a horribly regular occurrence these days. Someone won't be going home to their loved ones or perhaps it's the fact they didn't have any loved ones to go home to that affected their state of mind. I confess that in the past, I've been irritated by the inconvenience of a 'jumper', thinking only of the impact on my own plans. Now

I'm overwhelmed with sadness for the person or people involved, their families, their friends.

Instead of marching to the next station or calling for an Uber, I step out of the disgruntled crush of people, find a bench nearby and sit on it. I don't care that the rain seeps through my trousers or that it continues to pour down on my head. I've been through a terrible time, but I've survived and I'm still here. I have a lot in my life to be thankful for. I'm young – relatively speaking – I have a great job and a loving brother. I'm healthy and, by most people's reckoning, wealthy. I have life experiences and, for all the sad times, I've been blessed by an equal amount of good times. It's not all been plain sailing – far from it – but I've weathered the storm and have come out on the other side of it, battered, bruised, but not broken.

I look at London around me and wonder what on earth I'm doing here. I could be anywhere in the world where they don't stab strangers or desperate people don't jump in front of trains. Then I think that there's only one place that I'd like to be right now. The worst is behind me and, ahead, I can see blue skies and sunshine. If I think really hard then I can blot out the rain, the jostling crowds, the sounds of the approaching ambulance siren and imagine that I'm back at Cockleshell Bay. That's where I'd like to be right now with the sun going down on the water and the gentle sway of *Sunny Days* beneath my feet.

My phone pings and I sigh. I think it might be Chris, then remember I have his phone. I wonder if Della's told him yet that I know about them?

Yet when I look at my phone, the text is from Marilyn. At my moment of need, she's still there for me. The message says, *Wish you were here!* and there's a picture of the beach followed by a row of sunshine faces, palm trees, jet skis and a kangaroo.

I wish I was there too.

I don't know how long I sit here but I'm soaked through to the skin when I finally do move. It's a few miles, but as I walk home it gives me time to think.

Chapter Eighty-Four

Chris isn't in the apartment when I let myself in and I'm glad of that. I peel off my soaking coat and drop it in the hall on the tiles. I'll sort it out later along with the wet shoes I kick off. In the kitchen, I open a bottle of red, pour myself a big glass and take three hearty swigs. I have decisions to make and I definitely feel as if a hit of alcohol will help. I'm shivering now and head through to the shower.

The hot water helps to soothe me and all of the anger I previously felt has gone. Even my sadness has faded away and in its place there's a burgeoning sense of purpose. While I'm drying myself, I finish the glass of red. I get dressed in nice, warm clothes – a soft sweatshirt, my favourite jeans, cashmere socks – and, by the time I'm done, I feel almost human again. I deal with my wet coat and shoes then make myself a much-needed sandwich. I missed breakfast and lunch, but now my appetite has returned with a vengeance. When I've eaten it, I walk over to Ned's sculpture by the window and pick it up. As I always do when I hold it, I feel a sense of calm come over me. I know what I need to do and where I need to be.

Not long afterwards, I hear Chris's keys in the lock and,

instead of dreading him coming home, I feel positive for the first time in a long time. I put the sculpture down and wait in the living room for him to come in.

When he does, he looks at me, face drawn. 'I can explain,' he says.

'No need,' I tell him, sadly. 'We've both been out of this relationship for a long time, we just didn't realise it.'

'Della doesn't mean anything to me.'

'That makes it even worse, Chris. I hoped that you were in love with her. I think she loves you. In her own way.'

'She offered me some fun when our life was so bleak. You were so consumed by grief that I couldn't reach you.'

'I don't blame you.' I feel so calm that it's like someone else is having this conversation, not me. 'But we'd lost a child. I couldn't simply turn on being happy again. I just wish it hadn't been my best friend. I'll miss her.'

'She's very upset with you,' my husband says. 'Her phone is beyond repair. All her photos were on it.'

'I saw some of them,' I point out. 'I wish I hadn't.'

He has the good grace to redden. 'Someone took her knickers off the street and her Prada bag. She thought that was quite spiteful of you.'

I laugh when I probably shouldn't. 'I'm sorry, but I'm sure she'll get over it. I think she should count herself lucky that's all I did. I would have quite liked to throw her out of the window, too.'

'I'll end it with her. If that's what you want.' His face is lined with worry. 'Right away. I'll call her and tell her now.'

'She hasn't got a phone,' I remind him.

'Oh.'

'Besides, you'll need her. I'm going to pack a bag and leave. If you want to stay in the flat, we can organise for you to buy me out.'

357

He looks horrified. 'What are you saying?'

'I don't think that I need to spell it out. I'm saying it's over, Chris.'

'We should talk,' he says. 'Properly, I mean. Have counselling. Move somewhere else? I'll do whatever you want to do.'

'Make a go of it with Della,' I say, wearily. 'That's what I want you to do.'

'Don't go, Jodie. You're being hasty. We have so much to lose. I thought we were getting along fine since you came back from the Isle of Wight.'

'We weren't,' I say. 'We tried, but not hard enough.' I don't remind him that all the time he continued to have an affair with my best friend or that I had someone else constantly on my mind.

'You're not thinking straight.'

'On the contrary, I'm thinking straight for the first time in a long while.'

'What are your plans then?' Chris's expression darkens. 'Are you going back there to be with *him*? I'm not blind either, Jodie.'

'I don't know,' I admit. 'But either way, it's over for us.'

Then I go to the bedroom and pull my case out of the wardrobe once more.

Chapter Eighty-Five

I get an Uber and text Bill that I'm on the way to his place. Chris calls me three times while I'm in the car. I ignore them all and, eventually, my phone falls silent.

When I get to my brother's place, he takes one look at me and says, 'I can't have you sad again,' and immediately opens a bottle of champagne. 'This is to celebrate us winning the eco-hotel contract and to drown our sorrows at the demise of your marriage.'

I take the glass he pours for me, gratefully. 'I already have a base layer of red wine.'

'Never a bad thing.' Bill clinks his glass against mine. 'To the future. Whatever it may bring.'

'To the future,' I echo.

'So?' Bill leans against his kitchen cupboards and swigs his fizz. 'How did Chris take it?'

'He acted as if he was shocked.' I shrug. 'He says he doesn't love Della, that he wants me to stay. Honestly, I don't think he knows what he wants.'

'But you do?'

I nod. 'Let me get rid of this.' I glance at my suitcase standing forlornly in the hall. 'Then we can talk.'

'Food? I can order something in.'

'Chinese?' I say even though I've not got much of an appetite. 'Just a few picky bits for me. I had a sandwich a little while ago, so not much.'

As I head to stow my bag in Bill's spare room, my brother picks up his iPad to order dinner.

A short while later we settle on Bill's oversize couch, cartons of Chinese food spread out over the coffee table. Bill seems to have ordered most of the menu. I'm glad I didn't say I was hungry. While we pick at the various dishes, I tell him of my plans. 'If it's OK with you, I'd like to spend the summer at the houseboat. Maybe longer if things work out.'

Bill looks pained.

In all honesty, I'd like it to be permanent, but that seems to be getting ahead of myself. Maybe I won't be welcome there.

'This time I'll work, though.' I still have to earn a living. 'I know you'd prefer me to stay here, but I can work remotely,' I promise. 'You've still got one spare room empty. I could set myself up in there. You'll hardly notice the difference.'

'I like having you around the office.'

'There's Skype,' I offer. 'We can talk every day. Ten times a day, if necessary. And I can come back frequently if you need me for meetings or if you just want to check I'm still alive. I'll be a couple of hours away. That's nothing, these days. You could even come to visit me.'

He rubs at his beard. 'This is going to be a busy time. One of us will need to be down in the New Forest on a regular basis.'

'I can do that. I'll be even nearer to the hotel from the Isle of Wight. We can manage somehow. If we're both willing.'

Bill gives a resigned sigh. 'What does your boyfriend think about this?'

'He's not my boyfriend.' I risk a smile. 'Not yet. I'm doing

360

this for me. Last time I saw Ned, he was furious with me. I'm not even sure it's on the cards for us to get together.'

'You've not spoken to him?'

I shake my head. 'I've tried messaging him, but nothing back yet.'

'If you want him to quote for work on the hotel project, we need to get hold of him soon.'

'I know.' But what I don't know is why Ned is avoiding me so determinedly. I've messaged that it's about work. If nothing else, this contract could be worth a lot of money to him. Perhaps he just thinks it's a ruse to get him to speak to me.

'When do you want to go?'

'Tomorrow?' I venture. 'There's nothing to hold me here but you.'

'So soon? There's no point me trying to convince you otherwise?'

I snuggle against him. 'Not really.'

'You know you can be a total pain in the arse,' Bill complains.

I smile. 'But you love me anyway.'

He slips his arm round my shoulder and I lay my head against him. 'I do,' he agrees. 'And all I want is to see you happy. If that means you moving to the Isle of Wight, then so be it.'

'Thanks, Bill.' I daren't even look at him when I ask, 'Have you got any meetings in the morning?'

'Yes,' he huffs. 'But I can cancel them. I suppose you want me to drive you to the ferry too?'

'That would be lovely of you.' I might sound bold and determined, but I'd definitely like my brother to hold my hand.

Bill shakes his head. 'You've always liked your cake with a cherry on the top.'

Then we both laugh and hold each other tightly.

Chapter Eighty-Six

My darling brother drives me to the ferry port in Southampton and I buy a ticket as a foot passenger, once again choosing the Red Funnel to savour the journey.

We hug each other. 'Phone me the minute you get there,' he says.

'Thanks, Bill.' I squeeze him harder. 'For everything.'

'Go.' He wafts his hand towards the ferry. 'I don't want you to miss it.'

'I'll be back before you know.'

'Tell this guy that his gain is my loss.'

'I will.' If I get the chance.

'I can't watch you sail away,' Bill says. 'I'll blub my eyeballs out.'

'It's not goodbye,' I assure him. 'I'm a couple of hours away. I'll see you very soon.'

Bill's eyes fill with tears and, of course, mine do the same. 'Go on. Go.'

Then, before I change my mind, I leave him and head to the ferry, turning to wave to Bill as I go. It hurts my heart to be leaving my brother again so soon, but I know it's the right thing to do. At least, I hope it is.

This time, I stand at the rail on the ferry with a lighter spirit and hope in my heart. The clouds are like fluffy pillows and the sun is high in the bright blue sky. I lift my face to enjoy its soothing rays. As we leave Southampton, a plethora of colourful little boats bob along beside us and two crazy jet-skiers bounce in the wake from the ferry, twisting and turning their machines with exuberance. The day couldn't be more different than the last time I was heading away from the mainland. There's even a different mood on the boat too. I'm surrounded by crowds of holidaymakers, dressed in bright clothes and sunglasses. Children play on the deck, their shouts like music on the wind. I watch families enjoying themselves and, instead of experiencing the usual sickness in my stomach, I smile broadly at them. I feel as if I'm running towards something rather than running away.

An hour later, as we sail into the bustling harbour at Cowes, it seems as if the island is wrapping its arms around me. I can't wait to get off the ferry and head back to Cockleshell Bay. There's a warmth that spreads through me when I think of Ned and I hope that we can, if nothing else, resume our friendship.

Of course, I'm looking forward to seeing Marilyn and George too. I texted Marilyn this morning to tell her I was coming back and received three lines of emojis in return – everything ranging from a bunch of flowers to an octopus and an ice-cream. I take it from that she was excited.

When I disembark, I grab a taxi and we bounce across the island to Cockleshell Bay. If I'm going to stay here long-term then I should buy a little car so that I can explore more and use it when I need to go to the mainland. I can drive, it's just that I never really need to in London, but it would be nice to take it up again. I get a knot of nervous anticipation the closer we get to the harbour. I'm sure I'm doing the right thing, but what if I'm not? What if it's all a terrible mistake?

We come over the crest of the hill and, ahead of me, I can

see the blue, blue ocean sparkling for all it's worth. It's all I can do not to urge the taxi driver to put his foot down and speed towards our destination. Yet, soon enough, we're pulling up at Bill's houseboat. I pay him and take my case. Anxiously, I glance over at Ned's place, but I can't see him around.

When I let myself into *Sunny Days*, I sigh with relief. I'm here and that's all that matters. There's a sense of home-coming which feels good. The first thing I do is open the doors and go out onto the rear deck to drink in the view of the colourful harbour and, in the background, the reliable solidity of the imposing fort. I breathe in the fresh, salty sea air and, instantly, it seems to cleanse my body of the toxins of London.

Come what may, I can be happy here. I know it.

Chapter Eighty-Seven

I take my time to unpack my stuff to settle my nerves. Then I go and carefully place Ned's sculpture on the bookcase. 'This is our new home,' I say. 'I hope you like it.'

Then I brace myself to go round to Ned's and explain myself to him. I'm excited and nervous about seeing him. But when I go to the door of his boat, I can see that there's no one at home and a little of my excitement at being back dissipates. I won't feel entirely comfortable until Ned and I have cleared the air.

So, plan B is to walk down to the Beach Hut Café to see Ida. Perhaps she can tell me where Ned is. If I'm lucky, he might be on the beach doing some yoga or enjoying a coffee.

There's no need for wrapping up in a jacket and woollies today. The sun is high in the sky, bright and beautiful. I'm sure the temperature must be pushing into the twenties. I skirt along the harbour road and onto the esplanade. There's no sign of George on his usual pitch either and I wonder if he's still here or whether he's gone back to London.

I drop down to the beach and this couldn't have changed more since I was last here. The school holidays must have started as the beach is busy with families who look like they're set up for the duration with rugs, umbrellas, inflatables – all of the things you need for a good day out at the seaside. The little businesses that were closed up out of season are open and ready to trade. There's a queue for ice-cream at a cabin that I hadn't even noticed before and one next door selling lurid pink candy floss. The holiday rental properties that had mostly been closed up for the winter have their windows thrown wide and stripy towels hang over the balconies. The atmosphere is light-hearted and bustling. Summer is definitely in the air.

The Beach Hut Café is a hive of activity too. A quick scan tells me that all the tables are occupied, even my favourite one by the sea wall. Ida is busy behind the counter and two women who I haven't seen before are bustling about taking orders and delivering food. I'm not sure what to do now. Should I wait here until a table comes free or pop back later when it might be less busy? While I'm standing dithering, a man waves frantically at me and indicates a free seat opposite him.

When I look blankly, he shouts, 'Jodie!'

He obviously knows who I am, but I can't say that I know him. Yet, when he continues to beckon, I go over to the table.

'It's George,' he says.

'George!' I laugh with surprise.

'I guess you don't recognise me without my clothes on.' He flushes slightly.

'No. Oh, my God. No, I didn't.' I take in the handsome face, the mass of dark curls, his lovely hazel eyes and sweet smile. 'You look so different!'

'I think that's a good thing.'

Dropping into the seat opposite him, I still can't get my head round it. 'I'll stop staring in a minute.'

'It tends to have that effect on people,' he says. 'That make-up covers up more than you think.'

'It does. Wow.'

'It's good to see you back,' George says. 'I thought you'd gone for good.'

'So did I.' It makes me a little sad to admit it. 'Things didn't quite work out as I'd imagined. But I'm hoping to stay this time.'

'Me too.' George gives me an enigmatic smile and I can't tell you how nice it is to be able to see his face properly. 'While you were gone, I had a book deal come in.'

'George, that's fantastic.'

'It's not massive,' he adds quickly, but I can tell that he's very proud of himself. 'I don't think it will trouble the bestseller list, but it's a start. I've been able to give up the statue work to concentrate on writing.'

'That's great news. I really enjoyed it. Surely this is worthy of a celebration? Will you have another coffee with me? We could push out the boat and have some cake too?'

'That sounds great.'

I call one of the new waitresses over and we place an order.

When she's gone, George adds, shyly, 'It's really good to have you back, Jodie. It was weird without you.'

'Thanks, George.' I can only hope that everyone else feels the same about my return.

Chapter Eighty-Eight

Ida brings over our order. She looks harassed. She also looks great, though. The sun has tanned her skin and she's wearing her hair piled on top of her head and tied with multi-coloured ribbons. Her shorts are very skimpy and she has a baggy crochet top over a halter neck bikini. The biker boots that accessorise the look are very Ida.

She plonks our cake and coffee down in front of us. 'They say bad pennies always turn up again.'

'It's nice to be back, Ida.'

She grins at me. 'Good to see you. Ned thought you were gone for good. Me, I wasn't so sure. I thought you'd rock up at some point. I'm only surprised it's so soon.'

'I hadn't planned on coming back quite so quickly,' I confess. 'But I'm hoping to stay around. I'm just acquainting myself with the "new" George.'

'He's hot stuff.' Ida laughs. 'Look at how beautiful he is! How did we not know that?'

George blushes furiously and yet they exchange a look that says there might be more behind it than gentle teasing. He's a lot younger than her, but I don't think Ida would let a little thing that like stand in her way. She'd also eat him for breakfast. But then, George might like that.

She turns her attention back to me. 'You left Ned in a hell of state,' she says flatly. 'I've never seen him be such a miserable bastard.'

'I'm sorry,' I say. 'I didn't mean to.'

Ida shrugs, but I can tell that she's been concerned.

'Is he around? He's not at the boat.'

'He took off shortly after you did, a few weeks ago,' she says. 'Didn't say where he was going. He isn't answering texts. Twat. I've no idea what he's up to.'

'Oh.'

'It's not the first time he's done this. He buggers off for a while without telling anyone.' Another shrug. 'I'm not his keeper.'

'I've been trying to get hold of him too.'

'He'll turn up in his own good time.' She looks round at the counter. 'I'd better go. This place is madness now.'

'Perhaps the three of us could go out for a drink one night,' I venture. 'I'd like that.'

Both George and Ida look rather more keen than I'd anticipated – though I'm not convinced that it's the thought of my company that they're enthralled with.

'Yeah.' Ida sounds as if she couldn't care less whether we have a drink or not. 'I'm around tomorrow night.'

'Me too,' George agrees quickly.

'Tomorrow, then. Seven o'clock at The Jolly Roger?'

'Christ, no. We avoid the place like the plague now it's full of tourists. I'll text you the name of a quiet bar where the locals go.'

'OK, thanks.'

'He'll be back,' she says over her shoulder as she goes to leave. 'But you might have your work cut out trying to get him to trust you again.'

'Things have changed since then.'

She makes a huffing noise. 'Try telling Ned that.'

If only he were here, perhaps I could.

Chapter Eighty-Nine

When I get back to *Sunny Days*, Marilyn has returned. Bill must have been on the phone to her as soon as I left. He's such a good brother and I can't thank him enough.

The minute I walk through the door, my dear friend hugs me tightly to her fulsome breast.

'You've lost weight,' is the first thing she says – when I can assure you that I absolutely haven't. 'Good job I've brought you some shopping.'

When she puts me down, I say, 'I have missed you so much, Marilyn.'

'My darling girl, I've missed you like the desert misses the sun.'

I have to smile. Some things don't change, that's for sure.

'That husband of yours looked shifty. His eyes were too close together and he has a weak chin. I knew he wouldn't make you happy.'

I'm not sure that Chris suffers from either of these physical afflictions, but I'm not going to defend him. Marilyn's right. He didn't make me happy. And I didn't make him happy either.

I've heard nothing from him since leaving, but I hope that

we'll be able to sort out the sale of the flat amicably. If he wants to stay there, then I'm perfectly agreeable to that. We'll probably mostly communicate now through solicitors which is sad, but it still doesn't make me want to go back. I don't feel like a failure. I feel like someone who has decided life is too short to spend it being unhappy.

'Have you spoken to him next door yet?' She nods towards Ned's boat and her earrings jangle.

I shake my head. 'There's no one home. I walked down to the Beach Hut and talked to Ida. She said that Ned's gone away. He hasn't been around for weeks.'

'He'll be back,' Marilyn says with supreme confidence. 'As sure as eggs are peas.'

'I hope you're right.' But, whatever happens, I'm not going to mope around. I'm starting a new life on the Isle of Wight and I can't wait.

'You're going to need coffee,' Marilyn says. 'I've got a lot to tell you.' She searches through the pockets in her electric blue jumpsuit. 'I've got a list, so I didn't forget a thing.'

'Oh, good,' I answer with a laugh.

'Strap yourself in!'

So I sit at the table and stare out at the harbour while Marilyn clangs and bangs about with the kettle and some cups. I am going to be happy here. I know it.

Chapter Ninety

So what do I do for the next few weeks? I buy myself a second-hand runaround so that I'm mobile – it's a Peugeot something-or-another and is a vibrant shade of red that's had Marilyn's stamp of approval. I can nip round the island or hop on the ferry at will. I haven't driven for years and it does feel weird to be behind the wheel again rather than jumping into a cab or onto the Tube.

One of my first jaunts is to drive to the woods where Ned took me to his workshop. I park and enjoy a pleasant stroll through the surrounding meadows. It looks so different now. Grasses and wildflowers come up to my waist and there are butterflies in abundance, as he promised. As I walk, dozens of them flit round me, fearless and bold, as if I'm in a Disney movie. Then I go out to the peaceful salt marshes and sit alone in the quiet of a bird hide, watching the nesting black-headed and Mediterranean gulls feed their young and very demanding chicks. I miss Ned being here as he would have liked this.

For *Sunny Days*, I order furniture online to kit out Bill's spare bedroom as a serviceable office. Work is busy, so I'm pretty much occupied during the day. The eco-hotel project is gathering pace now and it's all hands on deck. I've been over to the New Forest a few times to check on progress and I've even managed to meet Bill down there so he doesn't think I've disappeared off the face of the earth. He's coping quite well with my new working arrangements and, as promised, we Skype every day. My brother also keeps vowing to come out and see me, but hasn't quite made it yet. Down at the hotel, the builders are getting on nicely – in fact, so well that I'm not going to be able to hold off on approaching other sculptors about doing the work here. I haven't had the nerve to pick up the phone and actually call Ned. It's disappointing, though, that Ned hasn't responded to any of my messages as he would have been ideal, but I've accepted that not everything in life is perfect.

Yet, despite work being busy, I feel as if I've stepped off the treadmill. Before I head to my desk every day, I go for a walk – either along the beach, round the harbour wall or along the esplanade. Some mornings, I've even practised a bit of the yoga that Ned showed me for half an hour or so, though I feel a little foolish doing it by myself.

I've also fallen into the habit of going out with George and Ida a couple of times a week. We head to a small bar in one of the backstreets, Old Salties, and have a few drinks together and maybe some supper. As you would expect in a seaside town, they do fantastic shellfish. George is great company – funny, witty and self-deprecating. I like him a lot. We all have a laugh together and I feel hopeful that Ida is softening towards me again. Nothing has happened between George and Ida yet – as far as I'm aware. Though I realise that I have form in not noticing what's going on right before my eyes. I do get the impression that I'm very much playing gooseberry as their looks of longing are ever more lingering.

At least one morning a week, I go out with Marilyn for a coffee and catch-up. As soon as she's finished the non-existent cleaning to her satisfaction, we head either head to the Beach Café or to one of Ida's many rivals in the town. She's good company and I love hearing her chatter about her family while she force-feeds me cake. Despite her many invitations, I haven't yet managed to brave meeting them all. But I will. Just not yet. I'm better. Much better. I'm just not sure that I'm ready to be knee-deep in McConaughey grandbabies. Marilyn has vowed never to stop asking me and I'm glad of that.

In the evenings, I read a lot. George's book has helped me to rediscover my mojo and I'm working my way through Bill's bookcase with a voracious appetite. I talk to Ned's carving of Lottie about what I might like to read. Then I sit on the deck with a glass or two of wine under the ever-changing sky and relax.

I think because my head's not so messed up and I have time in my life, the creativity that I once had at university returns. It's been sadly missing for a long time. I can call on it for work projects – that's not been a problem – but my personal creativity has taken a back seat. Now I want to paint again, just for the fun of it. So I found a little art shop in Ventnor where I bought some watercolour paints, brushes, paper and an easel. I set myself up on the deck whenever the mood takes me and, splashing about with my paints, attempt to capture the sunsets and sunrises, the little boats bobbing in and out, the sea birds sitting on the buoys. I'm rusty, but each time I paint, I'm getting better, rediscovering what works and what doesn't. I'm thinking about signing up for an art class, if I can find one near here.

I also paint one portrait. After flicking through the old family albums that Bill and I transferred to Facebook, I take a favourite photograph of me as a child and copy it in watercolours. I think this is, perhaps, what Lottie might have looked like too and it makes me happy to have an image of her – even if it's only one that I've created.

There's still no sign of Ned and no reply to my texts. Ida has heard nothing either. But I feel OK. Something inside me has shifted and there's a warmth around my heart, a feeling of wholeness that has been absent. I miss him being next door. I miss him being my friend. But, if he doesn't come back, I know that I'll be fine. This is a good, peaceful life. I could have loved Ned, very much I think, but if that's not to be then, in time, there might be someone else.

I'm content within myself and it's been a long time since I've known that.

Chapter Ninety-One

The summer is in full flow now. The climate here is very agree-able and the days have been long, hot and sunny. After years of living in London, I'm throwing myself fully into beach lifestyle.

Despite judicious applications of sunscreen, my legs are bronzed, my face freckled and my hair has lightened with natural highlights. Whether it's because I've relaxed or whether it's due to Marilyn's propensity for feeding me, I have filled out and I think I look better for it. Marilyn certainly says so. The bodycon dresses are left behind me in London and I spend my life in shorts and T-shirts. I've even been swimming in the sea – intentionally.

Today, even with the windows open, there's no breeze and the bedroom cabin is hot. It's set to be another scorching day, so I rise early and shower. Before settling to work, I decide to head to the beach. Despite not having Ned as my encouraging teacher, I've still been practising yoga reasonably regularly and watching yoga videos on YouTube to try to improve my tech-nique. If I'm feeling a bit brave, I might just try a sun salutation.

I head down to the beach and it's still quiet at this hour. There are only a few people dotted about, those eager to start their day and not waste a moment of precious sunshine. Then

I see, just ahead of me on the sand, a familiar figure and my heart lurches in my chest.

It's Ned. Of course. And he's not alone.

He's kneeling in the sand and, next to him, is a small child. It has to be Skye. She's wearing a frilly pink swimsuit and matching sunhat, and even at this distance, I can tell that she has Ned's hair, his features and, when she looks up, his eyes.

'Hello,' she says.

Ned turns to see who she's talking to and seems surprised to see me. 'Jodie.'

'Hi.' Emotion constricts my throat, but I manage to say, 'I see that you're putting your sandcastle-building skills to good use again.' I can't tell you how many times I've looked at that photo and longed for a moment like this.

'This little lady couldn't sleep,' he tells me. 'She was wide awake at four o'clock and couldn't wait to come down to the beach.'

'Is it exciting to be by the seaside?' I ask her.

Skye nods at me and keeps digging with her yellow plastic spade. She's so petite, so pretty that looking at her twists my insides. A tiny version of Ned. I get a pang, longing for the child of mine that might have been. But the new me smiles at the memory and lets it go.

'She's here for a week,' Ned says.

'That's really nice for you. I'm sure you'll have fun.'

'Yeah.' He looks at her with pride.

'I tried to contact you while I was in London.'

'I know,' he says. 'I went a bit off-grid for a while.'

'It was about a potential commission. An exciting proposition. Mainly.' Ned doesn't look convinced and I guess it's a conversation we might or might not have at another time. He might not even be prepared to work with me. 'I didn't notice that you'd come back.'

'Same here,' Ned says. 'We got back from the mainland last night. Though I did note the red car parked outside. Yours?'

'Thought I'd better be mobile,' I tell him.

We're shy with each other, hesitant. He doesn't know my situation yet and, let's face it, I don't know his either.

After a deep breath, I add, 'I'm back for good.'

'Just you?'

I know that the question is loaded. 'Just me. I have a lot to tell you.'

'I guess so.'

'It was a mistake for me to return to London. I worked that out pretty quickly. But I had to try.'

Ned acknowledges it with a nod, but says nothing.

'Perhaps I can explain it to you,' I say. 'One day.'

'Yeah,' Ned agrees.

'Come on, Daddy,' Skye says. 'Dig!'

Ned smiles at her and rolls his eyes at me. He picks up his spade again and doesn't ask me to join them on the sand.

'Well, I'd better leave you to it. Sandcastles fit for princesses don't build themselves. Lovely to see you. And Skye.'

I turn to walk away, digging my fingernails into my palms to deflect the pain in my heart. This is going to be harder than I hoped. It's clear that Ned is holding onto his hurt and I'm going to have to work hard to win his confidence again. So be it. I'm not going to give up easily and I have all the time in the world. I've only had to see him again to know that he's worth the effort.

For now, Skye needs his attention and that's fine by me. He should concentrate on his relationship with her while she's here.

Yet I've only gone a dozen steps when I hear Ned say, 'We're going down to Ida's for some breakfast. Come with us?'

I turn back to him and there's a lump in my throat when I answer, 'If it's OK with you both?'

'What do you think, Skye?' he asks. 'Shall we go with Jodie and find something to eat?'

'Will the princess castle be here when we come back?'

'Yeah,' Ned says. 'When we've had breakfast we'll be ready to build it bigger and fancier.'

'You're very silly, Daddy,' is her verdict.

'You're not the first person to tell me that,' he says wryly.

They both put down their spades and, when he stands, Ned looks deep into my eyes, but his expression is unfathomable. Then, with Skye running ahead, the three of us head along the beach to the café.

Chapter Ninety-Two

Ida's eyes light up when she sees Ned. I don't think that will ever change. She might be enjoying a flirtation with George, but will anyone ever fill the place that Ned holds in her heart? I hope so. It would be nice for Ida to find someone to love who loves her back. It would be nice for all of us.

'Where have you been . . . ?' Ida mouths an obscenity at Ned.

'I went to bring this little lady back,' he says.

'And they don't have mobile phone reception in Northampton?'

'Sorry,' is all he offers.

'Hey, Skye. I'm Ida – your daddy's oldest and most tolerant friend.' She looks pointedly at Ned.

He holds up his hands in surrender.

'So where are you going to sit, Princess?' Ida pulls out a chair for Skye and she jumps on. 'We have ice-cream and waffles.'

'Ice-cream! Can I, Daddy?'

'Ice-cream for breakfast?' He shakes his head. 'Don't tell your mama I let you have ice-cream for breakfast.'

'Yay!' Skye says.

'Ice-cream for you?' he asks me.

'I was thinking of the more conventional yoghurt and granola. A coffee too, please, Ida.'

Ned orders as well and, though there's so much unspoken between us, we mainly listen to Skye chattering away as we eat our breakfast. She's a delight – a bright and funny child. I wonder if it isn't too late for me to have a family. I might not get there by the usual means, but if I had a stepchild like Skye that would be just as wonderful, I think.

The child finishes her breakfast and says, 'Can I go and play on the beach?'

'Stay close,' Ned stays. 'Where I can see you.'

'OK, Daddy.' She pushes away from the table and runs down to the sand.

There's a few moments of silence between us and then I say, 'She's a lovely little girl.'

'Yeah. I'm really proud of her.' He pulls his coffee cup to him and ponders over it before he speaks. 'Thanks for making me get back in touch. It was the right thing to do. I went over to see Liberty to talk about having more regular access. She agreed.'

'I'm so glad to hear it.'

'I hung around with them for a while, getting to know Skye and their family again. It was awkward at first, but we all worked through it. I even did some carpentry jobs for them – fitting doors and skirting boards. I built a treehouse for the kids too. Liberty has let me bring her back here for a week. It's a big thing for us all. I have my fingers crossed that it goes well.'

'I'm happy to help. If you'll let me.'

'That would be great. She's a real live-wire. I'm out of prac- tice with this parenting lark. I'll be exhausted by tea-time.'

We both laugh at that.

Then the mood changes and I know that this is the time to tell Ned what has happened.

'I have a lot to tell you,' I say.

Chapter Ninety-Three

So while we both keep an eye on Skye, Ned listens while I let it all pour out. I tell him about the loss of my baby and how I struggled to come to terms with it, how the pain drove me to the edge of madness. I tell him about the difficulties between me and Chris and how we could never heal the rift. Then I talk about Chris's affair with my best friend and how that made me know that it was definitely over between us.

Ned listens to it all without speaking, just nodding in the right places.

Finally, I take a deep breath and say, 'I think I'm falling in love with you and the last thing in the world I intended to do was to cause hurt. Our night together at the festival was the best thing to happen to me in a long time and I'm so sad that it ended like it did. If possible, I wish you could find it in your heart to forgive me.' I let the breath out. There, I've said it. There can be no mistaking how I feel. 'And that's about it, really.'

When I eventually dry up and stop speaking, Ned reaches across the table and takes my hands in his. 'Let's start again,' is all he says.

Tears fill my eyes when I answer, 'I'd very much like that.'

Then Skye shouts, 'Come on, Daddy! Come on, Jodie! We have to build the princess castle!'

'We do,' Ned says. 'Though maybe we should call this one the diva castle.'

While we've been talking, the beach has filled up and so have the tables at the café. Ida is bustling about and Ned goes to pay her. She holds him a little too tightly when he kisses her goodbye and my heart hurts for her. Sometimes, we can't help who we love.

'Everything OK?' I ask.

'Yeah.' Ned presses his warm lips against mine. 'Everything's perfect.'

As we step onto the sand, Skye slips her hand into mine. It feels so tiny, so trusting, that it almost has me undone. I think of the other small hand that never made it into mine and my footstep falters, my heart tightens. Then Ned takes my other hand and squeezes it. His touch is so strong, so reliable that I know, in time, it will all work out just fine.

Acknowledgements

Thank you so much to Ian Freemantle, award-winning artist and wood sculptor, who inspired me with my hero's work in the book and was so generous with his time and knowledge. He is an amazing talent. Have a look at his art works at www.ian-freemantle.co.uk.

Apologies to the good people of the Isle of Wight for shamelessly messing with your geography. I was so spoilt for choice with super locations, that I thought I'd use a bit of them all. The houseboats we stayed on were both in Bembridge Harbour. Unfortunately, Cockleshell Bay doesn't exist but is a mash-up of Bembridge, Steep Hill Cove and Seaview with a few other bits and bobs thrown in for good measure. The forest where Ned works is based on the lovely area around Newtown National Nature Reserve. My advice is to go to the Isle of Wight and check it out. Don't forget your bucket and spade!

Don't miss Carole's gloriously festive sequel to her *Sunday Times* bestselling novel *Happiness for Beginners*...

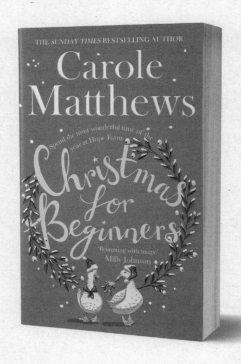

Coming in paperback October 2021
Available to pre-order now

Carole Matthews

 CaroleMatthewsBooks 🐦 CaroleMatthews

📷 matthews.carole

Check out Carole's website and sign up to
her newsletter for all the latest book news
plus competitions and exclusives!

www.carolematthews.com

LOVE TO READ?

Join **The Little Book Café** for competitions,
sneak peeks and more.

f TheLittleBookCafe 🐦 littlebookcafe

📷 littlebookcafe

Help us make the next generation of readers

We – both author and publisher – hope you enjoyed this book.
We believe that you can become a reader at any time in your life,
but we'd love your help to give the next generation a head start.

Did you know that 9% of children don't have a book of their
own in their home, rising to 12% in disadvantaged families*?
We'd like to try to change that by asking you to consider the role
you could play in helping to build readers of the future.

We'd love you to think of sharing, borrowing, reading, buying or talking
about a book with a child in your life and spreading the love of reading.
We want to make sure the next generation continue to have access
to books, wherever they come from.

And if you would like to consider donating to charities that help
fund literacy projects, find out more at www.literacytrust.org.uk
and www.booktrust.org.uk.

Thank you.

hachette
CHILDREN'S GROUP

little, brown
BOOK GROUP

*As reported by the National Literacy Trust